To CATCH a Husband

BALLANTINE BOOKS ~ NEW YORK

To CATCH a Husband

AN EX-WIVES NOVEL

LINDSAY GRAVES

To Catch a Husband is a work of fiction. Names, characters, places, and incidents are the products of the author's imagination or are used fictitiously. Any resemblance to actual events, locales, or persons, living or dead, is entirely coincidental.

A Ballantine Books Trade Paperback Original

Published in the United States by Ballantine Books, an imprint of The Random House Publishing Group, a division of Random House, Inc., New York.

This book contains an excerpt from the forthcoming trade paperback edition of *To Keep a Husband* by Lindsay Graves. This excerpt has been set for this edition only and may not reflect the final content of the forthcoming edition.

Library of Congress Cataloging-in-Publication Data

Graves, Lindsay.
To catch a husband : an ex-wives novel / Lindsay Graves.
p. cm.
ISBN 0-345-48548-3 (trade pbk.)
1. Divorced women—Fiction. 2. Mate selection—Fiction. I. Title.

PS3607.R3864T6 2006
813'.6—dc22 2006042797

Printed in the United States of America

www.ballantinebooks.com

987654321

Book design by Mercedes Everett

To catch a husband is an art.

—Simone de Beauvoir

Acknowledgments

I am extraordinarily grateful to my editor, Allison Dickens, for her discernment, inspiration, and enthusiasm; to Ingrid Powell, for terrific input; to my agent, Barbara Lowenstein, for just about everything; and to all the fabulous exes of Montecito—you know who you are!

To CATCH a Husband

CHAPTER *one*

A Sorry Excuse for a Divorcée

It is a truth universally acknowledged that a woman recently divorced and in possession of half the cheating louse's fortune must be in want of a new man.

Or so thought Jessica DiSantini when she saw Lally Chandler tilting toward her as fast as her Jimmy Choos could convey her at the Ladies Who Lunch fund-raiser for the Historical Society. Jessica had been officially divorced for only forty-seven days, from a neurosurgeon who'd left her for a thirty-year-old patient from whose brain he'd extracted a biscuit-sized meningioma tumor: Her final eye-popping bill from Oliver Dietch, Esq., had not yet been settled; the odd cross-trainer Skechers and the pasta alla cecca–stained tie still moldered in Michael's old closet; it was Mike's unctuous baritone still announcing, "Hey, it's the DiSantinis!" on her voice mail, for God's sake! But already she'd had to fend off half a dozen offers to match her up. And now here came Lally wearing that cat-in-the-cream expression that could only mean, *Do I have a man for you!*

Jessica turned her back and pretended to be absorbed in the exhibition. The San Carlino Historical Society was a formerly down-at-the-heels institution crouched at the bottom of Mission Hill that recently had begun mounting splashy shows with unabashedly lurid themes. Currently: "San Carlino Noir: Serial Killing, Deadly Passion, and Murder

For Hire" was packing 'em in. The fifty or so lunching ladies, dressed to the bleached teeth in pastel summer suits or fruit-salady sundresses, were circulating, schmoozing, and sipping a decent rosé among the mounted relics of grisly crimes past: yellowed newspaper clippings of killers staring hollowly from death row; old high school yearbook photos of beehived future victims; newsreel footage of a strangler in the forties who kept the eyeballs of his stranglees pickled like so many cocktail onions in refrigerated mason jars.

Jessica's contemplation of a montage of corpses chilling in a morgue was abruptly terminated by the insertion of Lally's live body between herself and the photos.

"Jessi*ca*!" Lally exclaimed. "I was hoping you'd be here! You are the very lady I wanted to see!"

There was something thematically Day of the Dead–looking about Lally. Perhaps the skeletal black-and-white motif of her tie-dyed Prada frock? Or the nearly fleshless length of her limbs?

Jessica inclined her face for the obligatory double air kiss. "Lally! How are you?"

"Absolutely super, darling. Isn't this an amazing event? So marvelously gritty; don't you just love it?"

"Oh, yeah. I've always been partial to grit," Jessica said.

Lally responded with a breathless laugh and a toss of her burnt sugar–colored ponytail. As everyone knew—or at least would know if they spent more than five minutes in her company—Lally had been a Bond girl. True, it was opposite Roger Moore in one of the lousier James Bond films, but it was the high point—and, as it happened, the final point—of Lally's early acting career; and it often seemed to Jessica that Lally had buried herself a bit too much in the part.

"You're hysterical, darling," Lally cooed. "But listen, what I wanted to tell you is that you popped into my mind this morning, and I had the most brilliant idea. I thought, my God, why don't I introduce her to Tommy? I'm an imbecile for not thinking of it sooner."

"Who's Tommy?" Jessica asked warily.

"My first husband."

This was novel enough to give Jessica pause. "The cinematographer?"

"Helmut? God, no, I wouldn't fix him up with a virus. The one before that, Tommy Bramberg. We were just babies when we got married. He was a hottie rock star back then, and I had dropped out of my first semester at USC."

Jessica wondered briefly how many husbands Lally had under her belt. Three, perhaps four . . . There was also a never-seen and rarely mentioned daughter who reportedly ran with a wild Eurotrashy crowd in Rome or Milan. Difficult to imagine Lally with a grown daughter; she looked so incredibly young.

Though not actually young, Jessica silently amended. More like *un*-young, which was kind of like the undead—eerily and perpetually preserved.

From a corner of her eye, Jessica spied a waiter cruising with bottle in hand. She shook her empty glass at him, like a witch doctor with a rattle, but the spell backfired—instead of approaching, he vanished. "Look, thanks for thinking of me, Lally," she said. "It's sweet of you, really. But the truth is, I'm just not ready to date yet."

An impatient little puff issued from Lally's coral-glossed lips. It was obvious to Jessica that Lally considered her a sorry excuse for a divorcée. Not only had Jessica shown no inclination to increase the square footage of her home or the cup size of her breasts, nor add a single tawny chunk to her light brown hair, she was in fact doing nothing at all to exploit the glamour of her situation.

Lally, by contrast, the second after shucking her last husband, the retired game-show host Artie Willman, had undergone a complete surgical overhaul, from butt to brow. Then she'd expanded her atrocious neo-Mediterranean on Polite Child Lane to a square footage approaching the Vatican. The pièce de résistance was a triple-story campanile that electronically and resonantly bonged out the first four bars of "*Non, Je Ne Regrette Rien*" every hour on the hour, until a testy note from the neighborhood association put a stop to it. And she'd gotten a tattoo! A half-dollar-sized sea anemone etched high on her right thigh, which she would readily hike her microskirts to display—a very jazzy and daring statement, Jessica supposed, except that it reminded her disconcertingly of a Girl Scout merit badge she'd once earned in Marine Life Identification.

Still she felt the need to defend herself from Lally's lofty disapproval. "I'm sure I'll feel differently in the future," she went on, "but right now I'm actually fine being on my own."

"Please. You know what's really the problem? You're in major denial. I know, darling; I've been there. But when you get lonely enough, or if you just plain get hot pants, let me know."

"You're on my speed dial," Jessica muttered; but Lally was already off, hello-ing a Jil Sander suit that had just emerged from the newsreel-viewing chamber.

Okay, maybe she had a point, Jessica conceded—about the hot pants, anyway. Lately, while flipping channels in the evenings, she'd found herself lingering on the WB, all those hunky young actors with their fantastic hair and luscious shoulders. Rowan was almost at the age of bringing home boys: Jessica had a sudden and terrifying vision of herself as a sort of Mrs. Robinson redux, hovering around her daughter's dates in tight toreador pants, nursing a Scotch, shooting seductive little jets of smoke their way from the cigarettes she'd obviously have to take up smoking.

The fleeting image of a drink made her feel like she was going to keel over right now, this very second, if she didn't get another glass of wine. Mercifully, lunch was being served. Women were streaming toward the saffron-clothed tables set up in the main gallery. She located her name among the place cards cunningly shaped like Weegee-style black-and-white flash cameras; Jessica McCready-DeSantini. That was weird: She'd jettisoned the limerick-sounding hyphenate when she had shut down her law practice directly after her daughter's first epileptic seizure. Who the hell had resurrected it now?

She sat down, noting with mild dismay that Lally's place card was right beside hers. Across the table was Caitlin Latch, a thirty-something who was divorced from an East Indian financial executive up north in . . . San Francisco? Seattle? Somewhere. He'd cracked up in some unspecified way. She was known behind her back as Caitlin the Snatch, in part because she had the reputation, justified or not, of trolling for other women's husbands, and in part, also, because she possessed a body that, even under last season's baggy peasant-look *schmatte*, was so spectacular as to border on the indecent. Caitlin was deep in conversation with Janey Martinez, a heavy-hipped fortyish woman with a round, peering face, *also* divorced, from a guy serving five and a half years in minimum security for cooking the books at his defunct pet food dot-com.

It's the table of the exes! Jessica thought suddenly. For some reason this struck her as extremely funny. She giggled.

"You really think that's amusing?" Janey Martinez demanded crisply. There were dark circles under her eyes. Janey famously complained of insomnia and had a reputation for swiping tranquilizers out of medicine cabinets. When you had Janey over, it was, "Honey, hide the Ativan!"

"Find what amusing?" Jessica asked.

"You probably didn't catch what we were talking about," Caitlin said with an ingratiating semismile. She was something of a social climber and almost always wore that same little smile.

"No, I wasn't listening," Jessica said. "What were you saying?"

"I was telling Janey that this exhibit, some of these photos here, made me think of this unusual case we had at the center over the weekend." Caitlin worked rather nobly as a coordinator of the local university-sponsored rape crisis center.

"Is there any such thing as a usual rape?" Jessica asked.

It was a flippant question—all that rosé was definitely having its effect—but Caitlin seemed to take it seriously: She momentarily compressed her lips into a deliberating pout. "Mmm, good point. I guess I mean unusual from the point that it wasn't actually a rape in the technical sense. And also that it happened in Colina Linda. It's our first victim from there, at least since I've been working."

Colina Linda was a village of multimillion-dollar properties directly north of the city; it was pinned onto the swank sea line like an expensively trimmed hat on a dowager. Shoot a gun off in here, Jessica figured, and odds were better than fifty-fifty you'd knock off a denizen of Colina Linda. Including, needless to say, herself.

And including Lally, who had just plopped herself onto the neighboring chair. "What? What happened in Colina Linda?"

"Someone was sexually assaulted inside her own home," Janey said. Her voice simmered over with drama.

"Who? Anybody I know?"

"Obviously I can't reveal her name," Caitlin said primly. "All I can tell you is that this woman woke up in the middle of the night last Sunday and there was a man in her bedroom, sitting in a chair. He was wearing a Spider-Man mask, she said, and he threatened her with a knife."

"Does anybody find Spidey as creepy as I do?" Lally cut in. "I mean, slime shooting from his fingertips? Is that a male ejaculation fantasy or what?"

"I don't think it's from his fingertips," Janey said.

"*N'importe quoi.* Okay, so if he didn't rape her, what did he do?"

"Well," Caitlin continued, "apparently he had a sexual aid. . . . You know, a vibrator."

"You mean a dildo," Lally said, with a note of delight.

"Well, yeah, okay. And he made her, well, fellate it while he watched. Then he left. Right out through the front door, apparently. Leaving her pretty well traumatized, as you can imagine."

"So he didn't want sex; he wanted to humiliate her," Jessica murmured.

"Rape is never about sex; it's about power," Caitlin recited.

"Oh, come on, tell us who it was." Lally's green-gold eyes were open wide and had a lubricious sheen. "We can keep a secret, right, ladies?"

Caitlin shook her head. "I've probably already overstepped the bounds of confidentiality. I just felt maybe I should be warning you ladies. I mean, I think we all need to be on the alert, lock our doors and windows and all."

"Wanna bet it was someone she knew?" Lally said. "Some Mexican, the gardener or a pool guy."

"No, it wasn't," Janey snapped. "Caitlin said he was British."

The others shot a look at Caitlin, who nodded. She was enjoying herself, Jessica realized—being the center of attention for a change. Caitlin the Snatch was, if not actually snubbed, then often rather benignly ignored.

"According to the victim, he had an upper-class English accent," Caitlin confirmed.

"Could have been faked," Lally scoffed.

"By a gardener? Give me a break!" Janey said. "Frankly, I find all this extremely disturbing. I happen to *live* in Colina Linda."

"So do we all, darling," Lally said. "But I don't scare very easily. I'm hardly going to worry about some English aristocrat breaking into my house. I don't care if he's dressed like Winnie the Pooh." She tossed her ponytail, intrepid-Bond-girl-style.

Fine for Lally, Jessica thought: her McMansion was surrounded by spike-tipped iron gates so imposing Jessica often felt she should doff her cap when she passed by. Even so, Jessica was inclined to agree with Lally—all their homes were nearly impregnable, what with walls and high-tech security systems and cruising rent-a-cops; it had to have been someone with some sort of familiarity with the house.

Anyway, she thought bitterly, you didn't need a masked intruder for a dose of humiliation. Try a fortieth birthday. A jiggle of cellulite on your behind. A husband sneering, "Hey, SpongeBob SquarePants, time to hit the gym."

Goddamned bastard shit.

The waiter appeared at her shoulder offering a choice of merlot or chardonnay. "Merlot," she said firmly. *Better pace it,* she warned herself. *You've been drinking a bit much lately.* In fact, she'd been systematically drinking her way through the half of Michael's wine cellar she'd received in the settlement: Every time she washed down a carton of leftover take-out pad thai with a three-hundred-dollar St. Emilion, or paired a '97 Château Mouton Rothschild with a Krispy Kreme, she could almost hear him squeal in agony. But wouldn't the bastard get the last laugh if she ended up every Tuesday and Thursday night at AA, acknowledging a higher power and sharing her story of revenge guzzling?

On her right, Lally appeared to be executing a kind of high-kick routine in her chair. Some old showbiz move? Jessica wondered. No, it was to show off her shoes, which were lavender with cutout stars, to Caitlin and Janey. Lally uttered the sacred name of the designer, and the other two dipped their heads in veneration.

Then someone sat down on Jessica's left: Rhonda Kluge, real estate agent to the well-to-do, and definitively *not* an ex—a diamond at least half as big as the Ritz coruscated above a matching band on her wedding-ring finger. She surveyed the four ex-wives and pursed her lips, as if savoring a particularly delectable piece of candy. "Girls, girls, girls!" she announced. "I have some amazing news!"

Four pairs of eyeballs immediately fixed on her.

"*Guess* who's split up with his wife?" Rhonda paused for a tantalizing effect, set elbows on the table, thatched her fingers, balanced her prominent chin on the thatching. "David. Alderson. Clemente."

An electric current shot around the table. "Are you sure?" Lally demanded. "I haven't heard a peep about it."

"It's all been very hush-hush, and it's all happened very fast. Susanna's run off with this art dealer in New York, a Belgian, and half her age, if you please. He was the one who finally found them their Rothko; you know how David's wanted one for ages."

"How do you know it's not just a temporary separation?" Lally pursued. "They might get back together."

"I don't think so. Susanna's already announced her engagement. There's a prenup, of course; she'll waltz away with thirty million or so. But that's small potatoes to what she's leaving behind."

There was a collective holding of breath. Jessica reached for her glass and discovered to her astonishment that her fingertips were tingling. *Don't be ridiculous,* she told herself. She glanced at the others. Lally was worrying the sea pearls at her neck as if they were prayer beads.

Janey's small, round mouth was parted, and her dark-ringed eyes blinked. Caitlin still wore her crescent of a smile, as fixed and pleased as a porcelain doll's.

For a moment Jessica felt almost sorry for Caitlin. Her spotlight had definitely dimmed. A sort-of rape, however close to home, was nothing compared to the news that a local billionaire was back on the market.

CHAPTER *two*

Nothin' Says Money Like Fieldstone

Caitlin Latch had to cut out early from the luncheon because it was her carpool afternoon. Jessica DiSantini's son also attended St. Matthew's, and her carpool day happened to coincide with Caitlin's, but Jessica had Help—one of those old family retainer–like Hispanic nannies who Could Be Counted On—whereas Caitlin did all her own schlepping.

She stepped out of the chill recesses of the historical society into a blast furnace—late September and still over ninety degrees outside. She fervently regretted now that she'd skipped the museum parking—seven bucks!—in favor of the free structure on Pinto, six blocks away. She slipped on sunglasses, double Cs adorning the hinges, the only authentic item of Chanel she possessed, and began the sweltering uphill trudge.

Caitlin the Snatch. Oh, yeah, she was well aware of her little sobriquet; more than once she'd been within earshot when one of those snotty pampered Stepfords had referred to her that way. But basically it didn't bother her all that much. The way she looked at it, her sexual presence posed a threat; and if it took a sniggering behind-her-back nickname to neutralize that threat and allow her to keep orbiting in at least the outer rings of their society, then so be it.

Truth was, whatever minor social position she did maintain in San

Carlino was on the shaky side, based as it was on a certain amount of fiction. As far as that queen bee Lally and the rest of them knew, she existed mainly on the alimony check she raked in from a financial hotshot of an ex-husband who'd suffered a nervous breakdown. What a joke! Okay, it was true Ravi had worked in the San Francisco office of Smith Barney, but only as a junior bonds analyst.

And there was no genteel nervous breakdown. He'd flipped out—and he'd flipped out big-time.

It had begun almost exactly six years after they were married. Little behavioral tics: scarfing cold clam chowder for breakfast, laughing like a hyena at the sad parts in movies. Then came the weeping jags, alternating with lunatic spending sprees that maxed out thirteen credit cards and sent the two of them spiraling into debt. Which was when he found religion. The Buddhist religion, to be exact—or anyway his own version of it. Shaved his head. Dyed all his clothes orange—jeans, Y-fronts, and tux included. Erected a nine-foot effigy of the Tantric Enraged Buddha in the living room, to which he made food offerings. Caitlin would return home each night from her job managing a day spa in Pacific Heights to the stench of rotting papayas and curdled milk.

His panicked family finally intervened and shipped him off to rich relations in Calcutta, where he was diagnosed with a galloping case of bipolarism and supplied with the right meds; but by then Caitlin had filed for a no-fault and whisked their six-year-old son Aiden to a fresh start in the exquisite old mission city of San Carlino.

It was the right thing to do. She was not about to have Aiden grow up in the shadow of his crazy father. She was determined to provide something a lot better for him.

But in the meantime, the amount of her monthly alimony check was actually zilch.

Not that she was fooling anybody into thinking that she was rich. Please. Her two-bedroom "character" bungalow was not even in Colina Linda proper, but a good half mile over the village line. But the way she saw it, you didn't have to be wealthy to hobnob with the right crowd. The key was simply to look like you exercised control over the way you lived. In other words, make it seem that your lifestyle was based on choice, and not grubby necessity. For example: choose to wear funky thrift-shop shit because you found it amusing and original, yada, yada—socially acceptable. Wear it because you had no other choice, your last dime went to repairing a leaking roof—social death.

And so she embraced dozens of little fictions. Why she drove a seven-year-old Volvo wagon. ("Safest car ever made, guys!") Why she employed no nanny, even part-time. ("I made the decision early on I didn't want a stranger raising my son.") Why she toiled forty hours a week at the rape center. ("I really feel the need to do something meaningful at this stage of my life.") With Ravi's folks chipping in the tuition for St. Mattie's and her daily secret little economies, like hunting out free parking, she was just able to pull off the illusion of a reasonably independent divorcée.

After only two blocks in the shadeless heat, she was sweating like a long distance runner. Her mind flashed to the others still lolling back there in frosty comfort, refusing second servings of lemon soufflé. Two hundred fifty bucks she'd shelled out for that damned ticket, and she hadn't even gotten her share of dessert.

But, she reminded herself, she'd scored something better—the interesting news about David Clemente. The thing about San Carlino was that it was dominated by women. The city was about flowers and colors and the sea; it was about cultivating heirloom tomatoes and restoring historical architecture and lunching al fresco in rose gardens. Women—particularly those whose souls were in need of soothing—took one look and said, "Aah," and made it their home. The city had divorcées the way rust-belt towns had abandoned buildings.

What it didn't have was unmarried men. There was no real industry to lure them: no Hollywood, like L.A., a hundred miles to the south; no Silicon Valley, which revved up San Francisco, two hundred and fifty miles to the north. Divorce was practically the only way a financially eligible local man became available, and when he did, he was snapped up lickety-split.

How long would David Clemente remain available? Half a nanosecond maybe?

Caitlin blotted her sweating forehead. This blouse was going to need dry cleaning. Meaning she could kiss what she'd saved in parking good-bye.

She returned her thoughts to David Clemente. What did she know about him? Pretty much what everybody did—that he had inherited a number of Los Angeles office buildings back in the eighties, when commercial real estate was in a deep recession. He'd hit on the idea of carving up the failing buildings into personal storage units of varying sizes, rentable by the week, month, or year. Caitlin couldn't help but admire the beauty of this plan: In a recession, when people were downsizing into smaller spaces, they needed storage for the stuff they no longer had room for; in a recovery they spent like crazy and needed storage to stash all the overflow.

David had then begun snapping up failed office buildings all over the West and constructing cheap facilities in the Far East. Eventually the Clemente Corporation began to diversify: sports franchises; a few high-tech firms; a greeting card company, etc. But it was the storage facilities that remained the heart of the empire. Caitlin imagined all those dark, airless spaces filled with moth-eaten easy chairs and baby pictures and ugly bridge lamps and albums by psychedelic groups from the sixties, and maybe even corpses and stolen masterpiece paintings.

And all of it adding up to a billion dollars.

She'd actually met David once. The Clementes had an adopted son named Noah who'd briefly attended St. Mattie's, a grade below Aiden. At some parent-teacher orientation thingy, she'd somehow wound up talking to David about the importance of phonics or some such pseudo-educational topic, until the principal, Myra Dearsoe, practically body-slammed Caitlin out of the way to salaam before her richest parent. Her toadying was in vain, though—the Clementes yanked Noah out a few months later and enrolled him in an even more exclusive school, the Learning Loop.

Caitlin summoned up an image: a medium-good-looking guy—or maybe a tad geeky, the sort of water-combed, side-parted hairdo once the staple of little boys dressed for company. (What was it about billionaires and bad hair? Did they think a salon cut cost two billion?) She remembered too that he'd kept his eyes fixed vaguely on her right temple, the way men did when they were trying not to stare at her tits. And after the toadying Dearsoe hustled him off, she'd caught him darting an over-the-shoulder glance back her way.

Nothing had come of the encounter, of course. Nor had she expected it to—though she did look up his Colina Linda estate in the school directory and pinpointed it on MapQuest. And she'd floated the idea to Aiden that maybe he'd like to have a playdate with Noah Clemente. "That guy? He farts a lot," Aiden had replied, and that had pretty much been that.

At last the parking structure!

She dragged herself into it and up the filthy metal staircase to the second level and bleeped open the Volvo. Blessed, blessed air-conditioning. She turned it on full blast, fluffed the damp copper tendrils matted at her temples, and refreshed her lipstick (Sashimi Mimi by MAC). Sufficiently revived, she backed out of the space. The gas needle trembled just above E. She gambled that she could make it through carpool and coast to the ARCO below the freeway entrance, nine cents a gallon less than the bloodsucking stations here in town.

Her cell rang as she swung onto Pinto Boulevard. She executed a pass around a poky diaper delivery van, then flipped the phone open.

"Hey, Cait." It was Juanita Bosco, a senior counselor at the center. "I hate to bug you, babe, but I'm having a problem with Cynthia Rudin. She's refusing to file a police report."

"Rotten hell! I spent practically all day yesterday working on her. She was fine about it when I left her."

"Yeah, I know, but now she says there was really no harm done. She says it was probably just some drunken kid playing a prank, and she wants to wipe the whole thing out of her mind."

Typical victim pattern. First response: *Find the bastard so I can rip his fucking balls off.* Then shame and humiliation come rushing in and it was: *I just want to go home and wash it all down the drain like a bad-hair day and not deal with it anymore.*

"Who's her counselor?"

"Korvitch."

Caitlin blew a silent raspberry. Andrea Korvitch was one of five therapists who volunteered time to the center, and to Caitlin's mind was barely a notch above a dimwit. The majority of the center's clients had little or no money: women from the rougher neighborhoods, Mexican or Nicaraguan mostly, or outraged or drug-dazed college girls reporting date rape. But this Cynthia Rudin was loaded; the Colina Linda house where she was assaulted was just a weekend place. "See if she'll do a private session. Recommend Benninhurst or Julie Greenberg."

"Can't. She's gone back to L.A. Says she's going to stick this place up for sale, 'cause she wouldn't feel safe there anymore."

"Yeah, okay. I'll call her when I get home. Thanks, Juanita."

Harmless drunk kid, my ass, Caitlin thought, flipping the phone closed. *Depraved little pervert, more like it.* Deserved to have his balls cut off, preferably in some public square at high noon. Except there was something not quite kosher about this particular assault, or Cynthia's reaction to it. Why would a wealthy woman haul herself way the hell across town to a scuzzy little college facility? How did she even *know* about the center . . . ? And the screwy, almost comical details of the assault itself . . . Caitlin wondered briefly if there was something a bit more to this story than Ms. Rudin was choosing to share.

Her thoughts were diverted as she arrived at the school. She slotted into the queue of cars on Manzanita, her Volvo one silver scale on a long metallic serpent. While she waited, she tidied the front seat; stashed an empty box of wintergreen Altoids (was it true what they said about these things and oral sex?) and a sleeveless Shania Twain CD in the glove compartment; briskly banished a composite of sand, Oreo crumblings, and some sticky greenish substance from the passenger seat with a slap of her palm.

The back door opened and Wanda Preston climbed in. She was a timid third grader with oversized black headphones clamped on her head like inverted Mouseketeer ears. "Hi, Wanda," Caitlin greeted her.

"Hello." Her tiny voice melded with the tinny beat from her iPod.

She slid her tush over to make room for Zander Loh, a half-

Taiwanese sixth grader with lush, girl-pretty lashes and a spoiled plum mouth. A real bully, given to punching and kicking other kids when he thought he could get away with it.

"Something stinks in here," he announced. "Like sweaty old feet with fungus."

Caitlin didn't reply. She'd caught sight of Aiden's head bobbing in the churning eddy of kids; and, as always when she glimpsed her son, she felt a confusing mixture of almost unbearable love and crushing disappointment. For the millionth time she wondered what had gone wrong. He'd been a beautiful toddler, silky dark hair and dumpling cheeks, a cheery little boy, and smart too—he knew words like *pleasant* and *cinnamon* and *gesundheit* and all of *Goodnight Moon* by heart before he was three; but now his hair had muddied—to the same damp-sand color her own would be in the inconceivable event she stopped tinting it—and what with his smallish eyes and almost succulent padding of baby fat, he had kind of a piggy look. She watched him shuffle up to the car, one shoulder sloped under the weight of his backpack as if it were crammed with bricks. He was only ten. Why oh why, then, did he remind her of some middle-aged man trapped in a dead-end job, ticking off the dull days to retirement?

He clambered heavily into the backseat next to Zander. "Hello, my sweet Aiden," Caitlin said, flashing him a tender smile.

Zander gave a snuffled laugh.

"Hi, Mom," Aiden said sullenly.

Okay, she'd embarrassed him. He was too old for public endearments; she knew that. But she couldn't help it; he just seemed so pathetically in need of a little loving; and she was sometimes terrified that no one else in the world was ever going to give it to him.

With a sigh, she swiveled back to the wheel. "Everybody buckled up?"

A raggedy chorus of yeahs.

She nosed out, keeping a worried eye on the gas needle, and headed north. Mission Street: soak-the-tourists antique shops, smugly stripped-down veggie cafés, handmade stationery boutiques with cutesy-lettered signs. Left on Jacaranda, live-music bars and taco-and-beer joints that would be jumping with college kids by nightfall. Over to Third, stucco-fronted lawyer and architect offices, second-tier antiques. Then a short-cut through the rucked streets of an upper-working-class Mexican neighborhood, every other house with a yawping mongrel dog and the bougainvillea growing wild.

"Mom, Zander hit me!"

"Did not."

"Did so, and now you're being a liar."

Hit him back, Aidey. Sock him right in his adorable little snubby nose.

There was a scuffle and a whomp, but apparently it was Zander still doing the socking. "Mo-om," Aiden whined.

Caitlin braked for the four-way light on Silver Creek Road and spoke into the rearview mirror. "Zander, cut it out right now, or else!" Or else what? Was there even the mildest form of capital punishment she could administer without prompting a hell-hath-no-fury call from Emily Loh? "I mean it," she added feebly.

"Yeah, yeah," Zander muttered.

The light switched to green, and Caitlin drove across Silver Creek Road and entered paradise.

She sure had to hand it to Colina Linda: It was the most picture-perfect little town she'd ever seen. Bowers of eucalyptus weeping over windy roads. Drop-dead-gorgeous haciendas, with flowering trees and hedges. It boasted the quaintest little village center with a historic hotel, all authentically restored Spanish tile and curly ironwork, and a Sleeping Beauty backdrop of hazy mauve and olive mountains. Even the sunshine seemed different here: not the white glare of downtown San Carlino, but a rippling silver and gold, as if somebody had been put in charge of shaving money into the atmosphere.

Two blocks off Silver Creek to the Prestons', a mustard-colored Tuscan villa distinguished by an abundance of white roses. Wanda marched in front of the car, as if in time to her iPod beat, and vanished into the flowers.

Another quarter mile to the Lohs on West Stonyhill. The homes began to swell ever larger and be sited farther and farther apart: A glimpse of a chimney top or sloping tiled roof was now all that was visible from the road.

As always, Emily Loh stood waiting on the curb. She anxiously yanked open the back door and clasped her precious son to her bosom. *You'd think they'd been separated a year instead of a few measly hours,* Caitlin thought scornfully.

Mother and child reunion complete, Emily waggled a cursory finger greeting to Caitlin, then shepherded Zander off to the unseen house.

Caitlin shifted out of neutral and started up the street. West Stonyhill forked: Right would circle her back toward Silver Creek and the freeway. As she approached the fork, a shaft of sun lit the windshield like a beacon of gold; and on an impulse, she veered left.

"Mom, what are you doing? Why are we going this way?"

"I just wanted to check out a little of this neighborhood. It's really gorgeous, don't you think?" This was an understatement. They'd cruised into the land of the killer estates, bona fide mansions with spring-fed swimming pools and chemically lush green lawns that rolled out to views of the sea.

"I've gotta take a whiz," Aiden announced.

Caitlin let out another and deeper sigh. The kid always had to take a whiz, couldn't go fifty minutes at a stretch without charging into the nearest john or Portosan or behind some poor soul's hibiscus bush. Nervous bladder, the pediatrician called it, one of about ninety-nine syndromes Aiden would supposedly outgrow. "You can hold it in for ten minutes. We'll stop at the gas station by the freeway."

"I don't think I can."

"Trust me. I know you can." She gave him an encouraging wink. "I've got confidence in you."

She hung a right. If memory served, Sierra Alta should be coming up nearby. Bingo, *a la derecha!* She turned left onto a heartbreakingly stunning little lane, bordered by fieldstone walls that frothed with profusions of honeysuckle and white morning glory. *Nothin' says money like fieldstone.*

"Mom, I've gotta go."

"Five minutes." She slowed the car to a creep. The lane ended in a towering pair of wrought-iron gates; they were festooned with an intricate pattern of leaves and tubular flowers that seemed a natural extension of the honeysuckle. No street number, needless to say. The estate, she recalled, had a name—Twelve Oaks or Seventeen Streams or some such—but nothing so tacky as to be displayed. You knew whose gates these were, or you had no goddamned business being here.

So was there any possible business she could drum up for herself—anything that could lead to some kind of contact?

The germ of an idea suddenly sprouted in her mind and within an instant rooted. Her heart pounded as she realized what she was about to do.

She braked the car. She reached up and snatched a hank of her hair to test that it still had some spring. Then, arm still crooked, she gave her pit a quick sniff. No discernible BO and just the faintest of sweat stains. She shot a glance over her shoulder to make sure Aiden was still buckled up.

The she tapped the gas, oh so gently, as she swung the wheel and veered the car at an oblique angle toward the gates.

Metal hit metal with a loud and sickening crunch. The sound of a shattering headlight merged with a jagged shriek from the backseat. She slammed the brakes, but the car had already jolted to a halt.

Jesus, God, she must have accelerated more than she'd intended.

"Mo-o-om!"

She unbuckled her seat belt and whipped around. "Aidey, are you okay?"

"You just crashed our car. What'd you *do* that for?"

He appeared to be fine, thank God, thank God! But for once his aggrieved whine was justified. What kind of monster mom deliberately slammed her car into an iron gate with her child strapped in back? Christ, she ought to be locked away!

"I'm really sorry, sweetie," she said, struggling to control her voice. "My foot kind of slipped."

"You're *stupid*! You wrecked our car. Now what are we gonna do?"

"Not wrecked. It's just a dent, no biggie." To demonstrate, she put the car in reverse. A second dislodgment of headlight shards sprinkled musically onto the asphalt.

"Mo-om!"

"It's okay, it's okay." And it was. Caitlin peered over the hood and saw no apparent damage. Apparently the Volvo really *was* the safest car ever made; wasn't that a hoot? The impact hadn't even been enough to activate the air bags.

She switched the engine off, slid out, and surveyed the front. The right fender and headlight were crumpled, as if they'd been punched by a superhuman fist, but that seemed to be it as far as damage went. She examined the area of the gates she had hit. Some scratches and flakes of silver paint, but otherwise hardly even a nick.

She began hunting for something that resembled an intercom amidst the bee-swept honeysuckle entangling the flanking posts. There was a sudden click, followed by a discreet rumble; and then, as if on her unspoken command—*Open sesame!*—the gates began to part.

A small silvery-green Lexus cruised up from behind the gates and came to a stop.

Jesus, of course, there must be hidden cameras galore. Delayed shock rippled through her, causing her to shake herself like a wet cat; it subsided into an internal vibrating little spool of dread.

What the hell had she gotten herself into?

She pasted her doll's smile on her face and walked with a deliberately measured step to the driver's window. At the wheel was a youngish, well-muscled guy with cocoa skin, his eyes canceled out by black-lensed shades.

"Hi, there!" she said brightly.

"Afternoon. Want to tell me what happened here?" Creepy security-guy voice, devoid of inflection.

"I'm afraid I just hit your gates. I didn't realize this was a dead end, so I tried to make a U-turn and, um, I guess I swung a little too far." She gave a little shrug: *klutzy little me.* "I'm really very sorry about this."

"Need a service truck?"

"No, oh, no, I just smashed a headlight. Your gates got a little scratched up, though, so I need to give you my insurance info and whatever." She was talking to her own face in his dark glasses—weird, like rehearsing a speech into a mirror. "And maybe I could, like, leave a note for Mr. Clemente? I mean, I know him. A little. My son is a good friend of Noah's; they were at St. Mattie's together."

"Your name?"

"Cait Latch. Caitlin. My son's name is Aiden; that's him in the car. He's kind of shaken up, if he could get, like, maybe a glass of water?"

The window whirred up. The driver embarked upon what appeared to be a conversation with himself, while Caitlin waited, shifting her weight anxiously from one foot to the other. The window whirred down. "You're to go up to the house. Follow me, please." Up scope again, and then the Lexus looped an effortless one-eighty.

She scurried back to the Volvo and started the engine. "What's going on?" Aiden demanded.

She pulled forward. "We're going up to these people's house for a minute. I need to give them my insurance and stuff."

"Mo-om."

"It'll just be for a flash." She trailed the Lexus through an archway bisecting a two-story stone gatehouse. They emerged onto a drive composed of some sort of translucent pink stone. *Like driving on crushed jewels!* she thought. The drive meandered through a lemon grove heavy with fruit, flowed through immaculately tended lawns, then pooled into a glittering circle in front of the main house. The Lexus stopped and idled meaningfully.

Caitlin pulled up behind. "C'mon," she said to Aiden.

"I don't want to."

"Get out of the goddamned car," she hissed.

She slid out and surveyed the house. English country baronial in style, with a venerable gray stone facade. Big—huge, even—but without seeming massive. The air was fragrant with honeysuckle, eucalyptus, and roses.

The front door swung open as magically as the gates had. A tiny old man with Mayan-mask features hovered in the doorway, the portal-keeper of some god-dwelling realm. He moved mutely to one side. Caitlin jerked a follow-me with her chin to Aiden and crossed the threshold.

Enormous vaulted foyer drenched with an almost ecclesiastical light. Carved and gilded wood. An Oriental carpet so threadbare you knew it had to be priceless. On one wall glowed a large painting, sad, floating rectangles of rose and violet—perhaps the very Rothko that had led to Susanna Clemente's abdication?

Another young man materialized from an adjoining room. With his fuzz of hair bleached platinum and his round dark blue eyes, he reminded Caitlin of one of those baby seals that are clubbed to death for their fur. "Ms. Latch, how do you do? I'm Barry Lewis." He extended a hand to shake. Soft, slightly squishy. "Sorry about your mishap; glad there was no real harm done. Mr. Clemente is very eager to see you."

"He's home?" Caitlin asked.

"Oh, sure, since he's become fully involved in the foundation, he prefers working from here. He's in the office wing, so why don't you just come along with me?" He swiveled like a ballroom dancer on the toe of one loafer.

Amazing! Her stupid little stunt was working out better than she could have wildly imagined. Instinctively and unconsciously she reconfigured her posture—shoulders back and down to thrust out her boobs, back slightly arched to highlight her butt. "Come on, Aidey," she whispered.

He crept up beside her, slipping his hand in hers. A pungent smell attacked her nostrils.

Fuck fuckety fuck fuck. There could be no hiding the fact that her son had peed in his pants.

CHAPTER *three*

One of the Most Desirable Women on the Planet

Fairy tales can come true; it can happen to you . . .

Sinatra's voice warbled thinly in Lally's head as she pushed herself through the last torturous five minutes on the elliptical machine, the one line repeating over and over, sometimes seeping into *da da dah, da da dah* before skipping back to the song's beginning and the fairy tale. Lally was halfway through her daily hour-and-twenty-minute workout in her peach-painted home gym. The lyrics competed with the guttural encouragement crooned by her personal fitness coach, Russell, who was crouched at eye level to her straining glutes: "C'mon, squeeze those abductors! Do it, give it to me hot, girl, tight buns, oh, yeah, tighter!" When she did focus on his voice, it led her to a knotty problem: How was she going to fire Russell as her lover and still keep him as her coach?

Fairy tales can come true. . . . It was four days after the historical society luncheon, and the fairy tale Lally had her sights on was a pleasant middle-aged man with a billion dollars to his bottom line. It was elementary, my dear Watson, *élémentaire,* that she would be seriously jeopardizing her chances by boinking a thirty-two-year-old fitness trainer on the side.

Brrrnng. The timer on the machine sounded. She collapsed over the bars in a sopping, muscle-quivering heap.

"Sen-sational." Russell handed her a plump white towel, and she blotted her dripping face. "Okay, hit the mat, belly down," he ordered.

She obediently hopped off the machine and stretched facedown on the yoga mat. Russell straddled the small of her back and placed the heels of his hands under her shoulder blades—such a marvelous touch!—and his fingers curled around her shoulders. "Lift and arch."

She lifted her chest and arched her back and lowered again, as the tune revolved in her mind: *It can happen to you. . . .*

Could it? Lally arched her back. Could it really happen to her?

Lally had grown up in a tract house in an unprosperous suburb of the San Fernando Valley. Her father, Howie, was a buoyant, exuberant man with half-moon green eyes who smoked Camels down to the filter and who changed jobs the way other fathers traded in cars—every two or three years, he'd chuck the old one and come up with something new. Among his many endeavors were: demonstrating a kitchen gadget called the Slice-o-Magic (Slice-a-Finger it turned out to be); breeding long-haired rabbits (they contracted bunny mange and lost their fur); cornering the market on stashes of 3-D glasses for the 3-D movie revival that never came; going partners in a soft-ice-cream franchise called Swirly's (kaput after a Carvel opened across the street).

Howie Siplowsky had plunged into each new enterprise with boundless optimism. "This is it, kiddikins!" he'd say to Lally, swinging her by the waist. "It's the pot of gold at the end of the rainbow! It's going to make us rich as princes." He made it sound like a fairy tale: Each time, Lally pictured him returning from an adventure in a dark forest or up a giant beanstalk with an iron pot brimming with doubloons.

She could never understand why her mother, Deena, refused to be swept up in his exuberance. "Oh, Howie," she'd murmur with a resigned little sigh; then she'd trudge off to her dreary breadwinner's job answering phones for an actuarial firm in Woodland Hills. Sometimes Lally thought it was her mother's doom-and-gloom that caused her father's ventures to fail—a sort of spell that worked a countermagic against him.

Lally was thirteen when Howie vanished from their lives. He'd been hawking novelty balloons to florists and party suppliers. It was a job that kept him traveling, and Lally had liked to imagine him, not inching his dented Fairlane down congested highways, but wafting freely through the air lifted by a huge bunch of red, pink, and yellow balloons. When he left for good, she knew perfectly well it was for a Peruvian woman in Rancho Cucamonga who baked erotic cakes for bachelor parties and fraternal lodge meetings using pink balloons for the breasts. Lally also knew well that it was by no means the first affair Howie had had over the years.

Still, she could never shake the idea that her father had been carried off by his balloons and was still somewhere being swept helplessly away through ever faster-moving clouds.

"Hands and knees!" Russell barked. "Now downward-facing dog!"

Lally scrambled to her hands and knees, lifted her tailbone high in the air, and stretched back on her heels. Holding the rigorous yoga pose, she still heard the melody: *Fairy tales can come true. . . .*

Three times in her life she'd thought it *had* happened, the fairy tale with the happily-ever-after payoff.

Three times she'd been bitterly disappointed.

Fairy tale number one: movie star. At the age of twenty-six and as a single mother of a baby girl, up-and-coming starlet Lally Chandler shoves aside Cybill Shepherd, knocks off Katharine Ross, vaults over Candice Bergen, to land the role of Priscilla Much in *Dying Is Easy.* Lally is the next Bond girl, which means she's been anointed one of the most desirable women on the planet, in the company of Miss Universe and the *Sports Illustrated* swimsuit-issue cover model. For a year she inhabits a magical land where people stir and flashbulbs pop wherever she sets foot, and her phone never stops pealing.

But what she doesn't know is that she is being hunted, stalked, and pursued by a wicked godmother who waves an evil wand and makes sure the film is a stinker—the worst James Bond ever made (unless you count the first spoofy *Casino Royale,* and most people did *not*). Her paper-thin character—who existed solely to wear a body cavity–clinging leotard and purr, "Oh, James"—erases any stature she might have acquired as an actress and replaces it with "babe"; and as everyone knows, the life span of a babe in Hollywood is approximately 10.6 seconds. Before the following year is up, Lally's career consists of hawking an apparatus called the Thigh Corrector on daytime infomercials.

Fairy tale number two: true love. She's living in Paris off the last of her Thigh Corrector money, stretching it to support her untamable daughter who is constantly getting expelled from Swiss and Austrian boarding schools, when Lally falls dizzyingly, passionately, dancing-on-the-moon in love with Helmut Grass, three-time Oscar nominee for cinematography, a caustic bon vivant with the looks of a ravaged Norse god—far giddier and intense than what she'd felt for her first husband Tommy, which now seems to her to have been just a teenage crush. They have a romping affair through the five-star hotels of Europe, Japan, and British Columbia, and are married by a monk in a seaside chapel in Monte Carlo.

The first time Helmut beats her, three months after the wedding, she blames it on circumstances: His father had just succumbed to pancreatic cancer and he'd been passed over yet again for an Academy Award. The second time, well, okay, he'd been out on the town with a Very Important Director who'd ordered up a pre–World War I Delamain, and though Helmut never could tolerate cognac, it would've been professional suicide to refuse it. The third time, in a hotel suite in Auckland, fracturing her cheekbone and cracking one of her canine teeth, she puts in a call to an old pal, a Teamster from the set of one of her early films; then she packs her bags and jets to Mexico for a quickie divorce, reading with satisfaction some weeks later that poor Helmut has been savagely pummeled by unknown assailants after leaving an after-hours dive in Tribeca.

Fairy tale number three: celebrity wife. She's still a knockout at thirty-eight when she snags Artie Willman, former host of the seventies and eighties game-show hit *Have I Got a Deal for You!*. So what if he's more than three decades older, his head beneath the custom toupee of a splotched pink dome, more grizzled fur on his back than your average bear? Or that he sleeps in a bed tilted up to keep down his acid reflux;

or that he needs triple-dose Viagra just to get a serviceable erection? The perks of being Mrs. Celeb make it worthwhile. She coaxes him out of Palm Springs—geezerville!—and they resettle in Colina Linda, where Lally bounds straight to the top of the social heap: chairperson of the opera board, even though she's tone-deaf and doesn't know *Aida* from Aunt Jemima.

But it begins to dawn on her that Artie is less of a bona fide celebrity and more of . . . well, a joke. She cringes when passersby yodel, "Hey, Artie, co-o-ome and get it!", the catchphrase from that ridiculous show. What she's actually become is Mrs. Running Gag, and this is ultimately unacceptable.

Sweet Artie. He's actually relieved when she calls it quits. Turns out he's been terrified that all that Viagra would lead to an in flagrante delicto cardiac arrest.

Three attempts at happily-ever-after. Three waves of an evil godmother's wand. But now, finally, as her forties are advancing with terrifying swiftness, the real thing has presented itself to her.

It can happen to you. . . . It wasn't just about the money—darling Artie had been more than generous. But ten figures got you more than just buying power. It got you *access*. Forget making a splash in a dinky little pond like San Carlino: Lally saw herself dazzling the world. Clad in Narciso Rodriguez, she would waltz into opening-night galas for the Covent Garden and the Met. Sit demurely between Charlize Theron and Princess Stephanie at the Paris collections. Lift a discreet paddle to bid on an important de Kooning at Sotheby's. She imagined herself whispering with Hillary, possibly getting goosed by Bill, and she knew she could bring tears to the eyes of an international assembly with her stirring presentation to Bono of the first Clemente Award for Humanitarian Services.

"Beauti-ful, baby." Russell's voice snapped her back to the present. They were the same words in the exact same tone of voice he'd employed two hours before, when he'd had his face buried between her thighs. "Okay, now roll over and we'll do some abs."

Perhaps the best approach was the direct one. She sighed, rolled over, and sat up."Russell, darling," she said. "I think we need to reconsider our relationship."

In the end it was easy. He was actually relieved—he'd been starting to worry that because they were having sex, she was going to begin demanding to be trained for free. It would have been flattering, Lally supposed, if he'd been just a little upset at getting kicked out of her bed, instead of taking it in such cheerful stride. But she was of a pragmatic mind—whatever worked! And anyway, she had a busy day ahead, no time to brood.

One P.M.: Lunch with the steering board of the Environmental Council at Ponte, soggy risotto and a brain-numbing discussion of erosion at Graypiper Bluffs.

Two forty-five: crucial pit stop at Saks lingerie department. Perimenopause—so gross—had caused her periods to go wild, leaking even through a super Tampax and wreaking havoc with her panties supply.

Three forty-five: Medical center on Despuesta, second-floor dermatological offices of Dr. Toshi Yoshimato.

Always a packed waiting room. There was her across-the-street neighbor, Aline Belkin, looking like death with a nose job. And eighty-something Celia Roederer, sporting a tennis dress, God help us. Lally flashed smiles at both women, then helped herself to a muddy demitasse and sloshed down a Valium (she despised injections). She settled herself on one of the mint-colored couches and flipped open her cell phone, scrolling down the IDs of five new messages. Four of these she summarily—even contemptuously—deleted. The fifth caused her to pause and stare at it a moment, feeling a rare prickling of guilt.

Tommy. She'd forgotten to call him back. She supposed he was pretty lonely, uprooted as he was from his beloved New England, and still grieving after his truly horrific tragedy. She would absolutely get back to him soon. She pressed KEEP AS NEW, then flipped shut the phone and picked up a copy of *W*. As she was studying a Valentino ensemble, wondering if all that gathering at the waistline would make her look like the Queen of Bloat, her new most intimate friend, Janey Martinez, emerged from the inner offices.

"Lally!" Janey squealed. Her round face, which was usually spackled with putty-colored foundation, now looked scrubbed and red-raw, the upper lip puffed to a startling degree.

"Darling, this is marvelous! You did it!" Lally rose. In deference to Janey's inflamed facial condition, they double air-kissed six inches from each other's cheeks. "So tell me, what exactly did you get?"

"Botox here and here . . ." Janey gingerly dabbed at the corner of an eye and between her brows. "And then here"—she traced the swollen bow of her upper lip—"I let him inject that stuff that comes from cadavers . . . ?"

"Alloderm, yes, it's fantastic."

"It kind of hurt. I look okay, don't I? I mean, I don't have blowfish lips or anything?"

Actually, Lally thought, they looked more in the grouper family; but she knew from hard experience that within a day the swelling would subside and a youthfully firm bow line would make its lovely appearance. "Darling, Toshi's a magician. Believe me, by tomorrow you'll look ten years fresher."

"God, I hope so."

Lally reached for Janey's hand and squeezed it. "You'll be dancing on air."

This newfound joined-at-the-hip status between herself and Janey had been soldered at the historical society luncheon. The two had been the last to leave, lingering at the table until almost five, gabbing mostly about Rhonda's bombshell. At some point Janey had voiced the obvious: "God, he'd be a great catch," and Lally had replied, with a coy flick of a brow, "Interested?" and Janey had responded with an emphatic shake of her head—not that she'd even be in the running, of course. But then she had ventured, "But Lally I'd think *you* could be his type," and Lally had modestly slanted her eyes downward and murmured, "Do you think? I mean, I've always admired him so much, what he's done with the foundation and all," and Janey had agreed, "Oh, yeah, it's great."

"Of course I'd love to get to know him better," Lally had continued, "but I hardly ever see him," and Janey had said, with just a hint of smugness, "I do. And I know zillions of people who see him all the time."

Lally's mind had started to tick away.

The thing was that Janey, despite her Miz Mouse demeanor, had amazing connections. Both she and her ex, the jailbird Robbie Martinez, were old San Carlino, meaning not only had they been born and raised here, but so had their parents, grandparents, and a goodly number of their great- and great-*great*-grandparents. Janey, if you could believe, had made her debut at the Colina Linda Jasmine and Roses Cotillion, which was infinitely more prestigious than the dowdy old soccer mom–ish Junior League. She belonged to the golf club—no big deal, anybody with a teacup to piss in could join Fairlawns—but also the Old Colina Linda Country Club, which forbade the wearing of denim on the premises, and the San Carlino Sailing Club, which, despite its rotting docks and clubhouse coated with mildew so thick it looked like moss, was so exclusive that (as the local joke had it) even God would have to marry into it.

Oh, yeah, Lally could use Janey's connections. Lally did have a nodding acquaintance with David Clemente. He wasn't a ghost—ghosts were what they called those people, celebrities and brand-name CEOs, who hunkered behind the walls of their estates and never engaged in the life of the town. The Clementes had fingers in many San Carlino pies: They just never happened to be the same pies as Lally's. She was opera; they were symphony. She was historical society; they were art museum. She was cerebral palsy; they were spina bifida. Etc.

And anytime Lally had ventured to invite them to dinner or a cocktail, she'd received a polite but hasty rejection from that pill Susanna.

Lally had scoured her mind for a tit-for-tat. "You know what I've always admired about *you,* Janey? You're just not obsessed with your appearance. You're so au naturel, not like the rest of us shallow creatures."

"What do you mean?" Janey had asked warily.

"I mean, here you've got the potential to be smashing, if you really put the effort into it, but it's just really never been your concern."

Janey had squirmed uncertainly in her chair. Lally seemed to be calling her a frump, meaning she ought to be highly affronted. On the other hand, when it came to looks, precious few people in Janey's life had praised even her potential.

"I suppose I ought to do a bit more with myself," she had allowed.

"Well, if you feel that way, you know what I think would be fun? Let me do a makeover on you. Nothing too glitzy, of course. We'd just make the most of what you've already got."

"So, like, what did you have in mind?"

"Well, for starters . . ." Lally's gaze had fluttered to Janey's forehead, where years of a tetchy disposition had etched a deep groove between the brows. Then she'd produced one of the Ladies Who Lunch invitations with its photo of a woman's decomposed arm waving from a partially dug-up desert grave, and on the back she'd printed the name of the artistic Dr. Toshi Yoshimato.

And so an unspoken pact was formed: Lally would take Janey under her wing, be her cosmetic *Queer Eye,* show her the sartorial ropes; and in return, Janey would coach Lally on how to worm herself into the Clemente consciousness.

The hush-voiced Asian nurse at the desk now inquired if Janey would like to book a follow-up. Janey responded with one of those irritable hand-snapping gestures she specialized in—*Not now*! Then she poured herself an espresso, dumped in a packet of Splenda, stirred it to a sludge, and tossed it back, like a drunk with a shot of whiskey. "I hardly slept a wink last night," she declared.

"You're a worrywart like me, aren't you? I toss and turn over the most trivial little things."

Janey hesitated. It wasn't worry that kept her awake. It was terror. She habitually bolted out of a deep sleep convinced she heard a footstep creaking on the stairs or someone jimmying a window on the bottom floor. Oddly enough, while she was married, it was Robbie who'd been the paranoid one. Kept a pistol stashed in his bedside drawer and a Winchester twelve-gauge in the closet, and scarcely a night went by when sometime between midnight and dawn he hadn't sat bolt upright and croaked, "I think I hear something!" Once during a Santa Ana wind, there was a noise out in the yard, and he'd actually grabbed the pistol and fired it—*blam, blam, blam!*—out the window—only to find in the morning that he'd shot the bejesus out of a market umbrella that had toppled in the wind.

But now that she was living alone, his paranoia seemed to have infected her, like some germ he'd left behind on the toilet seat. That story Caitlin Latch had told at lunch, for example: It had really creeped her out. In the dim, silent hours of the night, Janey could vividly imagine the hooded figure invading her room—although for some weird reason she pictured him disguised not as Spider-Man but as Kermit the Frog. Not even the sight of her two Cavalier King Charles spaniels, Brent and Brenda, curled peacefully asleep at the foot of her bed, would reassure her; she'd lie awake for hours, immobilized with dread, her stomach hollow and a taste like sour metal coating her mouth.

She couldn't tell this to Lally, of course. Lally would mock her mercilessly, those green-gold eyes lighting up with sardonic glee. "I suppose it's these new clients I just took on," she said. "They're driving me kind of nuts."

"Poor you, demanding clients can be such a bitch. Anybody I know?"

"The Dornholms? Warren and Marcy? I'm doing a room for them." After her divorce, Janey had audited a few horticulture courses at the college, and she now designed garden rooms for a few select acquaintances. A cachet job. All the exes had cachet jobs—something with which to reply to that most ubiquitous of dinner-party questions: "And what do *you* do?" Lally, for example, was a third owner, along with a pair of energetic septuagenarians, in a French-milled soap and candle boutique in Old Mission Plaza, which allowed her to burble on about "my shop" without ever actually having to set foot in it.

"Are they being impossible?" Lally prodded gently.

Janey let out a leaky sigh. "They keep saying they want something very Zen, but then they come up with catalogs for all this froufrou stuff, pergolas and gazebos and shit."

"I do know Marcy Dornholm, and she's about as Zen as a tuna-fish sandwich."

"What I thought." Janey plopped her wide hips down on the sofa beside Lally. "But if I don't do something about this insomnia, I think I'm going to lose my mind. You wouldn't happen to have anything, would you? Xanax, or something like that?"

Lally hesitated only the merest fraction of a second. "Would a little Valium help?" She plucked the vial from her Hermès tote and sprinkled several pills into Janey's open palm.

Janey closed her fist around them and stashed them in her own bag. Then, relaxing, she tilted her head back against the wall. "Actually, Lall, I was going to call you later. I had quite a long chat with my cousin Debba this morning."

Lally was all ears. "The one who's trustee of the Learning Hoop?"

"It's Loop. Learning *Loop*."

"Either way, it still makes it sound like they're going around in circles. Why don't they call it the Learning Rocket Ship or the Learning Freeway?"

"I don't *know*," Janey said irritably.

"Oh, well . . ." Lally gave a *n'importe quoi* wave of her fingers. "What did Debba say?"

"Well, naturally because Noah goes there, she's pretty cozy with the Clementes, so I asked her if she'd seen either of them lately, and she went on about how Dave's become totally obsessed over Indian education. He wants to fund a charter school on the Topanga reservation, and he's trying to drum up some sort of lobbying effort in Congress."

"Well, that is interesting," Lally said with studied casualness. "Did you know I've got some Indian blood in me? Apache. Going way, way back, of course."

"I'm not surprised. What with your cheekbones."

A nurse rustled in the doorway. "Doctor is ready for you, Lally."

Lally started to gather her shopping bags and bulky tote.

"Oh, leave it," Janey said. "I'll wait and we can walk out together. And then I can fill you in a bit more."

"Blessings, darling. Oh, I almost forgot. I set it up with my gal at La Rocha for you, noon on Tuesday. Marie-Celeste. Best bikini wax in town."

"That hurts too, doesn't it?"

Lally flashed on a recent memory of Janey sprawled on a chaise at the club pool, twin spumes of ginger-colored pubic hair frothing from the crotch of her swimsuit. "Believe me, darling, it's worth it."

CHAPTER *four*

Who Gets Possession of the Restaurant?

Jessica DiSantini walked stark naked into the glass-and-polished-blond-wood vestibule of the Five Cranes Café.

Okay, she wasn't *actually* stark naked. She was clad in a perfectly decent pleated light wool skirt and smoky-red cashmere mock turtleneck, not to mention burgundy leather boots, opaque tights, and assorted undergarments and accessories; but it was the first time she'd been to this restaurant since she'd removed her wedding ring, and it seemed to her that a spotlight glared on her denuded finger, casting it into high relief and throwing the rest of her in shadow. Should any of the diners happen to glance up from their crispy lavender duck or twice-simmered saffron noodles, she was positive that this was all they'd register: naked, naked, naked.

Five Cranes had been *their* restaurant. She and Michael had eaten here at least twice a month during most of the years of their marriage. They'd celebrated five of their sixteen anniversaries at their special table by the octagonal window; her thirty-ninth birthday, when they were still giddy with relief that the lump in her breast was not malignant; the heady occasion of Michael's promotion to chief of neurosurgery.

It was here, for God's sake, in the postage-stamp-sized and almond-scented ladies' room, that her water had broken the night Alex was born.

The place howled with the ghosts of her married life.

So what lunacy had prompted her to suggest it as a place to meet for a drink?

The fact was, she'd been startled by the invitation: She thought she'd made it crystal clear to Lally that she was absolutely, positively not in the blind-date business. So typical of Lally not to listen and give Jessica's number to her ex-husband anyway.

Thomas Bramberg had called a few days ago. The funny thing was, he'd sounded equally startled to be *making* the call. Jessica had been distracted by Rowan's twelve-year-old mynah Booter, who was supposed to live to about a hundred and nine, but was hunched up in a corner of his cage, emitting a sort of gargly sound that for all Jessica knew could have been an avian death rattle; and so she'd blurted out to Thomas Bramberg, "Fine, Thursday. How about Five Cranes? It's got a pretty nice bar," before hanging up and dashing Booter off to the bird-and-reptile vet, for the happy diagnosis that it was just the mynah bird equivalent of an adolescent sulk.

She glanced at her watch. She was late, but he was obviously later— there appeared to be no single man in the bar. What was it he said he did? Something to do with music, wasn't it? She pictured an aging hipster, affecting cool in a black leather jacket. Perhaps an earring, or a tattoo à la Lally.

Jesus, God. She must have been out of her mind.

The reservation desk was temporarily abandoned. She could see the owner and host, Jonathan Wing, in the main room, schmoozing the Albrights, an architect couple who, by virtue of being black, pretty much doubled the African-American population of Colina Linda. She could sneak out now, and no one would even have to know she'd ever been here. She turned, half determined to do just that, when the door swung open and in blew Michael and the Brain.

They were arm in arm, as giggly and mutually absorbed as a couple of teenagers. They stopped dead at the sight of Jessica. For a second all three stood jammed in the tight space, regarding one another with silent dismay.

Then Michael's face congealed into the shit-eating grin that had been his business as usual expression throughout the divorce proceedings. "Oh, ah, Jess," he mumbled. "Hi."

"Hello, Michael," she managed. "Hello, Amanda."

Jonathan Wing chose that moment to glide back up to the reservation desk. "Good evening, Dr. DiSantini," he began, and then faltered, as his eye fell first on the former Mrs. DiSantini, and then on the presumptive future Mrs. DiSantini. "Ah, um . . . table for three?"

"No," snapped the Brain. "We're not all together."

A floppy orange beret melted over the top of her head like some kind of surreal Salvador Dalí timepiece. Jessica wanted to imagine that its purpose was to disguise the crusted and oozing slice of raw scalp left exposed by Michael's inept sawing; but she knew that the Brain's abundant chestnut curls more than sufficiently covered any scarring that might remain.

"I don't need a table, Jonathan," Jessica said evenly. "I'm meeting someone at the bar." She turned with a less decisive movement than she would have liked and headed to one of the cocktail tables skirting the blond-wood bar.

Amanda. Uh-man-duh. She wasn't even that pretty. Sharp nose, drab skin. The curls were good, but hardly made up for enormous, Bozo-worthy feet and a crabby, perpetual-PMS temper. Nor was she any great shakes in the intellect department, as far as Jessica could determine.

So what was it, while rummaging around in the pulpy folds of her gray matter, that Michael had found so damned irresistible?

As if to answer that question, he suddenly came trotting up behind her. "Jess. Could I talk to you a sec?"

She stiffened.

"Listen, I'm sorry Amanda was a little curt. You just took us by surprise."

"Yeah, it's astonishing to find me in a restaurant I've been coming to for, what, fourteen years?"

"Okay, look, we both love this place. I guess we just have to deal with that." He smiled, this time in a non-shit-eating way—that sweet Michael smile that lit up his brown eyes and brought his dimples out.

She allowed herself to smile tentatively back. "So who gets possession of the favorite restaurant? I guess we should've covered that in the settlement."

"Yeah, I guess we should've. So . . . you meeting Taller?"

"No. Nobody you know."

"Oh." He nodded, as if he'd suspected as much. "Let's sit down a second, okay?"

She hesitated, then shrugged. "Okay."

It was a shock to discover how very familiar it felt to be seated across from him. He was *Michael.* That charcoal sweater—it was from a sale at Emporio Armani and had a tiny pull in one sleeve from when he'd snagged it on the mailbox. Those two freckles that made an umlaut above his left eyebrow—how many times had she and the kids teased him about it?

It all just felt so . . . well, normal.

Maybe he thought so too. The way he was gazing at her with that soft shine, maybe he was discovering that being here with her, in this particular place, made everything click back into its safe and rightful pre-Brain disposition.

"You know, it might be a good thing I've run into you," he said. "There's something I want to tell you." He smiled even more tenderly, and her heart turned over. "I'm getting married a week from next Saturday."

It was like a slap. She could feel the sting on her cheeks. "A week from Saturday."

"I realize we're rushing it a bit, but the reason is . . . well . . . Mandy's pregnant. Five weeks, we just confirmed yesterday. It's twins." He pronounced the word *twins* smugly, like a shopper who'd just scored some two-for-one deal on dental floss or raspberry-scented shampoo.

Jessica struggled to breathe. "Have you told Rowan and Alex yet?"

"No, not yet, but we will. I've got a feeling they're going to be pretty excited when they hear they're getting a couple of new siblings."

"You are an insensitive, selfish prick," she said.

His face flushed with anger, but just for an instant. It was that surgeon thing: You can accidentally slice open a vital organ, there can be blood gushing like Old Faithful, flatline on the monitor, and still you remain cool, calm, and in exquisite control. "I wanted to make this easy for all of us," he said coolly and calmly, "but obviously you're determined to make it as difficult as possible. So I'm just gonna lay this right out on the line. My circumstances are changing. I've got new mouths to feed, heavy new obligations. So I'm going to be seeking a pretty substantial cut in my support payments."

"You can't do that," she gasped.

"You're a lawyer, honey. You know damned well I can. I've already told Wiener to schedule an arbitration hearing." He got to his feet. "And know this too, Jessica. Nothing you do or say is going to spoil my joy in this event. And I can only hope that someday you find half as much joy for yourself."

He walked with an almost jaunty step back into the main room.

You could drop dead, buster. That would bring me a hell of a lot of joy.

It was what she should've said; and for a moment she nearly sprang to her feet and ran after him.

But she didn't. She remained in her chair, a chill numbness creeping inward from her fingertips. Outside, a train rumbled by, the Pacific Surfliner, halfway in its coastal run between San Diego and San Luis Obispo. It added a bass line to the insipid piping of the café's music. Train whistles and mission bells—these were the distinguishing sounds of San Carlino; and in Colina Linda, it was the train that predominated. Sometimes Jessica found this romantic. Old Hitchcock movies and all that. But right now it made her feel almost desperately forlorn—like a figure in an Edward Hopper painting, slumped in some end-of-the-line diner at three in the morning. . . .

Oh get a grip, she told herself.

Or better yet, get a drink. She swiveled to signal to the bartender.

"Jessica?" Someone suddenly loomed above her. "I am so sorry. Hope you haven't been waiting long."

There was a leather jacket—she'd gotten that right—except it was brown, not black, and battered to near shapelessness. Above that, a kind of rumply face. Prominent nose, wide, rubbery mouth. Salt-and-pepper mop top flopping over big ears. Not in a million years could she imagine a man like this with Lally, and for a confused moment she thought that perhaps he was a supernumerary, a messenger, maybe, or a driver, the real Thomas Bramberg waiting out in a car.

"You are Jessica, aren't you?"

"Oh, um . . . Yes, I am."

"Tom Bramberg." As if in some peculiar game of musical exes, he dropped into the chair vacated by Michael. "It took me ages to get across town. There's some kind of fiesta going on, kids whacking piñatas and a mariachi band in the middle of the road. I had to detour way around the mission."

"The Tijera Avenue street fair. We all know to avoid it. I should have warned you."

"Yeah. You know, I really expected you to look different. I was afraid you were going to be . . . I don't know . . . more anorexic."

She gave a faint smile. "I was expecting you to be different too. Flashier, I guess."

"Sorry."

"Oh, no. Believe me, it's fine." There was a pause. They looked at each other uncertainly. She suddenly remembered their phone conversation, what he'd told her he did: He was a composer, doing a year in residency at Moreland. "So you're at the college. Are you living on campus?"

"No, I've got a beach house. Rattrap with an ocean view."

"Oh." Another pause. From the adjoining dining room Jessica heard the Brain laughing. *Whoop, whoop, whoop*—unmistakably her laugh. To Jessica's horror, Rowan had lately begun imitating it, the other day watching a rerun of *The Fresh Prince of Bel Air,* going *whoop, whoop.*

She stood up. "Would you mind if we went someplace else?"

Tom rose as well, startled. "Whatever you want."

She strode rapidly to the door and threw herself outside. Scarves and petticoats of white fog drifted in from the ocean, like garments off some ghostly clothesline. Another train whistle mourned in the distance. For several moments they stood awkwardly on the sidewalk, not meeting each other's eyes.

"So, uh, do you know a place?" he said. "I'm not really familiar with this neighborhood."

Suddenly she could no longer help herself. She started to cry, great, heaving, convulsive sobs, punctuated with mewling little sounds of grief. She was dimly aware of his arms wrapping around her; she buried her nose in the lapels of his jacket, inhaling that masculine smell, leather and aftershave, sweat and soap. For three full minutes she bawled her head off.

When it stopped, it stopped suddenly. A last shuddering intake of breath and it was over. She drew back, pressing the heels of her hands against her inflamed eyes. "I feel like an idiot."

"Hey, don't think about it." He fished a floret of crumpled Kleenex from his jacket pocket. "This looks disgusting, but it's clean."

"Thanks." She mopped the snot streaming from her nostrils and blew her nose. Poor guy, not only had he drawn a prize loony case, but a pretty damned repulsive one at that. There was a damp spot on his jacket roughly in the shape of West Virginia. She stared at it, wondering if anyone she knew had witnessed her spectacle, and if so, had they gone inside and blabbed to Michael and the Brain?

She snuffled, blew again.

"I guess this really wasn't such a hot idea," she said.

"I guess not," he agreed.

It was only later, while driving home through the now-blanketing fog, that she seemed to remember that at some point in the middle of her sobbing fest, she had felt his lips brush the top of her hair.

But that couldn't be right. She must have simply imagined it.

"So he was a dog, huh?" Rowan was in the kitchen fixing herself a meal. Since proclaiming herself a strict vegan, she was frequently to be found in here, engaged in the chopping and slicing of things like jicama and organic Japanese eggplant; now she leaned over the table arranging thick chunks of produce in a wooden bowl. The ends of her lustrous long hair dangled into the food.

"No, he seemed perfectly nice." Jessica dropped her bag on a chair. She gathered her daughter's hair and swept it back over the girl's shoulders.

"Then why'd you ditch him so fast?"

Jessica hesitated. Oh, hell, the Brain would lose no time blabbing about it anyway. "I ran into your dad and Amanda at the restaurant, and it kind of bummed me out."

"That sucks."

"Yeah, it does. Where's Alex?"

"In Yolanda's room. They're watching some cartoon on one of the Spanish channels." Rowan whacked the heads off a bunch of some bristly-looking vegetable. The gold and silver links of her Medic Alert bracelet slipped over the wrist of her chopping hand; its silver charm, engraved simply with the word EPILEPSY and a number to call, beat gently against her pulse. She hadn't had a seizure since she was ten, almost four years now. She'd been eased off medications and officially pronounced in remission, but Jessica assumed the bracelet had become a part of her; that Rowan wore it the way some people adorned themselves with crucifixes or Stars of David—less out of religious devotion than as markers of personal identity. And Jessica was glad of this—there was always the rare, but terrifyingly real, possibility of a relapse.

"So are you gonna see this guy again?" Rowan asked.

"I don't think so. I've decided I'm really not interested in meeting anybody right now. I'd just rather hang out with you guys."

Rowan delivered one of those head-bobbling, eyeball-rolling expressions—*puh-leeze*—that she'd perfected since becoming a teenager. "You know, Mom, you can't keep moping around hoping Dad's going to come back. 'Cause he's not going to. He's with Amanda now, so you really ought to deal with it."

Jessica had the urge to smack her hard, epilepsy be damned. *Let's see how breezy you are, kiddo, when he shoves you aside for his new twin little brats,* she thought. For composure, she plucked a radish from the bowl and bit it.

"Nobody's moping, Rowan," she said evenly. "In case you haven't noticed, I've been extremely busy lately. I'm just about up to my ears in commitments. Running this house alone is a full-time job. If there comes a time when I feel I need more in my life, then I'll do something about it."

"Okay, okay. Whatever." Rowan dumped the bristly choppings in with the rest.

Jessica watched her a moment, still struggling to keep her temper. "I'm going to go tell your brother and Yolanda I'm home," she said. She turned briskly and headed to the housekeeper's room.

Hours later, when Alex was asleep and Rowan was ensconced in her bedroom instant-messaging her crew of friends and a burble of Spanish still muttered from Yolanda's TV, Jessica crept down to the wine cellar. Seventy-two grand they'd spent to convert it from a moisture-decayed storage space. Now it was all limestone floors and antique French tasting table and perfect humidity control. Michael would lead processionals of guests down here as if to some sacred catacomb, all speaking in hushed voices as they descended the winding staircase. Instead of saints' bones, amusing, hard-to-find vintages with dominant notes of elderberry, currant, saddle leather, and who the hell knew? Toe jam.

She browsed what remained of the reds. A 1983 Opus One called out to her, the last of a case sent to Michael by a grateful patient—though seeing as how it had been a sixty-nine-year-old retired oil magnate, presumably not one Michael had subsequently fucked. A bottle of this now sold for about five hundred bucks. Mike had treated it like molten gold.

She'd brought a mug down with her, the ugliest she could find, a chipped thing made of thick dirty-white ceramic and decorated hide-ously with a diapered kangaroo. She popped the wine cork. Filled the mug to the brim.

Here's to you, louse, she toasted, and took a deep gulp.

Lally had not wasted a second. By the time she got home from the dermatologist, she'd already had a dinner party in the works. She visualized it clearly: for twenty—no, make that sixteen—in her courtyard, under the stars, splashing fountains, and the sweet breath of night-blooming jasmine. Cobalt Sèvres. Buccellati flatware. Food exquisite but not ostentatious, perhaps one dish containing corn or pumpkin as a subtle reference to Native America. For atmosphere, that young Brazilian guitarist who was so haunting at Bennett Kleiner's last drinks party . . .

With the stage conceptually set, she placed the first call—to Washington D.C., the office of local congresswoman Mary Novacek. Mary was a dear, dear friend—at least since her last reelection campaign, when Lally had hosted a bagels-and-coffee, swelling Mary's coffers by over two hundred grand. Lally informed an aide that she was planning a small dinner in honor of David Clemente, head of Clemente International as well as the Clemente Foundation, and would like to coordinate it with a time when the congresswoman would be visiting her home district.

Mary herself returned the call within the hour. There was a recess the third week in October; would that jibe with Lally's plans?

Marvelously.

With Mary under her belt, Lally had her assistant, Perla, a morbidly fat young woman with a honeyed phone voice, place the second call—to Topanga tribal chief Ronald Elks Snelling and his wife, inviting them to dinner. They returned an immediate, if somewhat startled, acceptance.

The bait was firmly fastened to the hook. Now to cast it into the water.

Her people (Perla) called his people: "Ms. Lally Chandler wishes to invite Mr. Clemente to a private dinner in support of Topanga Indian education and welfare. Tribal chief Snelling and Congresswoman Mary Novacek will both be attending."

For two days Lally held her breath, tensing every time the phone rang. She was still dripping wet from her workout the morning of the third day when she saw Perla lumbering toward her, signaling a thumbs-up. "He's coming."

"Yippee." Lally clapped her hands and bounced on the balls of her bare feet. "Now we can start to work on the rest of the list. Give me fifteen minutes."

"They also said he's bringing someone."

Lally froze. "Who? From the foundation?"

"I don't know." Perla, who possessed a certain kind of fat person's implacable deliberation, took a maddeningly long time to consult her notepad. "Someone named Caitlin Latch. That's all they said."

The Snatch?

Lally was thunderstruck. Caitlin the Snatch? That climbing bimbo with the suspect tits and the god-awful pathetic kid? It was impossible; she wasn't even in his league. And how the hell could she have gotten to him so fast?

Lally tottered a bit, then realized Perla was still looking at her. She was working herself up over nothing, she told herself. This really wasn't much of a threat; the last few days had left her a little overwrought, that was all. Perhaps half a Valium, just to take the edge off—then she could digest this news clearly.

She went to get the pills, remembering she'd last had them at the dermatologist, in her Hermès tote. The very tote she'd left Janey Martinez to watch over while she went in for her shots—so it shouldn't have come as a surprise to find the vial was no longer there.

CHAPTER *five*

All Is Suffering

Basketball sneakers.

Those were the first things Caitlin registered when she led her reeking, miserable son into David Clemente's office. They were the old-fashioned kind, black and white with flaps that rose over the anklebone—high-tops were they called?—and David was wearing them, along with chinos and an Englishy pastel-striped shirt with a white collar, an outfit that gave him the look of a referee at some backyard lawn tennis match circa 1914. He had risen from behind a curvilinear glass desk on the far side of what might have been an intimidating room, with its soaring walls composed of multipaned windows and millions of dollars' worth of modern art; but as soon as she saw those nutty sneakers, she knew it was going to be okay.

"I've got to get my son to a bathroom," she blurted. Then flushed. What a gauche thing to start off with.

The aide, Barry, had swiveled and his nose twitched as it was suddenly assaulted by the tang of urine. "I'll take care of this," he declared, and scurried to one of the many phones in the room. A squat, motherly-looking Hispanic woman materialized. With much cooing and clucking, she gathered Aiden and formed a small parade, with herself and Aiden at the head, followed by Barry and another young man who'd appeared from God knew where. They marched swiftly out of sight.

"Poor kid," David had said. "I guess the accident really shook him up."

His hair was different, she noticed. Shorter. Better styled. "It wasn't that bad. He just has a nervous bladder. Sometimes he can't keep it in." Another brilliant thing to say. She was really blowing it.

"That's got to be tough. For a kid his age."

"Yeah, but . . ." She faltered. "All is suffering. That's what a Buddhist would say."

He glanced at her quizzically.

And the next thing she knew, she was sitting on a black couch under a painting of some blurry, howling figure (a Francis Bacon she matched later with a similar one in her copy of *The Art Book*) and telling him about Ravi's flip-out, his parading around in orange parkas and blazers and socks, and the gigantic Buddha in the living room, and how about twenty-six times a day he'd come out with the saying, "All is suffering."

"Not even just when he was unhappy or when things were going wrong," she said. "He could be wolfing down an entire box of chocolate cake and still be mumbling it, right through his chewing, with his mouth full of mashed chocolate and all. So finally I looked it up. It's kind of a boiling down of the Buddha's Four Noble Truths into one sort of general statement—all is suffering, or *dukkha,* as it's called in Sanskrit. There're three kinds of suffering, according to the Buddha. There's the obvious kind, like from cancer or a broken heart. Then there's the kind of suffering that comes from change—like even if things are great right this second, it still hurts to know it's not going to last forever. People leave, people die. Things fall apart, right? So then there's a third kind; it's called *samkhara-dukkha,* and it's harder to pin down, but basically it's when you make the mistake of believing in illusion. Like the illusion that the possessions of the material world really mean anything. . . ."

Here she'd broken off in some confusion. The last thing she wanted to suggest was that the stunning possessions in *this* particular material world were anything she was even remotely rejecting.

Illusion, shmusion.

"That's really fascinating," David said, leaning forward. "I've become extremely interested lately in different religions and ways of thinking."

At that point, Caitlin had settled back on the couch and exercised one of her primary talents, which was to let other people do all the talking: She murmured and nodded and gazed with absorption, and half parted her lips as if drinking in every word, while he talked on about . . . well, she could hardly remember what. Something about rituals, and Indians, and the problem of preserving indigenous cultures while still providing a first-class education . . . "Yes," she said breathlessly at the appropriate times, "that's absolutely true!" while at the same time a part of her mind rambled on its own: observing how exquisite the grounds were outside the expanse of windows with the sparkling blue band of Pacific Ocean beyond, and worrying about Aiden and thinking how much better David looked with his restyled hair.

Phones muttered continually while they talked; from time to time a disembodied voice spoke the name of a person or organization into the air, and he'd reply to the air, "We'll get back," or simply, "No." After about fifteen minutes, the voice pronounced a name that sounded like, but couldn't possibly have been, "Martha Washington."

"Yes," David said. He stood up and offered Caitlin a hand. "It's been a great pleasure. My son's in New York with his mother, but next time he's here, maybe we can get the kids together."

She realized she was being dismissed. "That would be wonderful," she murmured, and clasped his hand. Barry was already poised obsequiously in the doorway to guide her back through the sumptuous corridors to the entrance foyer.

A miracle! A happy, eager, talkative boy was waiting for her. He wore a pair of fashionably saggy jeans—so saggy, in fact, that he had to hold them up with one hand. His other hand clutched a shiny shopping bag, which would prove to contain his soiled pants and underwear, rinsed and folded and wrapped in plastic. "They let me play Halo on a forty-seven-inch plasma TV!" he burbled as they got back in the car, "and I beat this guy Carlton by seven kills, and they gave me a DoveBar and said I could keep the jeans—they used to be Noah's but he got too big for them, and they're Sevens like I always wanted!"

At the guardhouse, they were stopped by the multicultural security guy, who shoved a clipboard at her—a release, waiving any culpability on the part of the Clemente family. So that was what all this had been about—lavish a little attention on her, butter up the son, make sure she wouldn't annoy the poor little billionaire with a big fat nuisance lawsuit.

What the hell. She signed the paper and drove out of paradise forever.

Then another miracle.

Exactly one week later, she was upstairs in the cubbyhole that the rental agent had optimistically called a guest room, up to her ass in hats. Nearly every surface of the room was covered in hats, snappy fedoras and wide-brimmed straws, a flower-bedecked clip-on from the fifties, a moth-eaten cloche from the twenties, spangled hats with veils and ugly hats with feathers, and hats trimmed with mangy or luxurious fur; and any space that was left over was taken up by stuff to pack and send hats: cardboard boxes and rolls of transparent sealing tape and flour sack–sized bags of Styrofoam packing popcorn. It was the less lucrative of her two occupations: buying secondhand hats at garage sales and thrift shops and remarketing them as vintage headgear on eBay. She had just finished sealing a package containing a black Fendi floppy-brimmed number, circa the early nineties, which she happened to know had previously belonged to Jessica DiSantini, who had just done a radical cleaning-out of closets. That instinct to purge following a separation—it was something Caitlin knew well. Or to be more accurate, when you finally admitted the separation was for real, and all those souvenirs and knickknacks and gadgets you thought were some kind of glue that would keep the two of you together even over an ever-widening rift—now you just wanted to be rid of them as fast as you could.

Anyway, Jessica had dumped cartons and cartons of stuff at the

Women's Auxiliary League resale shop on East Mesa Road—all of it in pristine condition and bearing designer labels. Problem was, Jessica had too much *taste*—in vintage, it was the outré that tended to fetch top dollar. Score a genuine wig hat from 1969, and you could really clean up.

Caitlin was printing the address of the sendee on the Fendi parcel with a black Magic Marker when her phone rang. She waded through the shoals of felt and fur and straw and dashed into her bedroom to pick it up.

"Ms. Latch? This is Barry Lewis. David Clemente's personal assistant?"

At first she felt a jolt of alarm—what if they were going to sue *her* for purposely ramming their gates? But then his words began to filter through her panic. Lally Chandler. Caitlin's interest in the topic of minority education . . . Attend with Mr. Clemente?

"Yes," she said, barely suppressing a sigh of relief. "I believe I'm available that evening." As opposed to all her *other* evenings, which were clogged up with invites to the White House and Hollywood premieres.

A time was mentioned, a dress code (cocktail attire), a desire for Caitlin to have a wonderful afternoon.

She put down the phone and walked in a daze back to the hat room. She was agog with excitement. Was it actually a date? Would any guy go through an assistant to ask somebody out? For all she knew, the superrich did everything through intermediaries. As far as she was concerned, it was a date. End of discussion.

Screw the hats! She tore a piece of brown wrapping paper off the roll, grabbed a Magic Marker, and started jotting one of her innumerable lists.

Outfit. She'd need something new. Not that she could hope to compete with Lally, who'd be decked out in Saint-Laurent and dripping with important jewels. Caitlin would wear something simple, fitted, with just a hint of the tarty—plunging neckline, fishnet stockings. "*Mens sana in corpore* slutty" was her motto: a working brain in a body made for sex—it was a combination few men could resist.

Next to *Outfit* she wrote *Shoes,* underlining it twice. No skimping here. She'd have to bite the bullet and invest in an utterly fabulous, staggeringly expensive pair of fuck-me pumps. Blahnik, Prada, Jimmy Choo: the names babbled in her mind like a little mantra.

She printed another item on the list: *Charter schools info!* And then: *Topanga Indian Tribes.* She'd need to do some boning up in the next couple of weeks. She thought a moment.

Lally, she wrote. She punctuated the name and circled it: *Lally?!* Lally Chandler had never invited Caitlin to a single function, not even one of her famous Christmas buffets, at which she packed in everybody from the mayor to the butcher. She was not going to be thrilled when Caitlin sashayed in to this little soiree with the guest of honor. Caitlin needed to be prepared, arm herself with ways to flatter and mollify her hostess; and alternatively, she needed ammunition in case the going got rough.

She listed another item: *Center.* She'd need to arrange to take that entire day off at the rape center, to give herself plenty of time to prepare. And then under *Center* she added: *Cynthia Rudin.* She paused and tapped the name several times with the butt of the Magic Marker.

What the hell should she do about Cynthia?

Her last little chat with her had been pretty weird. Cynthia still wouldn't budge about filing a police report, though Caitlin had gotten her to spill a few more details about the assault. It turned out that the vibrator had belonged to Cynthia herself—some kind of high-design *objet* that looked like a miniature Brancusi sculpture. She'd kept it out on her coffee table as an amusing conversation piece. Turned out also that Cynthia was an Anglophile who frequently popped over to Jolly Old England and entertained a steady stream of upper-crust Brits. "So you see, it had to be somebody I know. Someone who's been to my house before. I can't possibly report it. It's a very tight-knit crowd; everyone would know."

"Is that why you came all the way up to the campus rape center?" Caitlin had asked her. "To avoid anybody you knew?"

"Well, yeah." Cynthia paused, then said, "And actually, I had your card."

"My card? You mean with my name on it?"

"Yes," she said. Then got all flustered, belligerent almost, and refused to say anything else.

Caitlin really ought to give her one more try. Except she knew the Cynthia Rudin type—it would be just like her to go over Caitlin's head and kick up a nasty fuss about being harassed or badgered or some such.

She scribbled Cynthia's name off the list.

Then she folded the paper in quarters and inserted it in her back pocket. Out of nervous energy, she began stuffing discarded packing material into a black plastic trash bag. She tossed it over her shoulder Santa Claus–style and took it out to the green recycling barrel that she shared with the dilapidated tract house next door.

The sight of this house never failed to irritate her. It was occupied by a family named Wynne: Pop was a retired plumbing company dispatcher with a malfitted artificial hip; Mom had been a dietitian at the local middle school until a couple of years ago, when she'd dropped dead of an aneurysm while scooping mashed potatoes. The place shrieked low rent. Farther down the block, a middle-aged gay couple named Jim and James had forked over ten times that for an almost identical house, gutted it, and rehabbed it into a little gem of mid-century Modernism. Those were the type of people the neighborhood needed more of, Caitlin reflected, but it would take something along the lines of a neutron bomb to dislodge the Wynnes from Despuesta Road.

A car with an iffy muffler gasped to a stop at the curb. Old green Pontiac with a plump purple ball impaled on the antenna. It was Otis, the youngest of the five Wynne sons and one of the two who still lived at home. He unfolded himself from the driver's seat.

"Hi, Otis," she called.

He veered immediately over to her. "Need any help?"

"No, but you're a sweetheart to ask." She stuffed the bag into the barrel and replaced the lid, then turned to him.

Pizza Face. It was what they used to call kids with complexions like that: ooey, gooey, tomato-and-mozzarella acne. You'd think he'd have grown out of it by now—he was in college, for chrissake! Besides, weren't there medications, Retin-A and whatever, to clear it up?

Because he wouldn't be bad-looking otherwise. He wore a crummy yellow T-shirt with the words I LEFT HOME FOR *THIS*? but there was the suggestion of a reasonably good bod underneath. And he had nice hair. Surfer hair, blond-streaked, thick and shaggy. If you saw him from the back or from a certain distance, you'd think he was cute. And apparently some chicks did, since he had a girlfriend, a beanpole of a creature named Baba, who was a fellow business administration major at the university. Coming home late one night, Caitlin had overheard them having sex in the back of the Pontiac, him grunting, her squealing, the car shaking and shivering as if it were getting in on the action.

Imagine kissing that pizza pie? *Ew.*

She immediately felt guilty for the uncharitable thought. She smiled brightly. "Just coming back from school?"

"Nah, I was working. And I gotta go back out in a while. My prick manager dumped me with a double shift today." Otis worked as a delivery person for the Plum Mart, a specialty (meaning rip-off) grocery store beloved by the housewives of Colina Linda. The kind of place where the pears come individually wrapped in tissue paper, and should you ever try using coupons at the checkout register, they'd have about sixteen strokes. Hence the purple plum on Otis's car antenna.

Caitlin raised an admonitory finger. "Now I know you need to earn money, but make sure you don't go neglecting your studies. Your college work has got to be your number one priority."

"Tell that to my manager," he muttered.

"I will if you want me to." She flashed him a flirtatious grin.

A gooney, lovey-dovey expression spread over his face. Girlfriend or not, the kid had a walloping crush on her. Caitlin didn't lead him on, of course, but on the other hand, she didn't go out of her way to discourage him—it was frankly quite convenient to have a worshipful young guy at her beck and call. Since she'd moved here, Otis had served as her Mr. Fix-it, her furniture schlepper, her errand-runner, and, on occasion, her freebie babysitter.

"You've got some stuff on your pants," he said.

"Yeah?" A few kernels of Styrofoam clung to the synthetic fiber of her capris. "Packing popcorn—it sticks to everything." She brushed them off, then twisted to examine the back of her legs. "Any more?"

"A couple." He hesitated, then in a bold motion reached down and plucked one from her calf and one from her upper thigh. "That's it."

"Thanks, you're a love." Okay, he'd had a little treat. Now for the payment. "Listen, Otis? I hate to even ask, but I wonder if maybe you could do me a huge favor?"

"Uh, yeah, sure. I mean, like what?"

"I've got some stuff I really need to do at the post office. Aiden's going to be home pretty soon. I wonder if maybe you could hang with him till I'm back? It should only be about twenty, thirty minutes."

"Yeah, no, it's no problem."

"You sure? I mean, I'd hate to make you late for your job. I don't want to get you in trouble with your boss."

"He can kiss my ass." The boast gave way to a self-conscious laugh. "And anyhow, I don't have to go back for an hour."

"You're an angel. Come on in." She headed back into her kitchen, Otis trotting after her like a Doberman puppy. "Feel free to raid the fridge. I'll be back down in a flash."

She scampered up the stairs to the hat room. She heard the front door open and close and stepped back onto the landing.

"Aiden?" She leaned over the railing. "Is that you, sweetie?"

"Hi, Mom." The miraculous bubbling of animation he'd displayed at the Clemente mansion hadn't lasted too long. He had quickly relapsed into prepube Willy Loman, whining about this and that and slumping his poor, poor little shoulders.

"I'll be right down. Otis is in the kitchen."

"Yeah, okay. Do we have any Tostitos?"

"Don't think so; check the cupboard. I know there's Cheetos."

"I hate Cheetos. Why do you *buy* them?"

"They used to be your favorite."

"No, they *weren't,* they always made me puke. I told you so."

"Okay, I'm running out to the post office, I'll stop at the 7-Eleven."

"But I'm starving *now.*"

Jesus H. Christ on a stick. Don't you know, kid, that all is suffering?

"There's nothing I can do this second," she said. "Get Otis to take a look; maybe he can find something you want."

"Yeah." The kid shuffled off into the kitchen.

"Rowr Raidren, rowr rarren?" she heard Otis say. His Scooby-Doo. It was Otis's shtick to do voices, mostly cartoon characters, Bullwinkle, Daffy Duck, Homer Simpson, sometimes real people, John F. Kennedy, Adam Sandler. Aiden used to adore it: "Do SpongeBob! Do the guy in the Jack in the Box commercial!" but lately he had proclaimed it one of the nine zillion things he considered lame. This time at least he laughed. A small, grudging hiccup of a laugh.

But nevertheless, a laugh.

Caitlin's throat tightened.

Smiling, she finished loading up shopping bags with the ready-to-go parcels. Nine hats sold: total profit two hundred and fifty-four bucks, or just slightly half the minimum amount she needed to spend on her big night fuck-mes.

She darted across the hall to the bathroom, moussed her spiky hair, gave it a finger comb, groomed her brows with a wet finger. She took a quick pee and emerged from the john, still zipping up her pants.

And found herself face-to-face with Otis.

Jeez Louise! She'd left the bathroom door open. He must have seen the whole works. "What the hell are you doing up here?" she shrieked.

His complexion bloomed to an unearthly shade of crimson. "I just, um . . ."

"Never, ever come upstairs again without my permission, do you understand me?"

He stared at her with the dumbstruck look of a kicked animal. Then he did something strange. Eerie, almost. He jammed his hands in his pockets, shuffled his feet, widened his eyes to circles. From his mouth issued a peculiar high-pitched cartoon voice: "Gee, boys and girls, I guess I really messed up this time. I sure hope Caitlin's not too mad at me."

Oh Christ. He was doing Mickey Mouse! He really was a priceless geek, when you got right down to it.

"What *are* you doing up here?" Caitlin asked again.

"Gee, Caitlin, I just thought—ha, ha, ha—that maybe you could use a little help."

Still with the Mickey Mouse. Okay, so he probably didn't actually see her on the john, she reflected. Obviously she would have noticed him looming in the hallway. She softened her tone.

"Look, I didn't mean to be harsh. But you've got to remember I need some privacy, okay?"

He nodded mutely.

"Okay, then. As long as you're up here, you might as well help carry these bags down." She gave his upper arm a conciliatory squeeze and his face glowed redder than a Christmas bulb.

CHAPTER *six*

I Forgot My Crown

"I forgot my crown."

Jessica patted her mother's knee. "It's okay, Mommy. We're going to church; you won't need it."

"How do you expect them to know who I am?"

Jessica sighed. Just in case her life didn't suck quite enough right now, her mother, Lillian McCready, was going intermittently gaga. She'd be perfectly lucid, sometimes for days on end; then whamo! She'd ricochet back to 1952, the year she'd been crowned Miss Pennsylvania after winning both the evening gown and talent competitions, and she'd create a ruckus about not being able to find her tiara or locate her custom-made strapless-backless brassiere. It was as if some essential part of her mind had been rejiggered and now operated on binary mode: Fantasy, reality. Past, present. Naughty, nice.

"They'll know who you are," Jessica told her. "You look beautiful."

Her mother placed a hand on top of her head, frowning as if mystified to discover a sparse and wispy white cap instead of the shimmering auburn cascade she'd been expecting. Lillian could no longer be trusted to drive alone: Several months before, she'd been picked up by the highway patrol just after dawn, tooling north on the southbound lane of the 804 on her way, she had crisply informed the officer, to an appointment with her vocal coach in downtown Philadelphia. Her residential village provided a shuttle to nearby St. Agatha, a newly built structure with a bird-on-the-wing design that Lillian had rejected as "kooky." So it now fell to Jessica to chauffeur her every Sunday morning to the ten-A.M. Mass at the acceptably neo-Mission-style Our Lady of Lourdes in Colina Linda.

"Our Lady of the Lexus," as it was popularly called. The parking lot was crammed with luxury vehicles. Jessica slotted her hazelnut-colored Saab wagon into a space between a Jaguar sedan and a shiny new Escalade. The church's adobe facade always struck her as more Taco Bell than authentic colonial—she half expected to see a take-out window doing a brisk business in burritos and three-cheese chalupas around the side; but the interior was lovely, all rough-hewn beams and gilt Madonnas and the smoky, transcendental light of a Caravaggio. Lillian's features cleared as she entered, and the binary switch flicked back to "present."

"I hope it's Father Hughes today," she whispered. "That new boy from Mexico is sweet, but I can't understand a word he says."

"Father DelMarco always says the ten o'clock. And I think he's from Guatemala."

"Well, wherever he's from, he might as well be speaking in tongues. His accent is unintelligible."

She strode toward her customary pew, exactly seventeen rows from the back on the right, Jessica following at a gingerly pace. A dull ache rose from the bridge of her nose and encircled her head like a too-tight helmet; her tongue felt plastered with wet sand; her eyelids, both upper and lower, were puffed like some sort of heart-healthy General Mills cereal. In short, she was hungover, and she looked and felt it. A pretty woman in the opposite section waved energetically. Jessica squinted and realized it was Janey Martinez sitting amidst a thicket of relations ranging in age from grandfather to toddler. Janey made one of those *I'll phone you* or *you phone me* gestures, hand at her ear, middle fingers clenched, thumb and pinkie outstretched, which translated as a) Let's have lunch; b) I'm hawking tickets to the arthritis/AIDS orphans/land mines ball; or c) I've got gossip that will make your hair frizz! Jessica nodded, then ducked her head and slid into the pew beside her mother.

With luck, she was too far away for Janey to have registered her appearance. Funny, though, that she hadn't immediately recognized Janey. Probably because Jessica had never thought of her as pretty before. New haircut? Or maybe she finally got a good night's sleep. Or was it that she finally got laid?

What was it about church, Jessica wondered, that seemed to turn her thoughts to sex? Sometimes it seemed all she needed was a whiff of incense and a mumbled amen to cue blue movies in her mind.

Maybe it was because the last time she'd attended church regularly, she'd been a hormonally raging college freshman. Then the following year she met a long-lashed premed student named Michael DiSantini who had no tolerance for any religion of any kind, and she'd let herself fall away from the whole thing.

She rose with the rest of the congregation for the opening hymn and added her voice to the melismatic, "Hallelujah," but she wasn't in a very prayerful frame of mind—unless it was to pray for the smiting of her ex-husband with some disfiguring, lingering, and ultimately incurable disease.

Bastard Michael! On Friday, her lawyer had called her with the details of the forthcoming arbitration. Basically, Michael was looking to cut support payments by a whopping sixty-five percent, which would no longer cover her monthly expenditures. One colossal bill after another rose before her eyes: the mortgage on the house, her half of tuitions and summer camps. Charitable obligations. Rowan's riding, Alex's tennis and speech therapist, Yolanda's salary. The exorbitant cost to keep her mother in the Sycamore Springs Independent Living Village, whose rates seemed to skyrocket by the second. The roughly two and a quarter million she'd received in the settlement had seemed like a reasonably cushy fortune at the time, but start chipping away at it, and it could dwindle to zilch in the blink of an eye.

Michael, of course, had this all calculated. And he had a solution: He proposed to buy out the house. Market rate, no contingencies.

She'd get the money, Alex and Rowan would have continuity, everybody won.

What a magnanimous offer! What a swell guy!

Jessica, however, would be booted from her home—the home she'd renovated and decorated and now viscerally loved, whose gardens she'd meticulously planned and planted; and henceforth it would be the Brain gathering *her* heirloom roses and Irish lavender, and frying up pork chops on *her* customized blue enamel Wolf range. Uh-man-duh soaking her bony buttocks in the Second Empire claw-foot zinc bathtub that she, *Jessica,* had spent a dozen Sundays searching for, sniffling and sneezing her way through every moldy and dust mote–infested antique shop in three goddamned counties.

The two of them could both go directly to hell!

She must have muttered this half aloud. Her mother shot her a frown; and in the row in front, a man in a blue cashmere blazer and black-framed glasses turned and gave an amused lift of his brows.

What do you know? It was the newly minted bachelor billionaire, David A. Clemente.

What was he doing at Lady of the Lexus? He and Susanna had been mainstays of the even more socially select All Blesseds Episcopal ("All Bentleys" was *its* snarky nickname). Jessica returned a sheepish grimace. Then she bowed her throbbing head to her missal, hoping to give at least the appearance of devotion.

At the conclusion of the Mass she bolted from the pew, hoping to avoid him. No luck: They emerged in the aisle at the same time.

He caught her eye and smiled. "Spina bifida?"

Oh, God, did she look *that* bad? Then she realized he was referring to the benefit she had cochaired with Susanna Clemente the year before, the Make a Difference Cabaret Night for spina bifida. "Yes, exactly," she said, smiling weakly back. "I'm Jessica DiSantini."

"Of course, Jessica." He appeared to take it for granted she'd know who he was. "And Michael, that's your husband, right? He's good, I hope?"

"I couldn't really tell you. We've split up. Officially, as of two months ago."

"Sorry to hear that."

"Yeah, well, it happens. I guess more often than not these days." Translation: *I know you're splitsville too.* She added quickly, "I didn't know you came to this church. I thought you were All Blesseds."

"I suppose technically I am. But my mother was Catholic. She died a few years ago, so I have a Mass said for her on every anniversary."

"Oh." Which would explain why the altar looked like a Rose Bowl float.

They shuffled in momentary silence along with the retreating crowd into the stone-floor vestibule. Jessica glanced back, looking for Lillian, but couldn't immediately spot her among the bobbing heads.

"Are you going to be in the cabaret again this year?" David asked.

"Oh, God!" She gave a short laugh. The year before, she and five other exhibitionist housewives had performed a loosely choreographed "One" from *A Chorus Line,* donning the requisite skimpy leotards, fish-net stockings, and bowlers, bravely showing legs and cocking hips and thrusting boobs, all, of course, for the worthy cause of ridding the world of spina bifida. "I think I'll stay behind the scenes this time."

"Too bad. I thought you were the only one who could really deliver Fosse."

"Thanks, but not really. Though I did take tap lessons when I was a kid. My mother kept entering me in child beauty contests, Little Miss Apple Festival and Little Miss Royale County, and tap dancing was my so-called talent."

"I'm guessing you won a lot."

"Actually, never. I'd get bored and start making faces. There are all these photos of me wearing frilly dresses and sparkling barrettes with these cross-eyed expressions on my face."

He laughed. The clunky black glasses were becoming, she decided—they gave a definition to his otherwise slightly ordinary features. It occurred to her that this was the first time she'd ever seen him on his own, without an entourage of assistants, flunkies and such, or else attached to his wife, the bulimic-bodied Susanna, whose constant mosquitolike voice dominated any conversation, deflecting any topic that didn't directly relate to herself.

"David, good to see you!" A gnomish, white-haired man in a hounds-tooth coat thrust out a hand. Others were glancing David's way. Jessica spied Janey Martinez and her extended clan gathering themselves, ready to emerge from the pews: The second they caught sight of him, they would engulf him like an amoeba with a particle of plankton.

And then she spotted Lillian in the throng, walking toward her. Or no, Jessica realized with dismay, not simply walking . . . she was *gliding.* Her chin was lifted, her eyes were widened to saucers, her lips were spread in a dazzling winner's smile . . . The digital switch had flipped again, and she was back in 1952, the famous evening-gown parade.

Jessica stepped forward, but too late: Lillian had already directed herself toward David. She gathered the edges of her skirt, lifted them slightly, and, in a move that had wowed them back in Philadelphia, dropped into a full curtsy in front of him.

"Mommy, please!" Jessica pleaded. David simply gaped.

Still smiling brightly, Lillian began to rise. Then she wobbled. Her arms cranked in a kind of windmill motion, she uttered a little gurgle of surprise, and down she went with a heavy thud onto the hard vestibule floor.

Kill me now, Jessica prayed.

A small crowd of people seemed to instantly materialize. Several, including David, crouched to help. Lillian was five-ten, with an hourglass figure that had thickened to a cylinder: It took considerable effort to hoist her to a sitting position.

Jessica knelt down to her. "Are you okay, Mommy?"

"I don't know."

Janey Martinez's face appeared in the crowd. "What's happened? Should I call an ambulance?"

"I don't think that's necessary." Jessica turned back to her mother. "Can you stand up?"

A group effort managed to raise Lillian to her feet. "My arm hurts," she whimpered.

"I think she fell on it," David said. "It could be sprained or broken."

"It could definitely be broken," echoed Janey.

How does my life suck? Let me count the ways. Jessica gingerly dabbed the sleeve of her mother's blouse. "Do you think it's broken, Mom?"

"Ow."

"Better take her to Mission Mercy and get it checked out," David said.

"Yeah, we should get her to the hospital," Janey said. "I've got the Mercedes right outside."

Jessica glanced at her: Close up Janey clearly featured the frozen brow of the unyoung; it was supplemented by a high gleam in her eyes. She was enjoying this, Jessica realized; she was reveling in this unexpected little spurt of excitement.

"It's fine; I can manage," Jessica said sharply. "It's probably just a sprain. Thanks, all of you, we'll be fine."

"Would you call and let me know how she is?" David said.

"Yes, call us and let us know how she's doing," chirped his faithful parrot Janey.

Another group effort was required to load Lillian into the Saab. Then a fifteen-minute stop-and-go, skirting the bustling farmer's market on Indio, to the hospital complex on the northwest slope of the hills. Mission Mercy: land o' Dr. Michael DiSantini. Though Jessica knew he wouldn't be there now—he'd taken Rowan and Alex sailing, the latest in a string of bribes, candy-colored iPods, brand-new pairs of Skechers, ice-cream extravaganzas, even cold cash, meant to cushion the news of Amanda's forthcoming blessed event. And it was working—as far as the kids were concerned, if a couple of new siblings translated to the latest Eminem and some cool new jeans, then bring 'em on.

Fortunately Jessica recognized the clerk at the desk in Radiology: a thick-faced woman named Renata with dyed-black hair and brows plucked to startled parabolas.

"Good morning, Renata," she said warmly. "I'm Mrs. DiSantini. My mother's taken a spill and injured her elbow, and I'm afraid it might be fractured."

"You Dr. DiSantini's wife?"

"Yes. Well, his ex-wife."

The parabolas ascended toward the inky hairline. "We got no call from him."

"No, he doesn't know. But it doesn't matter; we just need a quick X-ray."

"Without a doctor's order, you got to go down to the ER."

Jessica gave an exasperated sigh. "Try paging Dr. Lake. Mary Ellen Lake, in Neurology. Or Steve Lundholdt."

"I can't do that. I'm sorry, but you're gonna have to go through the ER. That's policy." The clerk crossed her arms and set her mouth in a stubborn slit.

Not so very long ago, when Jessica had been married to that awesome local deity, Dr. Michael DiSantini, any or all personnel in this hospital would have moved heaven and earth to attend to her mother's care. But apparently being the discarded ex of said deity counted for zilch.

"Come on, Mommy," she said, and led her mother back down to the ground-level emergency room.

It was mobbed, pandemonium, the floor littered with newspapers, discarded coffee cups, candy-bar wrappers. She deposited Lillian in a scratched plastic chair, then filled out a triage form thrust at her by a harried young Asian. "At least an hour, maybe more," he told her. "Since they shut down the ER at Benedictine, we've been swamped."

Jessica drank a cone of water, brought another back to her mother, and took a chair beside her. On one side, a ragged young man mumbled about honey bees. Behind them, a duet of squalling babies, a woman yelling in Russian into a cell phone.

"What does this mean? Am I going to be disqualified from the pageant?" Lillian suddenly demanded.

"No, Mommy, of course you're not."

"Because if I am, I don't think it's fair. My talent does not require the use of my arms. I'm not a ballerina. I'm not twirling a baton, like that conceited blond-haired girl from Allentown. I'm a vocalist. I don't need my arms to sing."

She sat up rigidly in her chair; for a moment, Jessica dreaded that she was about to start belting out, "I'm as corny as Kansas in August," as she'd done several weeks ago halfway through lunch at P. F. Chang's, to the acute mortification of her grandchildren.

But she didn't sing. Instead she crumpled back into herself, deploying her arm at an angle in front of her like a broken wing. "It really hurts a lot. I think I must've shattered a bone."

"They'll take care of it very soon." Jessica gazed in despair around the packed room.

Then suddenly she heard her name called. She popped to her feet and shot up a hand. It had hardly been ten minutes.

Jessica barely had time to wonder about this when a smiling orderly rolled a wheelchair over to her. "Mrs. DiSantini? You've got a mama who needs an X-ray?" He helped Lillian into the chair and, with jokes and breezy patter, began wheeling her back into the main building. The elevator whooshed them back up the seven floors to Radiology, where now a delegation led by a young cocoa-skinned resident in dazzling whites stood waiting for them. He introduced himself as Dr. Corcoran. "Let's get some pictures of that lovely little arm," he cooed to Lillian in a voice as warm and rich as healing itself, and Lillian beamed and fluttered as she was wheeled into the X-ray room.

Why the sudden star treatment? Jessica wondered. Could Michael somehow, magically, have gotten wind that they were here and put in a call?

Lickety-split, the X-rays were taken and developed and snapped onto a light box, and young Dr. Corcoran was pointing out the thin white jag of a hairline fracture. "We're fitting her with a removable cast that I think she'll find reasonably comfortable. And of course we'll give her something for the pain."

"You've been so wonderful," Jessica burst out. "I don't know how to thank you."

"Hey, there's no need. The Clemente Foundation practically keeps this hospital afloat."

It hit her like a bolt: It wasn't Michael who'd made a call. It was David. David Clemente was the true Supreme Being around here. The guy with the big bronze plaque in the lobby with his name on it, the one with the power to make or break the career of any doctor in the house.

Even, say, a lying, cheating, patient-boinking chief of neurosurgery.

And if she hadn't been mistaken, despite her morning-after-the-orgy appearance in church that morning—or maybe because of it—he'd been flirting with her. There had been a definite gleam of interest behind the clunky-cool glasses. An idea took form and became as insistent as the rhythmic stab of her headache: Perhaps she'd make that call to him after all and see if she could spark a little more than just interest.

CHAPTER *seven*

Isn't That What's Known as a Gigolo?

Lally forked a morsel of the unidentifiable fish that lay dead beneath a slick of oil and onions on her plate; she listlessly conveyed the fork halfway to her lips, then set it back down. Tommy, hunched in the seat across from her, had already demolished his moussaka and appeared to be happily grazing in an oversize bowl of pallid lettuce and mealy hothouse tomatoes. "Don't like your food?" he asked.

"Oh, no, it's fine. I'm just trying to drop a few pounds."

"You don't need to lose weight. Your shoulder blades stick out like chicken wings. If anything, you could use a little plumping up."

Lally smiled grimly. The famous Tom Bramberg tell-it-like-it-is—always one of his less endearing qualities. And apparently one that had not diminished over the years. For this and other reasons, Lally was beginning to regret having agreed to meet him for lunch.

The prime reason for regretting it being that he looked so definitively his age, which was almost exactly *her* age. All that salt-and-pepper and noble creasing and *weather-beating,* for God's sake, might be fine and dandy for a man—some might even say attractive—but as for herself, well . . . In the forgiving light of evening she could pass for early thirties, and in all but the harshest and most direct sunlight she looked no more than thirty-seven, thirty-eight, and that was the way she'd like to keep it, thank you very much, without a starter husband close at hand to advertise it otherwise.

Second, there was that air of tragedy about him, an illimitable sadness that pooled in Tommy's dark gray eyes and even seeped into his smile. Several years back, Lally had consulted a crimson-haired Brazilian psychic named Joacinda who claimed an ability to read and readjust people's auras; and though Joacinda had proved to be a thumping dud, nattering on about speckled fields and medium azure flashes, really just to push a fairly suspect line of her stinky spray-on "essences," Lally was nevertheless certain she could detect an aura around Tommy—it was brownish mauve in color and encased the entire periphery of his body like a translucent shroud. The aura of *le tragique.* It was her constant perception of this aura that made Lally feel she had to tiptoe oh so delicately in conversation, in constant fear of stumbling upon something, anything, that might possibly remind him that his entire immediate family—second wife, baby son, and (she believed) border collie—had blinked out of existence one rainy Tuesday evening, seven years ago come March.

And the final reason, as long as she was being brutally honest with herself, was because he was poor. Not rattling-a-tin-cup-on-street-corners poor, naturally, but by the measure of her own circles and circumstances, he was pretty goddamned penniless. *Par exemple:* That leather jacket he was wearing looked like something the cat dragged in. It was in deference to his restricted wallet that they were eating in a Greek dive called Proserpina of the Blue Aegean (Greek!) instead of Dolcino's or Umbrella.

Ah, the filet of hamachi with spicy starfruit and watermelon relish at Umbrella . . .

With a wistful sigh, Lally stabbed at an unpleasantly glistening rectangle of green pepper. It had lately become her custom to ask men to order for her, ostensibly playing to their sense of chivalry and power. But she had a feeling that Tommy sensed her actual motive, which was to avoid pulling out her reading glasses like some fusty, over-the-hill librarian, and as a wicked joke, he had selected for her the greasiest dish on the menu. She dropped her fork again, decisively this time, and reached for her glass of sparkling water—not Perrier or Solé, needless to say, not even Pellegrino, but some tepid substance with sluggish bubbles and an erupting volcano on the bottle.

Time to get down to business. "So, darling," she said with studied nonchalance, "I take it there were no sparks kindled between you and Jessica DiSantini?"

"You take it right. It was probably the shortest blind date in history."

"Tell me you did *not* wear that ratty jacket."

"This?" Tommy glanced at the garment with curiosity. "Don't know; I probably did. But I don't think it mattered; she seemed pretty upset when I got there. I think she's in an emotionally fragile state."

Not so fragile, Lally thought, that she couldn't be chatting up David Clemente in, of all places, Lady of the Lexus. Janey had dutifully reported witnessing the tête-à-tête. Lally wondered if David had become a regular in the congregation, and if so, would she have to start professing a sudden fascination with the moving and colorful rituals of the Catholic Church?

"I don't think you should give up on her," she said to Tom. "I've got a gut feeling that it could work out. And frankly, it wouldn't hurt for you to be with somebody who's got some money."

"Isn't that what's known as a gigolo?"

"That's not what I mean, darling. It's just that being a composer is so terribly underpaid. . . ." *Warning! Conversational land mine ahead!* Ever since *la tragédie,* Tommy had been unable to compose a single note, eking out a bare living on the pittance of an instructor's salary. She recovered quickly. "You deserve better, darling. And anyway, you do think Jessica's attractive, don't you?"

"Oh, yeah. You got that right, Lall. She's an uncommonly beautiful woman."

"Oh, well, she could probably stand to drop a pound or two, don't you think?"

Tommy gave her That Look—the one where his eyes narrowed to

rectangular slits and the corners of his wide mouth twitched up. Even after all these years, it made her feel so . . . what?

Exposed.

"I'd just really like to see you happy," she finished weakly. Was anybody ever really happy? she wondered. She quickly banished such an insipid thought from her head.

"Well, thanks, Lall. That's extremely decent of you."

He smiled almost sunnily. Lally was suddenly struck by an image of him when they first met: He was the lead guitarist for the one-hit-wonder metal band Frenzy Cat, all shoulder-length golden curls and slouchy could-give-a-shit attitude, a Marlboro perpetually stuck into his mouth, like a thermometer. Nobody was getting married in the seventies. Marriage was supposed to be a dead institution: You shacked up and then split whenever you felt like it. She and Tommy did it as sort of a stoned giggle. Down at city hall: Lally wore a fringed maxi and a little straw hat with daisies glued all over it, and the rings were flimsy bands made of that crappy Mexican silver that turns the skin of your finger black. In the months afterward, she got a real kick out of telling people she was Tommy Bramberg's wife, wriggling her finger to show off the cheapo ring. She accompanied him on all his gigs and bodily shielded him from groupies, and for a while at least it was . . . well, a glimmer of the fairy tale come true.

And then. And then . . .

Frenzy Cat's second album flopped. The drummer OD'd on meth, survived, and slunk back to his mom and dad in South Bend, Indiana. A roadie vanished with half the equipment. Everyone was constantly quarreling and pissing one another off. And Tommy started to noodle around with classical music, minimalist no-tune kind of stuff. He started talking about going back to grad school, scoring a Ph.D. in music composition. Lally was utterly nonplussed. Here she had thought she was getting Roger Daltry, but she was ending up with Mr. Chips!

And as soon as she realized that, she promptly slept with the bass guitarist, who was half-Swedish, half-Jamaican, and who—*whoops!*—knocked her up their first time in the sack and then immediately split to go on the road with a backup band for Elton John.

It had been a lousy thing to do to Tommy. She could see that now, of course. But she'd been hardly more than a child herself at the time. Tommy as well. Their marriage had been little more than playacting.

They had broken up, needless to say. Tommy had never seemed to hold her cheating on him against her; he even took a part in raising the baby, Sienna, helping to pay for the Swiss boarding schools, and taking her in with his own family for a couple of years when she was fifteen and at all-out war with Lally. Sienna had repaid him by dropping out of school at seventeen to run off with some Eurotrash fashion-sleaze photographer old enough to be her grandpa.

Which was Sienna in a nutshell.

Tommy at twenty, Lally thought again—such a dish. He had the prettiest penis, she remembered, pale and slender, nestled in a springy golden thatch of hair; and for a moment she wondered if she should take him home for a pity fuck. But then she recalled The Look. How truly dreadful would it be if afterward she couldn't figure out who was pitying whom?

"Are you talking to Sienna yet?" he asked suddenly.

She glanced up with a nervous start. "Not really. Have you spoken to her?"

"Not for months. Last time she called, she said she'd moved to Barcelona. I guess she's not living with that count anymore."

"Some count," Lally snorted. "Count Chocula is what he was."

"Is that why you stopped speaking to her? Because of her shitty taste in boyfriends?"

"No. Because she's a monster."

"Oh, come on. She's your daughter. Whatever it was, forgive and forget."

Lally gave an indifferent shrug. Then she looked down at her watch, a blur of platinum and diamonds, and pretended she could read the time. "Oh, my God, I'm going to have to scoot, darling. I've got to get to a terribly important appointment."

"And I've got to get me to a cigarette."

"I thought you quit. Ages ago."

"Yeah, I did, and three or four times after that. And I will again, but not right this second." He grinned. "Come on, don't tell me you never crave a Benson and Hedges?"

"Never." Lally crinkled her nose in distaste.

It was a gesture that made it Tommy's turn to flash on Lally at nineteen, a gangly, talkative girl with Cher hair, from a broken home in Tarzana. She looked like a sexy Olive Oyl, a triumph over gawkiness, stalking the bands on the Strip with a kinetic energy and the reputation (highly exaggerated) for Deep Throat–caliber blow jobs.

The image dissipated for him as a waitress shuffled over with the check and the present-day Lally reached for her bag. "Why don't you let me get this?"

"Fuck off, Lorraine."

She smiled at the sound of her real given name. Tom had to be about the last person on earth who even knew it. "Then thank you, Tommy. It's always a treat to see you." She unswirled a cylinder of lipstick and applied it to her mouth without benefit of mirror.

"You know, I miss your old nose," he told her.

"Fuck you, darling."

What's with all the "darlings"? Tommy was about to say. *You sound like a bad Billy Crystal routine.*

But he checked himself. He'd sensed something new and desperate about Lally. An almost pitiful vulnerability. Like a piece of marble with a hidden flaw, the slightest tap on just the right spot and she'd shatter into a thousand skinny shards.

"So what fabulous cause is your appointment about?" he asked instead. "Incurable disease or something in the arts?"

Lally smacked her gilded lips. "Rape," she said.

CHAPTER *eight*

Rape Is a Tremendous Problem There

Caitlin spotted Lally before Lally saw her. Of course, Lally was impossible to miss: six feet tall from the crest of her spuming ponytail to the soles of her four-inch Manolos; plus, she was sporting a papaya-colored Balenciaga jacket that, framed against the center's rather desperately cheerful canary-yellow walls, made her practically pulse, like an element of op art. The tiny director of the center, Grace Poyniac, scampered along beside her, her pop-eyed face tilted upward with a fawning grin, an invisible tail wagging vigorously behind.

Instinctively, Caitlin tensed. What the hell was Lally Chandler doing here?

Whatever it was, it couldn't bode well. By now, Caitlin figured, Lally had to know that she'd be attending Lally's exclusive little soiree on the arm of David Clemente—maybe this had so enraged the Queen Bee that she'd come here to get Caitlin fired. Even if that wasn't true and Lally's presence here had nothing to do with her, Caitlin still dreaded the possibility of Lally detecting her in her working environment. She'd worked hard to project the illusion that she'd taken this job motivated by the desire to do something meaningful—that it was just a tick away from the charity boards and benefit committees that consumed the time of the other divorcées. But one glimpse of this shabby little cubbyhole, with its take-no-prisoners lighting and tipping stalactites of stacked-up files, and it would be obvious to anyone that it was really just a paycheck.

Thank God! Lally and Grace swept by without a glance in her direction. They turned a sharp corner toward Grace's office and vanished from Caitlin's sight. Caitlin returned to what she'd been doing—sending a text message to Aiden.

DON'T FORGET CLARINET LESSON CANCELED GO HOME WITH CARPOOL. :) ILY.

I KNOW U ALREADY TOLD ME, he messaged back.

Jeez Louise. Aiden could convey a whine even in a simple text message. She sent him another ILY. *I love you.* If she spelled it out, he'd complain. For some reason the initials were acceptable. Go figure.

Then she plunged into a task she had long been putting off: coordinating the schedules of the center's many consultants and volunteers: Cops, shrinks, social workers, medical personnel—it was like trying to put together an elaborate jigsaw puzzle in which each piece was the exact same shade of gray.

She'd been working with intensity for some twenty minutes or so when her intercom bleeped.

"Oh, Caitlin," Grace Poyniac's voice chimed with an unaccustomed musical note. "Could you please join me in my office?"

"Could it wait a few minutes? I'm in the middle of wrestling with the consultants' schedules and it's a real bear."

"I'm afraid I need you right no-ow."

"Okay, be right there." Caitlin had another flash of paranoia—Lally definitely was up to something. She took out a mirror, refreshed her lipstick and mascara and examined her teeth for food particles, then gave the crown of her hair a quick back comb. Her navy pantsuit (Ann Taylor, last winter's end-of-season clearance sale) was in drastic need of a dry cleaning, but so what? Next to that Balenciaga, it would look like a pauper's rag anyway. She buttoned up her jacket and made her way to the director's office.

The Queen Bee sat primly in one of Grace's metal chairs, long, thin legs crossed at the knee. A Birkin bag sat prominently by her feet—the real thing, in green crocodile. Retail cost, roughly a third of Caitlin's take-home pay from this job. As it happened, Caitlin also owned a Birkin, bought for $79.95 from a knockoff designer stall on Olvera Street down in L.A.: The clasp had fallen off the first time she'd carried it.

However, she reminded herself, she did possess certain authentic items that with Lally Chandler were artificial—i.e., tits, jawline, and—*betcha anything*—those impossibly puffed-up lips. With this mollifying thought, Caitlin curved her own lips into her pleasant porcelain-doll's smile and advanced into the room.

"Why, Lally, what a marvelous surprise! What brings you here?"

Lally's green-gold eyes shifted leisurely in her direction.

"The most wonderful thing!" exclaimed Grace. "Ms. Chandler is becoming a benefactor of the center."

"Fabulous." Caitlin turned her doll's smile to Lally. "We're always so short of adequate funding. What made you think of us?"

"Actually, it was chatting with you at the historical society the other day. That terrifying story you told about the rapist dressed like Superman . . ."

"Spider-Man."

"Yes, right, Spidey. So creepy. And as a woman, naturally I feel this enormous sympathy for rape victims. I can't imagine anything more horrific than to be violated sexually."

How about bubonic plague? Caitlin thought irritably. *Or Lou Gherig's disease or terminal esophageal cancer?*

But she merely nodded and said, "That's a large part of the purpose of this center—to help the victims cope with the trauma."

"Yes, yes," Grace interjected, "but there's more. Ms. Chandler's not only pledging a generous contribution herself, but she's also sponsoring a program that will bring us in even more. Several days ago, I had a conversation with Ms. Chandler—"

"Please, call me Lally."

"Oh, all right, thank you, fine. Like I was saying, I was telling *Lally* about that series of seminars we conducted with the police, the purpose being to sensitize them to the needs of rape victims, and what a success it was—particularly with some of the male officers, who can be so clumsy and downright brutal in their treatment. Anyway, Lally was extremely impressed by this and . . ." Grace gave an excited little shimmy of her shoulder blades. "Perhaps you should explain from here, Lally."

Lally fluidly uncrossed several miles of legs. "I have a dear old friend, Melora Patterson, who resides for most of the year in Dunster, Arizona. She's married to Winch Patterson. You know who he is, of course?"

"Well, the name," Caitlin faltered, "but I don't . . ."

"Patterson Financial Management, number sixty-something on the Fortune Five Hundred. To make a story short, Melora has been searching for something to sink her teeth into, something beyond the usual charity committees. Apparently a place like Dunster, which is *swarming* with poor immigrants . . . well, there's a lot of drunkenness and machismo attitudes and violence of all kinds, especially toward women—and, well, rape is a tremendous problem there. So when I described these seminars to Melora and suggested that something of the sort might be useful in Dunster, she jumped all over the idea."

"We're going to help Mrs. Patterson set up a similar program of her own!" Grace broke in eagerly. "And in return, the Pattersons are going to contribute seventy-five thousand dollars to this facility."

"A kind of exchange program. It works out splendidly for everyone on both sides. . . ."

Lally paused uncertainly. Caitlin continued to fix her with that pleased little smirk, and honestly, it was starting to creep her out. In fact, the whole atmosphere of this place was creeping her out, from this bug-eyed munchkin of a director to the posters with their sickly-colored rainbows and fluttering Tweety birds. For a second she wondered if Caitlin had guessed the truth: Melora Patterson was a hyperneurasthenic woman married to a potbellied septuagenarian whose idea of a hot time these days was watching golf on the big-screen followed by a thick slab of Angus beef grilled medium well. Melora couldn't leave him; she'd be cut off without a nickel. And since—*poor darling*—Melora suffered from a vicious case of rosacea, a condition that made her cheeks flame and her nose as bulbous and red as W. C. Fields's, she could never hope to attract another even marginally wealthy guy. But she was going stark staring mad cooped up in nowheresville. "Tell you what, darling," Lally had said to her. "Swing this little project for me, and next spring, when the Le Freinets do their annual three-week barge trip down the Loire, I'll wrangle you an invite."

Melora promptly agreed. In fact, she would have wept with gratitude if weeping didn't make her nose an even gaudier red than usual.

But no, Caitlin could hardly suspect any of this, Lally assured herself. The Snatch simply didn't move in those circles.

Lally continued on, "The reason we called you in here, darling, is because I've requested that you be in charge of the project."

"Me?" Caitlin said warily.

Lally nodded her head. "My dear friend Janey Martinez told me what a super help you were in pulling together the Orchid Frolic a couple of years ago. She raved about how marvelously organized and *resourceful* you were."

"Really?"

"Oh, God, she couldn't praise you enough. She said the goody bags went absolutely down to the wire; they never would have gotten done in time if you hadn't burned the midnight oil to finish them."

That was a hundred percent true, Caitlin reflected. The Orchid Frolic was one of the first things she'd volunteered for after relocating to San Carlino, a dinner-dance held in a pavilion in the Botanical Gardens to benefit Down syndrome kids. She'd been a bottom-level schlepper, obediently following orders snapped at her by the imperious dowagers and divorcées who were running the show—and yeah, she'd stayed up till sunrise the night before the event, stuffing the frigging goody bags with several thousand dollars' worth (each!) of donated swag: Guy Laroche sunglasses and Ghirardelli chocolate samplers, Perry Ellis perfume and Coach leather billfolds and Tiffany travel alarm clocks, and so on and so forth.

Had she herself attended the benefit? Hell, no, not at seven hundred and fifty bucks a ticket.

Was she even allowed to take home a bit of the goody-bag loot, even some of the B-list items, like the candy-scented hair-care products or hideous chrome key rings that would just be shuttled directly to maids and nannies? Not on your life.

Had any of those tweezer-butt society babes tossed her so much as a thank-you?

You've got to be kidding.

She was astonished to hear that Janey Martinez had even registered the fact she'd been involved in the event at all. About the only interaction with Janey she could recall was when Janey had bitched that Caitlin was stuffing the Tiffany boxes too far down in the bottom of the bags.

"I'm glad Jane appreciated my effort," Caitlin said brittlely.

"Well she most certainly did, darling. And don't think *I* haven't noticed that you've been a dedicated worker bee on several of my own functions. Which is why I insisted to Grace that the Dunster project should be your baby."

For a moment Caitlin felt wildly flattered. Then she became immediately suspicious. This was Lally Chandler, after all, who never so much as wiped her ass without a hidden agenda. "Well, it sounds like an interesting project," she said. "But what exactly would it involve?"

"You'd work hand in hand with Melora Patterson and the local law enforcement to design the seminar program. And you'll conduct at least the first couple of them yourself."

"You mean in Arizona?"

"Well, yes," said Grace. "We want you to leave Sunday evening and start first thing Monday morning. You'll spend about two or three weeks there, all expenses paid, naturally."

"You'll have to work almost around the clock, but I think you'll find it an exciting challenge." Lally turned her face, all apricot complexion and wide-open eyes, to Caitlin.

She's getting me out of the way, Caitlin realized. *Shipping me off to East Boondocks, Arizona, and safely away from David's attentions, so she can have the field to herself.*

"I'm sorry," she said. "I'd love to do this—it's a terrific project—but I can't. I've got a ten-year-old. I can't just leave him for that long a time."

"Certainly not, darling. You'll take him with you. We'll arrange for child care."

"He can't miss that amount of school."

"He goes to St. Mattie's, doesn't he? They're used to this kind of thing over there. The Reichels just took their children with them for a month in Buenos Aires, and St. Matt's supplied them with advance lessons and they hired an English-speaking tutor when they got there. The kids were actually ahead of their class when they got back."

"So you see, there's nothing to worry about." Grace directed a hard look at Caitlin. The message was loud and clear: *Refuse and you're out of a job, sister.* It was a fairly lousy job, but it did have great benefits, and she desperately needed the medical, what with Aiden in and out of the allergist's office every other week and her migraine meds. . . . And it wasn't like San Carlino was teeming with great career opportunities . . .

Fuckety fuck.

"Well, then, sure, it'll be an exciting challenge," she said.

"Marvelous, darling. This is thrilling! Though I guess unfortunately you won't be able to make it to my dinner."

"Dinner?" Grace's ears pricked up.

"Just a little supper I'm throwing for another of my interests. Native American education. A friend mentioned he might be bringing Caitlin, but I suppose now that won't be possible."

"I guess not," said Caitlin.

"What a shame. I'd love to show you my house. You'll have to come over some other time."

"I'd love to." Caitlin gave a pleasant little smile.

A jubilant Lally drove out of the maze of university roads. She recalled a quote from Simone de Beauvoir: *Attraper un mari est un art.* To catch a husband is an art. Lally had always considered herself first and foremost an artist. To celebrate—*master brushstroke!*—she swung down to Neiman Marcus in the Conquistadora Arcade and treated herself to a smashing Judith Leiber crystal-studded handbag that had previously caught her eye.

Then she cruised on home and went directly into her office. A twinge of annoyance at the sight of Perla overflowing her chair and stuffing her face with Goldfish crackers.

"Do you have the seating arrangement done?" Lally snapped.

"Sure do." Perla handed her a diagram printed on pale green stock. Lally scrutinized it. Her name at the head of the table, of course. David properly situated on her right; on her left, across from him the Indian chief. Caitlin Latch at the far end, safely tucked between the congresswoman's husband (a CPA, dull as taxes) and Taller Kern, who was one of Janey (neé Kern) Martinez's zillions of relations—first cousin twice removed or vice versa; Lally never could remember which. Like Janey, a trustafarian—though Taller's trust fund came nowhere near the heft of Janey's, merely enough to keep him in modest luxury while dabbling in a rare-books emporium called Ex Libris on Manzanito Street. Lally had selected him for his old family pedigree and his considerable androgynous charm.

"There's a change in the guest list. Miss Latch will not be able to attend. If we aren't told of Mr. Clemente bringing anyone else by the night before, then please call Jane Martinez and issue her an invitation."

"Sure she'll be available?"

"Janey's always available."

"Wanna go over your messages now?"

"Please."

"Okey-doke," Perla said.

Perla lubricated her throat with a swig of bottled iced tea, then began chanting the phone messages: "Flower Power, can't locate any white peonies this time of year; the upholsterer, the Brunschwig and Fils fabric is on a four-month back order; Ms. Martinez; Sharon Meeker about golf on Wednesday; Flower Power again. And Sienna," she finished.

Lally went rigid. "What?"

"That's all she said. Sienna. Left a number."

Lally grabbed the message slip from Perla's hand: 310 area code, west-side L.A. She erased all emotion from her voice. "Call Flower

Power and tell Donald I want white peonies and if he can't find them through his regular sources then to use his bloody imagination."

Still clutching the message slip, she walked upstairs to her bedroom. She sank onto the edge of her canopy bed, and for several moments stared at a hazy square of dancing parabolas, the refraction of the sun off the water of the swimming pool down in the yard below. Then she picked up the bedside phone. To her surprise, she noticed that her hand was trembling.

She took a breath, then resolutely tapped the numbers. On the other end, the line began ringing, one of those peculiar office-type rings, *brr-bloop, brr-bloop, brr-bloop. . . .*

On the third one, Lally slammed down the phone.

CHAPTER *nine*

Ladies Who've Turned Forty Shouldn't Throw Stones

It was a wonder what loathing your ex-husband would do for your tennis game.

Through the entire match, Jessica had been playing as aggressively as a pro. All she had to do was picture Michael's smug, oleaginous face (*I've got new mouths to feed, baby*) sculpted on the approaching ball to send it smashing back across the net—which was exactly what she did now, returning Kimba Leary's serve, winning the match point.

Taller Kern, who'd been her mixed-doubles partner for the past eight years, tossed his graphite racket up in a little victory cartwheel. "That's the way I like it," he chortled.

Together they sauntered to the net to shake hands with their opponents, Kimba and her husband, Bob. Bob Leary, always a sore loser, muttered about a pulled muscle in his thigh, then stalked off to his Escalade, with Kimba scrambling to keep up. He was the kind of guy, Jessica reflected, who'd spend the rest of the day berating his wife for her lousy lobs and persistent failure to rush the net. It made her temporarily elated to be husbandless.

"You were in rare form this afternoon." Taller zipped his racket in its case and neatly stowed it in his burgundy Lacoste carryall. "Been taking extra vitamins or something?"

"Yeah, vitamin H for Hate His Guts."

"Good for you. It's about time you decided to come out fighting."

"Do you think I've been moping? Rowan told me I was."

"I don't know. Did Anna Karenina mope after Vronsky threw her over?"

"That bad, huh?"

"Sweetheart, for a while I was very nervous about you being anywhere around trains."

"Yeah, well, don't worry. I've finally seen the light. He's not going to walk all over me anymore."

"You are woman; hear you roar," Taller said admiringly.

"Damned right. So does that call for a martini?"

"You'd better believe it."

Taller squared his sweater over his shoulders and knotted it meticulously. It was a white cable-stitched sweater, V-necked with a contrast stripe, so classic as to be almost corny. Taller was someone who liked to pretend he'd been beamed in from another time and place—a time and place that vacillated between Edwardian England, Manhattan in the thirties, and a generic mid-America in the 1950s. Most people assumed he was gay because a) he was thin; b) he was fastidious and sardonic; and c) he had never been married. Jessica figured that sex just wasn't something that was high on Taller's list of favorite recreations; but when he did indulge, it appeared to be with females.

He'd actually made a halfhearted pass at her after Michael moved out. They'd been sitting on her couch watching a DVD of *All About Eve* and afterward, to her utter stupefaction, he'd made a lunge for her lips. Got a little sulky when she laughed out loud, but they had managed to make up.

They headed at a brisk clip to the clubhouse. The dining room had been recently redecorated in a vaguely thirties motif, all etched glass and chrome, which Taller had dubbed "Art Drecko"; in keeping with the spirit of it, he'd insisted they switch to martinis for their customary après-tennis drink. At first classic martinis, Stoli with double olives. Then they'd begun to branch out. Apple martinis. Chocolatinis. Bellini-martinis. There was the Sushi, with fresh pickled ginger that Taller brought with him from a market in Koreatown (weird). The Jalapeño, garnished with hot peppers (disgusting). The Jell-O shots made with lemon-lime Jell-O (kind of tasty).

Today's was apparently going to be something called the Flipper. "Grey Goose vodka, shaken with ice," Taller instructed the waiter, Luis, "and with a splash of Blue Curacao."

Jessica took a tentative taste of the frosty blue glass that appeared in front of her. The bittersweet nip of Curacao –it brought back memories of her honeymoon in Antigua. It had rained two of the six days, but she and Michael had gone down to the beach anyway, sitting in the thatch-covered bar, gabbing with the South African bartender who kept concocting exotic cocktails for them to sample. It was so strange, she thought—you could split up the shared possessions, but what did you do with the shared memories? Wouldn't it be a relief if you could split those up as well? *You take the one about the time our car broke down in that Irish forest, and I get the one about when the mockingbird got trapped in the attic.*

"Terra to Jessica. Are you there?"

"Sorry, what did you say?"

"I said, now that you've decided to move on with your life, what's on your agenda?"

"Well, a few things. I've signed up for a tap-dancing class at the college. I want to brush up to do the cabaret again next year."

"You go, Ginger."

"And, uh . . ." She gave her glass a casual swirl. "I'm thinking that I just might have a chance with David Clemente."

"Oh?"

"Yeah, I ran into him last week and he was kind of flirting with me. And he did a very nice favor for my mother. I called to thank him, but apparently he's in Asia on some business tour and won't be back till next week."

"Well, well. You're setting your cap for little old David."

"Setting my cap? For God's sake, Tall, what century are you living in?"

"Sometimes I wonder. But listen, you should know that half the gals in town are plotting to catch him, even as we speak. And from what I hear, Lally already thinks she's got dibs."

"Lally Chandler?" Jessica pursed her mouth in surprise. Lally was someone she hadn't even figured would be in the running. Too glitzy. Too *tall*. Too, well . . . Lally.

"Yeah, Lally Chandler. She's summoned me to attend an intimate little dinner party she's tossing for him, and it's obvious she's planning on eating up El Señor Clemente for her main course."

"Isn't she just a little, um . . . geriatric for him?"

"Which particular body part? Don't forget, my dear, that most of hers are just a couple of years old. And might I suggest that ladies who've turned forty shouldn't throw stones?"

"And may I suggest that gentlemen who are forty shouldn't be so damned bitchy?"

"Excuse me, but we're the only ones who are allowed to be. We've earned it."

"Yeah, right." Jessica gave a snort, then took another sip. This Flipper martini wasn't all that bad. "So do you really think Lally has a chance?"

"I've seen her work. She's a master." Taller giggled. "Or should I say mistress? She can turn strong men into quivering puddles of goo with just a flick of that ponytail. David could find himself snapped up before he even knew what happened to him." He traced a meditative *L* on the frosted surface of his glass. Then he traced a *J*. "Of course, you're a much more suitable match. My money would be on you, as long as you don't get in too late."

"You've got to help me out then. Can you bring me to dinner as your date?"

Taller's eyebrows rose to quizzical peaks. "Your date?"

"Why not? We could be developing a sudden infatuation with each other."

"Trust me: Lally's not stupid enough to fall for something like that. Besides, I'm clearly invited as the extra man. My job is to even out the boy-girl, boy-girl, while keeping Lally's status unambiguously single."

"Yeah, I guess you're right. So now what do I do? I can't call again; it will look like I'm chasing him."

"No, but you could throw yourself accidentally on purpose in his path."

"Maybe. But where?"

"Might I suggest the Para Los Niños Ball?"

"Sorry, but not invited. I'm not quite in that social strata. Especially now that I'm just another divorcée."

A greedy gleam lit in Taller's eyes. He was a notorious freeloader, famous for never picking up a tab if he could possibly avoid it. He had long ago given up his membership at the country club, since he could always count on being somebody's guest—Jessica was the one who always signed for the martinis. "If I were to pick up tickets, would you spring for them?" he asked smoothly.

"Well . . . okay."

"They're three thousand. Apiece."

Jessica winced. "No problem."

"Of course not. It's Michael's money, right?"

"Right," she said vaguely. "And listen. At that thing of Lally's—see what you can do to keep her from getting too close, okay?"

"I'll do the very best I can." He raised his blue glass to her in a toast.

At precisely that moment, Caitlin and Aiden were speeding down the coast highway to LAX, late for the Southwest flight to Phoenix, from which they'd make a connection to Dunster. There had been about six dozen crises before leaving: Aiden couldn't find his Game Boy; he'd forgotten to pack any socks; on the way out to the car he dropped the folder with the St. Matthew's lessons and they went scattering all over the front yard, blowing into the Wynnes'. It would be an utter freaking miracle if they made it through airport security in time.

Caitlin had already been in a lousy mood, beginning with the meeting with Lally in Grace Poyniac's office, and intensifying after she'd called David to cancel their date. She'd reached his assistant, of course, the mellifluous Barry, who crooned that Mr. Clemente was unavailable at the moment, but he'd relay the message, blah, blah, blah. She'd heard a big fat *nada* back.

Aiden began to wriggle and bounce. "Mom . . ."

"For chrissake, Aidey! We're gonna miss the blasted plane."

"I gotta. I'm not kidding."

There was an exit coming up. Caitlin veered across two lanes of traffic with an action movie squeal of tires, cutting off a red Hyundai that blasted its horn indignantly; then she tore onto the off-ramp at sixty-five miles an hour and swung onto a deserted strip near the freeway overpass, a gnawed-out patch of gravel and weeds. A three-wheeled shopping cart knelt nearby; it looked like a crippled animal, its basket still containing the detritus of some homeless guy's life. The air had a funk of oil, urine, and exhaust.

"Make it quick," she said.

Aiden slid out. "It stinks out here."

"Breathe through your mouth. Come on; make it snappy or we're gonna miss this plane."

He looked warily around, then unzipped his fly and began to tinkle. Her cell phone sounded, the first three bars of "Like a Virgin." If that was Grace Poyniac with one more bright idea for this frigging project, she was going to scream. She answered with a curt, "Yes?"

"Is this Caitlin? Dave Clemente here."

A joke. Somebody had put somebody up to playing a prank.

"Can you hear me?"

A noisy connection, but it did sound very much like his voice. "Yes, yeah, I can," she said quickly. "How are you?"

"Pretty good. I'm in Shanghai, of all places. I've been on a hop through the People's Republic, and your message just caught up with me."

China? Well, why not? They probably needed lots of storage there, what with all those billions of people. "It sounds fascinating."

"It is. Hell of a dynamic place. You should visit someday."

With you? she thought with a bubble of hope. "Listen, I'm sorry I've got to cancel out on the dinner. I'll be out of town on business."

"Where exactly are you going to be?"

"In Dunster. Arizona. In fact, I'm just now on my way to the airport." She presumed he could hear the drone of the traffic on the overpass, and if so, pictured her breezing down the road in the backseat of an airport limo, not parked in a bum's campground while her son took a whiz.

"Dunster? Well, hey, that's no problem. If you can get free at about four that afternoon, I can have you picked up."

"Do you have a Batmobile?" she said.

He laughed heartily. Aiden climbed back into the car. Caitlin put a finger to her lips.

"The office will firm things up with you. Oh, hey, I managed to visit a couple of temples while I was here. Very profound experience."

Temples? Why was he talking about temples? Then she remembered her babble about Buddhism and "All is suffering," and wondered if he expected her to start discussing all that again right this second.

But all he said was, "Looking forward to seeing you."

"Me too," she said and hung up, elated but utterly mystified.

CHAPTER ten

You're Lally Chandler. You are in complete control.

The kid delivering the cases of sparkling water from the Plum Mart had the most repulsive case of zits Lally had ever seen, at least since the nightmare days of junior high. She must have allowed her feelings to show, since the kid ducked his head and kept it lowered while he carried the cases into the kitchen. She couldn't help it; she was just the kind of person who felt physically assaulted by the sight of any sort of physical deformity. It was a flaw, she admitted it, but what could she do? And the kid certainly didn't help his case any, with that grungy T-shirt adorned with yellowed semicircular sweat stains and those jack-o'-lantern-orange cargo pants.

But she was also the type of person who, having gotten over the initial shock, went out of her way to be kinder to people who needed it. Look at all she'd done for Perla. And Imelda, her housekeeper, who had both a unibrow and a pronounced mustache.

In keeping, she tipped the kid a twenty. He stared at the bill for a moment as if not quite recognizing the denomination. Could he have actually expected more? But now other people were crowding into the kitchen, demanding her attention, and when she looked back, the kid had already shuffled away.

Everything was in perfect place for the dinner party. Her eighteenth-century Italian refectory table had been moved out to the center of the courtyard and was charmingly set with centerpieces of delphinium, white orchids, and pansies. Dozens and dozens of votive candles had been artfully grouped and were waiting to be lit. The chef, a temperamental, breadstick-thin young Belgian named Margarite had arrived in good time with her helpers and waiters, and the kitchen was suffused with mouthwatering aromas.

Even the weather was cooperating, promising to be clear and balmy with a light desert breeze.

The phone jangled. Lally tensed, as she did now each time she heard the phone ring, since the cryptic call from Sienna. Perla, who'd been attracted to the kitchen by the heavenly aromas, picked it up, dealt with whatever the caller wanted, and hung up, and Lally relaxed again.

She glanced at a clock. Yikes, almost five and she was still in her Juicy velours. She ordered Perla to keep an eye on everything and scurried upstairs.

Five-oh-five P.M. Lally soaks in a bath scented with lemon verbena, jasmine, and thyme, taking care not to moisten her hair, which she is wearing not in her trademark ponytail tonight, but piled on her head in a disheveled, seemingly careless arrangement that had taken her stylist, Raimond at Rai Carré, the better part of two hours to achieve. Before her hair appointment, she had dropped by La Rocha for the requisite waxings and . . . well, something she hates to even think about, but she has a little secret—several years ago, her pubic hair had begun to go prematurely gray and it requires a frequent touch-up of color. She's aware that among younger women it's become fashionable to shave the vagina entirely, but Lally finds this an unappetizing solution. Too *Hustler* centerfold. (Back in her Priscilla Much days, she had posed for a tasteful pictorial in *Playboy,* but had given *Penthouse* an emphatic N-O and would never have *dreamed* of doing *Hustler.*) At the spa, her color technician, Tilda, uses a vegetable dye formulated for men's beards because, as she explained, the skin of the face is a lot more tender than the skin on the scalp, and so beard dye is a lot gentler. It comforts Lally to glimpse the neat golden-brown strip swimming hazily beneath the green herbal slick of the bathwater.

Five twelve P.M. Rather reluctantly, she steps out of the fragrant bath and wraps herself in the lush terry-cloth bathrobe she had nicked from the Maui Four Seasons.

Outside the window, she vaguely notices that the fronds of the king palms have begun to sway. A breeze is picking up.

Five twenty P.M. Her makeup person, Marianne, arrives, somewhat earlier than usual, because the natural no-makeup look Lally has requested will take a bit more effort. "It looks like the Santa Anas are starting to blow," Marianne says; but Lally has detected in the pinkish light of the magnifying mirror a faint but brand-new little wrinkle, like a tiny comma at the end of the sentence of her eyebrow, and so she doesn't really listen.

Six ten P.M. Lally begins to dress. Simple elegance is her watchword for the evening. An ivory silk Armani tunic with fluted pleats skimming the knee. Two-carat diamond studs (Harry Winston—second-anniversary present from *sweet* Artie). Open-toed Rochas pumps in blond pony skin, adorned with cream silk roses.

And then fragrance: In the past, Lally has favored exotic and original perfumes—Wild Fig & Cassis from Jo Malone London, for instance—but she has lately returned to the classics, and now she applies a dab of Chanel No. 5 on the hollow of her throat, in the declivity of her breasts, and in the crooks of her elbows and knees.

One final touch: She selects a plain baby-blue silicone wristband from an assortment of various colors, each representing support and contribution to a noble cause: breast cancer, disaster relief, birth defects, etc. She forgets precisely which one the baby blue signifies (diabetes?), but it shows up well against the ivory pleats of her dress.

Seven fifteen P.M. She summons Perla upstairs to snap a digital photo. (There were certain women in town—Susanna Clemente had been among them—who never wore an outfit twice: After one airing, the clothes went straight to the consignment shop. Lally was not quite in that league, and so she always had a photo taken before a dressy or semidressy evening, to make sure she never duplicated the same outfit with the same people.) Perla has a dab of caviar clinging to the upper of her two chins, revealing that she's been sampling the hors d'oeuvres, but since she's had to stay so late, Lally lets it slide.

Seven thirty P.M. The banks and towers of votive candles have been lit, and, bathed in their flickering glow, the courtyard has never looked beautiful. Lally is confident that she too will appear to full advantage. A strong gust of wind comes up, causing the candlelight to flutter and shiver, casting mysteriously mobile shapes and shadows that only enhance the romantic atmosphere. With the crenellated tower of the campanile rising behind, it could almost be Tuscany: Lucca, Pisa, Livorno . . .

Everything is going to be perfect.

She reviews her talking points for the evening. She has done her due diligence vis-à-vis David's ideas for reservation schooling. He supports the idea of breaking up the system into very small schools, a hundred students or less, with each school having a theme: archaeology, health and traditional medicine, tribal customs and language. Lally is impressed by these ideas and is genuinely excited about discussing them.

To her surprise, the doorbell chimes—who could be so gauche as to be arriving right on the dot? But she's ready. She poses herself with a radiant smile, as the cater-waiter ushers in a man with shoulder-length gray hair and a woman in a wheelchair, who is so enormously fat she would make Perla appear svelte. The Topanga chief and his wife! Lally's smile falters for only the most undetectable fraction of an instant—how the hell is that contraption going to be wedged into the tightly seated table?—and then she steps forward with both hands extended in greeting.

"Chief Snelling! Mrs. Snelling!" she coos. "How lovely of you to come!"

Seven fifty-eight P.M. All the guests have arrived except the most important one. Janey was the second to clock in, twelve minutes after the Indians, overdressed in Escada and the kind of chunky gold necklace last seen on slave princesses of ancient Babylonia. (Lally makes a mental note to herself: *Janey—accessories!*) Close on her heels was Taller Kern, impeccable in chalk-stripe Yves Saint-Laurent and a forties-era tie whimsically patterned with jazz notes. He was followed by the congresswoman wearing a blue-cheese blue dress with a swirly belle-of-the-ball skirt, accompanied by her husband, the CPA, who appears to be furtively scoping the place for IRS-allowable deductions.

All the others except David Clemente arrived in a sort of loose pack. Two of the men are megamillionaires in their own right: Steve Kostolakis, retired Coca-Cola exec, and Les Neiling, who owns several thousand acres of prime Santa Ynez wine country. Both come equipped with aging trophy wives, one (strawberry blond) a former Lufthansa first-class flight attendant, the other (honey blond) a former Elite model widely known to have briefly been a star of the Bel-Air Madam's high-class stable of hookers. The final couple is the Rubinsteins, Christopher and Laura, a yo!-ing, horseback-riding, his-and-her financial team who manage half the portfolios in town.

Four of the women and two of the men are featuring plain silicone bracelets on their wrists, one white, two pink, and a classic Lance Armstrong yellow.

The Native American guests of honor are introduced around, cocktails and hors d'oeuvres circulate freely, and Lally begins to feel a touch of alarm—what if David is a no-show?

Plus the wind is definitely getting stronger. It's a genuine Santa Ana now, hot, dry, gritty with the dust of the desert. An intense gust causes the king palms to nod and sway as if in lamentation. The candles sputter, and several of them blink out. The women's hairdos are blown to bits, and the congresswoman holds down the sides of her billowing skirt, Marilyn Monroe–style.

Eight fourteen P.M. At last, the rent-a-butler ushers in David Clemente. Lally swivels with relief. He looks handsome, much better looking than she remembers him. Their eyes meet, and his seem to widen, as if he's thinking the same thing about her. An uncharacteristic sensation grips Lally, something that makes her heart beat faster and causes a flutter in the pit of her stomach.

Then she immediately freezes—behind David appears Caitlin

Latch. Lally gapes in an astonishment that turns quickly to dismay—Caitlin is wearing a little black chiffon frock that clings like crude oil to her contours and exposes a significant amount of truly spectacular cleavage. For a moment, every man appears to be riveted by the sight of Caitlin's half-bared bosom. David drops a proprietary arm around her shoulder.

Suddenly there's a mighty whoosh of wind. A vase topples. Somebody lets out a little scream, and a fourteen-foot king palm frond comes crashing down onto the center of the table, taking with it some two or three thousand dollars' worth of Sèvres and Waterford.

Chaos ensues. Lally, who has always prided herself on being able to rise to any occasion, finds her brains almost melted by the sequence of events. She stands rooted to the spot, unable to speak or move. Then Taller, bless his heart, takes over. "I'd suggest we take this show inside, folks," he announces, and personally begins wheeling Mrs. Topanga Chief through the French doors into the adjoining great room. One of the wheels gets stuck in the crevice of the door and won't budge, no matter how hard Taller shoves the chair. It's Caitlin Latch who, by deftly manipulating the wheel, finally manages to unhinge it.

Mrs. Chief is rolled inside. The other guests follow in a nonplussed body, while the waiters and butlers scurry to salvage what's left of the tableware and cart the table back into the dining room.

Lally remains in the blustery outdoors for some minutes to direct the proceedings. Janey pops up at her elbow to assist: She's displaying a preternatural calm, courtesy, no doubt, of the Valium she purloined from Lally's bag. Lally has the feeling that should they suddenly be caught up in the vortex of a tornado—table, courtyard, palm trees, and frigging all—zonked-out Jane wouldn't turn a hair.

Lally shoos her away, then follows the table inside, replacing the broken crystal and china with mismatched pieces, doing what she can with the flowers. She glimpses at herself in the mirror above the Provençal sideboard. Eek! Her wind-whipped hair has gone from artfully disheveled to Bride of Frankenstein!

She gallops upstairs and effects a quick reconstruction with a dollop of Bed Head gel, while silently reciting a mantra: *You are Lally Chandler. You are in complete control.*

Eight twenty-seven P.M. As she hurries back downstairs, a cater-waiter waylays her and informs her that dinner is ready to be served. "Not yet!" she exclaims, and races into the kitchen, where the chef, Margarite, is stooped over the Viking range.

"Hold everything up for about twenty minutes, would you please, Margarite?" Lally tells her.

Margarite straightens up, her entire body vibrating like a struck tuning fork. "Excuse me. But you told me to serve at eight thirty."

"I know, I know, but we've had this crazy disaster happen, so just give it another twenty minutes. Okay?"

"Okay, fine. Why not? I can hold it up for twenty minutes. And at that point my lamb will be mutton, and my blue-corn soufflé will be cornmeal mush. And I can't even begin to describe to you what's going to become of my baby artichokes!"

"Okay, okay," Lally appeases her. "We'll eat now. Five minutes."

Eight thirty-four P.M. Lally heads into the great room to announce that dinner is served, only to find that the cater-waiter has beaten her to the punch. Taller, who's somehow become self-appointed master of ceremonies, is in the act of herding everyone into the dining room and is directing them into chairs. Lally's carefully wrought seating plan has been thrown to never-never land—before she can object, she somehow finds herself wedged between Taller and the shiny ironsides of the Native American woman's wheelchair.

Caitlin Latch, she notices, is nestled between the two married multimillionaires, who are already being attentive enough to attract glares from their wives.

And David is way, way down at the foot of the table, sandwiched between the congresswoman and the chief, and already conferring cozily with both.

Lally thinks of the facts and figures she's so arduously memorized in order to dazzle David: the average high school dropout age among Native Americans, the correlation between enrollment in charter schools and acceptance into a four-year college, etc. But she's too demoralized to go into any of it now—she'd have to bellow it down the entire length of the table. She's too demoralized even to give her customary toast welcoming her dear, wonderful guests into her home. She hunches over the blueberry soup that is the first course and slurps it disconsolately.

"Bon appétit," Taller says. There's something just a bit snide in his voice that makes her look at him sharply.

But then on her left, there's a sudden sound like a seal barking. *Ork, ork, ork, ork.* It's Mrs. Topanga Chief. She thumps herself on her prodigious chest. "I've got this nasty cough," she confides.

Ten fourteen P.M. The beignets with homemade coconut sherbet have been consumed with attendant coffees and teas. Lally is hoping to herd the guests back into the great room for postprandial cognac, and this time she is bound and determined to position herself strategically.

But no: The congresswoman must attend a crack-of-dawn prayer breakfast at the Knights of Columbus and has to leave. David regrets he must leave as well—something about getting back to Arizona?—and thanks Lally profusely for what has been an informative evening. The Snatch simpers her thanks as well—"I've had such a lovely time"—and trots off triumphantly on David's arm.

Within ten minutes, the rest of the guests have also departed. The cater-waiters and the rent-a-butler whip through the cleanup. Lally hands out lavish tips and profuse thank-yous.

After they depart, she totters into the den and throws herself onto the fennel-colored leather sofa in utter exhaustion and defeat. *Quel désastre!* She figures she's dropped about seven grand tonight, counting the breakage of the china and crystal and all. Seven thousand dollars to listen to Taller Kern bubble on about nothing in particular and to a fat lady bark like a seal.

As she rubs her knee, which she had banged twice against the wheelchair, something else catches her attention. The glass-fronted Arts and Crafts cabinet set against the far wall . . . Its door is slightly ajar. Even from here, she can see what's missing.

Her golden gun.

The mock gold-plated Beretta that was her signature prop in *Dying Is Easy.* Every poster of the movie (there's one hung right beside the cabinet) had prominently featured her with the gun tucked into the top of her vinyl thigh-high boot. It's one of her most cherished possessions!

She leaps up, flings the cabinet door open all the way, and frantically searches the shelves, but it's definitely gone.

One of the cater-waiters pinched it, no doubt. But which one? And how could she ever hope to prove it?

Hell's fucking bells. She sinks back onto the sofa, then picks up a silver-framed photo of herself posed with Jane Fonda at an antiapartheid rally (happier days) and hurls it like a ninja star into the opposite wall.

CHAPTER *eleven*

The Expression on Lally's Face Was Priceless

Caitlin snuggled cozily into the capacious leather seat that faced the aisle of the jet and giggled to herself. The look on Lally Chandler's puss when Caitlin had sashayed into her candlelit courtyard in the company of David Clemente was, as that MasterCard commercial put it, priceless. And when the palm branch came crashing down, she thought Lally was going to pee in her pants. All in all, an amazing evening. Now, feeling comfortably sleepy from the wine and rich food, Caitlin contemplated the events of the past week.

The seminar project was pretty much a bust. The cops she was expected to "sensitize" were a bunch of cowboy yokels, rowdy, given to crude jokes and hawking gobs of chaw tobacco on the floor while complaining in four-letter language about how pissed-off they were about not getting paid overtime. She'd have had better luck sensitizing a herd of local cows.

But the majority of her time had been monopolized by Melora Patterson, a woman with a startling Rudolph the Reindeer nose and more turquoise adornments than your basic Aztec god, and who really just wanted to use Caitlin as an audience for her endless recitative about how unfair and boring her life was stuck in this backwater town. *Give me your dress allowance for a year, lady,* Caitlin thought, *and I'll be happy to put up with a hell of a lot of boring.*

And then there was Aiden. At first he'd been enchanted by the novelty of living in a hotel—room service! kidney-shaped swimming pool! tiny shampoos in the bathroom!—but he quickly became disenchanted, neglected the prepared lessons, whined that his tutor was *stupid,* the pool was *freezing,* and there was nothing to do, that he was missing all of his most favorite video games—*Why did you make me pack so fast? I brought all the wrong ones!*—and the cable TV in their room didn't get the cool channels, only the channels that sucked.

She could sympathize. She wasn't exactly thrilled to be here either. "It's for my job, sweetie," she said. "Try to understand. I know it's a drag, but we'll be home before you know it."

In the meantime, she'd had a number of communications with David's assistant, Barry, though she had never worked up the nerve to ask how exactly she was going to be "picked up." This morning he'd told her "the car" would be at her hotel at four fifteen, so it seemed that it was a Batmobile after all.

She hadn't brought the right clothes, of course; but in exchange for sympathizing with Melora's account of how impossible it was to find a halfway decent gardener in this town, Melora let her raid her closet. Not much fit—Melora was a scrawny five-foot-two—but Caitlin managed to find a scoop-necked black cocktail dress that was just a shade too tight. On the other hand, she could wear Melora's size nine and a half pumps—black satin Bottega Venetas—only by stuffing cotton in the toes. She'd hinted about jewelry, but Melora had chosen not to take the hint, and so her workaday strand of cultured pearls had to do.

Having enlisted one of Melora's army of housekeepers to stay with Aiden, she went down to the hotel lobby at the ordained time. It was not a Batmobile that collected her, but an ordinary hired car. A Chevy, not even a Town Car. The driver poked at a leisurely pace through town, leaving Caitlin even more mystified—at this speed it would take about two and a half *days* to make it back to San Carlino.

The car veered into a kind of industrial-wasteland part of town, and she had a quick jolt of fear. She didn't really know whom she was dealing with here: What if he were some kind of psychopath? What if this were some kind of freaky, twisted plot to abduct her and have her tortured to death in some freaky, twisted way and leave her body dumped in an abandoned warehouse?

Her skin prickled as the car pulled up to what looked exactly like an abandoned warehouse. She leaned forward. "Where are we going?"

"Airfield," the driver mumbled.

She suddenly noticed a discreet blue-lettered sign centered above the warehouse door: GENERAL AVIATION. Right, of course. Billionaires had private planes. How could she have been so dense?

Inside the warehouse, in a bare-bones waiting room, she was greeted by a Barry clone, a blandly handsome young guy dressed in a snappy gray uniform. "Good afternoon, Ms. Latch. Perfect weather for flying. Ready to depart?"

Yeah, she was ready to depart. He whisked her out through tall glass doors on the other side of the waiting room (no tedious security lines here!). A gleaming white jet was idling its engines on the runway. She ascended the movable stairway into a mocha-and-mint decorated interior. Both the pilot and copilot introduced themselves. The Barry clone brought her a glass of fizzy water and filled her in on the plane: Gulfstream V, seated fourteen, the former Mrs. C. had redecorated it just six months ago and added the bidet in the lavatory.

The jet took off, was aloft, and almost immediately began to descend.

"Going down already?" she asked.

"We're picking up the Wildcats in Tucson."

"The what?"

"Mr. Clemente's basketball team? We're dropping them in Burbank. They've got a semifinal game in L.A. tomorrow night."

She vaguely recalled reading that, among his many assets, David owned a basketball team. Still, she was surprised when the jet filled up with immensely tall, impressively muscular, and mostly African-American women. The Wildcats were a women's basketball team! A rowdy gang, hollering and whooping and hooting insults at one another for the fifty-minute flight into Burbank, where they tumbled out in a noisy, jostling mass.

A twenty-minute wait on the runway due to heavy traffic, then another rapid up and down, landing on an airfield in the outskirts of San Carlino that Caitlin hadn't even known existed. This time, as she disembarked, a limo was waiting right on the tarmac. She plumped herself regally in the backseat. *Oh, yeah. This really is the way to travel.*

The car swooshed down the coast highway to Colina Linda, then purred through those heartbreakingly lovely little lanes to the Clemente estate. As they passed through the gates, Caitlin looked for some evidence of her crash, but all traces had already been removed.

And then David was sliding into the seat beside her. "Hello, heard you had some traffic in Burbank; really sorry for that. You look stunning, by the way." His eyes journeyed briefly to the plunging neckline of the tight black dress.

"Thank you, and so do you," she replied. Which he did, in a charcoal cashmere jacket and a shimmery pale green tie. No high-tops tonight, but a luscious pair of softly shined black oxfords. The only jarring note was the glasses, a peculiar black-framed pair that reminded her of Elvis Costello.

But hey, if he wanted to crown himself with antlers and whistle "Yankee Doodle," she wasn't about to complain.

"So what did you think of the Cats?" he asked. "Terrific bunch, aren't they? If we win tomorrow night—and I'm confident we will—we'll go to the finals." For the rest of the half-mile trip to Lally's, he enthused about the team, practically bouncing in his seat as he described a game that went down to the final free throw; even without the high-tops and striped shirt, Caitlin was again struck by the image of an old-fashioned referee.

The limousine snaked up the drive to Lally Chandler's house in all its ersatz Mediterranean glory, and then they had waltzed into the entertaining spectacle of all that wind and the palm branch making mincemeat out of that fancy table.

Her only disappointment was that she didn't actually get to spend that much time with David. Her two dinner mates were pleasant and attentive and obviously rich, and one, Les Neiling was handsome in a bland-faced golfer way, but they both came with wives who monitored their every move.

And then she and David were back in the limo, and no sooner had it pulled out than they both dissolved in laughter.

"We sure made quite an entrance," he said.

"Yeah, amazing."

"I swear I didn't stage it just to impress you."

"You didn't? Well, now I'm disappointed."

They burst out laughing again. She was surprised—she hadn't expected him to have a sense of humor.

"The chief's a fascinating guy, though," he said. "Told me they'd been having trouble on the reservation from local Klan types. Letters threatening to kidnap children and burn down schools. Mary Novacek is going to launch an investigation."

Here was an opening for Caitlin to show off some recently acquired Native American lore—like Lally, she had done some quick cramming. But David suddenly reached into his jacket and pulled out a titanium-colored pager. He looked at it and grunted. "Sorry to be rude, but I'm going to have to deal with this." He picked up the limo phone and, without dialing, seemed to be magically connected.

While he talked in a low, intense murmur, Caitlin stared politely out the window. They had turned onto Despuestas: She wondered if they were going to his place, and if so, did he expect her to go to bed with him? And if he did, would she agree to? She'd never slept with anyone in his league before, i.e., a guy who could afford to sample any number of exotic mistresses and might therefore expect . . . well, specialties . . . or have a few bizarre kinks himself. She thought of an old roommate of hers, Pamela Moseley, who'd dated the scion of some superwealthy San Francisco family; she'd told Caitlin that the only way he could have an orgasm was if during sex, he speed-dialed his mother in Pacific Heights so he could be chatting with her while he came, his mother, of course, not suspecting a thing. . . . Caitlin wondered how she would even handle such an event.

But the car swung onto the highway and in a jiffy had returned to the private airfield, so whatever strange sexual bridges needed to be crossed remained, at least for now, in the future. David terminated his call and rather formally escorted her into the little terminal. The Gulfstream was revving up its engines on the runway.

"I had a terrific time," she said. "Thanks for inviting me."

"Thank you for coming," he said stiffly.

Her heart sank: She'd obviously struck out.

"Listen," he added, "would you like to go to a Cats game? Provided they make the finals?"

Her heart rose. "I'd love to."

"Good." He leaned in for a kiss. Nothing too slurpy, but with a proprietary bit of pressure and just a little tongue.

Surprise number two: It left her tingling.

And now here she was back up in the stratosphere. Might as well enjoy it, she told herself, before she had to get back to Aiden. He'd no doubt still be awake, ready to bombard her with complaints: His stomach hurt; the sitter smelled funny; when were they going to go *home*?

"You got some assistance from an act of God," Taller said.

Jessica had dropped by his bookshop, Ex Libris, and found him lounging with weary grace in a leather armchair, one arm of which had been clawed to coleslaw by Boswell, his Jack Russell terrier. Chair and dog were just a couple of Taller's English aristocrat–wannabe affectations.

"I heard a palm frond blew down and wrecked the table."

"Yeah, and when it did, poor old Lally just about lost it. After that it was easy for me to divide and conquer."

"So David's safe from her clutches."

"For the time being. Thing is, though, you've got another contender to worry about. This girl Caitlin Whoosis . . ."

"Caitlin Latch."

"Where the hell did she pop up from?"

"She's been around. A bit of a social climber. She tries hard, but most people don't take her very seriously."

"From the way David was admiring her assets, I'd say you might have to take her extremely seriously."

Jessica had an image of Caitlin at the historical society luncheon. That va-va-voom body. Those pillowy lips lifted upward in that pleased-to-meet-you crescent of a smile.

And one other thing.

One other huge thing.

She was young. Thirty-three or -four, making her not much older than the Brain. Jessica felt a sudden and visceral flash of hatred for both of them—for all the laugh line–free younger women who'd lost none of the plumpness in their cheeks and didn't have to starve to keep it off their tummies.

"Urumph." Taller cleared his throat. "Did you, ah, bring the check?"

"Yes, Taller. I brought the check."

He rose and plucked it from her hand. Six grand. It had required a call to her financial manager, Laura Rubinstein, to transfer enough funds to her checking account to cover it; it was, in fact, Laura who'd given her the first account of Lally's dinner party. "What was Lally thinking, setting up outside in a Santa Ana? If that palm frond had hit a person, I'd sure hate to think of the lawsuit!"

Laura had also pointed out that Jessica's portfolio was down this month, her positions in pharmaceuticals were in the toilet, and was she sure she wanted to withdraw these funds?

No, she wasn't sure at all. For a moment she nearly snatched the check out of Taller's fingers, but he slipped it into his billfold as smoothly as a magician palming a quarter.

"Congratulations. You've just purchased a pair of insanely hard-to-get tickets to the glamorous and exclusive Para Los Niños Ball."

"Are you sure about this, Taller?"

"Of course I'm sure. I was there last year. It's fabulously exclusive."

She made a face at him. "You know what I mean. Are you sure he'll be there?"

"He's on the board; he's purchased a table. That's all I can say for sure." Taller shrugged. "But it'll be a who's who of the city, and Lally Chandler's bound to be there. I can tell you now, she's going to come out swinging."

After leaving Taller's shop, Jessica drove to her mother's assisted-living village. Lillian was enjoying her broken arm. It had the strange effect of keeping her rooted in the present; and in the present she made constant and very specific demands: *Move this rocking chair closer to the window; find my pink slippers with the pom-poms; make me some scrambled eggs with milk and Muenster cheese and some scallions in them.*

"You're getting fat, aren't you?" Polishing off the scrambled eggs, Lillian eyed the open snap above the zipper of Jessica's jeans.

"Just a couple of pounds, Mama." She hadn't made a trip down to the wine cellar in five days, but previous sojourns had had a noticeable effect on her waist. Five hundred calories, give or take, in a bottle of pinot noir—the equivalent of two extra pieces of chocolate cake a day. She sucked in her stomach and snapped the snap—but in doing so, her elbow brushed her mother's plate, which in turn got egg on the front of her T-shirt. As she was futilely trying to wipe it off, Mr. Swimmer, the retired nursery owner who occupied the cottage two doors down, rapped at the door. Lillian went into her fluttery, flirty mode, and Jessica was able to make her getaway.

She then made the hateful trip to Michael's new home to pick up Alex—it was a cramped ranch-style house in a second-rate Colina Linda neighborhood for which Michael coughed up an exorbitant rent. No mystery why they were panting to get their mitts on Jessica's house.

As usual, Alex was sitting on the front stoop waiting. Amanda never had the guts to face her. Rowan was at lacrosse practice, so mercifully this afternoon Jessica wouldn't have to listen to her effusions about all the cool new additions to Amanda's clinging-to-adolescence wardrobe, the implication being that Jessica could take a few tips to spice up her own appearance.

"Hey, Mom, you know what? Amanda's scared of hummingbirds.

She thinks they're giant bugs, and she screams when they fly too near her."

That the Brain had no brains was no news to Jessica. "They're not insects; they're tiny birds, and they're very beautiful and completely harmless."

"I know, I told her, but she won't believe me." He produced a Three Musketeers (junk food had become one of Popular Parent Michael's favorite bribes) and began to unpeel the wrapper, shooting a sidelong glance to see if she, Unpopular Parent, was going to forbid it. She didn't have the energy to protest. He wolfed a big bite and said through the mush of chocolate and nougat, "Can we go to Amoeba? I want to get CDs for Evan."

Another weekend, another extravagant birthday party at which some spoiled princess or princeling, who already owned enough toys and games to stock a local branch of FAO Schwarz, would be lavished with dozens more. But it was the custom of the country; and so she dutifully headed with Alex to the music superstore that had recently opened on the outskirts of town.

Alex made a beeline to the rap section and began thumbing through the gangsters on the covers. Unpopular Parent should be monitoring his choices, nixing the most violent and obscene, but again she felt entirely sapped of even rudimentary strength.

"The new Ludacris is excellent. His best rhymes since *Back for the First Time.*"

A man in a leather jacket was proferring a CD to Alex. Jessica turned to glare at him.

"Hi, there." He smiled. "Remember me?"

She blushed deeply. It was Tom Bramberg, Lally's first ex and her aborted blind date. He was wearing the same scruffy leather jacket she had blubbered all over. "Of course. Nice to see you again. This is my son, Alex."

"Hey, Alex. Looking for anything in particular?"

"Birthday present for my friend Evan, but he's already got that Ludacris; he's got everything."

"Betcha I can find a few things he doesn't have." He flipped through the racks and pulled out a couple of albums with seemingly identical scowling, motley-clothed groups on the covers. "These guys are outstanding. Go check them out."

"Cool." Alex took them and headed to the sampling booth.

"Are you a big rap fan?" Jessica asked in wonderment.

"I'm a big all-kinds-of-music fan. Guess you'd say I have eclectic tastes. I'm like a pig in shit in this place." He handed her the clutch of CDs he was holding, and she looked through them: Benedictine chants; a Mongolian throat-singing group called Altai-Hangai; *The Who Sell Out*, remastered; Saint-Saëns, *Carnival of the Animals;* a girl rock group called the Donnas; a Brazilian samba trio; *Die Zauberflöte* by the Zurich Opera . . .

"*The Magic Flute*. My favorite!" she exclaimed.

"You like opera?"

"Love it. Or actually, I used to. My ex-husband hated it; he called it fat people howling in pain, even though most of the singers aren't even fat anymore, are they?" She gave a little laugh. "Anyway, this reminds me how much I really do love it. I'll have to start going again."

"If I've turned you back on to Mozart, then I've done my good deed for the day." He grinned. That overstretched mouth, those soulful, sad gray eyes—he shouldn't have been good-looking, except somehow he was.

She suddenly had the strangest sensation: that right here in the middle of the hip-hop section of Amoeba, he was about to gather her up in his arms.

For a moment she desperately wished that he would.

"These are both outstanding; I want to get them." Alex popped up at her elbow.

"Then I guess I've done two good deeds today," Tom said. "You two take care, okay?"

"Yeah, you too," said Jessica.

Tom Bramberg carried his haul of new CDs to the register, where a teenager with triple nose rings began to ring them up. He'd noticed Jessica's unsnapped waistband, what looked like egg yolk stains on her shirt, the faint unerased-by-toxins frown lines crumpling her forehead. It was wonderful, he thought, to see a gorgeous woman who still looked natural, not like she spent twelve hours a day in a rejuvenating salon or as if she ran to the toilet to throw up every time she ate a carrot stick.

Which made him think of Lally. Why should he even care about her? Their absurd little playing at marriage was another lifetime ago. But somehow he did care; he had thought of at least one thing he could do for her, and he had already put it in motion.

CHAPTER twelve

You Could Get a Little Augmentation

Lally had bounced back.

To begin with, she'd had an extrastrenuous workout the morning after the disastrous dinner, Russell flexing and arching her acrobatically over the Swiss exercise ball until she cried out for mercy. Afterward, she received a call from Sylvie McPherson, who'd been a bosom buddy of Lally's back when Sylvie had been a starlet named Sylvia Davis, inviting Lally to a shooting weekend at her second husband's family castle in Lockerbie: exactly what Lally needed—to scoot over to Europe for a posh, single-malt-Scotch-soaked long weekend. A complete change of scene would help her recover; also it would give her a nifty chance to wear that stunning new hooded Black Watch cape from Burberry that was frankly just a little too dramatic for the likes of San Carlino society.

She directed Perla to make travel arrangements, then tottered her quivering limbs into the sauna. She had just begun to luxuriate in the sweat-inducing temperature when Janey rang on the gym line to wax enthusiastically about the night before.

"Darling, it was a fiasco. I'm mortified."

"But you shouldn't be. I mean, I know it's the kind of thing that seems like a total nightmare while you're going through it, but then later on it makes a sensational story."

"That sensational story cost me seven thousand dollars. At least. I was wearing that new pair of Rochas. The pony-covered ones with the silk roses? They got completely ruined while I was out there helping them move the table. So that really makes it closer to eight thousand."

Janey was momentarily taken back by the sum. "Oh, well, what's that, really? A Chanel suit."

Lally snorted. Easy for Janey to be blasé about money; she was born into the stuff. Those such as herself who'd had to scramble and sacrifice and work like dogs for it—or at least, until they found a source to marry into—would always be acutely aware of the value of a dollar.

"But the important thing is that everybody's going to remember it," Janey burbled on. "The night the palm tree fell at Lally's dinner! David's going to remember it. And he'll also remember that you looked incredibly stunning. Everyone thought so."

"You think?" Lally blotted the sweat pooling under her breasts with an Egyptian bath towel.

"Oh, my goodness, yes. Even Greta Neiling, who's such a bitch—she never has anything but bitchy things to say about other women—she told me she couldn't figure out how you managed to look exactly the same for twenty-five years. Which I guess *is* kind of bitchy, but also a compliment, don't you think?"

Lally did think. Her spirits rose another notch. "Oh, but one more thing. One of those bastard cater-waiters pinched my gold Beretta."

"Your little James Bond gun?"

"Yes, darling. It's gone."

"So typical. The last catered affair I had, I was missing so many things I can't even tell you. Three of my best pieces of Meissen. At least your gun wasn't valuable."

"It was to me, darling. And I think you'd be amazed what a collector would cough up for it."

"But you could have it replicated, couldn't you? You must know somebody who could copy it. I mean, what with your Hollywood connections."

That was a point. Lally mentally ticked off several film wardrobe designer friends who would surely know how to duplicate a gold-plated 1970s-issue Beretta. And who would be the wiser that it wasn't the original, so long as she didn't tell?

She suddenly felt so good, she decided to blow off her decorator, Marky, who was coming by with veneer samples for the poolhouse commode, in order to take Janey to meet her secret jeweler, a brilliant little man from Oaxaca who could reproduce any piece for a fraction of what you'd pay at Tiffany.

By the time she showered and dressed, she was almost ebullient. Janey was right: The important thing was that she'd made an impression on David. The opening salvo had been fired: Now she could engage the campaign for real. And the more she thought about it, the more she considered that it was a good thing he'd hooked up with Caitlin Latch. He was on the rebound from a claustrophobic marriage; he needed to screw his brains out with a bimbo or two, get that well out of his system. After which he'd be ready—no, make that eager—for a more appropriate relationship with someone of his own social station and experience of the world.

All she had to do now was be ready to pounce when he was.

It was a spectacular day, seventy-two degrees, a booming blue sky swept clean of smog by the winds of the night before. She whirred down the top on the Mercedes convertible and pulled out of her gates, reveling in the soft warmth of the sun on her face and hair.

A ratty blue car idled on the street outside, a purple Styrofoam plum impaled on the antenna. A delivery from the Plum Mart, and it looked like the same acne-faced delivery boy as yesterday. Poor kid. Obviously a hard worker. Deserved a little kindly consideration.

She waggled her fingers in a greeting to him as she accelerated by.

Otis waved back. It was a reflex motion; he had not planned on being spotted by Lally, and particularly not on engaging her attention. He was making no delivery today. In fact, he wasn't even on the job at the moment: Technically he was slumped in the last musty row of Gunther Hall, dozing out over a crap lecture on Principles of Product Distribution 101.

This was reconnaissance.

Lally had been on his radar screen for some time. One of the first of Caitlin's "Stepfords" he had actually put a face to. Before that, he'd been operating on a sort of generic paradigm, the Colina Linda rich bitch, the high-and-mighty society babes who Caitlin said treated her like poor trash. Then one day, while he was over at her house, Caitlin was thumbing through a copy of *San Carlino Magazine,* the pages that had photos of the society parties, all those people grinning at the camera so damned pleased with themselves for being so filthy rich and exclusive. There was one babe with a brunette ponytail who popped up in almost every photo. He recognized her—she was a regular charge-account delivery of the Plum Mart.

"The Queen Bee." Caitlin snorted. "She buzzes around every hive, and all the little drones bow and scrape and feed her honey."

From the way she talked, Owen could tell that Miss Ponytail had been particularly snotty to Caitlin—which was confirmed by the way the lady had reacted to *him* yesterday. So he had problem skin, big fucking deal. It was a temporary condition; he'd grow out of it in a couple of years. Women like Caitlin got that and could appreciate him for what he would become. The caterpillar in the chrysalis and all that crap.

But this Queen Bee had acted like he was the Elephant Man or something, like if she had to look at him one more second she was going to puke all over her expensive pink floor.

Which ultimately proved to be a positive thing—her taking her eyes off him. Gave him the opportunity to do an interior reconnaissance. With all those people milling around, it had been a snap to shoot upstairs and get the lay of the rooms. The Queen Bee's bedroom was easy to identify, half the size of his family's entire house and all in white, like she was the virgin fucking Queen Bee.

One tricky moment after he came back downstairs. He turned left down a hall instead of right and got a little lost. But that led him into the room where he found the gold gun, which was a truly sweet score. A tactical error, however, to leave it out on top of his dresser after he got home. He woke up this morning to find his bastard brother Tim pointing it at him, going, "Bam, bam, bam." Then laughing like the shithead hyena he was. "Hey, Neo, where'd you get this? What, did it fall out of the Matrix?"

Asshole. All four of his asshole brothers still called him Neo, even though he hadn't been into *The Matrix* since he was fifteen—hell, he hadn't even *liked* the third film in the trilogy. But just try to explain that to those losers. As if they could give a shit, so long as they had some sweet way to put him down.

Screw his asshole brothers.

And screw you, Queen Bee.

Pepé Le Pew. The character came to him in a burst of inspiration. The lover-boy French skunk. Awesomely perfect.

He tried on the voice: "Ah, my great beeg bund-del of sweetness. Eez eet not love at first sight? Can you not kees your Pepé?"

He pursed his lips and made Pepé Le Pew kissing sounds—mweh, mweh, mweh, mweh—at Lally's big pink house.

Was Lally putting her on? Janey wondered. Dragging her to this grubby little shop between a Dunkin' Donuts and a Vietnamese nail salon in a strip mall in a sleazy commercial area near the 191 . . . And the proprietor, this peculiar little man with Elvis sideburns and puffy black eyes, scuttering back and forth between a Plexiglas counter and a wall checkered with photos of ancient Mexican movie stars . . .

No way Lally bought her jewelry here.

But apparently she did. The Elvis guy produced a blue velveteen case, snapped it open, and removed a delicate necklace of peridots set in gold filigree. Lally took it from him and fastened it around her long neck.

"Ramon, you're a genius!" Lally swung around to show Janey. "Isn't it gorgeous? It's modeled on the one Nicole Kidman wore to the last Golden Globes, but with a slightly more intricate design. I described what I had in mind to Ramon, and he got it instantly."

"Very pretty," Janey allowed.

"I told you he was brilliant. Ramon, what do you have that would work with the outfit my friend is wearing now?"

The peculiar man ducked wordlessly into a room in back.

"I don't know if I want to get anything right now," Janey said. "I mean, this isn't exactly—"

"Look, for your really important pieces, you'll still want to hit Rodeo Drive, but for everything else, why pay those prices? And what Ramon can also do is take the stones from some of those clunky old pieces you've already got and reset them in a better design. Something more contemporary and understated."

"Mmmm." Janey wasn't sure she wanted to be understated. Surely the purpose of owning big gems was to show them off? Besides, some of those "clunky" pieces had been passed down to her from her grandmother and great-grandmother—certainly she shouldn't go messing around with family heirlooms.

Thing was, though, that so far everything Lally had prodded her into doing had been absolutely correct. Her newly plumped-up face with the clean, feathery eyebrows. Her shorter swingier bob with auburn streaks. The long, slimming jackets that definitely mitigated what her mother used to refer to as "the family pear"—a body narrow on top, broad in the beam.

For the first time since probably even before she had married her third cousin Robbie at the age of twenty-one, she was attracting glances from men. One of them had even made a pass: Warren Dornholm, her so-called client. She was overseeing the installation of a gazebo in the garden room for him and Marcy when he backed her up against a wall of azaleas, planted his slobbery mouth on hers, and clamped her hand on the bulge in his Diesel jeans—at which point a couple of the gardeners came back into the yard dragging a slab of painted lattice and Warren had scuttled away. He was a scuzz, of course, with a potbelly and sardine breath, not to mention married, and if he tried it again, she'd quit the job cold.

Still, it had been weirdly flattering.

Ramon returned from the inner sanctum with several more velvet cases. He glumly set them on the counter and flipped them open.

Lally eyed the selections. She chose one, a rope of rather small rubies cut in multifaceted teardrops and fashioned into a lariat. "Let's try this on you." She fastened the loop of the lariat around Janey's neck. "I love it!"

Janey turned to a mirror. It did sparkle prettily, but such teeny-tiny stones—her mother would have sneered and made some sotto voce crack about "decoration for poor relations."

"You don't think it's a little too, um, insignificant?"

"Nope, it's perfect. Rubies are luscious with your coloring; they make your eyes go a much richer brown. . . . And wait till you hear the price; it's only . . ." Lally turned a questioning glance to Ramon.

"Nine hundred and fifty."

"Can you believe it? It's a steal!"

The price only confirmed Janey's suspicions that she was getting something cheap. Another thing that bothered her—the dangling tail of the lariat pointed like an arrow to her absolute lack of chest. She wasn't even an A cup—she was more like a *minus* A—and the last thing she needed was a sparkling arrow pointing to this humiliating concavity.

But it seemed to be a done deal. Lally was telling Ramon that her friend would wear the necklace out, handing him the velvet case to wrap up, and Janey had no choice but to produce her platinum American Express. Something odd happened as she signed the receipt: She had the distinct sensation that her hand was melting. Like the Wicked Witch of the West, it was dissolving into a watery puddle. Amazing that the pen didn't fall clattering onto the counter surface, but continued to form the letters of her name in her looping, Catholic-school script. She had a Valium tucked in the change pocket of her wallet, the last of the ones she'd swiped from Lally, but she was hoarding it for a real emergency. Some vague notion that her hand was liquefying didn't quite qualify, did it?

Lally steered her out the door and back into her silver-green convertible, gaily proposing lunch at Tra Monte. She had never mentioned missing the vial from her bag. Maybe she'd never noticed. . . . Or perhaps she thought she'd lost or misplaced it and had had the prescription refilled. . . .

Janey felt a wild lurch of hope: Could she possibly hit Lally up for a few more?

No, of course she couldn't. Nor could she think of anyplace else she could immediately get any more. Forget her doctors: Her internist, old Ralph Cathaway, also treated half her family. If she mentioned wanting even the mildest sedative, he'd go broadcasting to the lot of them that she was turning into some kind of drug fiend. Ditto for her gynecologist, Dr. Weitz. Her dentist was good for Vicodin, but only when she actually had major dental work done. And though lately she'd been able to surreptitiously poke into several people's medicine cabinets, she'd come up short. Her friends suddenly and mysteriously seemed to be coping splendidly without any sort of pharmaceutical assistance.

Later, she had the same weird *I'm melting, I'm melting!* sensation when she picked up the menu at Tra Monte.

"Are you okay?" Lally peered at her.

"Yeah, fine. My dogs wouldn't let me sleep last night. They kept making a racket, like somebody was right outside the house. I even called the security patrol. It was about two A.M. by then, so I'm, like, exhausted." Janey punctuated this statement with an exaggerated yawn. The heaving of her chest made the tail of the ruby lariat swing between her no-breasts. Lally's green-gold eyes followed it like a cat's fixed on the twitching tail of a mouse.

"God, I hate being so flat-chested," Janey blurted. "I'm, like, almost concave."

"You don't have to be, you know."

"I'm already wearing a padded bra. I guess you'd never even know it."

"Darling, I mean you could get a little augmentation. It's really a very simple procedure. I didn't need it, fortunately—I'm a perfect thirty-four B—but if I did, I certainly wouldn't hesitate."

Janey did hesitate. "Don't silicone breasts give you cancer or something? Because of leakage or whatever?"

"Good Lord, no, not if they're done by the proper person." Lally smiled. She had to admit, it was fun doing this makeover on Janey. Rather like playing Henry Higgins in *My Fair Lady*. Not that Janey would ever be called *fair*—not with those close-set eyes and lamentable haunches—but she'd certainly come miles from the Frump Girl of just a few weeks ago.

Lally now leaned forward and dropped her voice to a conspiratorial murmur. "Look, you may as well know I've had a little bit of nip and tuck."

Janey choked back a laugh. As if everybody didn't know that Lally Chandler was the San Carlino poster girl for plastic surgery. "Oh, really?" she managed.

Lally nodded. "Nothing major, just a bit of freshening up. But I had it done by the very best, Bruce Goodmayer, down in Santa Monica. You'd be crazy to go to anybody up here; there's nobody in this town I'd trust within a hundred yards of me with a scalpel. Bru's got a waiting list long as my arm, but I know I could slip you right to the top."

Janey had a sudden vision of herself making an entrance into Lally's next dinner party wearing Caitlin Latch's clingy black dress and displaying Caitlin Latch's cleavage. No, even better and bigger cleavage. She heard every man gasp with lust and desire, and she saw every woman's complexion turn green with envy; and then she pictured the tip of the tail of the ruby lariat necklace disappearing completely into the vast, nearly fathomless valley of her boobs.

"Well, maybe," she said.

It had not been difficult to find out where he lived.

Jessica had a friend who taught premed anatomy at the college who had a close friend in the music department who often had coffee with the composer in residence and knew the address. It was in a section of San Carlino known as the Portofino, an entanglement of little lanes, alleys, and dirt roads on a south-side bluff overlooking the ocean. Mostly decrepit little shacks and salt-rotted bungalows crammed cheek by jowl on tiny plots of land; but lately these had begun to disappear, giving way to sleek two-story Euro-design contempos that to Jessica looked like capped teeth set incongruously in a mouth of scraggly, broken molars and incisors.

Plus every street name had at least three incarnations: trying to find 10310 Sand Dollar Lane, she found herself on the dead-end Sand Dollar Trail, then stymied by the equally dead-end Sand Dollar Court. She doubled back on Sand Dollar Drive and still almost missed the correct turn. But then suddenly there it was! One of the scraggly old teeth—a formerly gray weathered-to-no-color little shingled house with a lopsided roof and an ancient cedar that blocked sunlight from the front yard. But it was sited on the seaward side of the bluff; and even from where she now was, parked across the road, Jessica could tell that it commanded a zillion-dollar view of the ocean.

So what was she doing here?

Stalking, obviously.

Just in case he happened to appear and notice her, she had a story concocted about having a friend who lived nearby and getting lost. She even had a street map folded to the right section, so she could look as if she were studying it. . . .

Then, to her astonishment, he did appear! The front door opened and he stepped onto the saggy little porch.

She reached for the map and spread it over the steering wheel and ducked her head. But he didn't notice her, for the simple reason that he was totally absorbed in someone else. A twenty-something girl had emerged from the house with him, an exquisitely beautiful creature who looked as if she had been dipped in gold. She had the kind of long legs that her jeans were designed for, and her skimpy tank top set off her golden skin. But it didn't matter—she could've been wearing a burka, a nun's habit, a Mother Hubbard, and she still would have shimmered.

Tommy put his arm around this vision's shoulders, and the vision put her arm around his waist. There was no denying the affection between them. They walked to a car in the driveway, a midsized black Audi, not new, not old. They got in and drove away.

Jessica felt strangely relieved—as though a decision had been made for her. She tossed the decoy map aside, waited a few minutes, and then also drove away.

CHAPTER *thirteen*

I Hate You! I Hate You!

It was marvelous to be in Scotland. The bracing air. The sense of history embedded in the walls and rooms of the castle. The long, rambling walks over heathery moors and grassy pastures studded with black-faced sheep. All utterly smashing. Lally had constantly congratulated herself on her decision to come.

The Burberry cape was a huge success, as were the Ralph Lauren mossy green gabardine trousers and the Tod's whiskey-colored lace-up boots, though the boots did pinch rather painfully on those long, rambling walks—and sheep shit proved stunningly difficult to scrape off Italian leather soles. Sylvie had gathered a fascinating mix of people—a bit of politics, a smidge of finance, a few theater types. And naturally she had provided an eligible man for Lally, Sir Wallace Kauferman, divorcé and a muckety-muck at the BBC. Unfortunately, Lally had already had a fling with Sir Wallace, back in her post–Bond girl days when he was plain Wally Kauferman, producer of one of those British talk shows where everyone sat on high stools and spoke with their jaws clenched. Flabby thighs and a habit of humming—mainly Elton John tunes like "Rocket Man"—during foreplay. Funny what you remembered about old lovers.

She shuddered to think she had reached the point where men were being recycled for her.

She and Sir Wallace grinned and mugged at each other and said, "Fantastic to see you again," and then they had avoided each other like the plague for the rest of the weekend.

And by Sunday, other things began to get just the tiniest bit tedious. The constant gloom of overhanging clouds. The bone-chill that was also embedded in the castle's historic walls. The tap in her bathroom in which scalding and cold water ran out in thick streams side by side, never really mixing.

And the way everyone sprang up at dawn to go blast away at pheasants. Lally didn't participate in the shooting, of course. She found no pleasure in killing creatures (though she didn't at all object to consuming them—she supposed this made her something of a hypocrite, but *c'est la vie*). Problem was it was impossible not to be awakened by the stomping and hearty bantering of the departing hunters, not to mention the racket made by the dogs.

On Sunday afternoon, she decided to cut her visit short. "Darling, my housekeeper called and there's a little emergency. A pipe burst in the guest bath and I've got to get back and attend to it." Sylvie, who had already slugged back half a bottle of Laphroaig, just smiled blearily, and Lally changed her plane from Tuesday to Monday.

She woke in her Virgin Upper Class sleeper seat during the descent into the brilliant blue California afternoon. She felt revitalized, ready to throw herself back into the fray. She was on the phone the second the car pulled out of the LAX terminal. Only gone less than a week, but so much had happened.

Juliet Shapiro diagnosed with in situ breast cancer . . .

The Morellis' Dutch au pair decamped in the middle of the night with their Bose audio components and the best of Christine Morelli's jewelry . . .

Madeleine Sweet rumored to have begun a wild and woolly affair with her personal trainer . . . (Russell! Lally felt a tiny pang of jealousy.)

She finally tracked down Janey at the vet having those two neurotic spaniels of hers dewormed. "Poor babies," Janey said, "that's what was making them so agitated and everything. Yesterday I was out walking them and scooped their poop, and I finally thought to look, and sure enough, it was full of these disgusting big white worm sections. I'm such an idiot; I should've realized sooner."

"Mmm," Lally murmured impatiently. She was hardly interested in the infernal dogs. "What else is going on?"

"Oh, there was a big item in the *Register* yesterday. The Clemente Foundation is giving fifteen million dollars to launch a tutoring program on Indian reservations. So you see, your dinner was a success after all."

That *was* interesting. "Seeing as how I made the connection, I guess I really ought to follow up on it."

"If you mean with David, you're going to have to wait. His son's coming out from New York. You know, the kid they adopted, Noah?"

Lally had, in fact, forgotten about this appendage. "Is Noah coming to stay?"

"I don't think so. I think he's got a school break for a couple of weeks, and David has custody." There was a ruckus of yelping and barking in the background. "I need to take my dogs home. I'll call you later. Oh, by the way," Janey added, "I did it! I made the appointment."

"Appointment?"

"With Dr. Goodmayer. I'm driving down for a consultation tomorrow."

"Marvelous, darling. He's the best."

Lally was no longer listening. She was too busy chewing over the visiting-son information. If only she had a child anywhere near Noah's age, she could arrange a playdate. It had always seemed intrinsically unfair that she was excluded from such a major facet of San Carlino social life as networking through kids.

But then a thought struck her: She might not have a young child, but she had godchildren galore! She and Artie had participated in baptisms and brises at least a dozen times. Okay, so technically they were trophy godparents. It was intrinsically understood that they were not expected to be the kind who kept the kids' photos stuck with magnets on the fridge, that there would also be another pair of *actual* godparents, nice, solid aunts and uncles who lived in places like Torrance or Topeka, or former Pepperdine U. roommates of one of the parents. The purpose of trophy godparents was twofold: to deliver lavishly on birthdays and Christmas; and to provide that extra little social edge—letting Mom and Dad casually remark to acquaintances, "Well you know that Artie Willman is Barnaby's godfather. Yes, *the* Artie Willman. And Lally Chandler is his godmother. Yes, remember? In the Bond movie, *Dying Is Easy*?"

But even a trophy godmother was entitled to take an interest in her godchildren some of the time.

With that thought, she settled back happily for the rest of the ride.

Home sweet fabulous home. The limo driver carted her bags into the front hall, and Lally heaved a sigh of luxurious relief. Heated bathrooms! Unlimited hot water! Lightbulbs stronger than forty watts, so you didn't have to grope and squint, even in the middle of the day . . .

Then suddenly she caught the faint odor of cigarette smoke.

Impossible. Nobody was allowed to smoke in Lally's house. It was an inviolate rule—anyone who worked for her knew they'd be sacked immediately if they broke it.

She followed her nose into the great room. The tobacco stench grew stronger. She gaped as she saw an ashtray brimming with butts; they overflowed onto the coffee table and—*oh, my God!*—one was stubbed out on her two-hundred-year-old Tabriz carpet!

Plus there were glasses and dishes and newspapers strewn over the furniture. And—*oh, bloody fricking hell*—somebody with dirty shoes had put their feet up on her just-reupholstered couch—a scuff mark like a hideous scar slashed across the silky Brunschwig & Fils fabric.

Somebody's head was going to roll!

Lally stalked back into the foyer. "Imelda!" she bellowed. "Imelda? What the fricking hell's been going on here?"

No answer. It was Monday, she realized. The housekeeper spent every Sunday and Monday with her sister's family down in Alhambra. Lally spun furiously and began storming toward her office, then remembered that, in a fit of ill-placed generosity, she had given Perla the day off as well. She had the number of Imelda's sister written down somewhere. . . . Where? Maybe in the Filofax she kept by her bed.

She stomped upstairs to her bedroom and was zapped by an even greater shock. This room also reeked of stale tobacco. More appalling, somebody had been sleeping in her bed! The sheets and coverlet were twisted and half thrown on the floor, the pillows mashed and bunched. Jesus, God, it looked like an orgy had taken place on it.

And there were clothes—Lally's *own* clothes!—strewn and flung about everywhere. She picked up a delicate Christian Lacroix silk-and-lace shirt wadded in a ball against a leg of the bed. Ruined—and she hadn't even worn it yet.

Quivering with rage, she rummaged for the Filofax and began searching for the number. Then she heard the chirp of a cell phone, followed by the sound of a female voice. She leaped over to the window and looked down at the terrace of the pool.

A golden girl was stretched faceup on a chaise longue, completely naked except for a pair of Dior shades that Lally recognized as her own. Strands of the girl's long gold-brown hair snaked over her breasts Lady Godivaishly. Lally couldn't see the phone, but she could catch a word now and then in Sienna's flat, mocking voice: *Shithead. Positively putrid. Thursday. I want . . .*

Then the girl turned over on her side, still droning a monologue into the phone, but Lally could no longer make out what she was saying.

Run away. That was Lally's first instinct. She could go to the club, burrow in there, call her security company, and have them roust the girl from the house.

But she was Lally Chandler—she never ran away.

She changed with deliberate motions from her travel-rumpled shirt and trousers to a crisp linen sheath and a never-worn pair of Gucci sandals. She grabbed a terry-cloth robe from the linen closet, and strode out to the pool.

Sienna's expression didn't alter as she saw her mother coming toward her. "Gotta run," she muttered into the phone, and abruptly clicked it shut.

"Well," she said to Lally. "I'm surprised you've even noticed me. That's so not like you."

Lally tossed her the robe.

"You've gotta be kidding. It's sweltering out here."

"Just put it on. A lot of people come in and out of this yard."

"Pool boys?" Sienna gave a lascivious smirk.

Lally waited.

Sienna sat up fluidly and reached under the chaise for a long, gauzy shirt that Lally also recognized as belonging to her. Sienna shrugged it on. Through the semisheer material, her nipples were visible, as was the neat golden strip between her legs—no furtive little trips to the spa colorist for her.

She groped around in the moat of litter encircling the chaise—dirty dishes, mangled Starbucks cups, half-chewed and deliquescing fruit, cigarette butts, used Kleenex, squeezed-in-the-middle tubes of gloss, and magazines that lay in the tents formed when she had tossed them down—Sienna, for all her ethereal beauty, was a total slob. She found the pack of Gauloises she was searching for, lit one with a lime-colored Bic, and blew a leisurely jet of smoke at her mother. "Nice dress. Prada?"

"Sonya Rykiel."

"You used to have such crappy taste. What happened? Did you get touched by the style angel?"

She's not going to get to me, Lally told herself. *Not this time.* "What are you doing here?" she demanded.

"What are *you* doing here? Your blimp of a secretary said you wouldn't be back till tomorrow. You know, she didn't even know you had a daughter." Sienna made a mock-mournful face.

"You haven't answered my question. Why are you here?"

"Will you please sit down? Or stand someplace else? You're blocking my sun."

Lally stood her ground.

Sienna smiled again. "I've been in L.A. for a couple of weeks with my boyfriend, Gogo. He's a filmmaker; he's doing a movie in New Zealand, and we're all flying out there tonight. Another hour and I'd have been already gone. So you can just relax."

"So it's not that phony count?"

"God, no. You're way behind the times, Lally." Sienna leaned her head back to blow a smoke ring. It wafted for a moment like a halo searching for a saint, then dissipated in the sparkling air. "Look, I drove up the other day to see Tommy and he insisted that I come over here. So I did, and Miss Blubber said you were away. Sob, sob."

"Her name is Perla."

"Yeah, sure, whatever. She was very happy to let me use the place. It was her idea really. It's very swanky, by the way. You must have soaked old Artie good."

With extreme difficulty, Lally kept her temper in check. "I'll be in the house, if you have anything of substance to say," she said, and turned sharply. Inside, she headed directly for the butler's pantry, where the liquor was stored. Empty bottles everywhere. All the Scotch was kaput. Ditto for the vodka and tequila. It appeared that only a few bottles of the nastier liqueurs were left. She poured a finger of Tio Pepe and tossed it down.

She went back into the kitchen and found Sienna sitting in a chair, languorously blowing smoke.

"I don't allow cigarettes in here," Lally said.

"So who are you, the surgeon general?" Sienna raised the Gauloises deliberately to her lips.

"Did you drink up all the liquor?"

"Well, not personally. A few people came up from L.A., and we had to give them something. For chrissake, you're rich now, Lally; you can spare a few bottles of booze." She glanced sardonically at her mother. Her green-gold eyes were almost identical to Lally's in color and shape. "Look, I did call you. You didn't call back."

"Oh, yes, well, I was insanely busy. And then somehow the number got misplaced."

"The dog ate it. Oops, you don't have a dog." Sienna flicked her cigarette into the dregs of coffee in a cup. "Let's cut to the chase. Tommy said you really wanted to see me."

"Did he? Well, that was his opinion. I never said anything like that." *Damned Tommy.* He always did have a Good Samaritan complex. Probably thought the second she and Sienna beheld each other they'd fall weeping into each other's arms, begging mutual forgiveness.

Strange thing, though—she did have an urge to touch the girl. To pet her glimmering hair and stroke her golden skin.

Instead, Lally began to briskly gather up dirty dishes and carry them to the sink. When was the last time she had washed dishes? She couldn't even remember—certainly way before she married Artie.

"So, at any rate, you've seen me and I've seen you, and now I've got to go pack." Sienna languidly rose and moved toward the stairs.

Lally attacked a plate with an SOS pad and scrubbed it vigorously. Her phones were ringing; people were calling; her busy, glamorous life was demanding her attention. She ignored them and kept on scraping and scrubbing dishes.

Why had they always been at each other's throats? Practically since the moment Sienna popped out of her in that gloomy Presbyterian hospital in Sherman Oaks, howling and scarlet with rage, they had been more like enemies than mother and daughter, Sienna crying and wailing and sometimes even beating her head against the floor if Lally so much as said boo. "I hate you, I hate you!" Sienna would shriek, and Lally would find herself yelling back, "I hate you too!"

There were rare moments of truce. The times they played dress-up, Sienna's favorite game. Those were the happy times, Sunday afternoons when Lally would festoon the little girl with her scarves and beads and bracelets and Sienna would slip her tiny feet into Lally's shoes and shuffle around the room with crows of delight—the most adorable thing you could possibly imagine.

"Nenna" was how Sienna pronounced her name as a baby, and for a while it stuck. "I'm Nenna."

The first word she ever said was *Lally.* And that stuck too: she never said *Mama* or *Mommy* or *Mother.* Always *Lally.*

Remembering all this, Lally felt something sharp knife through her. "Nenna," she whispered to herself.

Sienna reappeared, dressed in jeans, a white tee, and the Dior shades and carrying a Louis Vuitton satchel that had seen better days. Lally removed her hands from the soapy water and dried them. "Those sunglasses really suit you, darling," she said. "Why don't you keep them?"

Sienna smiled sardonically. "Thank you, Lally. That is sooo generous of you."

Clearly she had never intended to give them back. Lally was positive that the Vuitton bag contained a number of expensive designer items filched from her closet; and undoubtedly most of whatever *else* was in the bag would have been shoplifted from boutiques and *magasins* in Paris, Rome, and Barcelona. Whatever momentary softening toward her daughter she'd been experiencing instantly hardened up again.

The lies. The stealing.

And those photos that Lally would never be able to erase from her mind. She could still see them vividly, in every X-rated digital detail.

"Do you need a cab?" she asked coldly.

"No, I've got a car. It's in the garage. Next to the two of yours. You wouldn't want to give me that darling little Mercedes, would you?"

Lally said nothing.

"Didn't think so. Well then, later, gator."

Sienna turned fluidly and headed toward the foyer. The phone rang and Lally snapped it up. "Yes, darling, I'm fabulous; I had a sensational trip," she said to Rhonda Kluge on the line. "I'd adore to do lunch tomorrow."

She barely flinched at the sound of the front door closing.

CHAPTER *fourteen*

You'd Think Dating a Billionaire Would Be More Fun

You'd think that dating a billionaire would be a little more fun, Caitlin reflected.

Like maybe he'd whisk you up to San Francisco via his private jet for a fabulous evening at the opera, in the manner of Richard Gere with Julia Roberts in *Pretty Woman.* Or, like Richard and Julia, he'd present you with a credit card and give you carte blanche to go wild at some exclusive little boutique, showing up the snobby salesgirls who tried to high-hat you. And then, once you were properly outfitted, he'd escort you to some glamorous sporting event like the races or polo, or include you in an elegant business dinner where you, à la Julia, could act the muse while your billionaire engaged in shrewd negotiations.

Truth be told, the bulk of Caitlin's expectations about rich guy–poor girl relationships came from *Pretty Woman.* Naturally she wasn't so naive as to expect real life to completely mirror a simplistic Hollywood fantasy. It was just that so far her experience with David had been so completely non–Richard and Julia as to be almost baffling.

Second date: Instead of Thoroughbred racing at Del Mar, there'd been the Wildcats play-off game at the Burbank Center. Caitlin had perched on a hard stadium seat on the edge of the court, chugging Bud Light and munching a hot dog, while David paced courtside and conferred anxiously with the coach. At one point, one of the players had come tumbling directly toward Caitlin, causing her to execute a Wildcats-worthy jump of her own, sloshing beer on her new winter-wheat linen slacks, a stain that did *not* look like it was going to come out. The Cats lost fifty-seven to sixty-eight, precipitating a postgame shouting match between their coach and the ref; and then David had jumped into the fray, informing Caitlin he had to stick around and smooth things out. After a flurried good-night kiss, she drove herself home (two and a half hours due to nighttime construction on the northbound 101), paid the babysitter, and raided her own refrigerator, since she was still starving after the one lousy hot dog.

Third date: one week later. She did accompany David to a business affair; but this was not an elegant gathering of CEOs at Café Cygne. It was the launch ceremony of a decayed-neighborhood high school arts program that the Clemente Foundation was funding, and it had entailed glamorously stepping over broken glass and puddles of urine to get to a graffiti-desecrated auditorium for a succession of stultifying speeches and interminable thank-yous delivered by a drab bunch of education types. The dinner that followed was in a local dive called the Chicken Shack with the same people who'd made the boring speeches. Once again, Caitlin had to cut out early and make her own way back to Aiden.

Fourth date: a screening of an artsy-fartsy Chinese movie in David's private home theater. She and David and a half dozen of his employees, including the baby seal–resembling Barry, and Eduardo, the scary butler, watching a three-and-a-half-hour movie in Mandarin with ungrammatical subtitles. Dinner this time was Szechuan ordered in from the Five Cranes on Kittredge and eaten with chopsticks straight from the containers.

Afterward, as if on some prearranged cue, the help had melted away, and it was finally just the two of them alone together, sipping Cakebread chardonnay and chatting (though David did most of the talking; Caitlin deftly made sure of that). Which quickly led to snuggling and making out. Things had developed and they'd drifted into his enormous paneled bedroom and tumbled in between the Pratesi sheets on his bed.

The sex wasn't extraordinary. The earth didn't move or anything. But there'd been nothing weird or kinky either, thank you, God: no bizarre requests or introduction of fuzzy objects or phone calls placed to relations or priests or whatever in the middle of things. If anything, it had been a little too plain-vanilla, which she hoped didn't reflect badly on herself.

One thing that surprised her: He was in terrific shape. Fairly flat tum, firm ass, nicely muscled shoulders. When she complimented him, he'd laughed almost shyly. "I've got this trainer who used to be a navy SEAL, which is just another way of saying sadist," he'd said. Then he'd told her that her body was ravishing, which was more or less what men always said to her. She figured she had ten more years before gravity would cancel out the raves. Fifteen, maybe, if she really worked at it.

Almost immediately afterward, David had bounded out of bed to place a few calls overseas. "If you'd like to stay the night, that would be very nice," he said, knotting the belt on a silk robe, "but I'm afraid I'm going to be up for quite some time." She could tell he really wanted to get to work without having her knocking around; and besides, she had enlisted Otis to stay with Aiden, and he sulked if she got back too late.

So she got up and dressed and, just for a change, drove herself back home.

Otis was sulking anyway. He sat hunched on the sofa, barely lifting his eyes from Conan on her old Magnavox when she rushed in. "You said you'd be back by twelve," he grumped.

"It's only twenty after," she said.

"Twenty-eight after."

Caitlin had the creepy feeling he could tell she had just crawled out of bed with a guy, even though she'd told him she was going out with her friend Juanita from the center. Not that any of it was his freaking business. Jeez Louise, it was like coming back to a jealous boyfriend, that slit-eyed, how-could-you-betray-me look on his pimply face.

This was absolutely, positively the last time she was going to ask him to stay with Aiden. She didn't give a rat's how much a regular sitter cost.

And this time, she meant it.

~

A busy signal?

Lally hung up and redialed Tommy's number. The same unnerving noise—*bamp, bamp, bamp*—accosted her ear. Yep, a busy signal. When was the last time she'd even heard such a thing? Most people she knew would rather miss a meal than a call: They had two, three, even four lines, with rollovers and call waiting and sophisticated voice-mail systems that integrated with their mobiles.

A busy signal was so damned . . . primitive.

She waited several hours, then tried his number again. Still the infernal *bamp, bamp, bamp.*

No doubt he'd taken his phone off the hook. *Que c'était primitive!* And so annoyingly typical of Thomas Samuel Bramberg. And unless Lally wanted to leap in her car and drive over to his cottage-slash-hovel way up there in the Portofino and pound on his door like some mustachioed silent-movie rent collector –which he *still* probably wouldn't respond to anyway—she'd have to wait until he reemerged to discuss exactly why he had seen fit to spring Sienna on her.

The hell with it.

She slapped the phone down on the teak poolside table at which she was currently sitting. Then she strode to the edge of the pool and dove crisply in, swimming twenty furious laps in quick succession. She climbed out, pulled the Speedo cap off, and shook out her hair. Something was entangled in the long strands. She reached up and pulled out something slithery.

Oh, God! A used condom.

She shrieked and hurled the repulsive thing back in the water. "Imelda!" she screeched.

The housekeeper raced outside, one hand held over her fast-beating heart. "What is it?" she said. "Are you all right?"

"No, I am not all right. Call the pool people and tell them to get here immediately! I mean right now!"

"Yes, Mrs. Lally." Imelda scurried back inside.

It was simply too much. Lally sank down weakly on a chaise to collect herself.

She had slept in one of the guest rooms the night after Sienna had left. First thing the following morning, she'd had Imelda call the Merry Maids, who had sent a crew to scrub and air and polish every inch of Lally's own bedroom. She had been tempted to instruct them to burn the soiled sheets, but it was several thousand dollars' worth of antique Irish linen in question, and in the end she just had Imelda cart them to the French hand-laundry on Village Road with exhortations to have them use the most stringent cleaning process possible.

After a few days, the appearance of her daughter had begun to seem more and more unreal, like some jet lag–induced hallucination. Lally might even have managed to convince herself that she'd imagined the entire thing, except she kept discovering tangible evidence of Sienna's presence throughout the house. Cigarette burns in the weirdest places: on a maid's room curtain; on one of the Pilates mats in the gym. A La Perla bra, thirty-four-B, pale pink turned grubby gray from lack of laundering, bandaged around a leg of the dining room table. A crumpled pack of towelettes with an Austrian brand name wedged into one of the Donghia slipper chairs in the great room.

There was the even more eloquent evidence provided by the things that were *not* there. The girl had first class taste; Lally had to grant her that. Sienna had taken only the choicest items, Chanel, Prada, Hermès.

But this loathsome . . . thing . . . in the pool was the final straw. Sienna was a selfish, twisted creature. Lally had done her best, but she was through tormenting herself with guilt over any failure on her part.

So resolved, she got up, went inside, and luxuriated in a long, steamy shower. Feeling cleansed, she slipped into a fresh matched set of pale green silk underwear, then sat down at her dressing table. She opened the top drawer. Inside, she discovered a tiny pyramid of silken face powder, in a shade of gold several degrees tawnier than her own.

Lally dabbed the pyramid with an index finger. She stroked the silky powder on the back of her hand; and as she did, she felt that knifing pain slice through her again.

~

Dr. Bruce ("Call me Bru") Goodmayer, plastic surgeon, was a consummate testimony to his medical specialty. He looked about twenty-three years old, all blond gee-whiz good looks, adolescent-slim beneath his snugly fitting pullover and tight black jeans. Unless, of course, he *was* only twenty-three, some sort of Doogie Howser who'd whipped through med school while still a preteen—though Janey somehow doubted that this was the case.

Anyway, here she was, rather astonished to find herself sitting in his neo-midcentury-decorated Santa Monica office, nervously clutching a cut-glass tumbler of sparkling water. Directly in front of her was a large flat-screen TV that was currently tuned to a profile of her own body in all its concave-chested glory. "Micromastia," Bru called it—the medical term for lack of bosom endowment. Though in her case, Janey thought sardonically, "micro" was the overstatement of the year.

Bru sat at a Plexiglas desk, manipulating a computer mouse as dexterously as she imagined he would a scalpel. "Okay, ready? Now here's how you would look with a B cup."

Janey giggled as her boobs on the monitor swelled, like popovers rising in an oven. Her fuller-figured profile rotated: left, full frontal, right.

"That looks pretty good," she said tepidly.

"Uh-huh. Now let's try out a C."

Janey's TV breasts expanded again. She felt like Alice eating from the Wonderland mushroom: *One side makes you larger. . . .* She giggled again.

"So?" Bru beamed at her expectantly. "What are your thoughts? Are you digging the B or the C?"

"Which do you think looks better?"

"Hey, it doesn't matter a dot what I think. Or anybody else either. The only opinion that counts is yours, Jane. Whichever silhouette would give *you* the most confidence and personal satisfaction is the one that's right for you."

Janey nodded.

Bru flipped the screen between the B cup and the C. Pop up. Pop down. She bit her lip, thought a moment.

"Let's try a D," she said.

Caitlin had expected to receive something from David to mark the occasion of their first time making love—some romantic gesture, like a blizzard of orchids delivered to her home, or even one perfect rose nestled in a pure white florist's box. But *nada*. Instead, a couple of days later, a message on her phone: David, informing her that his son, Noah, was arriving from New York and they'd be going camping for a couple of weeks. He'd speak to her when he returned.

She was still stewing over this news when she got another call, this one from the scary butler, Eduardo. Mr. Clemente and his son would be returning to town for Halloween and he, Eduardo, was organizing a trick-or-treating playdate for Noah. Caitlin was invited to bring Aiden.

Yes! She accepted the invitation with elation.

But the more she pondered it, the more she realized it had pluses and minuses.

On the plus side: David wanted his son to be involved with hers.

On the minus side: Aiden.

There were only about a thousand ways the kid could screw things up.

Jeez Louise! She immediately felt disgust with herself. What was she thinking? Was she the world's shittiest mother or what? Why couldn't she just have the teensiest bit of confidence in her son?

Besides, Noah Clemente, during his brief stint at St. Mattie's, had been even more unpopular than Aiden, if that were humanly possible. So maybe—just maybe—if he and Aiden spent time together, they'd find a common bond. Maybe even become buddies. She just needed to think positively.

She'd have to buy Aiden a fabulous costume, of course. Something that could compete with what the richer kids would be sporting. Luckily she'd just had a little windfall—she'd unearthed a vintage 1964 Mary Quant newsboy cap in mint condition, as once featured by John

Lennon, at a garage sale up near the university, and the bidding for it on eBay had gone totally wild. She had earmarked the check for a second hand Electrolux to replace her ancient Hoover that did little more than redistribute the dust, but that could wait. This was far more important.

And as for her own costume . . .

She worried over it for several days, considering and rejecting one idea after the next. Then, just when she was despairing of ever having an inspiration—*bam!*—it hit her—a conversation she'd had with David about what kind of movies they'd liked when they were kids, who their favorite characters were, yada, yada. Suddenly she was seized by the most brilliant idea! A costume she knew he'd absolutely adore. And it was something she could pretty much make herself, so it wouldn't even cost that much.

It was so obvious, she was amazed she hadn't thought of it right off the bat.

CHAPTER *fifteen*

It Was a Single-woman's Order

October brought the kind of stunning weather San Carlino was famous for: one breathtaking, cloudless day after another. Instead of autumn leaves, there were crimson and blood-orange displays of bougainvillea; and who needed frost when the air was just chilly enough at night to let you wear the season's chic new jackets trimmed with fur?

By the second week of the month, Lally was thoroughly immersed in reigning over the frenetic fall social season that had now officially kicked into high gear. Days were a whirlwind of benefit committee breakfasts, art auction luncheons, charity lingerie fashion shows. Every night, a dizzying choice of A-list events, opera galas, theater openings, elaborate private dinner parties for twelve or twenty or fifty, black-tie mob scenes in the name of the Sciatica Foundation, or Doctors Without Borders, or Save the White Rhinoceros. Lally also had an array of escorts, culled from the best of the city's acceptable extra men, i.e., charming, good-looking, and gay; or boring, ancient, and rich.

But there was not a glimpse of David Clemente at any concert, dinner, or event. It was as if he had vanished in a poof of smoke.

"He's taken Noah saddleback camping in the Sierras," Juliet Shapiro told her.

"Oh," Lally said. "So that explains why I haven't seen him around."

Lally was treating Juliet to lunch at the Café Cygne, in an attempt to cheer Juliet up while she waited for the results of a biopsy of a lump in her left breast. Juliet was a fragile-looking woman with gamine-cut black hair and a voice like a church bell. She had given up a career as prima ballerina with the Seattle Ballet to marry Deke Shapiro, a guy with a slippery smile and wiry, no-color hair, who was the heir to a chain of pancake-and-waffle houses. While Juliet stayed home bringing up four children and cultivating Technicolor-striped strains of heirloom tomatoes, Deke dabbled in real estate development and in sleeping with a succession of willowy twenty-five-year-old "assistants."

Over the first course, Juliet had wept softly, tears plopping onto her untouched Coquille St. Jacques, while Lally assured her that she knew dozens and dozens of women who had licked breast cancer. "In fact, every single one is alive and kicking," she remarked. "It's not like ovarian, which is so insidious it's usually too late by the time they even find it."

"But what if I need a radical?" Juliet faltered. "I mean, do you think that would make Deke find me physically repulsive?"

Good Lord, she was worrying if that bastard was still going to want to squeeze in some sex with her between the rest of his extracurricular activities. Lally narrowed her green-gold eyes. *Tell the creep if he has a problem he can bugger off.*

But then, responding to a more charitable impulse, she gave Juliet an encouraging smile. "Oh, darling, don't worry. If it should come to that, it's amazing what they can do with reconstruction these days. I know a surgeon in Santa Monica who can perform miracles. He'll make you look even better than you did before."

That had succeeded in perking Juliet up—enough so that, by the time her second course of wild salmon had arrived, she was happily chatting about other things. With Juliet, that inevitably meant her children. She told Lally that her son Conner had been invited to a playdate with Noah Clemente, and that led to the news about the Clemente's saddleback trip.

Now Lally picked up her glass of Montrachet and said casually, "Did anybody else go on the camping trip with them?"

"Gosh, I have no idea. I just found out about the whole thing from Eduardo. You know that ghastly butler the Clementes have? The one Susanna hired because she thought a rude butler was classy?"

"Oh, yes. I most certainly do."

"Well, he's the one organizing the playdate. Apparently he's been put in charge of Noah's schedule because Noah's nanny was hired in New York and doesn't know the scene here. It's actually more of a party than a playdate, some sort of trick-or-treat expedition for a group of boys and their parents."

"Oh, really?"

"Yeah. Deke's going to take Conner, and I'll do Halloween with my other three."

"You know, I've always adored Halloween," Lally mused. "I guess it's the actress in me. I still have a hankering for getting into costume."

"Me too." Juliet lifted her face. She had those huge doe eyes set in an oval head that were de rigueur for ballet dancers, eyes that were now deep lagoons of reflected feeling. "You want to know something? Sometimes I get out my old ballet clothes, my practice tutus and leotards and pointe shoes, and I put them on and just stare at myself in the mirror, thinking I can't believe it—I can't believe this used to be me. And then maybe I'll try a simple entrechat or *changement de pieds* and I'll look about as ridiculous as the hippos in *Fantasia* and nowhere near as graceful. So I'll take off the damned stuff and toss it back into a closet and spend the rest of the day trying not to cry."

"I know exactly what you mean," Lally said eagerly. "You feel like once upon a time you were living this fabulous fairy story, and then some wicked godmother or . . . I don't know, an ogre, came along and stole it all away."

"Yeah, exactly." Juliet gave a short laugh. "My daughters don't even take ballet. They think it's lame. They're into karate and lacrosse."

Lally made a sympathetic sound.

Juliet ate silently a moment. "Tell me the truth, Lally," she said. "Do you think I caused this cancer myself?"

Lally set down her fork. "Darling, what are you talking about? How on earth could you give yourself cancer?"

"I've heard that people who keep their feelings locked up inside them can make themselves sick. Particularly with cancer—there's a theory that it's a symptom of unexpressed anger or grief." The doe eyes welled up again. "I know that Deke's been unfaithful to me, and I've always looked the other way. I mean, I've always thought that it's just a flaw in some men, that it's just impossible for them to stay faithful. But maybe I've really had all this rage pent up inside of me, and now it's expressing itself in the form of a tumor."

Lally was silent a moment, thinking of her mother, Deena. She'd never said a word about Howie's little flings, never letting on she even knew about them, right up to the day when he ran off for good with the erotic baker lady. Two months after Howie's final departure, Deena was diagnosed with the colon cancer that, despite the surgery and many months of radiation and chemo, would come roaring back almost exactly five years later and kill her.

So maybe there was something to Juliet's pent-up-rage theory.

But there was one thing Lally definitely did know—that when people said things like "I really want you to tell me the truth," it meant they wanted to hear anything but. She grasped one of Juliet's sparrow-boned hands and gave it a tender squeeze. "Here's what I believe, darling. I think it's just something that happened, and that you had nothing to do with it one way or another. You didn't cause it, and nothing you did could have prevented it. It could happen to any of us, anytime."

"You think?"

"Absolutely. And here's what else I think: You're going to deal with it, and everything is going to be fine."

"Oh, God, do you really think so?"

Lally gave an intrepid flick of her ponytail. "I'm positive. It's all going to work out for the best."

Juliet's face lit with relief. "I'm so glad you coaxed me out, Lally. I haven't been eating much lately, and I'm absolutely starving." She dug a fork into her salmon. "Oh, hey, speaking of David Clemente... Did you hear the Brubecks are breaking up? I think Chloe Brubeck has her eye on little old David."

By the time they had finished dessert (a shared pear financière made with mango and lychee sorbet), Lally had formulated a plan. She raced from Café Cygne to show her face at an Opera Guild meeting, popped in for a speedy upper-lip waxing at La Rocha, then hurried home in time to put in a call to Grace Poyniac at the Rape Crisis Center.

Grace was all agog, her voice as hoarse as a bullfrog's. "Oh, Lally, it's a good thing you called. I think you need to know. There's been another one!"

"Another one what, Grace?"

"Those assaults. In Colina Linda."

"Oh, my Lord! You mean the Spider-Man guy?"

"We think so. But this time he was wearing the mask of a character from the movie *The Incredibles,* which I personally have never seen, but I've been told was very good. Anyway, it was the same kind of case: He broke into a house where a woman lives alone and made her perform a sexual act with some sort of object."

"Yikes! Anybody I know?"

"Well, you realize I can't give out the names of victims. And anyway, this particular woman didn't come to us. We learned about it from the Colina Linda sheriff's department, so *we* don't even know her name. I just thought you should be informed so you could take all possible precautions."

"Yes, thank you," Lally murmured. She had a crawly sensation of... not fear, exactly. More like unease. She no longer felt as invulnerable as she used to—maybe because her home had just been invaded by Sienna and her repulsive friends. She made a mental note to call Protec Security and have them test out her elaborate alarm system, just to be on the safe side.

She felt a sudden flash of anger. Why was it that she always had to look after herself? Maybe, just for once, she didn't want to be the intrepid Bond girl.

Maybe, just for once, she wanted to be the princess rescued by the knight on the powerful white horse.

Which snapped her back to her reason for calling Grace Poyniac. "By the way, Grace," she said, "is Caitlin Latch working this week?"

"Yes, she's here. You did get the copy of her report, didn't you? The Dunster seminars were a smashing success. Mrs. Patterson was extremely pleased with them. Do you want me to transfer you over to Cait?"

"No, that's not necessary. If Melora was satisfied with her work, then I am too."

Lally hung up. She was totally satisfied to hear that Caitlin Latch had not gone saddlebacking with David and Noah Clemente. Things had obviously not progressed that far.

Which meant Lally was free and clear to make her next move.

Jessica did not consider herself a true Plum Mart customer. Shelling out the twenty percent extra they charged to enfold your fruit in tissue paper struck her as ludicrous, and the specialty items—the mobcapped little jars of black-currant preserves and swanky, illustrated tins of Cyprian figs marinated in port—was stuff her kids wouldn't eat if they were threatened with imminent starvation. But she did maintain a charge account there. Michael had frequently developed whims—generally twenty minutes before dinner was ready—for certain and specific tastes, such as Irish clover butter, or picholine olives, or even sometimes something junk-foodish, like chili-cheese Fritos—and after a hard day drilling into people's skulls, he had to have his whims satisfied or there'd have been holy hell to pay. And for the price of the marked-up item, plus the $7.95 delivery charge, plus a respectable tip to the delivery person, making a standard-sized bag of Fritos shoot northward of twenty bucks, the Plum Mart would be happy to whip it right over to you.

Lately, however, Jessica had found herself dialing the Plum Mart number more and more frequently, particularly on days like today, when Rowan and Alex were at Michael's and she just needed to feed herself. The thought of pushing a grocery cart around the vast and bustling Albertson's was overwhelming; and worse, at the smaller El Ranchito Market over on Camrose, she stood a good chance of encountering the Brain.

Besides, she told herself, if she was going to go broke, she might as well go broke in style.

And so once again, she picked up the phone and recited a litany of items to a lisping Plum Mart dispatcher. Her call waiting beeped. She quickly gave the dispatcher her account number and clicked to the other line.

"Mrs. DiSantini? This is Eduardo Dia speaking. I'm in the employ of Mr. David Clemente." It was a voice with such an exaggerated affect of culture, a prissy clipping of consonants and broadening of vowels, she immediately suspected a prank.

"Come on, Taller, knock it off. I'm really not in the mood."

"Pardon me?"

She glanced at the caller ID screen. It displayed an unfamiliar number. "Oh, I'm sorry," she said quickly. "I thought you were someone else. Who did you say this was?"

"Eduardo Dia." *Idwahdo Deeah.* "I'm calling on behalf of Mr. Clemente. His son, Noah, wishes to have your son, Alex, join him and several other boys for a playdate."

Noah Clemente was inviting Alex to come over and play? Noah had been two grades above Alex and could hardly even have known him, much less consider him a friend.

Was David behind the invitation? She felt a prickle of excitement. "What day did Noah have in mind?"

"On Halloween. There's to be a gathering at the house at twilight, followed by a trick-or-treat expedition by limousine."

Jessica hesitated. When she'd divided up the holidays with Michael, she had gotten Halloween, but the kids would naturally want to be out with their own friends. Alex had at least two other party invitations that she knew of. But what the hell—she could drag him by the Clemente "gathering" beforehand.

"Sure, that would be fine," she said. "Please tell Noah that Alex would love to get together with him."

She hung up, suddenly oppressed by the very idea of Halloween. Would Michael get into costume this year? she wondered. He liked to go as a doctor, ha, ha. Carried an old-timey black bag with that old-fashioned round reflecting thing doctors used to wear on their foreheads.

So did that mean the Brain would dress up as a brain? Outfit herself as a giant medulla oblongata?

Jessica suddenly realized what she wanted to be for Halloween.

Somebody who didn't have a Brain.

How cathartic and cleansing that would be! The more she thought about it, a character without a brain, the better and more buoyant she felt. The doorbell rang—her Plum Mart delivery—and she was grinning as she went to answer it.

It was a single-woman's order. Otis could tell that at a glance.

One Italian-style marinated chicken breast, no skin. Small-container-size portion of Caesar salad, nix the anchovies. One bunch of organic baby carrots, feathery tops intact. One hefty slice of double Dutch-chocolate layer cake with chopped hazelnut topping. Plus two bottles Acqua Panna springwater, one thirty-five-ounce Cascade dishwasher detergent, one packet "sandstone" linen-quality paper dinner napkins, and a not-quite-ripe casaba melon.

No condiments, chips, beer, or red meat, meaning it probably wasn't for a straight guy. Baby veggies of any kind could signal single woman or gay—but the hold on the anchovies (Plum Mart's were famously imported directly from the island of Sardinia) pointed to female. Same for chocolate anything.

Double chocolate spelled double lonely.

The rest of the items, Otis knew, were filler, to make it sound like it was actually grocery shopping and not a pathetic loser take-out order for dinner for one.

Pretty house, though. Seemed more like something you'd find in the vicinity of Cape Cod or Vermont. Not that he'd ever been within three thousand miles of either vicinity—he'd been rejected by every Eastern school he'd applied to, even the ones he thought were his safeties, which was how he ended up going to the lame-fuck local university. But he sure as hell could imagine what a swanky New England residence would look like. This one fit the bill.

Pretty lady too. Had a little more meat on her bones than most of the anorexics-bulimics-whatever-the-fucks he delivered to. Probably from scarfing down all that double-chocolate cake.

She didn't flinch either when she got a full blast of his crappy complexion. Kept a pleasant smile tacked on her lips as she reached to take the two magenta-colored sacks from him.

Otis tightened his grip on the bags and authoritatively barged past her. "These go in the kitchen, right?"

"Oh, um, yeah, that would be fine."

He instinctively navigated his way to it—*turn left and head past the peach-tinted dining room*. He noticed gaps between the pictures hung on all the walls. Definitely a divorce: When the hubby split, he took half the art.

The big open kitchen actually looked like people cooked food in it. He loved the shiny blue stove with the many different-sized burners and all the dinged-up pans dangling from that heavy old rack. And the floor was made of a cool, rough-looking stone of a pinkish color that made him think of a deserted beach.

There was a bottle of wine on one of the counters. It was covered in dust, meaning it must be pretty damned old, which spelled a certain amount of class right there.

This was exactly the kitchen and this was exactly the kind of house he was going to own himself one fine day when he started to pull in the big money. For a moment, the image of Caitlin faded from his mind, replaced by a shadowy, younger version of this lady here. Someone who exuded class and upper crust.

A vacuum cleaner began to growl somewhere upstairs. *Maid on board!* Otis presented the receipt to the lady for her to sign. She held out some folded bills, which he pocketed.

"Have a good one," he said, and turned to leave.

"Um, wait," she said.

Otis turned back.

"Uh, my husband, my *ex*-husband, he's a doctor, and well, you know, there are some excellent medications that could help your skin condition."

He felt his face catch on fire.

"He's not a dermatologist," she went on. "He's in neurology, actually, but all doctors get free samples. I know that prescription treatment can be expensive." She gave a no-big-deal kind of laugh. "One benefit of having been married to an MD is you end up with a closet full of free medicine. Let me get you something."

She darted out of the kitchen.

Who the hell did she think she was, frigging Mother Teresa and he was some goddamned leper or something? Otis heard her upstairs saying something to the maid, the two of them exchanging a laugh, probably at his expense. Yukking it up. Reminded him of that thing that happened on campus the other day. He was crossing in front of Lutheim Hall and got accosted by a bunch of asshole DKE pledges. Said they were on a scavenger hunt and had to bring back a "redskin," racist fucking bastards. Told him he could qualify. Yuk, yuk, yuk. The only thing that stopped them from hauling him bodily back to their suck-ass frigging frat house was a couple of old professors doddering out of Lutheim and giving them fishy looks.

Screw them all.

He glanced around the kitchen for something to steal. How about that dusty bottle of wine? Too noticeable—she'd realize it was gone right away and be on the phone to his boss before he was even out the door.

The lady came back into the kitchen clutching a handful of little white boxes. "Give this a shot," she said. "If it works and you want more, let me know. I could probably get you into some sort of clinical trial. It won't cost you a thing."

"Yeah, thanks," he mumbled.

Damned bitch, he thought.

CHAPTER *sixteen*

I Used to Imagine Running Off to Oz

Lally quickly procured an invitation to bring one of her godsons to the Clementes' Halloween playdate.

As how just about everything got accomplished in San Carlino, it had been simply a question of pulling a few strings. The ghastly Clemente butler, Eduardo Dia, had a socially ambitious wife who had campaigned long and hard to get their daughter into the Jasmine and Roses Cotillion. The girl had been speedily rejected: Despite the fact that Eduardo Dia pulled down a fat six-figure salary, was a graduate of the prestigious Cornell University School of Hotel Administration, and had his suits hand-tailored in Hong Kong and his shirts custom-made in Jermyn Street, he was nevertheless . . . a butler. After the rejection, Lizabeth Dia had spent weeks trying to ferret out which member of the cotillion committee had blackballed their daughter, which Lally had found rather touching—Lally was not on the committee, but from what she'd heard, the decision had been unanimous.

But of course, many of the members of the committee were friends of Lally's for whom she had done a share of favors in the past, and it was not hard for her to twist a few arms. After Lally's intervention, Lauren Luisa Dia was retroactively declared an alternate for the cotillion. And since rumor had it that Bebe Twilling's mother was a shoo-in to become the new ambassador to Iceland, meaning the Twillings would be imminently relocating to Reykjavík, Lauren Dia had better-than-even odds of actually being in the assembly.

The following morning, Lally received a call from Eduardo. He understood she had a godson who was Noah's age? Noah would be pleased to invite him for Halloween. . . .

Lally's next step was to procure the godson.

Jake and Jasper Hendricks, who were identical twins, were the right age. Technically, Lally was only Jake's godmother—Jasper had a trophy godmother of his own, a former tennis star who was now a prominent lesbian activist—but apparently the two boys came as a matched set. And frankly Lally had never been able to tell them apart—she lavished affectionate hugs and overcompensating gifts on both of them, hoping no one would actually notice.

Abbie Hendricks was thrilled that Lally was giving some non-holiday attention to the boys. "They'd love to go," she volunteered. "I mean, they had something lined up, but Noah Clemente was in their class at the Learning Loop until he moved to New York, and, well . . . I'm sure they'd absolutely love to see him again."

"Fabulous," Lally said. "I'll pick them up at a quarter to five."

Okay, all was set. Now she had only to decide on a costume.

What she'd told Juliet Shapiro was true: She adored dressing up, and when she did, she plunged herself completely into the role. The year she attended parties as Delores del Rio, sporting a sarong and a pineapple on her head, she'd perfected an authentic Brazilian accent and practiced the samba for weeks before. Perhaps her greatest triumph had been three years ago, at a Halloween shindig of Taller Kern's, when she was so convincing as a Carmelite mother superior that a drunken Frank Helvigson actually confessed his sins to her.

This year she wanted to be . . . well, something special, obviously. Something that would strike a deep chord with David. Possibly even a subliminal one.

She set Perla a task: Root out whatever she could about David Clemente's personal likes and dislikes.

Perla spent half a day Googling and reported back her findings. "The author he most admires is John Steinbeck," she began.

Henry Fonda in *The Grapes of Wrath*? Or, God forbid, Ma Joad as portrayed by Jane Darnell? "I don't think so. Go on," Lally said.

"He's very into Thai food. He once contributed a recipe for *gang gung sapparot* for a cookbook put out by the Assistance League."

Hmmm. Anna in *The King and I*... Possibilities there. Lally could fix her hair in ringlets and wear a scrumptious Victorian gown, something taffeta with six full crinolines. But would David make the connection? Doubtful. "What else?"

"As far as music goes, he likes Mozart and old Motown stuff."

A powdered wig? Aretha Franklin? "Keep going."

"He's got three golden retrievers and a collie mutt. He loves fly-fishing and claims he always ties his own flies. And he says his favorite movie is *The Wizard of Oz.*"

"Ooh!" Lally's eyes shot open. Now, here was something she could work with.

In fact she knew exactly which character of Oz would suit her: Glinda, the Good Witch of the North! Beneficent, lovable, and gorgeous, yet also wielding a certain amount of power.

Perfect!

She hustled down to L.A. to see her friend Patsy Dearn, who was working wardrobe on the latest Spielberg. Patsy obligingly jiggered up the costume: the gauzy pink gown with its jeweled brooch and poufed diaphanous sleeves; the glittering tall crown; the magic wand topped with a silvery five-pointed star. At home, Lally rehearsed the Glinda voice, high-pitched and merry, with the rounded vowels of the thirties. "You've always had the power to go back to Kansas, my dear," she pronounced. "There's no place like home."

Halloween fell this year on a Thursday. Lally canceled her engagements for the night before and arose fresh and rested in the morning. In lieu of her taxing workout with Russell, she did a two-hour private session at the Bikram yoga studio on Village. Her hairdresser, Raimond, bless him, made a rare house call, setting her hair on skinny hot rollers so that it undulated in shiny Glinda-like cataracts to her shoulders. Her makeup stylist, Marianne, drew on Glinda-like arched brows and painted her lips candy-apple red.

Lally stepped carefully into the pink confection of a dress and placed the tall crown on her head. She picked up the wand and turned to the mirror.

She looked amazing.

For a moment she almost believed that all she had to do was wave the star-tipped wand and she could make her own fairy tale come true. She swirled the wand over the high points of her crown and chanted: "Lally Chandler, you will live happily ever after."

Then, just to make sure, she gave the wand a second swirl and repeated the spell: "You'll live happily ever after, Lorraine Siplowsky-Bramberg-Grass-Willman.

She swung by the Hendrickses' house on Lantana Court and scooped up the twins, Jake and Jasper. She had not taken the Mercedes convertible, but had chosen instead the Range Rover that she and Artie had purchased the last year of their marriage for the purpose of hauling large objects. Such a purpose had never really arisen—all of her large purchases were swiftly and efficiently delivered—and for the most part, the car squatted unused in the garage. But it was ideally suited for her domestic role this evening.

Both boys were costumed in *Star Wars* stormtrooper outfits, complete with voice boxes that when activated made them sound like throat cancer survivors. But at least this time Lally had a means of telling them apart: Jake's lightsaber glowed stop-sign red and Jasper's acid green.

They gawked at Lally's silver crown, then clambered into the backseat and lapsed into an almost comatose silence.

"This is going to be really fun," Lally declared as she backed the cumbersome vehicle out of the driveway. "First there's going to be a terrific party, and then we'll all head out and trick-or-treat."

"Do we have to give the money we get to UNICEF?" said Jake.

"UNICEF sucks," said Jasper.

"Don't you want to help kids who are poor and have nothing to eat?"

Silence.

"Okay, I'll tell you what," Lally said. "Donate the trick-or-treat money to UNICEF and I'll give both of you the same amount to match."

"You ought to give *me* more," said Jake. "You're *my* godmother, not his."

"It's not your birthday, dickwad."

"Diarrhea breath."

"Dickwad. And you hurl chunks from your butt."

"Okay, stop that!" Weren't identical twins supposed to have some sort of mystical bond between them? Lally wondered. Something that united them against the rest of the world? If so, the news didn't seem to have reached this pair.

She took a right on Paseo Verde. "How well do you guys know Noah Clemente?" she asked.

"He was in our school last year?" said Jake. "And the soccer coach made him do twenty push-ups, and he could, like, only do eleven? And he started crying?"

"Boo-hoo-hoo," went Jasper.

The mystical twin thing seemed to finally kick in. They both mercilessly started imitating the sobbing Noah: "Boo-hoo. Boo-hoo-*hoo*."

"Hey, I want you to be nice to him, okay? It's his party, and you're his guests."

"One time there was an assembly?" continued Jasper. "And he, like, farted and then said it wasn't him, but everybody knew it was?"

Illustrative flatulent sounds issued from a twin set of stormtrooper voice boxes.

"Okay, listen," Lally broke in. "If you guys act friendly to Noah, I'll give each of you a hundred dollars."

Silence. In the rearview mirror, she watched them exchange looks.

"You mean if we just, like, hang out with him?" said Jasper.

"Yes, and behave like you're actually his friends. That can't be so terribly hard to do, can it?"

"A hundred dollars for each of us?" demanded Jake.

"Okay, yes."

"And the UNICEF money?" said Jasper.

Mercenary little creatures. "All right, *and* I'll match the UNICEF money."

A second exchange of looks.

"I guess. Okay," said Jake.

"Yeah, sure," said Jasper.

"Okay, then. I'll be counting on you." Lally swung the car onto the eucalyptus-bowered lane that led to the Clemente estate.

The gates swung open rather majestically at their approach. She drove to the guardhouse, her name was ticked off a security guard's handheld, and she was waved forward onto the glittering pink-stoned drive.

The twins were suddenly jolted out of their sullenness.

"Whoa!" exclaimed Jake.

"It's like Disneyland!" put in Jasper.

It absolutely was, Lally had to admit. The drive was populated on both sides by enormous automated Halloween figures: Towering skeletons jiggled and danced; black cats the size of water buffaloes arched their backs; ghosts taller and more gaunt than street lamps raised and lowered their spectral white arms. From hidden speakers arose a sound track of dismal moaning and wailing and the *clink-clank*ing of chains.

The Range Rover ran the gauntlet of these automatons, then swept into the circular drive in front of the main house. A hearse was parked in front of the door—a stretch hearse. Could there actually be such a thing? Lally wondered.

On closer inspection, she could see that it was actually a superstretch Hummer tricked out to resemble a hearse. A squadron of monsters came shuffling out from behind it and approached the Range Rover.

A heavyset mummy tapped on her window. "Welcome," it intoned, and yanked open her door.

A Dracula unfurling a dramatic cape appeared at the back door and bared a set of fangs at the twins. "Cool!" they chorused.

"You're all gathering in the playhouse," the mummy informed them in sepulchral tones. "Follow me, please."

They dutifully trooped after him, the twins imitating the stiff-legged mummy walk. To the boys' increased delight, he packed them into a flamingo-pink golf cart. They jolted off through a gated arbor and entered the grounds of the estate.

It was truly one of the most beautiful estates in Colina Linda, Lally reflected. The sun was starting to set: The turquoise sky was streaked with hot-pink clouds underlit with gold, like a painted Technicolor backdrop. Lally had the thrilling feeling that she was back on a movie set: that first day of shooting, at the crack of dawn, stepping out of the makeup trailer into a world of make-believe, everybody from the stars to the grips to the best boys abuzz with the anticipation that something extraordinary was about to happen.

Her spirits rose higher as they skirted the beautiful lagoon pool with its lilies and cascading waterfall, then shortcutted through the sculpture garden (no corny marble statues here—it was all twisting and cantilevered shapes of polished metal or rough-hewn wood). The cart veered away from the path that led to the tennis court and barreled toward several smaller buildings that echoed the Georgian style of the main house. The smallest of these was the playhouse. It was transformed now into a haunted minimansion, all dripping cobwebs and spooky, flickering lights.

Inside, the illusion was intensified—more cobwebs and spooky lights galore, stacks of fiercely carved glowing pumpkins, and a huge steaming cauldron stirred by a coven of cackling witches. Some half dozen boys were racing around whooping and happily slaughtering one another with realistic-looking revolvers, ray guns, and AK-47s. The twins bounded instantly into the action.

Lally moved toward a gaggle of costumed parents who were standing near the cauldron. She air-kissed a D'Artagnan, who was Rhonda Kluge's husband, Sandy, and then Deke Shapiro, who was dressed as

Robin Hood (*yeah, right*), and Myron Rose as Friar Tuck, and finally Lynne O'Rourke, who was a smidge too big in the butt to pull off her Little Mermaid.

"Nice getup, Lally." Deke Shapiro smirked. "But I never thought of you as the fairy-godmother type."

"I'm a witch, darling," Lally said.

"Is that with a W or a B?"

"That depends on the circumstances. You probably wouldn't want to find out."

Sandy Kluge whistled. "Tell it, babe."

"I think you look charming, Lally," Myron Rose said. He was a tiny, balding, rather fluttery guy who had exchanged the ulcer-inducing life of a studio executive for the milder pastures of academia. It apparently suited him: He had risen in just a couple of years to chairman of the San Carlino University graduate film arts department. "You've captured the character of Glinda intrinsically. And for my money, she's the most interesting character in the movie. On one hand, she's kind and good and beloved and so forth. But on the other, she rats Dorothy out to the Wicked Witch of the West."

"Two-faced woman," said Deke.

"No, a complex character," Myron said. "If she were only sweetness and light, she'd make you want to throw up."

"Thank you, Myron." Lally laughed. "I'm glad I don't make you vomit."

"Did you hear the news, Lally?" Lynne O'Rourke cut eagerly into the conversation. "About Hilly Sutter getting assaulted?"

"Is that who it was? I'd heard it was somebody in Colina Linda."

"Yes, it was Hilly. And she's only two blocks away from me!"

"Do they have any leads on who did it?" Lally said.

"It was Mr. Incredible," sniggered Deke Shapiro. "So it couldn't have been all bad." He gave a suggestive thrust of his pelvis, causing his green tunic to ride up over his waistline.

He really was a despicable guy, Lally thought. *Un homme méchant.* Juliet would be a thousand times better off if he did leave her.

Myron Rose said, “The cops are saying she didn’t lock up, but knowing Hilly as I think I do, I believe that’s highly unlikely. She’s a security freak.”

“So it must have been someone she knew,” Lally said. “Someone with a key.”

“How many men out there have *your* key, Lall?” Deke said with an insinuating chuckle.

“You don’t, darling. But I have your number, and it’s a pretty pathetic one.”

The others laughed. Deke muttered something under his breath and sidled off. The rest of the little group drifted apart.

A menagerie of waiters dressed as gorillas, armadillos, and kangaroos were circulating with trays of soft drinks. Lally accepted a lemonade. As she sipped, her eye was caught by a clown working the far side of the room. Wearing baggy pants, candy-striped shirt with green suspenders, a bowler hat perched on a bright yellow wig, he clumsily juggled four colored balls in the air. *You’d think David might have sprung for higher-caliber entertainment,* Lally mused.

The juggler fumbled a ball, but caught the rest and jauntily pocketed them. He turned, and Lally saw to her surprise that it was David.

She waved and he came over, waddling in his floppy clown shoes. His square black glasses worn over the garish clown makeup gave him an impish look that was not at all displeasing.

“The Good Witch of Oz, I presume,” he said.

“Yes, my dear. I’m Glinda, the Good Witch of the North.”

“I’m extremely pleased to meet you. Allow me to introduce myself. I’m Klampers the clown.” He produced the three remaining balls and sent them up in wobbling loops.

Lally smiled. “I knew you had many accomplishments, but I didn’t know juggling was one of them.”

“Yep.” He repocketed the balls. “I spent two summers as a kid at a circus camp up in Salinas. I was a flop on the flying trapeze, and the elephants kind of intimidated me, so they shuffled me off into clown activities. Which was good, because I found my niche. I was a real whiz with a squirt bottle."

She laughed. "When I was little and my mother was giving me a hard time, I used to fantasize about running away and joining the circus. I was going to be one of those ladies in a tutu who ride standing up on the back of a horse."

"That's funny, because I used to imagine running off to the Emerald City. It's my favorite movie. I think I've seen it about fifty times."

Lally adopted her Glinda voice. "Then just close your eyes and click your heels together three times and say, 'There's no place like Oz,' and you'll find yourself there, my dear."

"In these?" He glanced down at the floppy blue-and-yellow clown shoes. "I think they'd just take me back to Salinas."

Lally laughed again. Strange, all the times they had crossed paths over the years, at all the glamorous events at which she'd seen him in tuxedos and bespoke British suits and designer tennis wear, and she had never found him nearly as attractive as she did right now with his nose painted purple.

"So is that your hearse parked out front?" she teased.

"No, that's a rental hearse. Mine's in the shop."

"You must be planning quite a huge funeral."

"God, I sincerely hope not." He grinned, his painted mouth stretching literally ear to ear. "Here's the plan. We'll let the kids use up a little energy here; then we'll pack them in the Hummer for trick-or-treating. The rest of us can follow in our own cars."

"I don't think I've ever actually met your son. Which one is he?"

"That tall drink of water in the pirate costume over there. He grew three inches this year alone. Noah!" he called. He flapped both hands over his head to signal semaphorically.

The boy slouched over. He was big for his age and gawky, Lally thought—one of those kids whose body had grown faster than he could learn to control it, so that every time he made a gesture, you worried he was going to poke himself in the eye. His pirate costume was authentic in every way, from the plume on his tricorn hat to his cuffed and polished leather boots and the musket tucked into his wide white sash.

"Yo ho ho!" Lally greeted him.

He eyed her with mild alarm.

"I'm Glinda the Good Witch, my dear. You look extremely dashing in that costume. A buccaneer of the high seas."

He made a sound like *urgh* and ducked his head.

Lally persevered. "I hear you went camping with your dad. That must have been terrific fun."

"He got a touch of altitude sickness the first night, so we had to strike camp and come back down to Tahoe." David put his arm around his son. "But we had a blast down there, didn't we, kiddo?"

"Dad, you're bending my sword." The boy jerked awkwardly away.

"Sorry, kiddo."

Lally inclined toward Noah and treated him to her most dazzling smile. "I'm here with my godson, Jake Hendricks, and his brother, Jasper. They said they're good friends of yours."

"Nah." Noah violently shook his head.

"They are; they told me so. Why don't we go over and join them?"

"Excellent idea," said David. "You don't want to just hang around us old folks."

"I don't know any of those guys too well."

"But Jake told me he was looking forward to seeing you. And so did Jasper. Come on; let's go say hi."

Before the boy could protest further, Lally linked a firm arm through his and began steering him toward the twins, with David in tow. Jake and Jasper were in the rear of the main room, engaged in noisy mayhem with two other boys. One had slightly Asian features and a sneery plump mouth, possibly Emily and Winston Loh's kid (Sander? no, Zander). The other was Simon Shapiro, who had his mother's emotive doe eyes and his father's wire-terrier hair.

"Hey, guys," Lally said brightly. "Have you said hi to Noah yet?"

Zander Loh and Simon Shapiro exchanged smirks. Simon made a low farting sound and Zander guffawed.

Lally directed a meaningful look at the twins.

"Hey, Noah," croaked Jake through his laryngeal voice box.

"Cool costume," rasped Jasper through his.

"Yeah, it's wicked cool," said Jake.

"Yeah?" Noah peered at them a bit suspiciously. "You guys look cool too."

"Hey, Noah, gotcha!" Jake aimed his flashing lightsaber at Noah and made a ray-gun shooting sound. Noah obligingly clutched his chest, emitted a loud death rattle, and fell down, mortally wounded. Then he propped himself back up, pulled out his musket, and aimed it at Jake. "Pow, pow, pow!"

With a gurgle, Jake elaborately toppled over. Endorsed by the twins, Noah was accepted into the battle, which now resumed energetically.

David turned to Lally with a look of astonishment. "What did you do, put a spell on him?"

"Maybe just a little one." She smiled.

"More than a little. He's usually not much of a mixer. I'm forever pushing him to get more involved, get out and make a few friends, but it usually backfires. He just ends up hating me."

"I'm sure he never hates you," Lally said. She had the sudden image of Sienna at four, writhing on the floor of her bedroom, shrieking, "I hate you! I hate you!" and her own twenty-four-year-old self yelling back, "I hate you too!" She had the impulse to blurt this out to David.

But before she could say anything, Deke Shapiro materialized at her elbow. "Holy shit, we've got the whole damned movie here!" he exclaimed.

What the hell is he talking about? Lally wondered, furious at the interruption.

But suddenly it seemed everyone was looking in the direction of the front door, where two new arrivals were hovering: Caitlin Latch and Jessica DiSantini. And, if Lally could believe her eyes, Caitlin was dressed as Dorothy and Jessica as the Scarecrow from *The Wizard of Oz*.

~

"You didn't tell me Zander Loh was gonna be here," Aiden whined as they stepped into the swirling milieu of the party. "And those guys Jake and Jasper. They hate me."

"They don't hate you," Caitlin said.

"Yeah, they do. Don't you *remember*? That time they stuck gum in my hair, and you had to cut it all off to get it out, and I looked like a total dork till it grew back."

"Well, then, stay away from them," Caitlin said. "Just hang out with Noah."

"He's *with* them. They're all, like, over there together."

Caitlin sighed. Already just about everything that could go wrong had gone wrong. She'd planned to arrive at the party early and stake a firm claim on David, but with her usual brilliant luck, the Volvo had had a flat. She'd had to recruit Otis to change it (making him late for his Plum Mart job, but he didn't seem to care); but then after he finished it, he got all sulky that they were going out trick-or-treating without him. Then on the way here, she'd been held up at the railroad crossing on Mordecai Road by a freight train that was about as long as the freaking Empire State Building.

And neither of their costumes had turned out quite right. She was a trifle too busty for Dorothy's blue-striped pinafore, but so was Judy Garland, so that was okay. The problem was her ruby slippers: She'd made them herself by gluing red glitter on a pair of worn-out Naturalizer pumps, but a bit of it came off every time she walked, so that she left a little trail of gooey glitter behind her like a snail or something. And Aidey . . . well, she'd hoped he'd want something really original, but no, he'd insisted on Harry Potter, like a million, trillion other kids in the world. Still, she had gone whole hog, bought him the Quidditch robe and the purple-and-yellow-striped scarf and a flying broom; but the broom turned out to be too cumbersome to carry, and the glasses didn't look quite right; they were too big for his face or something, giving a kind of crazed-scientist-trying-to-destroy-the-world look to him.

Think positively, she told herself.

She shifted the basket she was carrying that contained a stuffed "Toto" dog from her left arm to her right and gave Aiden's shoulder an encouraging squeeze. "Look, you don't have to play with any of the kids if you don't want to. There's some video games here, so you can just do that if you want."

"I need to take a whiz," he mumbled.

"Okay, go find the bathroom."

He shuffled off to find the john. She noticed that his Quidditch robe was too long and trailed on the ground. She sighed again.

Then she realized that people were staring in her direction, grinning at her, some even clapping their hands. *Shit.* She really was too busty for this costume.

"This is too funny," somebody said beside her. "They're going to think we planned it."

Caitlin turned. It was Jessica DiSantini, looking totally adorable in a wide-brimmed pointed hat and a tunic cuffed and collared in straw. She was with her son, a beautiful kid with the same creamy skin and wide-set eyes as Jessica's.

Jessica laughed again. "I don't believe it! There's Lally Chandler dressed up as the Good Witch."

Caitlin looked over. Yep, here came Lally done up to the dazzling nines as Glinda, practically radiating movie-star glamour. Was it ridiculous or what that they were all wearing costumes from the same movie?

Caitlin simply could not believe her rotten luck.

Lally, quickly recovering her aplomb, had realized that the only way to make the best of the situation was to take charge of it. She came swooping up to the other two women. "This is fantastic!" she cried out. "We're all on the same wavelength. Who's got a camera; we need a photo of this!"

Everybody had a camera. A cluster of people pointing a variety of lenses quickly coalesced around the three women.

A photo op! Here was something Lally could always rise to. She linked arms with Caitlin and Jessica and maneuvered them to face the cameras. She tilted her face to its most flattering advantage and opened her eyes wide—*swock!*—and then she subtly thrust out one shoulder and one hip to give herself prominence in the picture. "Say 'Yellow Brick Road,' girls!" she exclaimed, and bared her perfect white teeth.

She suddenly found herself jostled roughly aside. Caitlin inserted herself in the middle of the shot. "I think Dorothy should be in the center," she declared. "She is the star of the movie."

"Yes, that's true," Lally said. She stepped back, treading a high heel on the toe of one of Caitlin's balding ruby slippers.

"Ow!" yelped Caitlin, and gave a little hop backward.

Leaving Jessica's Scarecrow in the forefront of the group. Digital lenses clicked; camcorders whirred.

And to Lally's utter astonishment, Jessica began to tap-dance.

Lally goggled at her. It was a basic shim sham step, amateur but competent, and it was greeted with whistles and whoops and applause from the gathered photo takers.

And it most definitely did not escape Lally's notice that David, standing at the front of the group, was clapping most enthusiastically of all.

After Jessica's spontaneous performance, all three women linked arms again and grinned and shouted out, "Follow the Yellow Brick Road." More pictures were taken, and then everyone went back to the mingling and milling they were engaged in before the distraction.

Lally found herself momentarily isolated. She wandered a few steps toward a tower of trick-or-treat bags that were to be given out to the guests. No cheapo paper shopping bags for this gang. No, sirree! These were huge black-and-orange satchels made of the best-quality canvas, embossed in silver with the triangular logo of the Clemente Corporation. Disconsolately, she opened one. It was already partly stocked with treats: lollipops the size of dinner plates in swirling colors and exotic flavors. Humongous movie counter–sized Almond Joys and gargantuan boxes of Good & Plenty.

She flashed back to the dingy Halloweens in the working-class neighborhood she grew up in. The candy apples that nobody ate. The sick-making candy corn. Those peculiar strips of pallid sugary dots that everybody ate but nobody really liked. She had a sudden and intense nostalgia for such stuff. She peeled the wrapper of an Almond Joy, which was the closest thing, and began munching it glumly.

She now had two significant rivals, she reflected, licking coconut off the back of her teeth. Caitlin was younger, determined, and had that eye-popping body in her favor. But Jessica—Donna Reed with skin like poured milk and a tart sense of humor—was perhaps the more dangerous.

Lally needed to make a move and make it fast.

She looked around the room and located David, not at the moment with either Jessica or Caitlin, but talking with a wildly gesticulating Sandy Kluge. *Good.*

Her crown was askew. She positioned it firmly back on the center of her head and strode purposefully in David's direction.

Suddenly there was the sound of a commotion: high-pitched boys' voices yelling furiously at one another. Lally swiveled, turning just in time to catch the extraordinary sight of Aiden Latch socking Noah Clemente square in the solar plexus.

The raised voices also immediately caught Caitlin's attention. Instinctively, her stomach clenched. She hurried toward the commotion.

She saw at once what was going on. It was one of those gang-ups that happen among kids, where one of them was somehow designated the odd man out, giving the others free rein to torment him. This time it was Aiden who was the odd man. He was backed up into a cob-webby corner. His Harry Potter glasses had fallen off, and one end of his long striped scarf trailed on the floor. Five other boys formed a crude semicircle around him and were hooting and hollering. Noah was among them: He wore the dismally triumphant look of an un-popular kid who was being at least temporarily tolerated by the popu-lar ones.

Zander Loh yanked off Aiden's scarf.

"Cut it out!" Aiden yelled.

"Why don't you make me?" Zander jeered.

Aiden tried to push his way through the knot of boys, but they closed ranks, not letting him pass. He turned helplessly, caught be-tween his tormentors and the wall. Zander jabbed him in the back with the barrel of his plastic semiautomatic.

Hit him back, Aidey, Caitlin thought automatically.

And astonishingly, he did.

Aiden's face mashed up in a fury. He whirled and balled his fist and socked at Zander, who ducked nimbly out of the way. The punch caught Noah instead in the center of his frilly pirate shirt.

"Oof," Noah said.

He sat down with a thud that bent his pirate sword in two. He began to bawl.

The two awful twins in the stormtrooper costumes pushed their way forward, elbowing one another and sniggering loudly.

"Boo-hoo," said one.

"Boo-hoo-hoo," said the other.

"Shut up," Noah sniffled.

"Boo-hoo-*hoo!*"

Aiden glanced fearfully over at Caitlin, shaking his head. *I didn't mean it,* he mouthed.

It was almost funny, she thought. The one time in his entire life that Aiden asserted himself, and it cost her a billion bucks.

She threw back her shoulders and arched her back, and she curved her lips up in her pleasant doll's smile. Then she walked over, picked up the smashed glasses, and put her arms around her son's slumped back.

"It's okay, Aidey," she said. "They were picking on you; I saw it. You had a right to get mad."

CHAPTER *seventeen*

What a Little Moonlight Can Do

The punch in Noah's gut pretty much put a damper on the trick-or-treating-in-the-Hummer plan.

Lally didn't see exactly what happened next—only that Noah was quickly surrounded by a delegation of fawning adults, and that Caitlin and Aiden melted off into the night immediately afterward. Still sniffling, Noah was ushered into the main house by a kangaroo, a tiger, and his father; and then the rest of the party thinned out pretty quickly, with most of the guests grabbing the black-and-orange satchels as they departed.

Lally continued the Halloween rounds on her own with the twins. For two hours they rang the doorbells of the swankiest houses in Colina Linda, yelling, "Trick or treat!" to mostly housemaids, butlers, and grandparents who were doing duty. Finally the satchels were bulging and the twins, who'd been cramming candy in their mouths the entire time, started nodding off to sleep.

On the way back, Lally detoured to a Wells Fargo cash machine and withdrew the promised two hundred dollars. She thought about claiming breach of contract—the twins had ended up being mean to Noah after all. But she could imagine the whining and arguing that would ensue. What the hell—it was easier just to pay them off.

She slipped a Billie Holiday CD into the dash player—*What a lit-*

tle moonlight can do . . . and began mulling over the events of the evening.

She really did feel sorry for Caitlin and her poor, depressing son. That nasty little bully Zander Loh deserved to get the wind knocked out of him—it was just rotten luck for the Latches that it was Noah's tummy that took the punch. Safe to say that Dorothy had been shipped back home to Kansas; Lally honestly couldn't feel too desolate about that.

She thought with further satisfaction of her triumph in giving Noah that little boost with the other boys. She recalled David's look of astonishment and gratitude. A guy who had parlayed a modest inheritance into a staggering fortune almost wept with joy just because a few spoiled, smart-assed kids were nice to his son. . . . It was . . . well . . . *endearing* was the word for it.

Her thoughts skipped to Jessica's impromptu little tap dance, stealing the photo shoot. Lally had studied tap, as well as jazz, ballet, modern, and ballroom. She could have worked up a routine that would have left Jessica's little amateur performance in the dust.

She suddenly pictured Jessica waltzing off into a fairy-tale marriage with David and felt almost sick with alarm.

And amazingly, it didn't seem to have anything to do with his staggering fortune. It had a lot more to do with how extremely appealing he looked in those glasses and that silly clown makeup.

Startled by this realization, she made a wrong turn heading back to the Hendrickses' house. Jake sleepily opened his eyes. "You're going the wrong way, Aunt Lally," he said.

He looked sort of sweet, with the silly helmet off, his hair mussed and damp, and his face flushed. This had been fun, really. She should do things with the boys more often.

"You're right, darling," she said. "Silly old me."

She swung a U-turn, nearly colliding with an old wreck of a car. It had a purple Styrofoam plum impaled on its antenna.

Plum Mart delivery, she registered vaguely. Lately they seemed to be everywhere.

~

"You were dead right about Lally Chandler," Jessica said to Taller. "She's definitely got him in her sights."

"Told ya." Taller took a fastidious sip of their martini du jour, a concoction called a "Woo Woo," made with cranberry juice and peach schnapps. He puckered his finely etched lips. "Revolting. Tastes like Kool-Aid."

"I kind of like it."

"Honey, your taste buds must be ossifying. What I think we need to do is go back to basics for a while and clear our palates." He raised an index finger to summon the waitress, and ordered two Bombay martinis, extra dry. "Shaken not stirred," he said archly.

While they waited for the fresh drinks to arrive, Jessica filled him in on the events of the Clementes' Halloween party, Taller laughing a bit too heartlessly, she thought, over the dustup that ended with Aiden socking Noah. "But before that happened, I definitely picked up vibes," she said. "From David, I mean."

"Maybe he's got a thing for scarecrows."

"Maybe he's got a thing for me." She gave a deprecatory little laugh. "I danced for him."

"You what?"

"I tap-danced. Lally and Caitlin Latch and I were posing for a picture: the girls of Oz. He was standing sort of right in front of me, and I thought of how he'd complimented me on the Fosse routine at last year's spina bifida cabaret. So suddenly, I just did it. A little thirty-second shim sham shimmy."

Taller hooted. "It's always you demure types who are the exhibitionists at heart."

"I don't know what came over me. But he did seem to go for it."

"Okay, so now it's advantage, Jessica. Ball's in your court, baby. You gotta follow through."

"What do you suggest I do?"

"I suggest that you send him something."

Jessica looked at him quizzically. "Like what, a present? What could I possibly give him that he doesn't have twenty of already?"

Taller leaned back in his chair and half shut his eyes, like a drowsing cat. "A pair of your panties," he pronounced.

"What?"

"He doesn't have twenty of those already, does he? If he does, I've been missing something here."

"No, he does not," she said emphatically.

"So then it's simple. You send him a charming little bread-and-butter note thanking him for his lovely hospitality. You add something to the effect that you're so very much looking forward to seeing him again soon. Perhaps at the Para Los Niños Ball? And you underscore your point by including a wispy little pair of undies." He hoisted his eyelids and looked directly at her. "Preferably in black."

"I really don't think so," Jessica said.

"Suit yourself. But my sources tell me that Lally looked smashing. Apparently *she* didn't need to be stuffed with straw to hide a few figure flaws."

"People who wear hats to cover up their nonexistent hairlines shouldn't throw stones," she flared back.

"That's not why I wear hats," he said smoothly. "I'm simply partial to them."

It was impossible to ruffle Taller. "When I get desperate enough to start sending my panties all over town, I'll let you know," she said. "Till then, I think I'll just wait to see him at Los Niños."

"And hope that Lally doesn't get her hooks into him in the meantime." Taller assumed his feline look again. "Of course, we could put her out of circulation for a while."

"Yeah, how? Kidnap her and keep her tied up in a basement for a couple of weeks?"

"Not bad. But I was thinking more along the lines of giving her a social disease."

Jessica gave a startled laugh. "Now I *know* you're insane."

"Not literally, of course. I mean we could spread it on the grapevine that Lally Chandler is being treated for some not very serious but extremely unpleasant condition. I once knew a girl who came down with venereal warts."

Jessica made a face. "That is totally disgusting. Could we please just change the subject?"

"I didn't know you *had* any other subjects these days."

She stuck out her tongue at him. He stuck out his, which was longer and slightly pointed, back at her.

When she returned home, a Jaguar convertible roughly the color of the Woo Woo martini was gliding out of her driveway. Michael bringing back the kids. Early again. The bastard was whittling down his time with them a little more each weekend.

She idled at the curb until he'd driven out of sight. Then she pulled into the garage, reminding herself for the fortieth or fiftieth time that the automatic door made a sound like an elephant in labor and needed to be looked at, and then headed inside. She found Alex parked in front of the family room tube absorbed in the Cartoon Network.

"Hi, sweetheart." She kissed the top of his head, inhaling the loamy, unwashed fragrance of his hair. "I missed you. Did you have a good weekend?"

He barely raised his eyes from the garish images. "Was okay."

"What are you watching?"

"Codename: Kids Next Door."

She stared for a moment at the stupid cartoon. "You can watch the end of this show, then no more TV, okay?"

"Dad lets me watch all I want."

"Well, I don't. So turn it off after this, okay? You've got schoolwork."

Alex grunted unhappily.

She sighed. Bad Parent once again. She gave him another kiss, then went upstairs and tapped at Rowan's door.

"Yeah?"

Jessica pushed open the door. Rowan lay stomach down on her

bed, headphones covering her ears, a silver-blue DVD player propped on her pillow. She lifted her chin an inch and said, "Hi, Mom."

"Hey, honey. Is that new?"

"Yeah. Daddy bought it for me."

"But you've already got one, don't you?"

"Mom, it was two years old. It didn't even record."

"Oh. Okay. Well, I just wanted to say hi." Jessica moved toward her, bending to give her a kiss. Then she froze. "Where's your bracelet?"

The gold-and-silver Medic Alert bracelet, which had adorned Rowan's wrist for nearly ten years, was missing. Her pale arm looked almost obscenely naked without it.

"I took it off. Dad said I didn't need to wear it anymore."

"He doesn't know that for certain. There have been cases of relapse after more years than you've gone." Jessica felt the blood pound in her veins. She drew a deep breath and measured her voice. "I really think you should continue to wear it, just to be on the safe side."

Rowan turned over on her side and directed a look at her that was pure Michael, both aggrieved and condescending, with a twitchy lift of the brow. "Mo-om. I don't *need* it. Amanda says you're becoming totally overprotective. She says that always happens with the parent that gets left behind."

A rage rose inside Jessica, so intense and all-consuming that for a moment she thought she might spontaneously combust. She lunged for the DVD player with the intent of grabbing it and smashing it against the floor.

Rowan scrambled to a sitting position, clutching the machine to her lap. "Okay, okay. I'll wear the stupid bracelet if it makes you happy. It's no big deal."

"It would make me happy," Jessica said. She turned and, still breathing rapidly, walked out of her daughter's room.

She managed to keep her temper through dinner, even though neither of the kids ate much because Michael had stuffed them so full of junk. Sometime after midnight, she crept down to the wine cellar and selected a bottle.

The last of the Medocs: a 2000 Pauillac, velvety maroon in color, with a faint palate of violets. Jessica poured it into a cracked coffee cup and took a gulp. Went down so deliciously easy. She finished the bottle within an hour.

She didn't feel drunk, though she figured she was—such was the effect of superb French wine. What she *did* feel was exuberant, intrepid, ready to blow all caution to the wind. She felt like calling Amanda and saying something extremely coarse about the Brain's anatomy, and then getting Michael on the phone and hexing him with that pustulating skin disease.

She felt like following that up with calls to all her divorced friends and encouraging them to exact a similar revenge on all their ex-husbands.

Drunk dialing. An occupational hazard among exes. More than a few times, Jessica had been the recipient of a wee-hours call from some ranting friend.

The fact that she could identify the syndrome and thereby prevent herself from succumbing to it proved she wasn't drunk. Tipsy, maybe. Pleasantly buzzed.

Meaning she was able to perceive with crystal clarity what she really, truly ought to be doing—which was exactly what her very best friend, Taller, had suggested.

She directed herself upstairs to the den and turned on her Mac laptop. She typed a proper, breezy thank-you note to Mr. David Alderson Clemente, mentioning that she was very much looking forward to seeing him at the Para Los Niños charity ball.

A brilliant note. Perfectly done. She was so proud of herself that she dashed an e-mail to Taller, telling him she had gone ahead and taken his advice.

Terrific advice. Bet he never thought she'd really do it.

Then she printed out the thank-you note and scribbled her name with a flourish and folded it in precise thirds into an envelope. She looked up the address from the St. Matthew's parents' directory from the year before and printed it on the envelope. She wrote *Personal* underneath this and underlined it twice.

Then, walking very, very steadily, she went to her bedroom and opened her panty drawer and searched for a wispy little thong.

Problem: She wasn't the wispy-little-thong type. She was the all-cotton-briefs-with-patterns-of-hula-girls-or-Tweety-bird type. She tried stuffing a pair (hula girls) along with the note, but it resulted in a peculiarly bulgy envelope. Even in her present state, she could tell it did not have the desired erotic effect.

She opened her bra drawer and picked out her skimpiest. It wasn't very skimpy. She tossed it back.

Panty hose?

Ew.

She had a sudden brainstorm. When she had performed in that spina bifida tap number, she had worn a pair of black fishnet thigh-highs held up with garters. She was positive she still had them. She rummaged through more drawers, flinging items onto the floor and furniture, until she finally unearthed them, buried under a Pilates unitard that hadn't seen the light of day in a year.

One of the pair had a jagged rip in it, but the other was in perfect shape. She folded it into the envelope. Still a bit bulgy, but it would do.

She licked the seal of the envelope and dug up a stamp. *I'll just pop out a minute,* she thought. It would be fine—Rowan was fourteen and extremely responsible, and Alex was sound asleep. Then, to make certain she didn't lose her nerve, she got into her car and drove cautiously, very cautiously, the seven blocks to the mailbox outside the post office on Jardinera.

Furtive as a cat burglar, she dropped the envelope into the slot.

CHAPTER eighteen

A Bond Girl Is Like a Superhero

Taller read Jessica's e-mail while finishing his wake-up double cappuccino at the Café San Remo on Manzanita, across the street from his bookshop. *Well, well,* he thought. This should stir the figurative martini up quite enjoyably.

He wondered if it was true that Caitlin Latch had been eliminated from the competition. Too bad if it was—one less player in what had so far been a highly entertaining competition. The stage now seemed set for Jessica, though he wasn't altogether certain yet that he wanted her to win.

He glanced at his watch. Almost eleven. He stretched languorously and stood up. Time to mosey on across the street and give the appearance, at least, of being in business.

At least the letter was handwritten, in navy-blue ink on heavy cream-colored stationary, embossed with the same triangular Clemente Corporation logo that had embellished the trick-or-treat satchels. It had been delivered to Caitlin's house by a private messenger service, along with a tissue paper–wrapped package that was roughly and intriguingly the size and weight of a luxury jewel case. Caitlin already knew what the letter was going to say before she slit open the envelope: *It's been swell knowing you, babe, but seeing as how your kid punched out mine, I guess it's sayonara.*

Of course, it was phrased a lot more elegantly than that, but the gist was pretty much the same. She skimmed it quickly, her eyes blurring by the time she read the last sentence:

I remember that you mentioned F. Scott Fitzgerald
was your favorite writer, and so I thought you
might enjoy owning this.

He signed it, *All fondest regards, Dave.*

When the hell had she ever said she liked Fitzgerald? Oh, yeah, right, at the Chicken Shack dinner after that ghetto school thing—the principal with the beard striped like a skunk had asked her what writers she most admired and she'd blurted out the first nontrashy one she could think of.

She ripped open the tissue paper.

It was not a jewel box. It was a used copy of *Tender Is the Night.* The cover was a drawing of a pastel Riviera village nestled on a cove behind a stand of tall purplish-blue tree trunks. It was slightly dog-eared at the top corner. She opened the book in the middle and sneezed violently—she was drastically allergic to book mold—then shut it.

It was a lovely, thoughtful gesture, yeah, yeah, yeah. A sapphire-and-diamond bracelet would've been an even lovelier one.

It occurred to her that maybe the book was valuable, a first edition or something. She eagerly flipped past a few pages to the title and copyright pages, scrutinizing them, but found nothing to indicate it was. She sneezed again, even more violently, and again closed the book.

She dropped it onto the kitchen table, and tears plumped at the corners of her eyes. *Don't be an idiot,* she told herself. *It's not like you're any worse off than you were before.*

She should look at it as a learning experience. If and when she was ever presented with another entrée to the upper class, she'd be better prepared. Like you always said *car and driver,* not *limo and chauffeur,* and come over to *the* house, not to *my* house, and you always downplayed things of importance with a light little dismissive comment.

Oh, fuckety fuck!

Somebody tapped on the kitchen window: *Shave and haircut.* Otis. He had an uncanny radar for sensing when she least wanted to see him. As always, he let himself in without waiting for anything so trivial as an invitation.

She swabbed her eyes with her knuckles, squared her shoulders, and managed a smile.

"Hey, Cait. Wassup?"

She gave a shrug. "Same old, same old."

Maybe her eyes were a little blurry with tears, but it seemed to her that his complexion had improved. His face was still zitty, but not quite as pizza gooey.

He stood by the table, jiggling a sneaker on the linoleum-covered floor. "So, I just thought I'd see if there's anything you need doing. Like I've got some time right now, before I've got to go to class."

"Thanks, Otis, but I can't think of anything right this second."

He squinted in an exaggerated manner at the copy of *Tender Is the Night*. "F. Scott Fitzgerald. You like his stuff?"

"He's a great writer," she said.

"Can I borrow this? To, like, read, I mean."

"Sure. Be my guest." Her voice trailed off, and she squeezed her eyes shut.

Otis put on a voice: "Aw you depwessed? Don't be depwessed, Caitwin. I don't wike it when Caitwin's sad."

Oh, good Lord, he was doing Elmer Fudd.

"I'm not depressed," she said quickly. "I've just got a bit of a headache. I've probably been working too hard."

"My mom used to have killer migraines. I'm good at giving rubs. Want one?"

"Thanks, no, it's okay. I'm fine."

"C'mon, let me show you." He sloped over to her, placed his hands on her shoulders, and began to knead the muscles.

She jerked away. "I said I'm fine, for God's sake! Are you deaf or something?"

He backed off with a stricken look.

Please, please don't go into Elmer Fudd again, she silently pleaded.

Mercifully, he didn't. "I guess you just kind of want to be alone for a while, huh?"

"Yeah, Otis. If you don't mind, I could use some time by myself."

"Sure. Hey, I understand." He picked up the book and tucked it under his arm. "I'll bring this back after I read it. Maybe we can discuss it or something?"

"Yeah, sure. That would be great." She forced herself to keep smiling till he was securely out the door.

So Lally did get thrown temporarily out of circulation.

Tizzie Caldwaller, one of Lally's septuagenarian partners in the chic little Mission Plaza soap-and-candle shop, had suffered a small stroke and probably would never recover full use of speech. Martha Franke, the third partner and Tizzie's longtime friend, was tending her twenty-four-seven, and so Lally was called upon to man the shop. Or, to be more accurate, Lally reposed in one of the overstuffed dahlia chintz armchairs, kibitzing with customers over poor Tizzie's condition. She agreed it was wonderful that Martha was so devoted and faithful, and deflected all insinuations that the two old women were anything but platonic friends—though Lally had sometimes wondered herself, given the way the two called each other by pet names—"Tiz-Tiz" and "Frankie"—and had such a comfy-old-couple rapport. A college junior named Chia with flowing lavender-streaked hair did the actual ringing up and gift-wrapping of purchases.

At the end of the week, after a long, tearful conference with Martha and Tizzie at Tizzie's bedside, Lally arranged to sell Savon Et Bougie to Candy Campbell and Rochelle Landis, two thirty-somethings who were in need of cachet occupations now that their kids had entered middle school, and who planned to turn the shop into a spiritually correct center for aromatherapy.

Problem: This left Lally without a cachet occupation of her own.

But lo and behold! When one door closed, another was opened. Such were the kinds of things Lally's mother used to continually say—happy little truisms to gloss over the real and inevitably disappointing untidiness of life. Though it had certainly seemed to Lally that once a door slammed shut on Deena Siplowsky, it remained firmly shut forever.

But as she grew older, Lally had to admit there was a certain amount of truth in some of these old saws. No sooner had she relinquished the keys to Savon Et Bougie than she received a call from Myron Rose down at the university. "Seeing you do Glinda gave me a brilliant idea," he told her. "How would you like to lead a session of my graduate directors seminar? You could take the approach of how an actor creates a character, drawing from your own experiences. I'm sure my budding young directors could benefit from that kind of insight."

Interesting proposal. Lally's instincts told her that this was precisely the type of thing that would impress David. She could imagine dropping it casually into her conversation the next time she saw him: "I was up on the SCU campus the other day teaching a graduate seminar. . . ."

"Well, sure, I think that would be fascinating," she told Myron. "When did you have in mind?"

"How about next Monday? It's short notice, I realize, and I apologize, but I had a cancellation. Les Weingrod—you know, the indie producer?—I'd recruited him to lead the class, but he's embroiled in some kind of crisis on a set in Santa Fe and can't get away. Do you think you could prepare in time?"

"I'm like a Boy Scout, darling." She laughed. "I'm always prepared."

It was marvelous to be back in the spotlight—even if it wasn't on the red carpet at a premiere at Mann's Chinese, but in a classroom in decrepit old McCreely Hall smelling of sweat, chalk, and something like spoiled fruit. Lally was encircled by a dozen fresh-faced young men and women who were hanging onto her every word, and she was loving it. Inspired by their rapt attention, she gave a vivid and hilarious account of how she had constructed the character of Priscilla Much, from suggesting the high-spouting ponytail (originally supposed to be a Farrah Fawcett–like shag) down to finding the exact intonation of murmuring, "Oh, James" (besotted, but slightly campy). She described her epic fights with a director who thought she should be wearing pointed falsies (she won) and with a lighting designer who wanted to bring out "the money-green tones" in her skin (she lost); and how long she had to practice before she could effortlessly reholster her golden gun in the top of her boot without stabbing herself in the groin.

"A Bond girl is like a superhero," she summed up. "The best ones have cool costumes, silly names, and they keep you guessing while they straddle the line between good and evil."

The students ate it up. The two-hour seminar stretched to three as they besieged her with questions, and even then they didn't want to let her go. Those who didn't have to get to another class coaxed her to the café in the basement of the building, where, for another hour, she continued to hold court.

Another group congregated at a table kitty-corner to them. Lally looked over and gave a start. It was Tommy with a clutch of worshipful students of his own. He did a similar double take when he spotted her. She waved and he raised a hand back in greeting.

When both groups finally broke up, she and Tommy drifted toward each other. "So, what are you doing here?" he asked.

"Same thing as you. Teaching a seminar."

He gave one of his maddening, enigmatic smiles. Could it be he'd forgotten she had gone to UCLA on a full scholarship? she thought indignantly. Granted, she had dropped out after the first semester, traumatized by the death of her mother—and frankly, more interested in rock and roll than Milton and Shakespeare; but still, he should know damned well that she was no airhead. She could have excelled academically if she'd chosen to. "It was one of Myron Rose's graduate classes," she elaborated. "I seem to be very good at it. I'm thinking of proposing to Myron that I give a course of my own."

"It'll be nice to have you on the faculty," he said.

Was he being facetious? So impossible to tell with Tom Bramberg. He had really let himself go lately, she thought: His chin was rough with several days' stubble, and his hair looked like he'd cut it himself. And that outfit! Baggy no-color sweater. Ancient jeans. And—*be still my heart!*—brown dress oxfords with no socks.

But she admonished herself not to criticize. "Which one of your classes was that?" she asked.

"Advanced composition. I assigned them a Pierrot cycle, and we were discussing their efforts. Most of them had no idea that Schoenberg lived and taught in Los Angeles back in the thirties."

Lally gave an imagine-that murmur, knowing vaguely that Schoenberg was an avant-garde composer of the kind of pieces the symphony played first, making you eat your spinach before rewarding you with Tchaikovsky or Brahms for dessert. "I've been trying to call you," she said abruptly. "You've had your phone off the hook."

"Yeah, probably."

"Does that mean you've been working?"

"Yep." He glanced at his watch. "I've got to get to a section meeting. Are you heading out?"

They strolled out of the glass-fronted McCreely onto a broad brick promenade shaded by century-old live oaks. Several students greeted Tommy as they passed, flicking curious or startled glances at Lally. She had chosen suitable campus attire—slim-legged jeans, silk sweater, mules—but the fact that the jeans were skintight, the sweater a lavender Marc Jacobs that slipped off one shoulder, and the three-inch-high Gucci mules were the color of overripe key limes ensured that she didn't exactly blend anonymously into the collegiate crowd.

"Those kids seemed surprised to see you with somebody like me." She laughed.

"I think they're surprised to see me with anybody. They seem to have some idea of me as the mad hermit composer working away in feverish isolation."

"I can't imagine why they would think that! When was the last time you used a razor?" Lally started to hook her arm teasingly through his. But then she remembered she was mad at him, and she stiffened. "The reason I was calling you," she said, "was because I was furious at you for siccing Sienna on me. You might have at least given me a little warning."

"For God's sake, Lally! I thought you'd be happy to have your daughter pay you a visit."

"Excuse me. She didn't pay me a visit. She moved herself into my house while I was away. Then she invited all her trashy friends, who treated my home like a trailer park. I came back from Europe exhausted and completely jet-lagged and found the place a total wreck. And then I stumbled on her sunbathing in the nude."

Tommy gave a delighted laugh.

"I'm sure it sounds funny, but believe me, it wasn't."

"Oh, come on. She's your daughter. What could be so shocking about seeing her naked?"

"That's not the point. The point is, I was totally unprepared. And then naturally she was her usual vicious self."

"Christ almighty!" He whirled to face her. They were in front of Granger Hall, a tall stucco building decorated with Mayan carvings. Lally, startled, took a step backward into a leering sun god. "Okay, look," he said. "Exactly what did Sienna do that was so incredibly vicious that you feel you have to cut her out of your life?"

"I don't think it's any of your business."

He gave her That Look.

Lally took a breath. "Okay, if you really want to know . . . After I split up with Artie, I met another guy. His name was Robert; he was somebody I really liked. I had high hopes for the relationship. I spent the summer with him at a villa he was leasing in Porto Ercole, and Sienna showed up. After she left, we had a cocktail party and I was taking pictures with Robert's camera. I flipped it backward to look at the previous shots. And, well . . ." Lally looked away. "I came across pictures of my daughter. That obviously he had taken."

"Let me guess. She was sunbathing in the nude."

"She wasn't sunbathing," Lally said icily.

"Okay, so she seduced a guy you were trying to snag, and now you can't forgive her."

"It wasn't the first time. She had done it twice before. Once when she was just seventeen."

" 'You know what I mean,' " he recited.

"What?"

"Nothing." He laughed again. "A line from an old Beatles song."

"You don't take anything I say or do seriously." Lally pouted.

"That's not exactly true. I take a lot of things you do very seriously. But let me ask you—did Sienna remain with any of these guys? I mean, for any length of time?"

"Of course not. It was just for the fun of breaking things up between them and me. I told you, she's perverse."

"Was Artie one of them?"

"Absolutely not! Artie isn't like that. He would never, ever . . ."

"Exactly my point. Did it ever occur to you that maybe you were picking the wrong kind of guy? If they were sleazy enough to let themselves be seduced by their girlfriend's daughter, maybe she was doing you a favor by snatching them away." He added in a low voice, "She might really have been trying to rescue you."

"You've always taken her side," Lally said stiffly. "You just don't know her like I do."

"Oh, yeah? How much do you really know about her? Did you talk to her the other day? Find out what was going on in her life?"

"As a matter of fact, I did. She's got a new Eurotrash boyfriend. She's off to New Zealand to hang around a movie set. Same thing as always."

Bells started clanging stridently in the tower above them.

Tommy gave a harsh little laugh. "You don't know anything, Granny," he said.

He turned and hurried up the steps into the Mayan-bedecked building.

Lally stared after him with indignation. If he thought he was going to provoke her by making cheap digs at her age, it wasn't going to work. She wasn't exactly ancient. She still looked utterly fabulous. To prove her point, she flashed a flirtatious smile at a good-looking professorial type who was sauntering by. He blushed, almost stumbled, and smiled back in a goofy manner. Instant enrapture.

Take that, Tom Bramberg! she thought smugly.

Except one thing nagged her: Tommy, so famous for telling it like it was, had never been given to cheap digs.

CHAPTER nineteen

Oh, My God, It's Hooterville

The first rain of the season. A storm had cartwheeled into town in its classic Pacific Ocean pattern—for several minutes water sheeted down so hard it was impossible to distinguish between the land and the sea; and then just when you thought the entire city would be submerged, it would taper off into a gentle spray. And then as you were about to close your umbrella or switch off your windshield wipers—*shwhoosh!*—down slammed another blinding curtain of water.

The first rain always made people drive crazily, either creeping along fearfully at about six miles an hour or weaving and bobbing in their lanes as if trying to avoid the drops of moisture. *You'd think it was pouring frogs or salamanders,* Lally thought scornfully as she navigated her Mercedes down the coast highway. This was nothing—she had once driven the autobahn from Vienna to Berlin in a deluge so intense she couldn't see the hood of her own car in front of her, and she hadn't braked once. Now she tooted her horn at a poky PT Cruiser and swept around it, sending up a majestic fan of water, and veered onto the exit for Venice Beach.

It was hardly the ideal weather in which to go shopping for a formal gown. Lally had promised Janey they would go dress shopping at Penelope Sylbert, but Janey had been incommunicado for several weeks—

vanished on some mysterious trip. She had finally called yesterday and been irritatingly vague about her whereabouts. It was cutting it close—the Los Niños Ball was only nine days away, and Penelope required at least a week for alterations.

Penelope Sylbert was another of Lally's discoveries, a darling hole-in-the-wall boutique located in the old warehouse district of Venice that was now the province of installation artists, glassblowers, and found-object sculptors. There was no sign on the shop, nothing to distinguish it except a persimmon-colored door. You had to know about it, be recommended by another client, like a speakeasy, and be booked for an appointment. Inside the shop, there was no merchandise on racks or shelves, just a few Italian-made armchairs, several dressing alcoves shielded by gauzy gentian-blue curtains, and an enormous bank of triple-view mirrors. How it worked was that you conferred with the dramatic-looking Penelope about what you were shopping for—something cocktail-festive, or sportif, or dressy-casual. Penelope would rather rapidly size you up, and then she and her assistants would begin materializing garments from unseen storerooms, accompanied by full suites of accessories.

Lally arrived on the dot for her eleven-o'clock appointment. No Janey. Lally had forcefully emphasized the fact that Penelope did not brook tardiness, suggesting that Janey drive down with her; but Janey had muttered something about heading down early for an appointment in Santa Monica beforehand and insisted on meeting Lally at the shop.

Could Janey be having an affair with someone in L.A.? Lally wondered. Some married man she had to keep under wraps?

More irritating mysteriousness.

Lally accepted a cup of chai tea poured from a glazed celadon pot by one of the assistants, a Japanese girl who dressed like a fourth grader. "So what are we looking at this season?" she asked Penelope.

"Sexy, that's the big news." Penelope's eyelids were greased a royal blue, a dozen enameled bracelets clattered musically on each arm, and her voice, with its unidentifiable accent, was cured by tobacco. "The dresses are letting it all show, shoulders, cleavage, the curve of the behind. I hope you're not frightened by clingy fabric?"

"Darling, I live for clingy fabric," Lally laughed.

"That's good, because some of my clients are squealing like piglets. 'Too revealing,' they complain. 'Well, it's not the fault of the dress,' I tell them. 'It's the fault of the body that's being revealed.' "

Lally grinned. Penelope was such a diva—but her taste and imagination in clothes were flawless.

The door flew open and a sopping Janey burst in. "Thank God I'm in the right place. I got totally lost in these little alleyways, and with the rain and all I could hardly see." She was wearing an oversized yellow slicker and nor'easter-style rain hat, like the girl on the Morton salt box. Lally thought: *It never rains but pours.*

"Where are the clothes?" Janey's eyes darted around the shop.

"They bring them from the back," Lally said.

"I provide everything," Penelope said. "You're going to be perfectly satisfied; don't you worry about a thing."

Janey still looked dubious. "Everyplace you take me, Lally, they bring things from the back."

The Japanese grade-schooler scurried over and helped Janey off with the slicker. Underneath the slicker she was wearing a man-tailored white shirt and gabardine pants.

And underneath the man-tailored white shirt, she was sporting an enormous, eye-popping pair of boobs.

Lally nearly choked on her chai tea. "Oh, my God! So that's what you've been up to!"

Janey beamed proudly. "Bru did them week before last. I didn't want to tell anybody till I was sure everything was okay. I just came from his office and he said it's all fine."

"And, uh . . . what size did you get?"

"D cup. I guess they look bigger right now, but Bru says they'll get a little smaller and start softening up in a few more weeks."

"You see?" Penelope said smugly. "This year it's all cleavage, cleavage."

Cleavage? Lally thought. *You could stick the Ventura Freeway between those tits and still have room to maneuver.*

Janey regarded her anxiously. "What do you think? Is it too much? Did I go overboard?"

"No, no, no," Lally assured her. "I'm sure they're going to be exactly what you want."

Janey wasn't a hundred percent certain they really were what she'd wanted. There had been so many decisions to make. Smooth or textured, round or teardrop-shaped? Implanted over the muscle or under it? An incision through the armpit or navel?

The first couple of days after the operation in the little recovery hotel off Montana Avenue had been pretty rough. The staff had danced attendance on her—as she had expected them to at $850 a night, room service and tips extra—but the pain had been pretty intense, and the painkillers made her agonizingly constipated. Her upper body had been trussed up like King Tut, and there'd been constant pressure, as if a hippopotamus were squatting on her chest. On the morning of the third day, when Bru removed the bandages, she had almost fainted. Two shiny beige beach balls stuck straight out from her ribs. It was horrible, freakish! She'd made a hideous mistake!

Bru had clucked and murmured like a mothering hen. "Now remember what I said. They'll loosen up, get a little smaller, and look much more natural in just a month or two. Everybody has your reaction at first. But trust me, you'll forget all about this once they take the proper shape."

She stayed three more nights at the Hotel Briarcliff. Gradually the stiffness and pain abated, and without the pain pills, she was able to go to the bathroom. And yes, hallelujah, the beach balls deflated slightly.

The weirdest thing was that, at Bru's order, she had to squeeze them for fifteen minutes several times a day to keep them softening up. It didn't seem right to fondle her own breasts. Almost perverted, even. She thought with sudden kindness of her ex-husband, Robbie—how he used to sneak glances at girls with big chests. *You don't know what you're missing, Rob,* she thought with a giggle. Perhaps she should run up to that country-club prison of his in Petaluma, arrange for a conjugal visit, and let him have a good, long squeezing session to make up for all he'd been deprived of while they were married.

But she didn't, of course. And by now things had improved: The breasts had dropped and softened somewhat and assumed something of a more natural shape. Yesterday she put on a T-shirt with no bra and looked at herself in the mirror, and this time she almost sobbed with joy.

She looked . . .

Well, for starters, she finally looked like a girl.

"Ladies, undress, please."

Penelope had become all business: Time was wasting; other clients would be arriving at their appointed hours. Lally and Janey were ushered into the Arabian-tentlike dressing spaces. Pamela's assistants darted in and out of the curtains bearing armfuls of evening bags, stoles and scarves, brooches and hair clips. Jewel-colored gowns waved from tufted hangers like battle standards, and shoe boxes formed towers waiting to be scaled.

Lally was having a blast. She was Cinderella and Penelope was her fairy godmother outfitting her for the ball. It was magic: *bippity boppity boo!* Each ensemble Penelope brought was more spectacular than the one before: a Paco Rabanne chiffon strapless; a flirty, knee-length silk Dior.

And finally one that made her almost faint. A satin Galliano slip dress the color of amethyst, which was her birthstone and which glowed against her tawny skin. It was clingy, with a plunging neckline, and accented by a bunchy satin wrap. Very vamp. Very Jean Harlow.

"I love it!" Lally exclaimed.

"This is the one," Penelope agreed. She made a minute adjustment to the bunch of the wrap and twitched the fabric just so over Lally's hip.

"I've got to show Janey!" Lally parted the curtain and twirled out, just as Janey emerged from her own tent. For once Penelope's genius had been defeated. Janey was encased in a rose-red strapless gown that made a heart over her huge breasts, like a grotesque valentine.

Lally couldn't help it. She burst out laughing. "Oh, my God, it's Hooterville!"

Janey recoiled as if she'd been slapped. "I guess I look ridiculous," she muttered.

Lally got hold of herself. "No, not at all. I'm sorry, Janey; it's just the dress . . ." Her lips twitched again, and she ducked back into her dressing tent, where she doubled up with silent mirth.

She could no longer see Janey's face. And so she didn't know she'd just made a lethal enemy out of Janey Martinez.

Four days of rain. The first fresh feeling of relief the storms brought after the many months of relentlessly dry skies was now beginning to give way to a universal anxiety in town over mudslides, leaking roofs, and the problem of getting around in open-toed shoes. Jessica had a perplexing leak—one that seemed to originate from nowhere, a welling in the center of the living room ceiling that was like one of those portals to evil dimensions that were forever opening up in horror films. Her regular plumber, Gary, was booked up for the next several days. So were the three other plumbers she called from the Yellow Pages, and a fourth didn't even respond at all. She paged Gary again and begged him to fit her in. He agreed finally to come around six, but he'd have to charge overtime rates—which, Jessica reflected, put him on a pay scale roughly equivalent to the salary allotted to the vice president of the United States.

She was excruciatingly attuned to salaries at the moment, being in the middle of her torturous monthly bill-paying session. She switched to Bob Marley from the Prince CD that had just ended and continued systematically working through the heap of bills that had accumulated in the old Easter basket she'd tossed them into. The rip-off tree trimmer—a hundred and sixty dollars just to lop off a dead eucalyptus branch. Two hundred and twenty to Expert Extermination to get rid of the silverfish in the bookshelves. Those flabby-assed sewer guys who Roto-Rootered out the line—they were zapping her for five hundred bucks.

She worked by rote. A band of heavy rain hammered the roof and lashed the windows at the same moment the phone rang. She continued working, letting the machine pick up.

"Hello, Jessica? It's Dave. Hey, I got your note and the, um, present and, well, I appreciate it very much. I really look forward to seeing you too. I took the liberty of moving you to my table at Los Niños. Hope you don't object. See you there."

Jessica leaped up and scrambled across the kitchen to lunge for the phone. Too late—the hang-up clicked in her ear. She kept clutching the receiver, wondering if she should try to call him back using star-69.

The problem was, she couldn't remember much about the note she had sent him. She had only a hazy memory of driving to the mailbox and stuffing the envelope down the chute. Returning home, she had lurched the car too far into the garage, whacking the front of it into Rowan's Schwinn. No real damage done, but it had scared her enough to stay out of the wine cellar ever since.

But what had she written in the note?

And more important, what had she included with it? Panties, wasn't that what Taller had suggested? If so, she hoped to high heaven that a) It was a pair with no rips or holes; b) It was *not* a pair of her old Calvin boxers with saggy elastic; and c) Whatever pair it *was,* they were freshly laundered.

Oh, God! It was too humiliating to even think about.

Perhaps she shouldn't go to the benefit. Duck out on the whole thing. If she were a no-show, that would retract the message that she was flinging herself and her intimate garments at David.

Except she'd still need to explain the whatever-it-was she sent him. Could she say it was just a joke, ha, ha? A malicious prank played on the two of them by somebody else?

Or simply a mistake—she had meant to send just a bread-and-butter note and—*whoops!*—her panties, diaphragm, bra, whatever it was somehow found its way into the envelope.

She groaned. She had succumbed to something worse than drunk dialing.

She was a drunk mailer.

Get a major grip, she told herself, *before you do something even stupider than that.*

She returned to the computer and threw herself back into the bills. The sprinkler company—a small fortune to repair the patio drip system. Dr. Momo Ruiz, pun-loving, premium-charging orthodontist. Neiman Marcus. It seemed like she never bought clothes anymore, so how had the balance run up to nearly a thousand bucks?

What was a thousand dollars to a billionaire? About twelve seconds' worth of interest?

Unworthy thought. She pushed it from her mind.

She finished her work, noting that the rain had finally tapered off to a weepy drizzle. A car crunched up the gravel driveway. She peered out the kitchen window to find out if it was Michael or Amanda driving: Seeing Michael, she grabbed a baseball cap, slapped it on her head, and went out to speak to him.

Alex bounced out of the backseat. "Mom, we went to the Renaissance Faire and look what Dad got me!" He brandished a cheap-looking wooden mandolin. "Dad said I can quit piano and take lessons on this if I want."

"We can talk about that," Jessica said.

Rowan slouched out of the front, reeking of some spice-heavy perfume and gripping a turquoise-colored shopping bag. "It was really lame this year. They had to have it under a tent, 'cause of the rain, so a lot of stuff wasn't there."

"Too bad. Listen, guys, go on inside, 'kay? I want to talk to your dad a second."

Rowan and Alex exchanged looks of mingled hope and wariness. When they had entered the house, Jessica walked around to Michael's window.

"You're going to get wet," he said.

She pulled the cap brim lower on her forehead. "Your attorney hasn't responded to our request to postpone."

"That's because it's a bullshit request. You've had over a month, for God's sake; how much more could you need?" She noticed that he had his own souvenirs of the fair—a fake gold medallion hung around his neck, more Henry VIII than Elizabethan, and a plastic scepter lay on the seat behind him. So appropriate. He was Michael the First, King o' the Hospital. Sovereign of all he surveyed.

"I need a few more weeks," she told him. "Whether you realize it or not, the expenses for the kids have been escalating lately, and they're going to continue to go up. I think that has to be taken into consideration. I'm barely getting by as it is."

He gave a nasty laugh. "From what I hear, baby, you're getting by just fine. I happen to know what you shelled out to take yourself to Los Niños."

Trust Taller to blab about that all over town.

She had a sudden inspiration. "I don't know what you mean by that," she said breezily. "Maybe you didn't hear that I'm going to be at the Clemente table. I've been invited by David. In fact, he was on the phone just a few minutes ago."

The effect of this statement on her ex-husband was gratifying. Michael's jaw dropped almost to the medallion on his chest. His Adam's apple worked. He ran a hand through his Fekkai For Men–gelled hair.

"David Clemente?" It came out hoarsely.

"Uh-huh."

"I didn't know you were, uh . . . I mean, how long have you been seeing him?"

"Oh," she said, "for a while."

"I didn't . . . I mean, I knew Alex went to the Halloween thing there, but you and David . . ."

Jessica could imagine the thoughts spinning furiously through Michael's mind. Powerful board member of Mission Mercy Hospital interested in ex-wife . . . Meaning ex-wife could exert influence affecting head of neurosurgery's future . . .

Meaning ex-wife was currently a force to be reckoned with.

"Well, hey, give David my regards," he added with a sickly grin.

"I will."

"And listen, I'll talk to Stan about that postponement. It shouldn't be that big a deal. A couple more weeks, right?"

"Right," Jessica said.

CHAPTER twenty

You Got Yourself a Girdle

As recently as a decade ago, a parvenu like Lally Chandler would never have been invited to attend La Noche Para Los Niños Indigentes de Colina Linda Benefit Ball, no matter what size check she pledged to donate. (The fact that there were no actual indigents, child or adult, residing within the town lines of Colina Linda—unless you counted those people who had maxed out their platinum cards and were behind on their Porsche payments—was beside the point: The net contributions were distributed among several international children's charities). Held in the celebrated azalea gardens of the venerable Broadmore Shores Hotel, the ball had been a carefully guarded old-money event: Dowagers weighted down with nectarine-sized jewels fox-trotted with polo players and ambassadors to banana republics; the heirs to household-cleanser fortunes mingled with the occasional member of European royalty.

It was always held on a Monday night, which was itself a marker of class: If you were a workaday person, enslaved to the idea of weekends versus weekdays, this event, my dear, was not for you.

But the new money wasn't to be denied. For one thing, there was so damned much of it pouring into San Carlino, snapping up the old Colina Linda estates, or constructing châteaus, which would have boggled the Sun King, on sea bluffs formerly inhabited by pelicans and spiny lizards. For another thing, new money was . . . well, just so much more fun. Who wouldn't rather dance cheek-to-cheek with a buffed and beautiful movie star or an Armani-clad venture capitalist than the jowly scion of some dwindling shoe-polish dynasty?

And so now, while the Los Niños was still the most exclusive event of the year, old and new San Carlino wealth were about equally represented, with perhaps the new gaining greater ground each year. The ultimate victory of the parvenus had been achieved the year before, when the venue of the ball was switched from the century-old, ever-so-slightly-ramshackle Broadmore to the new and ultraopulent Four Seasons.

But it was still held on a Monday night.

This would be Lally's fifth year of attending. The twenty-five grand she'd pledged had entitled her to a number of preball events: a multicourse dinner the evening before at the Roger Thornleys; a champagne breakfast at Van Cleef & Arpels; an auction and caviar brunch at the Native American Hall. She had declined them all, in the interests of appearing fresh and rested for the ball itself.

But then Janey had rung her up, asking her to pop over for a light lunch. Lally had turned her down as well—she had earmarked the midday hours for relaxing with an iced antifree radical facial mask.

But Janey was insistent. "I really need to talk to you about something," she said. "It's extremely important."

Lally, who was still stung with guilt about laughing at Janey's monumental boob job, reluctantly agreed to come. "Just a quick bite. Then I really have to get back for a couple of hours' nap."

"You'll have oodles of time," Janey promised.

Janey lived in a hundred-year-old Craftsman-style house on Gertrude Court, one of the original streets in Colina Linda—it had been paved only twenty years before, and over the objection of the residents who preferred the decayed-gentry illusion of a dirt road. Janey's decor had been shabby before shabby had become chic: wing chairs with wobbly legs and Empire-backed sofas with faded slipcovers, all of it shredded by a succession of spoiled dogs. She did have a few beautiful heirloom pieces. Lally had always coveted the eighteenth-century walnut lowboy that Janey used essentially as a repository for spare change and homeless junk.

Now they sat out in the backyard at a scabby old picnic table (Janey had a lot of crummy stuff as well). Her housekeeper, an elderly Hungarian named Magda, had concocted a Nicoise salad of sorts, using Bumble Bee tuna and bottled lemon juice. Lally picked at a slice of petrified egg and kept her eyes firmly averted from Janey's new Dolly Partonish silhouette. "So what's the big emergency, darling?"

"I just don't know whether I should go tonight. I'm thinking of not."

"Don't be silly. You always go. Didn't your great-grandmother found it or something?"

"My great-aunt Florence Wickersham. She was *one* of the founders—there was a whole ladies'-club type of thing that got it started. I guess I've gone almost every year since I came out. The only time I missed was when I had that ruptured appendix."

"So what's the problem now?"

"I don't have an escort. I had my cousin Logan lined up, but he shows champion Yorkies, and one of them's got some strange disease, poor baby. Its fur is coming out in clumps. So Logan's got to fly him up to some specialist in Palo Alto who's connected to Stanford."

Lally clucked sympathetically. "Well, there must be plenty of men you can call up. What about Taller? He'd kill to get to Los Niños."

"He's already going, can you believe? *Nobody's* available. For some reason, all the extra men in town have been snapped up."

One of Janey's dogs snuffled its nose into Lally's lap. She pushed it firmly away. "Well, if that's your only worry, it shouldn't be. *I'm* going solo this year."

"That's different. You're doing it on purpose. You've got an agenda."

Lally pursed her lips. That wasn't precisely the way she wanted to look at it. "The point is, we'll both know just about everybody in the room. So what difference does it make who's with anybody or not? It's not 1955. Nobody thinks in terms of stags and wallflowers and that kind of rubbish."

"My family does," Janey said. "Most of them will be shocked if I turn up alone."

You've just acquired a pair of size-D bazooms, Lally had the urge to point out. *It might be a little late to start worrying about shocking your family.*

But she merely said, "I think it would do you good to show some independence. And it would probably do them good as well. They need to start seeing you as your own person and not just an extension of themselves."

"I suppose you're right," Janey said.

"I'm absolutely right, darling. And besides . . ." Lally gave a little laugh. "I want you to be there. If you want to know the truth, I'm a little nervous about tonight."

"You? I doubt that."

"No, really." Lally was about to tell Janey how much she'd been thinking about David since the Halloween party, about his casual charm, and how touching she found it that he worried so much about his son, and how very attractive his gray eyes had looked behind those glasses . . .

But Janey leaped up and reached for the salad plates. "Finished?"

"Yes, thanks. It was delicious."

Janey carried the plates into the kitchen, where Magda was ensconced at the breakfast bar watching *General Hospital.* Janey scraped the leftover egg and anchovies into the dogs' bowls, then went to the refrigerator and took out two large cups filled with chocolate mousse, one blue and one green.

What she'd said to Lally wasn't true. She'd never had the least intention of skipping the Los Niños ball. In fact, she was eagerly looking forward to it. She had discovered that a lot of men found her new figure as sexy as all get-out. She could hardly walk down a public sidewalk without their eyes flicking to her chest—one guy in an Audi had almost rear-ended the car in front of him, he was so busy gawping at her. Her dry cleaner, Manny, while pulling plastic over her ready-to-pick-up sweaters, had inquired whether she was busy Saturday night (she'd turned him down). And Teddy Brimmer, whom she'd known since kindergarten, and who'd ignored her since the first grade, had out of the clear blue called her up and suggested they "hook up" sometime (she said maybe).

She shot two dollops of whipped cream from an aerosol can into the chocolate cups, replaying in her mind the scene in the boutique. Lally having a big, fat laugh at her expense. The whole nasty Hooterville thing.

If Lally thought Janey looked ridiculous . . . well, the attention Janey was now getting only proved one thing—Lally Chandler was full of crap.

She brought the cups outside and placed the green one in front of Lally.

"I couldn't, darling. You know how tight my dress is. I can't afford even the tiniest little bulge."

"It's just a small portion. The Julia Child recipe. I stayed up last night cooking it because I know it's your favorite."

Lally had an image of Janey doggedly following the elaborate recipe, laboriously chopping the chocolate, melting it slowly over simmering water, stirring and stirring until it was exactly the right consistency. She had another twinge of guilt.

"Well, maybe just a bite." She nibbled a spoonful.

Janey watched, brows knitted. "Is it good?"

"Delicious." Lally really did have a weakness for chocolate mousse; before she knew it, she was scraping the bottom of the cup. "Yum."

"I'm glad you liked it." Janey took a nibble of her own.

Lally ran a finger around the sides of her cup, wiping up the last residue. It had an aftertaste, she realized, licking her finger. *A chalky undertaste*—wasn't that what Mia Farrow said about Ruth Gordon's chocolate "mouse" in *Rosemary's Baby*? This wasn't so much chalky as metallic. Must be just nerves. Lally had been experiencing mild butterflies in her stomach all morning.

"It was perfect, really," she said.

Janey smiled. She happily spooned up the rest of her own mousse, which she had made with very expensive imported Swiss dark chocolate. Lally's, however, she had cooked using half Swiss chocolate and, for the rest, eight squares (quadruple dosage!) of extra-strength chocolate Ex-Lax.

Because, she told herself, *Ex-Lax is what you feed somebody who's full of crap.*

Jessica called Taller in a panic. "I can't get my dress closed."

"Oh, my God! What are you wearing?"

"It's my Carolina Herrera. The ice-colored with the bow . . ."

"Yep, I know it. Very becoming, but it was always just a tad snug on you. In the hip department."

"Really?" Jessica ran an exploratory hand over the curve of one hip. "But now it's tight in the tummy."

"Even when you suck it in?"

"Yes, Taller. Even when I suck it in."

"What else have you got? I always liked that smoke-colored Ralph Lauren."

"It got a salt stain in New York last winter. I wore it to the opera, and afterward we couldn't get a taxi and had to walk back to the St. Regis through all this banked-up snow. I gave it to Yolanda for her niece's *quinceañera.*" Jessica paused. "I've got that blue Chloe with the fluted skirt."

"Oh, my God, goddess gowns! That's so five years ago. Tell you what, don't do anything yet. I'm just about ready, so I'll be right over."

Jessica hung up. She tugged again at the closure of her dress. Taller was right. If she sucked her stomach in and *held* it in, she could probably get the zipper up, but one good belly laugh and it would split the seam.

She resisted the urge to dash down to the wine cellar and open a bottle. True to her resolution, she hadn't had a drop of anything alcoholic since the lost posting-the-whatever-it-was-to-David night. She wasn't going through withdrawal, exactly. Nothing so dire as DTs or the shakes or anything. Just this frequent, goading desire to sneak down the winding little stairs.

The doorbell rang.

She heard Alex scamper to answer it and then his piping, eager voice mingled with Taller's arch tenor. Clutching the back seams of her dress, she padded out to the landing and peered down.

Taller was exquisite. Vintage dinner jacket, from the fifties, judging by the narrow satin lapels. Receding hair slicked back from his forehead, Bogart-style. Face bronzed and far better moisturized than her own.

He glanced up with a mirthful spasm of his lips. "Somebody needs to start counting carbs."

"If you're just going to make fun of me . . ."

"Nope, I'm here to save the day." He high-fived Alex and then bounded up the stairs two at a time. He experimentally tugged at the back of the dress. "Not so bad. There's a little room to move these hooks. Can Yolanda sew?"

"Sure. She's a great seamstress."

"Alexander?" Taller called down. "Would you go get Yolanda, honey? Tell her to come up here *rápido.*"

"Do you think moving the hooks will be enough?" Jessica said.

"I'm not done yet." Taller turned and marched authoritatively into her bedroom. Jessica watched anxiously while he rummaged through dresser drawers, tut-tutting a little at the untidiness of her stored things. "Aha!" he said, removing a pair of Lycra tights.

The gesture jogged Jessica's memory. Fishnet stockings! That was what she had sent David!

She suddenly recalled it clearly, liberating the pair from the bottom of a drawer. But was that better or worse than a pair of undies?

"Got a pair of scissors?" Taller said.

"Scissors?"

"Yeah, you know, the thing that goes snip?"

Jessica retrieved one from her dressing table. Taller unceremoniously scissored off the legs of the tights and handed her the pantylike top.

"Are you kidding?" she said.

"Nope. You got yourself a girdle, honey."

By the time Lally had finished dressing, the butterflies in her stomach had metamorphosed into hyperactive gerbils. Ridiculous. She had never suffered from stage fright. She was an intrepid actress, public speaking held no fears, and in her youth, she had crashed A-list parties in Manhattan, London, and Rome with perfect sangfroid.

So what the hell?

She swallowed some homeopathic pills left over from that bout of Montezuma's revenge she'd contracted last spring at the Sheffields' *casa* in Zihuatanejo, with its woefully inadequate plumbing. While waiting for the pills to work, she scrutinized herself in the mirror, satisfying herself that, rampaging gerbils notwithstanding, she looked as near to perfection as possible. The sapphire chandelier earrings brought out honey-gold glints in her eyes. And the Galliano was amazing—Penelope Sylbert had triumphed again. The silk flowed like water over the contours of Lally's body, which displayed not one extra ounce of fat, despite her pigging out on all that mousse at lunch.

The thought of the mousse made the gerbils do vigorous somersaults.

She was certain now that she had not imagined that metallic undertaste. The chocolate had been stale or gone bad somehow. Trust Janey, who could squeeze a nickel till it shrieked, to use stuff that had been moldering in her pantry for decades.

Lally muttered a low curse.

Perla's voice suddenly reverberated on the intercom: "Lally, the car is here."

"I'll be right down."

Thank heavens she had hired a car for the evening—driving right now, with her insides in this kind of distress, would be unthinkable.

She sat for a moment and took several fire breaths, drawing in slow and deep through the nose, expelling hard and fast through the mouth. Then she closed her eyes and visualized a placid mountain lake.

No waves. No shadows. No turmoil.

Either the pills or the visualization seemed to work—the gerbils stopped tumbling and instead began just wandering aimlessly. *You've performed under worse circumstances,* she reminded herself. On that set in Romania in freezing rain with a fever of a hundred and two . . . Or the time she'd had to clown through an off-off Broadway production of *A Night at the Opera* with an excruciating ingrown toenail stuffed into pointy-toed shoes . . .

She could do it. She was prepared to dazzle.

She bunched the satin wrap artfully around her shoulders, picked up her bag—a Judith Leiber minaudière in the shape of a jeweled tortoise—and glided downstairs.

"Wow!" Perla exclaimed.

"Like the dress?"

"It's sensational. But are you okay? I mean, you look kind of in pain or something."

Damn! Lally made an effort to relax the muscles of her face. "Just cramps," she fabricated.

"Again? You had bad cramps last week."

"Perimenopause, darling. Dr. Schlobel says it can go on for years."

"Did you take any Midol?"

"I don't need it. I'll be okay."

"Don't be such a blasted martyr. I'm going to get you some."

A couple of Midol couldn't hurt, Lally reflected. It might actually be what she needed. "Okay, but please let's make it snappy," she said. "I'm already running late."

Lally had perfected the art of the entrance.

She habitually timed herself to arrive precisely between forty and forty-five minutes after the appointed hour. By then the majority of guests would have already arrived and been through the first flurry of meeting and greeting. Those who drank would have imbibed just enough for things to have acquired a rosy tinge, but not so much that they'd lost their powers of discernment; and the teetotalers would be feeling a little heady simply from the buzz of the room. At this point, Lally, taller than most women and a good many of the men, would enter briskly, causing many heads to turn. She would pause for just a fraction of a moment at the edge of the crowd with a yearning, somewhat distant look on her face, as if searching the assembly for a long-lost love. Then she'd plunge in, confident of being the center of attention.

True to schedule, she emerged from her hired Town Car at eight forty-two. The seven-minute drive from her house to the Four Seasons had felt like seventy minutes. The gerbils had undergone a growth spurt: They were now raccoons foraging on heavy paws.

Just a few hours, she told herself. *Not a problem.* She put on a radiant smile and walked regally into the hotel.

The theme of the ball this year was "Heaven." Huge pearly gates were constructed at the entrance to the gardens. A beatific-looking Saint Peter was ticking off the names of the blessed guests, while a retinue of young angels of both sexes waited to escort them into paradise. An equal number of devils stood by—burly security guys in red sweatshirts with horns fastened to their heads and wires worming from their ears, ready to eject any sinners.

Inside the gates, a high, billowing tent encased the gardens. Under the tents, a breathtaking scene. Lally took a step forward. A kaleidoscope of jewels, gowns, flowers, and wings-and-halos swirled before her eyes. "Angel Baby" throbbed in the background. Something above caught her eye. Acrobats recruited from the Cirque du Soleil and costumed as seraphim and cherubim swooped and fluttered on nearly invisible wires.

Slam, bash! The raccoons suddenly turned her stomach into a mosh pit and began doing an enthusiastic slam dance.

Lally let out a moan. She doubled over and began to tear a zig-zag path through the crowd. Familiar faces went flickering by: the Shapiros, the Kostalakises. Taller Kern arched an eyebrow in surprise. Janey Martinez, grinning with what appeared to be glee.

Lally staggered by them all, intent only on making it to the glassed-in corridor in the rear that contained—blessedly contained—the ladies' lounge.

CHAPTER twenty-one

You Look a Little Green Around the Gills

"That was some entrance!" exclaimed Taller.

"Truly memorable," Janey agreed. "Lally should be thrilled. She's always anxious to make a memorable entrance."

Taller regarded his cousin with interest. What had happened to turn Janey so suddenly and decisively against Lally Chandler? he wondered. Though it was so typical of Janey's relationships: one minute, bosom buddies; the next, mortal enemies.

And speaking of bosoms, he could hardly believe what Jane had seen fit to do with hers. Those protuberances! Together with her unfortunate thunder thighs, she resembled some sort of root vegetable, a rutabaga, say, or a turnip, wrapped up in chartreuse taffeta.

But Taller was in a mellow mood. At this particular moment in time he was in the exact place he wanted to be—sipping a flute of a stunning Krug Grande Cuvée, surrounded by the cream of San Carlino society, and with a bevy of eye candy in halos for added visual pleasure. He allowed that he was not the best person to assess his cousin's new attributes—but since both Ted Brimmer and Brant McCleary had been hovering near her, drooling like Saint Bernards, he supposed she'd achieved the desired effect.

More power to ya, Jane! he thought benevolently.

He supposed he ought to seek out Jessica and make sure she was doing okay, and so he dutifully scanned the crowd for her. *Bingo.* David Clemente had not only found her but was attached in a rather proprietary way to her side. With them was a tall man, a kind of male *jolie laide,* attractive in an arty-ugly, ears-too-big way. He wore a ratty tuxedo, but so what? Taller knew an inordinate number of wealthy eccentrics whom you might take for homeless if you didn't know any better. His great-uncle Buster Wickersham, for example, looked like he picked his clothes out of a Salvation Army reject bin, and old Buster was rolling in loot.

Taller considered joining Jessica. He could find out whether David was satisfied with his purchase of that first edition of *Tender Is the Night.* But then, why wouldn't he be? The book was in very fine condition, with the extremely rare first-issue dust jacket and signed by F. Scott on the front free endpaper. An expert collector might have haggled another fifteen or twenty percent off, but it was still worth all of the fifty-four thousand dollars David had sprung for it.

A boy with teeth as white as his wings and a rakishly tilted halo materialized at Taller's shoulder. "Would you like a sevruga blin, sir?" he murmured, proffering a tray.

Sevruga. Now this was heaven. "I'd love one," Taller murmured back, and decided that Jessica was doing just splendidly on her own.

Jessica had attended her fair share of black-tie benefits over time, but this one, she had to admit, was a doozy. Maybe heaven didn't actually look like this, but that would probably be heaven's loss. How, she wondered, had they managed to get lighting that bathed every face in the kind of glow usually achieved only after marathon sex? Or those rainbows that washed overhead in colors that Monet would have sold his sister for? The billowy white tables that actually seemed to be floating on an azure sky? And the pièce de résistance—the after-dinner entertainment was going to be Rod Stewart, who'd been Jessica's very first passion and whose name still gave her a residual adolescent thrill.

She blinked as a flashbulb went off in her eyes.

Another difference between this event and others in her past—about every two minutes, one of the dozen roving photographers snapped her picture.

Well, okay, technically they were taking David's picture. But since David had glued himself to her side, they couldn't photograph him without getting her own grinning face in the frame as well. David seemed to take this endless documentation for granted. He didn't turn or pause a beat in conversation. But with every click and flash, Jessica looked up, a little startled.

She glanced at Tom Bramberg, who, by some subtle movement, usually managed to stay outside the shots, even though he was clearly a part of their conversational group. She still couldn't get over finding him here. It scarcely seemed to be his kind of scene. Amid the squadrons of modish custom-tailored tuxedoes, his seen-better-days dinner jacket and slightly frayed bow tie were an almost exotic sight.

"Don't you like getting photographed?" she asked in a teasing tone.

"Not really," he said. "I think I agree with the cultures that believe having your picture taken steals a little bit of your soul."

"Not me," David put in. "I'd say it's just the opposite. If you lend your face to a cause and it leads to more people digging into their pockets, well, that's got to be good for the soul."

"Yeah, but you see, there's the problem. The sight of my face is not going to make anybody reach into a pocket."

"Hey, come on. You're being modest. You're a celebrated composer. That's got to seem pretty glamorous to most folks."

Tommy shrugged dismissively. There was a crackle of animosity beneath their exchange, Jessica noticed—some sort of male head-butting thing going on. It was not complimentary to either of them: It made Tommy seem almost priggish and David rather insufferably folksy.

Was it over her? she wondered. And if it was, how did she feel about it?

Concerned, of course. And upset.

Bullshit. It was flattering as hell.

Then she reminded herself that Tommy was probably here with that exquisite girl who'd been so lovingly entwined around him outside his house. Jessica glanced around the crush of faces, half expecting to see her appear and claim him. But it was someone else who suddenly linked her arm through his: Celia Roederer, wearing a bit too much blusher for her eighty-something years and arms, neck and ears dripping with diamonds.

"There you are," she trilled. "Having a good time?"

"Yes, a wonderful time, Celia," Tommy said politely. "Thanks for inviting me."

"It's my pleasure." Celia turned with a flutter of bejeweled fingers to David and Jessica. "Did you two know that our symphony has commissioned a brand-new piece from Tom? A piano sonata . . ."

"Concerto."

"Yes, exactly, an absolutely brilliant piano concerto, and we're going to have the world premiere in April. We've signed up a young Korean pianist who's won scads of competitions to be the soloist."

The mystery of Tommy's presence was solved. Celia was a heavyweight on the board of the San Carlino Symphony, and she'd obviously glommed on to Tommy Bramberg as a local prize.

"How exciting," Jessica said.

"You bet it's exciting! It's the first piece he's written in . . . how many years?" Celia glanced at Tommy.

"A few." He smiled tightly.

"Many, many years! But of course, David, I don't have to tell you any of this. After all, it's your grant that's paying for it."

"Oh. Right." It was David's turn to smile tightly.

"It's a real coup for us," Celia burbled on. "It's going to get our little orchestra international attention."

"I can't wait to hear it," Jessica said.

Tommy shot her a glance that made her blush.

Celia began tugging him away. "You can't hog him, David. There are scads of people I want him to meet."

"Looks like I've got to go sing for my supper. Pleasure to meet you,

David." Tommy and David curtly shook hands. Tommy gave a last lingering glance at Jessica, then dissolved into the crowd with Celia.

Jessica felt strangely flustered. To mask it, she raised her champagne flute to her lips and drained it. An angel miraculously appeared at her side, exchanging her empty flute for a filled one. *Number three,* she reminded herself. *Better watch it!*

David inclined his head intimately toward her, his face relaxed now. "By the way," he said in a low voice, "I haven't thanked you yet for that gift you sent me."

Jessica blushed again, bright red. "Oh, God! I'm sorry about that."

"Don't be. It was very charming."

"No, I feel like an idiot. I'd had a bit too much to drink and, well . . . it was just a dumb thing to do. Please tell me you got rid of it."

"Nope. It's framed and mounted with your name on it on my living room wall."

"Oh, God, now I'm totally mortified." She laughed, and he laughed with her.

But David couldn't talk for more than a few seconds without someone approaching him, and now a new group engulfed them, men with silver hair and expensive watches, and tawny-maned women who'd stopped aging at twenty-eight. David made introductions, but the names fluttered by Jessica—they were denizens of a Colina Linda society several strata above her own. He was quickly caught up in a ping-pong of business and social references that she couldn't join.

She melted, Tom Bramberg–fashion, several steps back. A redheaded angel offered a tray: dollops of scallop ceviche served on Buccellati soup spoons. She accepted one, swallowed the delicious mouthful of ceviche, and replaced the spoon on a tray proffered for that purpose by a second angel.

Taller came swimming by in the current of the crowd. He paused to hiss in her ear: "We've been upgraded! We were originally at table sixty-six, which was Nowheresville, but now we're at table three!"

"I know," she hissed back, but he had already paddled away.

The band smoothed into a rendition of "My Blue Heaven," and the lighting became drenched with a radiant blue pierced by shooting stars. People gasped in delight. Jessica glanced back at David and saw one of the tawny women tuck a folded piece of paper into his pocket.

So this was what it would be like to be with him, she thought. An unending round of flashbulbs and meaningless introductions and younger, thinner women slipping him their phone numbers. She felt a painful pressure in her stomach.

Then she realized that what was causing her the pain was not really the idea of sharing a life with David—it was the damned makeshift girdle. She should never have let Taller bully her into wearing it—moving the hooks on the dress would have been sufficient to get by. If she was going to make it through a five-course dinner without suffering, the damned thing had to come off. "Excuse me," she murmured to David, and slipped away.

She asked one of the waiter-angels where the ladies' room was and was directed to a glassed corridor encompassing the far end of the gardens. Inside the lounge she ducked into one of the four stalls, hoisted her skirt, and rolled off the Lycra garment. *Blessed relief!* Maybe it left her with a bit of a tummy, but so what? She was a woman, not a teenage boy with breasts.

A low moan issued from the neighboring stall. "Hello?" Jessica called. "Are you okay?"

"Fine, thanks," was the faint reply.

"Lally? Is that you?"

An affirmative croak.

"It's Jessica DiSantini. Are you sure you're okay?"

"Yeah, just a touch of food poisoning. I'm fine."

Food poisoning? From those exquisite hors d'oeuvres? Jessica emerged from her stall and stuffed the cutoff tights in the trash. Lally emitted another groan.

"Are you sure you don't need anything?" Jessica asked.

"No!"

"Okay, then. I guess I'll see you out there." Jessica shot a last look of concern at Lally's stall, then went back out into the corridor.

Somebody grabbed her by the wrist. Before she could react, a door pushed open and she was pulled out into a fragrant, moonlit courtyard. She smelled aftershave and tobacco and leather as arms encircled her and drew her close. Hard lips pressed hungrily against hers and she found herself kissing them just as hungrily back.

After a violent twenty minutes, Lally tottered out of the stall. She peered in a mirror and uttered a rattle of despair. She looked like the bitter wrath of God! But at least the stomping raccoons had shrunk back to gerbils and she felt able to navigate the rest of the evening.

She set about repairing the damage to her appearance, availing herself of the toiletries laid out on the commode, finishing with a vigorous swish of mouthwash. A couple of other women burst into the lounge, animated, chattering, high on the night. Lally directed a vivacious smile at them—*Isn't this such super fun!*—and then propelled herself back into the gathering.

The band was playing a swing version of "Stairway to Heaven," and a number of couples were twirling and dipping on the dance floor.

"Care to take a spin, Lally?" A beaming Myron Rose held out his hand to her.

Spin. Wrong word. She goggled at him in horror.

"Maybe later?" he said quickly.

"Yes, later would be lovely, darling." She got a grip on herself. "It looks like we're about to be fed. Where are you seated?"

"Fifty-nine."

Siberia. Myron was just a minnow in this sea.

"And you?" he asked.

"I'm at three. The Clemente table."

He looked suitably impressed. "Well, enjoy. I'll catch up with you afterward. I'm going to hold you to that dance."

Lally nodded, smiled, headed to her seat. It was no accident she'd been placed at David's table. She'd had her pick of seating, for the simple reason that she had been instrumental in providing Rod Stewart.

Some years back she'd had a fling with the head of his current record label, a diminutive man named Harold who aspired to tall women like a mountaineer to Annapurna. He was happy to do Lally a favor now and again.

Table number three was a puff of white gauze set with cut crystal and blue-and-gold Limoges, with a sumptuous centerpiece of rare ghost orchids and out-of-season white tulips. Lally had arrived first. She hunted for her place card. *Damn!* Four seats away from David. She might as *well* be in Siberia.

She glanced quickly around; then she palmed her card and exchanged it for one to the right of David. Then she scurried back and set the purloined card in her original place.

With a shock, she realized that Taller Kern was suddenly sitting directly opposite. Had he seen her make the name-card switch? He was gazing at her sardonically, but that meant nothing: Sardonic was his usual expression.

She calmly slipped into her self-assigned place. Then she leaned with an insouciant air toward him. "Taller, darling! How great that we're at the same table."

"Super-duper!" Taller plucked an orchid and substituted it for the browning gardenia in his lapel. "But what a shame we're not sitting closer," he added archly. "I'd love to be able to dish."

The message was loud and clear: He'd seen her make the switch. But really, so what? "Yes, it is too bad. But I'll call you tomorrow, and we can compare notes."

"Can't wait." He grinned, showing his teeth. Sharp little teeth, like those on the kind of tropical fish that would eat up all the others if you added them to your aquarium.

Fortunately his attention was diverted to a woman sitting down beside him—Paula Kazzle, the forty-something heiress of what she referred to as an adhesive manufacturing company and everyone else called a glue factory. Then Joe Riesenthal, CEO of Browner Aluminum, claimed the seat at Lally's right. He was a cadaverous-looking guy with the habit of groping the thighs of his dinner party seatmates. (Years ago he'd tried it with Lally. She'd stabbed his knuckles with her salad fork, and they'd gotten along quite pleasantly since.)

A host of heavenly bodies began serving the first course; a terrine of truffled duck foie gras on lamb's tongue and mâche. Lally, nodding without really listening to something Joe Riesenthal was declaiming about the Supreme Court, stared at the food with distaste. The gerbils milled and strutted ominously.

"Oh, Lally . . . Hello."

She glanced up to find David hovering at his chair. The same quick thrill she had felt at the Halloween party shot through her—though now it had to battle with the milling gerbils. In fact, she realized, she wasn't quite sure what she was experiencing. David, for his part, looked perplexed to find her beside him, and not enormously pleased.

"Why, hello, David," she said warmly. "How nice to see you! Isn't this a fabulous affair?"

"Yes, spectacular." He peered at her place card. "I uh . . . thought I was sitting next to somebody else." He glanced down the table.

Lally pulled a mock-sorrowful face. "No, it's just me. I'm sorry to be so disappointing."

David recovered his social poise. "Oh, no, not at all. I'm delighted to have your company."

"Why, thank you, sir." She tilted her head flirtatiously.

He sat down and she asked, "How's Noah? Back in New York, I suppose?"

"Yeah, he is. I don't get him again until Christmas. We talk a lot, and when I'm in New York I grab some time with him, but it's still pretty damned hard to be separated. Every time I see him, he's changed in some little way."

Lally nodded vigorously. "Yes, I remember that with my daughter. I'd be gone for even a short time and then when I came back—" She broke off in confusion. She would come back to discover Sienna had grown an inch or developed breast buds or picked up a few dirty words in French, but in the most important respect hadn't changed at all. There would continue to be that fierce and undeclared war of wills between them. "I know exactly what you mean," she finished lamely.

"Hey, you know, Noah was asking about you," David said.

"Really?"

"Yeah. He wanted to know if I'd seen the lady who was dressed up as the Good Witch. He said, and I quote, 'I think she's hot.'"

Lally gave a startled laugh. "Well, hey um . . . I'm flattered."

"I should tell you," David added, "that he's a kid with extremely discerning tastes." He grinned, teasing, and that electric thrill shot through her again. *What about you?* she wondered. *What do you think of me?* She felt almost desperate to know.

Suddenly flustered, she looked away. Reaching for a roll, she broke it into pieces, furiously slathered them with the truffle-studded foie gras, and took a bite. Big mistake. The gerbils began their unsettled shuffling again.

Taller leaned diagonally across the table, his face creased with a great show of concern. "Lally, are you okay? You look a little green around the gills."

"I can't imagine why," she said crisply. "It must be the lighting in here."

"Yeah, it is a little harsh down at that end of the table."

She realized suddenly that everybody at the table had heard their exchange and was now glancing her way.

She went on the attack. "I've been meaning to ask you, Taller," she said. "Since it wasn't Janey who paid for your ticket, who are you sponging off tonight?"

Paula Kazzle giggled. Somebody else gave a quick cough.

Taller continued to grin. "You mean who invited me?" he replied smoothly. "Why, it was Jessica DiSantini. You know, the person whose place you're sitting at? At least, it *was* her place before you switched cards."

"You bastard!" Lally hissed. Without thinking she hurled the hunk of roll she was holding at Taller. It hit foie gras–side down on the skinny lapels of his tux.

"This tux is vintage!" he yelped, and smacked it off.

"Oh, my God, a food fight!" squealed Paula Kazzle. She grabbed a roll and flung it in Lally's direction. It sailed by Lally and landed in David's lap.

Joe Riesenthal gave a snort of laughter.

"Could we all please just control ourselves?" Taller said pompously.

"You bet we can," Lally said, and hurled a second piece of foie gras–smeared bread. It struck Taller directly between his foxy eyes.

Taller gurgled with outrage. Joe Riesenthal laughed louder.

The gerbils in Lally's bowels expanded once again into raccoons, and they began to stomp. She rose unsteadily to her feet.

"Lally, you really don't look well." David regarded her with concern. "Do you need any help?"

"No, thanks. I just need to get a little air."

"Are you sure?" He placed a hand on her shoulder and gazed with deeper intensity at her. "At least let me come with you."

A part of her wanted to cling to him. But no, not in this grotesque condition. "No, really," she said, shrugging his hand off. "Please, just let me go!"

For the second time that evening, people were treated to the sight of Lally Chandler staggering rapidly through the crowd. What the hell did it matter? She'd made a first-class fool of herself in front of David, not to mention every other person at the table. The best she could wish for now would be never to see any of them again.

Plunging into the glass corridor, she doubled over and lunged for the door of the ladies' lounge. Except it wasn't the right door—this one opened onto a little enclosed courtyard.

And her condition was apparently making her hallucinate, because she seemed to be staring at an apparition of Jessica DiSantini, with her skirt bunched above her knees. And Lally's first ex-husband, Tommy Bramberg, appeared to be clutching Jessica's well-endowed ass.

Jessica looked up in a near swoon as the door swung open. A weirdly hunched-over Lally Chandler stood there looking as startled as if she'd seen a ghost. And then someone materialized directly behind

Lally, a guy in black square-framed glasses whom Jessica vaguely registered as David Clemente. *They make an attractive couple,* she hazily thought.

Are you crazy? she immediately reprimanded herself. *Are you seriously going to toss away the chance of catching a billionaire in favor of a near-starving composer with big time emotional issues?*

Apparently she was, since all she wanted to do at the moment was get her tongue back down Tommy Bramberg's throat.

"Hey, guys?" she murmured to Lally and David. "Would you very much mind closing that door?"

CHAPTER twenty-two

That's Absolutely Wicked-stepmother

It was a frigging boring book. It had started out promisingly enough with this hot little movie-star babe hitting the Riviera. But she had her mother with her, for chrissake. And then there were all these boring people who talked, talked, talked about stuff nobody'd given a shit about for, like, a hundred years. Then there was this bunch of snobs who considered themselves so extremely cool and sarcastic that they sat around lording it over everybody else. You were supposed to admire them, but to Otis they just seemed like self-important shitheads, the kind you ran into no matter where you went; it sure didn't have to be in France.

He couldn't understand why Caitlin was so crazy over this book, seeing as how these were exactly the kind of people that if they ever met her would treat her like a zero. It was probably what was making her so depressed. There was that one character with a string of pearls down her tan-alicious back, like that was supposed to make her so special. Nicole was her name. Otis had never known a Nicole who wasn't a stuck-up frigging snob.

He ran a vivid little mental movie of just what he could do with that Nicole Diver and those pearls of hers. *How tanned and superior would you be then, babe, huh?* In his imagination, she resembled the lady in the New England–style house who had laid the zit cream on him. But then suddenly he got confused. The zit cream was working: For the first time since puberty, he could detect a little clear skin on his crappy face, and so he guessed he had to be thankful to her for it.

He switched the face of Nicole Diver from the zit-cream lady to that of the Queen Bee. He assumed his Pepé le Pew voice: "Just a leetle kees for your Pepé." He placed the open book to his groin and humped it hard several times.

Then he lobbed the book over to where it belonged—onto the Mount Trashmore of junk piled up and around the Huey, Dewey, and Louie Duck wastebasket that had been in his room forever.

Some lousy fairy tale.

Lally had spent the better part of the past three days either staring at the marble tile in her bathroom or curled in a semifetal position on her bed. If fairy tales could indeed come true, then the Para Los Niños Ball should have been it—the night it happened for her. She reviewed it all obsessively. The breathtaking decor. The beautiful faces and gorgeous clothes. The tinkling of crystal and the babble of cultured voices and the sparkle of a first-class dance band. And, of course, the prince who was supposed to sweep her into the happily-ever-after.

The prince who had looked so totally crestfallen at the sight of Jessica DiSantini in a gropefest with another man.

At that point, Lally had wished she could just vanish. *Poof!* Like a genie back into a lamp. But David had chivalrously insisted on escorting her to her Town Car. The second her driver had pulled out she'd shrieked at the poor man to step on it. He'd put pedal to the metal and made it back in five minutes flat. She'd shot into the house and had been as sick as a dying dog ever since.

"Ohhhhh." She groaned again as Imelda crept into the bedroom with a tray of chamomile tea and white toast.

"Feeling better now?" Imelda set the tray on Lally's lap and parted the curtains at the bay window. Afternoon sun slanted into the room.

Lally averted her eyes. "You want I should close them again?" Imelda said.

"No, no, I could use some sun. Maybe a little air as well."

Imelda opened the doors to the balcony and then bustled out of the room. Lally slowly sipped the flowery tea. She had unplugged the phone in her bedroom, but she could hear the lines chiming in the house and office below. Perla had reported that everybody in the world had been calling, concerned for her well-being.

Yeah, right. What they really wanted was to gloat. By now everybody in town knew that Janey had played some malicious prank on her—some people claiming that Janey had spiked Lally's champagne with a knockout drug; others insisting it was ant poison on the foie gras. And everybody had heard about Lally pelting Taller Kern with food, though once again the rumors outstretched the truth: The story had it that Lally had dumped the entire entrée—pheasant à la reine; soufflé of cremini, cèpe, and morel mushrooms; and baby white bok choy—on Taller's natty head.

Basically she was the laughingstock of the town. Instead of kissing the frog, she had become the frog.

She despondently set down the teacup. She heard the distant sound of the gate bell, and several moments later Imelda reappeared in the room. "Mrs. Lally, a man is here to see you."

"Tell him to go away. I don't want to see anybody in this city ever again."

"Don't be an asshole, Lorraine." Tommy Bramberg strode uninvited into the bedroom. "Jesus almighty, you look terrible."

"Do you always have to be so damned honest? Would it kill you to tell a white lie now and then?"

"Maybe. I never really tried it." He sank onto the bed next to her and reclined against the pillow. He always took the left side of the bed, Lally suddenly remembered. And he made a kind of sighing sound in his sleep. She had a vivid flash of being nineteen: For a moment she was certain that if she turned her head, she'd see golden curls spilling on Tommy's pillow.

"So you and Jessica," she said flatly.

"Could be." Tommy gave a wry smile. "So you and Richie Rich."

"You mean David? Nope. I had some hopes, but I was just kidding myself. I've done a lot of that all my life, haven't I?"

"Haven't we all?"

"I don't know, I think I've done it more than most. I've had this romantic notion of what life was supposed to be. Everybody else could have problems and troubles, but I thought I was meant to live some wonderful fairy tale. And then in the end, what did it come down to? Three days in the bathroom hugging a goddamned toilet."

Tommy laughed. "Most fairy tales have a dark side, you know. Kids get eaten up by witches. Little mermaids turn into the foam of the sea."

"Yeah. And wicked stepmothers get what's coming to them."

He darted a glance at her. "You're not a stepmother. And you're not wicked, if that's what you're implying. So don't go giving yourself airs."

"Yeah, you're right. I'm just a particularly lousy mother." Lally shook her head. "The past few days I've been thinking a lot about Sienna. The way I kept foisting her off on all those nannies and boarding schools. That's absolutely wicked-stepmother behavior. No wonder she hates me."

"For the hundred and twentieth time, she does not hate you," he said sharply. "Can't you get that through your head? If anything, she really needs you right now."

"Why right now?"

He paused. "I mean now as much as any time."

Lally rolled on her side to stare at him. "No, something's changed. You're not telling me something."

Tommy drew an exasperated breath.

"Come on, Bramberg. Out with it."

"Jesus, Lall. Don't be so fucking dense. I already told you."

Lally was still a moment. "Oh, my God!" she whispered. "At the university, when you called me Granny—you weren't just being facetious, were you?"

Tommy hesitated, then shook his head.

"So I really am a grandmother?"

"I wasn't supposed to tell you. Sienna made me swear on my soul not to. But she also swore to *me* that she was going to tell you herself."

"Which means you're even. So come on; spill it all."

"Okay," he said. "You've got a three-year-old granddaughter named Chiara."

Lally's heart leaped to her throat. "Who's the father?"

"Remember that count Sienna was with?"

Lally gave a snort. "That phony, you mean."

"You were dead right about that. Turns out he grew up in South Paterson, New Jersey. His family's got a plumbing-supply business there. Sienna's left the baby with them while she's off on this latest spree of hers."

"You mean she just ran off and dumped her with them?" Lally said angrily.

"Sound familiar?" He gave a harsh chuckle. "Look, I'm not going to go blaming you for the way you raised Sienna, so don't you go blaming her now. I think she's been dying to tell you, but she wasn't sure what your reaction would be. She probably thought you'd hate the idea of being a grandmother. She figured it wouldn't jibe with your image."

"That's ridiculous."

"Oh, yeah? Are you sure about that?"

Lally wasn't sure of anything at the moment. She had the childish desire to pull the covers over her head.

"The thing is," Tommy went on, "I've always pretty much felt Sienna was my daughter as well as yours. I told her she could leave the baby with me, but we both knew that with the state of my life right now, that would be insane. So it's kind of up to you, Lorraine."

Lally sat straight up. "The people she left the baby with—who are they? How do I find them? Do you have their phone number?"

"Sorry, I don't. But one way you could find out—you could have a chat with your daughter." Tommy swung his long legs off the bed, got up, and dug his wallet out of his jeans. He removed a folded piece of lined notebook paper. "Her cell phone. It's about nine in the morning in New Zealand, so if you call right now, you'll probably wake her up." He leaned over and kissed Lally's forehead. "Eat something. You're skin and bones."

He left as abruptly as he'd come in.

Lally sat very still on the bed, legs crossed under her, clutching the folded piece of paper. She was suddenly very hungry, she realized. Famished. When she was sick as a girl, her mother would serve her chicken noodle soup. Lipton's: She could distinctly remember the taste, somehow both bland and salty. She pressed the intercom, and her voice reverberated throughout the huge house. "Imelda? Do we have any chicken noodle soup?"

Imelda sounded startled by the request. "No, Mrs. Lally. We have a jar of consommé madrilene. Do you want me to heat it up for you?"

"No, I'd really like some chicken noodle. Maybe you could call the Plum Mart and see if they'll deliver some. Lipton's if they have it, but any brand."

Then she stared at the scrap of paper with the number written in Sienna's careless scrawl. It seemed suddenly so clear to her now that all these years she'd been pursuing the wrong fairy tale. Another, truer one was formulating in her mind.

She took a gulp of the chamomile tea, which had gotten cold, and then reached for the phone and dialed. Her chest constricted as she heard it pick up.

"Yeah, hello?" Sienna's voice was husky with sleep.

Lally shut her eyes. "Sienna? Nenna? Hello, sweetheart. It's Mom."

There were going to be cutbacks; everybody at the center was aware of that. The only questions were, when was the ax going to fall and on whose neck?

Caitlin was about ninety-five percent certain that it was going to be on hers. An arctic chill had set in between herself and Grace, which Caitlin was also certain had something to do with Lally Chandler's meddling. Grace no longer summoned Caitlin into her office or dropped into Caitlin's for minisessions of policy brainstorming or kvetching fests. Her current pet was Juanita Bosco, the other full-time staffer. Caitlin had glimpsed Grace just this afternoon parked in Juanita's cubbyhole, the two of them cozily splitting a bear-claw pastry.

Yeah, the writing was on the wall. It was just a matter of time before Caitlin would be scrambling once again for a job with suitable pay and precious benefits. In the meantime, she needed to build a cushion of cash in case she had to coast on savings for a few months. No way she was going to register for unemployment—if anyone she knew saw her going into the grubby unemployment office, it would be instant social death.

She was mulling all this over as she picked up Aiden from the rehearsal for the Luminaria Procession and ferried him to his second appointment with a children's therapist, Dr. Wintra Cohen. Caitlin had maneuvered Aiden into a subsidized program—four free sessions—designed to keep underclass minority kids out of gangs. Aiden was not a member of the underclass. Being a quarter East Indian didn't make him much of a minority. And despite his rather professional right hook to Noah Clemente's frilly-shirted abdomen, he was in little danger of hooking up with the Crips or the Bloods or the Norteños.

But it was becoming increasingly clear to Caitlin that he was miserable, and that she couldn't do anything about it. Maybe this shrink could dig up the cause somewhere deep in Aiden's psyche and find the key to lightening him up.

Dr. Cohen's office was located above an Indonesian import furniture shop on Palos Verdes Street. The first session had been with Aiden and Caitlin together, half of it taken up with paperwork, but after that Aiden had gone in alone.

Now Caitlin waited in a narrow room painted in Crayola colors. The only magazines were old copies of *Parenting*. She really didn't need to read about the many ways in which she failed at being the ideal parent; and so she sat near the window with her legs crossed, chewing Altoids and staring out at the traffic, counting the number of Rolls-Royces that went by.

After forty-five minutes, seemingly to the dot, Dr. Cohen ushered Aiden back into the waiting room and beckoned Caitlin into the inner sanctum. This was another crayoned room, hung with posters of Victorian urchins running with kites.

"My feeling is that Aiden is very depressed," Dr. Cohen announced crisply.

"I know that. That's why I brought him here."

The therapist gave a tolerant smile. "I'm speaking in a more clinical sense. He suffers from deep feelings of inadequacy and low self-esteem."

"I know he does. I can tell that. I just don't know why. I mean, I'm always telling him how special and terrific he is, and I compliment him whenever he does anything well. Or even a lot of times just for trying."

"Yes, I'm sure you do, but it goes deeper than that. For one thing, he has issues about his father being absent from his life."

Caitlin tensed. She hadn't mentioned Rav's bipolar flip-out. She had just spoken in vague terms about his leaving and her getting a divorce. "So what do you think I should do?" she asked quickly.

Dr. Cohen smiled again. She was a dramatic brunette, dressed in a designer taupe pantsuit accented by a choker of pink-tinged pearls. San Carlino was the type of place where almost all the shrinks had independent means and worked just for the "fulfillment" of it. Wintra Cohen's husband, Caitlin happened to know, owned an extensive network of FM radio stations. "We have only one more session," she said. "My feeling is that Aiden might benefit from medication. I can refer you to an excellent psychiatrist for an evaluation."

"Medication?" Caitlin's chest tightened. "You think he's got some kind of mental illness?"

"Depression is a form of mental illness," Dr. Cohen said gently.

Caitlin pictured Ravi setting a plate of quivering raw tofu in front of the giant Buddha in their living room. Squandering thousands on an antique deep-sea diving suit. Curling into a fetal position among the dust balls under the bed, weeping like a baby.

Aiden wasn't crazy. Not like that.

"He doesn't need meds," she said sharply.

Wintra Cohen glanced at her watch. "Tell you what. Why don't you think about it, and we'll talk about it next time."

Dismissed, Caitlin walked heavily back to the waiting room. "Ready to roll?" she said to Aiden.

"Yeah." He actually seemed a little more buoyant than usual. At least he wasn't dragging his feet as if his Adidases were filled with wet sand.

"So do you like Dr. Cohen?" she asked as they settled in the car.

"She's okay."

"You like talking to her?"

"Yeah, I guess. We don't just talk. We play games and stuff. Sometimes she has me draw stuff."

But do you talk about me? Caitlin was dying to ask. *Do you say good things or bad? Does she tell you that I'm the cause of all your problems, or does she help you to see how really, really hard I'm trying?*

But he didn't volunteer anything more, and she figured it was better not to press him.

She drove for a moment in silence, then asked, "How was the Luminaria rehearsal?" The Luminaria Procession was an annual event at St. Mattie's school. At dusk on the first evening of Advent, a procession of students dressed in white and carrying tall lit tapers wound through the streets of the old town district singing carols in Spanish and English.

"It was good. Except that a wind came up and kept blowing out all our candles, so Mr. Landross says we're going to switch to a different kind that won't go out so easy."

"Oh, yeah? Good."

"I need seventy-five dollars," he said suddenly.

"Jeez Louise! What for?"

"To be in the Luminaria."

"Seventy-five bucks for a candle?"

"It's more than just *candles.* It's, like, for the robe and afterward there's gonna be hot cider and doughnuts." He shot a worried look at his mother. "You *promised* I could be in it."

"Yeah, okay. Don't worry. I just wanted to figure out where it was all going, that's all." The damned school was a money sucker. One extra expense after another.

At home she instructed Aiden to go up and practice his clarinet (wet sand instantly refilled his sneakers). Then she hit the computer to track her current eBay listings. She'd had high hopes for two items—a Cubs cap signed by Sammy Sosa and a Marlene Dietrich–ish felt fedora that just needed a little blocking to look like brand-new. So far both were just pulling in under-reserve bids. She spent the next forty-five minutes scanning in photos and writing up enticing descriptions of her remaining hats. But she couldn't kid herself—they weren't going to bring in a hell of a lot.

What else could she put up for sale? She had some old family treasures—an ivory fan that had belonged to a great-grandmother; a tarnished old gold pocket watch from some no-longer-remembered relative—but these were things she didn't want to part with except in the direst necessity.

Maybe some of Aiden's baby toys had acquired vintage status . . . or something in the box of old books and CDs from her life with Ravi that she still hadn't unpacked . . .

Maybe that old copy of *Tender Is the Night* was worth a few bucks. She Googled the title, then scrolled through several dozen headers before clicking on one: *Wish List: F. Scott Fitzgerald.* The posting was by a rare-books dealer in San Diego, a short list of editions the dealer was looking to acquire. She clicked on *Tender Is the Night.* A book jacket shimmered onto her screen: a Riviera sea cove peeking behind a stand of tall, bright blue tree trunks.

Her heart beat quickly. She dashed off an e-mail to the dealer:

> I own a copy of this book with this cover on it. It didn't say first edition, though. Could it still be worth anything?

To her surprise, the reply came back almost instantaneously:

> If it does indeed have this jacket, it's almost certainly a first. In the thirties, Scribner marked their firsts with a capital A on the copyright page. Please verify. Value would depend on condition. For very good to fine, roughly forty to sixty-five thousand dollars. If your copy is authentic and you wish to sell, we have a client who would be interested in purchase.

Caitlin felt dizzy. *I'll get back to you shortly,* she replied.

She jumped out of her chair and hurried out to the hall. Where the hell had she left the book? Somewhere down in the kitchen, where it would be acquiring grease stains and losing thousands of dollars by the second.

No, worse. Much worse. She had lent it to Otis.

She paused by Aiden's door. From behind it came the bleeping of a video game rather than the faltering notes of his clarinet. "Aidey? I'm going next door a second," she called.

She raced across the weedy patch and pounded on the Wynnes' back door. Otis's father (Frank? Fred?) cracked it open and gawked silently at her. "Is Otis here?" she asked.

"Nope."

"Do you know when he'll be back?"

"Not a clue. Probably not till late."

Shit. Caitlin lifted her lips in her pleasant china-doll's smile. "I really hate to bother you, Mr. Wynne, but I lent Otis a book and I really need it back. I wonder if it might be somewhere around the house? Maybe up in his room?"

"The black hole of Calcutta? Take a look if you want. But if you can find your own nose in there you're nothing short of a miracle worker." Mr. Wynne shuffled aside to let her in.

She entered gingerly. It was the first time she'd actually been inside the house. You could tell it was an all-male establishment, all clutter and dust bunnies with a smell like wet dog.

"It's the room at the back of the hall," Mr. Wynne directed.

He wasn't exaggerating about the black-hole part. Otis's walls were painted not quite black but a kind of eggplant color that seemed to suck in all light. The room was so messy it made the rest of the house look almost Spartan. Even the smell was worse in here. Wet incontinent dog. Wearing rotten socks.

Where to even begin looking? In the junk that littered the desk and bureau? Under the grungy unmade bed?

Instinct pointed her to a large mound of stuff lurking like a discouraged beast in a corner beside the desk. Her instinct proved correct: Beneath some crumpled junk-food wrappers she uncovered the pastel book. She grabbed it, wiped it with her sleeve, and flipped to the copyright page.

Yes, there it was! A capital letter A.

"Hey, whattaya think you're doing?"

She looked up with a start. One of Otis's loutish older brothers had come into the room and was staring at her in a menacing way.

"Hi, I'm Caitlin." She smiled. "From next door? I'm just picking up something I'd lent to Otis. Your father said it was okay."

"Yeah? What are you 'picking up'?"

What did he think, that she was in here stealing Otis's priceless belongings?

"Just this book," she said.

"Oh, a book." His tone indicated that a book was worth somewhat less than one of the dust bunnies. He shifted his gaze from her to the rest of the room, staring at it as if encountering it for the first time. He shook his head with lordly disgust. "Look at all this shit. Don't know where he gets half of it." He picked up a shiny bright red garment crumpled at the foot of the bed and dangled it between the tweezers of two fingers. "The dickwad thinks he's Superman."

"That's not Superman," Caitlin said, staring at the red cloth. "It's Mister Incredible."

"That's him, all right. The Incredible Dickwad." The brother let out a guffaw and dropped the garment back onto the floor. "So, you gonna wait for Otis, or what?"

"No, I was just leaving. I've got the book; that's all I need." Caitlin bolted past the brother, scrambling downstairs and out into the sweet fresh air.

She slipped back into her kitchen and leaned on the counter, trying to calm her fast-beating heart. *Okay,* she told herself, *it doesn't have to mean anything.* A lot of people could own that costume. A couple of years ago, every other kid came dressed as Mr. Incredible for Halloween.

It didn't have to mean that Otis was the guy breaking into Colina Linda homes and assaulting single women.

Nevertheless, she decided to call one of her contacts in the Colina Linda sheriff's department. It couldn't hurt to have them check it out.

The Plum Mart did happen to have in stock not Lipton's but a can of Wolfgang Puck organic roast chicken with homemade egg-noodle soup. The packer, a phony snot who out of the blue had changed her name from Sharon to Winona, handed Otis the magenta bag in which the can lay nestled in tissue-packed splendor.

"This is the whole order?" he said.

"It's all the lady wanted."

Shit. What kind of tip was he going to get on one lousy can of soup? If it was a guy who was the customer it might be different: A guy wants delivered one pack of Winstons or a couple bottles of pre-chilled Molson, and to make up for the shittiness of the order, he's likely to double or even triple the amount of the bill. But a female thinks, Tiny order, tiny tip.

He glanced at the address on the dispatch slip: 1655 Polite Child Lane. He recognized it as the address of her highness, the Queen Bee. Naturally. She was the type to think nothing of ordering people to drag their butts all over God's earth just to bring her a can of frigging soup.

But he'd been waiting for quite some time for exactly this dispatch. "This has got to be my last run," he told Sharon-Winona. "I've got a seminar in risk analysis that got changed from yesterday."

"You better watch out, Otis. Mortie's really pissed off at the way you've been slacking off lately. I think he's thinking of firing your ass."

"Yeah, well, you know what? Mortie can *kiss* my ass."

Otis whirred up the window and peeled out. Instead of hanging a left on Alta Vista into the Colina Linda residential section, he turned right and fired up the coast road to his own neighborhood. He slammed to a stop in front of his house and galloped up to his room.

The mask and the little golden gun were in his closet, packed in a burlap bag originally containing a Plum Mart shipment of organic Hawaiian onions. It had been impossible to find a Pepé le Pew mask. Guess the little lecher wasn't as popular as he used to be. Otis had finally settled on a generic skunk-head mask from a kinky sex Web site that catered to people who got their kicks from dressing up as furry animals.

There sure were a lot of weirdos in the world.

He grabbed the bag, practicing his Pepé voice: "I have been waiting a long time for zees, my leetle petunia."

"Hey, Meat! Your lady friend was here looking for you."

Otis jumped. His brother Timmy stood in the hall outside the doorway, stuffing barbecue chips like quarters into the dumb slot of his mouth.

"The hell are you talking about?" Otis said.

"That hot little piece from next door. Caitlin. She was up here in your room. She seemed really disappointed you weren't home. I think she was looking for a little action."

Otis stared at him, dumbfounded. "Caitlin was in my room?"

"Isn't that what I just said? Jeez, listen up." Tim put the empty chip bag to his lips, puffed it, and exploded it with a punch.

"So what did she say?" Otis said. "Am I supposed to call her or something? Does she need me to do something?"

"Hell if I know. She took off in a big hurry."

Otis considered this news with despair. What was she doing in here? Tim was an asshole with pork sausage for brains, but maybe he was right in thinking Cait was starting to be interested in him. His complexion had been clearing up in leaps and bounds, and God knew he'd always been 100 percent there for her, whenever she needed him.

So it wasn't out of the question that she'd start to feel a little itch for him.

But why did she have to come into this room? Otis had no illusions—it was a frigging hellhole. And it stank—how come he'd never noticed that before? She must have just about puked when she walked in.

He'd never have allowed her to come upstairs, never, ever. If he'd been home, he could've stopped her.

He kicked at a pile of moldering underclothes and let out a string of obscenities aimed at the room, his luck, the whole turd-infested world.

Then he tightened his grip on the onion bag. He had lied to Sharon-Winona about having to go to the risk analysis class. It was a course he'd taken last year—got a lousy C-minus, because the professor was the type of frigid old bitch who always had it in for him. Still, it had been a valuable class. It was studying the principles of risk analysis that had shaped the idea of how he could strike back at all the frigid bitches and stuck-up snots and Queen Bees, not only for himself, but for Caitlin as well.

How risk analysis worked was pretty simple—once you got a plan of business, you measured the probability of certain things going wrong, and then you took steps to avoid them. For example, in his current enterprise, high-risk factors included: dogs, frequent male visitors, live-in help with rooms on the same level as the master bedroom, and women who chatted you up when you made a delivery—the ones who tried to establish some phony-friendly connection with underlings.

Low risks were the women who never even deigned to acknowledge his existence. The ones who acted like he was the Invisible Man.

The Queen Bee he labeled medium-high risk. She had no dogs or even cats, and the maid's room was not only on a different floor but in a whole different wing. And he was fairly sure he'd never registered as even a blip on her radar screen.

But on the downside—and it was a big downside—she was just the type to have some dude staying the night, in which case he'd have to totally abort, or if he didn't find out in time, he could have serious trouble.

But the principles of risk analysis stated that the greater the reward, the more risk it's acceptable for you to take. The reward for bringing down the Queen Bee would be huge—one compensating blow against the shitheap of injustice that constituted his life.

And the bonus was that she, like the other ones, would probably go crawling to Caitlin up at that counseling place of hers for help. He couldn't help giggling to himself. If only Cait knew how much business he was throwing her way, she'd be freaking amazed!

Substantially cheered by these thoughts, he slung the onion bag over his shoulder and hurried out to his car.

He made it to Polite Child Lane in less than nine minutes. Parked four blocks away, plucked the Styrofoam plum from the antenna, then jogged back to the big pink Mediterranean, carrying the soup delivery bag in one hand, the onion bag hooked over his other shoulder. He was buzzed in through the gate, and a pleasant-looking Filipina answered the door.

"Plum Mart, afternoon, ma'am," he drawled. Friendly as folks. Like Woody, the cowboy in *Toy Story*. "Sorry for the delay. We've been extra busy today. Must be something in the air." He gave an aw-shucks, friendly-like chuckle. Then he strode confidently past the maid into the house. "Kitchen, right?"

As he was certain would happen, she didn't protest but trotted meekly behind him. He set the plum-pink bag on a kitchen counter and handed her the receipt. She handed him a pair of twenties without examining the bill.

"Thank you," she said softly. "You can keep the change."

"Thank *you,* ma'am. Is there by any chance a rest room I could trouble you to use? It's been such a heck of a busy day, I haven't had the opportunity."

The maid hesitated only momentarily. "Yes. Through that hallway."

It was the maid's-room john—no fancy guest powder room for the likes of him. He emptied his bladder, conscious that he wouldn't get another chance for many hours. He flushed, then emerged briefly in the kitchen, where the maid was already busying herself with opening and heating the can of soup. "Thanks a heap, ma'am. You have a wonderful afternoon now."

As he knew she would, she let him find his own way out.

Which made it a snap, after opening and slamming shut the front door, to duck into a coat closet and hunker down, silent as a statue.

CHAPTER twenty-three

Intrepid-Bond-Girl-Style

Lally woke up with a start. She was wearing her Juicy Couture sweats, not pajamas, and the room was dark except for a milky patch of moonlight seeping in the bay window. How long had she been asleep?

She pressed the glow button of her clock: eleven forty-nine.

It seemed like she'd just shut her eyes when it was still daylight. She reconstructed the afternoon. The phone call to Sienna, who'd almost hung up on her—it had taken Lally fifteen minutes of apologizing, coaxing, babbling reassurances before Sienna had told her all about Chiara and grudgingly given Lally permission to go and see her. They had ended the call . . . well, not exactly reconciled: Sienna had still been mocking and resentful. But a little break had opened in the wall between them, and Lally was determined to keep chiseling at it.

Shortly afterward, Imelda had brought her the chicken soup, which she'd gobbled down, along with dry toast and more tea. Imelda asked to spend the night with her sister, and Lally told her to go ahead. Then she'd lain back, telling herself she'd just take a little nap.

Somehow eight hours had slipped by.

A shape stirred to the left of the bed, just beyond the patch of moonlight. Lally felt a shiver of alarm. "Who's there?" she said.

The shape moved closer to her, looming now at the foot of the bed.

"Imelda?"

Lally switched on the lamp and let out a squawk of fear. It was a stranger, a man—and he was wearing some kind of cartoon costume. Or rather, just the head of the costume, in the shape of an animal with a tall crest—a skunk, judging by the white stripe.

"*Bonsoir,* my leetle flowaire," he said.

A French accent? There had to be only one reasonable explanation—she must still be asleep.

She realized he was holding something. It was her stolen golden gun!

Now she was sure she was dreaming. A Frenchman in a skunk mask with her lost golden gun. She'd have to call her former shrink, Irv Shaye, and tell him about this. He was an old Freudian—he'd have a field day with the symbolism.

She squeezed her eyes shut. The problem was, when she opened them, the symbol was still standing there, in full living color. It took a step closer. She caught a whiff of a smell that was weirdly like the onion tart at Café Cygne.

"Who are you?" she said hoarsely.

"I am your Pepé, my leetle flowaire. I theek we have a leetle fun, *oui, ma chérie?*" He made a disgusting kissing sound through pursed lips.

"Va te faire foutre, trou de cul!" Lally spat.

"What did you say?"

"Ha! I knew you weren't really French." Lally crossed her arms triumphantly. "I said that you could go screw yourself, asshole!"

"Shut up, Queen Bee!" he yelled.

She gave another squawk of fear and shrank back against her pillows. Why did he call her Queen Bee? Was that what *he* was supposed to be, a bee, not a skunk? Confusion made everything all the more terrifying. "Where did you get my gun?" she whispered.

He reverted back to the lousy French accent. "Your preety leetle gun. You love eet so, eh? You will show me how you love eet."

He dangled it out to her. She grabbed it and pointed it unsteadily at him.

He laughed harshly. "What do you think you're gonna do with that? It's got no bullets, you stupid bitch." He seemed to have dropped the lousy accent again.

Of course the gun wasn't loaded. It never had been—it was just a prop. Lally threw it at the skunk-head mask. The intruder easily dodged it, and it clattered against the mirrored bank of closets.

Okay, don't panic, she told herself. The thought made her remember: the panic button! It was on the security panel mounted on the other side of the bed: Pressing the red panic button automatically summoned the police. She lunged to reach it.

Skunk Head roughly shoved her back. "No fucking way!"

"Connard!"

"I told you to shut up!" He reached for something resting on one of the tufted chairs. "See this?" It was a knife with a long, serrated blade. "Let's get this straight. I'm in charge here." He gave a demonstrative slice of the air that reminded Lally eerily of her father's brief stint demonstrating the Slice-o-Magic.

This had to be a nightmare.

"What do you want?" she whimpered.

Skunk Head scuttled back several steps to where the little gun had fallen and kicked it over toward the bed. "Okay, this is what I want. You're gonna get your ass off that bed. Then you're gonna take off your clothes, and we're gonna see just how much you love that precious gun."

Lally began to slowly inch herself off the bed.

"Come on, move!" He gave the air another Slice-o-Magic swipe.

Something suddenly took over Lally. She was no longer in her bedroom; she was in a martial-arts studio in Koreatown down in L.A., in training for the role of Priscilla Much in *Dying Is Easy.* Here was her instructor, Lee-Kwan Yan, a merciless black belt, taunting her, calling her a jellyfish, telling her she had noodles for arms, bean curd for legs, employing all manner of food imagery to insult her until she could kick high and hard enough to whap Roger Moore's stunt double in the head.

Which was what she did now. She bent down toward the gun; but instead of picking it up, she torqued her body, then uncoiled it fast and hard. "Kyee-op!" she screamed and lashed out her leg to kick.

She was no longer twenty-five. She could no longer kick as high as the Skunk Head. The heel of her bare foot struck his non-knife-slashing arm just below the shoulder.

"Wha!" he yelled, more from surprise than pain. He staggered a step backward.

Reflexively, Lally kicked a leg out from under him. He went down hard on his backside, and this time he did yell in pain.

She turned and raced from the room. She propelled herself downstairs, stumbling a little at the bottom step. Her kicking heel hurt like hell. Had she fractured it? She couldn't deal with it now. She righted herself and began half running, half hobbling as fast as she could.

It was only when she found herself in the great room that she realized that she had gone to the back of the house instead of toward the front door. *Idiot!* She could go out the French doors, but that would trap her in the courtyard. Across the hall, the library led out to the pool, but that yard was also enclosed, and in the pool house she'd be a sitting duck.

Imelda's room! It had a window that looked onto the service alley, which in turn gave onto the street. Lally began to hobble-run back toward the service wing. As she rounded the corner, her heart seized. There he was, standing at the end of the hall!

How the hell could he have gotten there? Materialized out of thin air?

It wasn't him, she realized suddenly. It was just that damned totem pole she'd bought in Vancouver last year. It was supposed to have been authentic Inuit but turned out to be tourist trash, so she'd stuck it in the service wing and forgotten about it. In the dim light, she'd mistaken the carved eagle's head at the top for the crest of the hideous skunk mask.

She nearly giggled with relief.

Something went crash in the den. She jumped and her heart started pounding again. The ground-floor windows had heavy-duty security screens, she remembered. Even a karate kick with a non-fractured heel couldn't dislodge them.

Her only chance was to get to another security panel. There was one downstairs in the gym that she could get to by the back stairway at the end of the service hall. As quietly as she could, she hobbled toward it. Damned heel—it felt as if she were walking on jagged glass.

She pulled open the stairway door and carefully shut it behind her. She groped for the light, then limped down the stairs, placing each foot as soundlessly as possible. She switched the overhead lights on in the gym.

"Oh, shit!" she muttered.

The security panel was on the wall beside the sauna, and some complete idiot had pushed the Bowflex machine up against it. Then she remembered that the complete idiot was herself—after one excruciating session on it, she'd thrown a fit, saying she hated the damned thing, and made Russell push it out of the way.

She hobbled around the obstacle course of weights and equipment and began pulling at the heavy Bowflex. For a second it refused to budge; then it did, with a deafening screech against the floor.

Immediately footsteps sounded above her. She froze: It was just a matter of seconds before Skunk Head found the front stairway leading down here.

She was right—she immediately heard the clattering of descending feet. And she still couldn't get to the panic button—pulling the Bowflex had just resulted in wedging it obliquely up against the panel. She glanced around for some kind of weapon. There was a small steel rod on the floor, the kind that attached to one-pound weights. Not much, but it was better than nothing. She grabbed it, then ducked down on her stomach behind a small stack of mats.

The door at the opposite end of the gym swung open. She heard footsteps stalking across the room. Her heart was slamming so hard against her chest, she was amazed he couldn't hear it.

Then suddenly she got a glimpse of him reflected in a far mirror. She gasped. He had taken off the skunk-head mask: She realized she'd imagined he was grotesquely deformed behind the mask, like the Phantom of the Opera. But he was just an ordinary-looking young guy. Overgrown blond hair. Slightly pocked complexion.

In fact, he looked vaguely familiar.

He stopped. Rather girlishly, he put his hands on his hips, his gaze sweeping the far end of the gym. It rested on the angled-out Bowflex. He approached it, examined it. Then he looked at the door of the sauna beside it.

That's right, she silently urged him. *Go ahead; check out the sauna.*

He stepped toward it, tried the latch, seeming a little surprised when it opened easily. He cautiously cracked the door and peered into the blackness.

Lally burst out from behind the mats. "Kyee-op!" she screamed again, and shoved him with the full force of her weight. With a yawp, he went sprawling into the sauna.

She slammed the door shut and stuck the rod through the latch.

"Hey! Hey, let me out!" He began pounding on the door and rattling the latch. "Open up this fucking closet!"

"It's not a closet; it's a sauna. So just relax." Lally switched on the heat and turned it up to high. "That's what it's for."

He continued to pound and yell.

Pain flashed intensely in her foot. She hobbled up to the kitchen, wrapped some ice in a dish towel, and pressed it to her bruised heel. *I need to call the police,* she thought, and reached for the phone.

Before she could dial, the outside gate rang. She gave a nervous start and pressed the intercom. "Who's there?"

"Colina Linda sheriff's department. Everything okay here?"

Had she somehow managed to hit the security panic button after all? "I think you'd better come in," she said, and buzzed the car through the gates.

She pulled her bedraggled hair up into a high ponytail and fastened it with a rubber band. Then she limped to the front door and opened it to two deputies. "Good evening, Officers," she said. "I'm glad you're here. I've got something you might be interested in."

And she gave her ponytail a toss, intrepid-Bond-girl-style.

CHAPTER twenty-four

You Know, I Have This Plane

A neighbor four blocks away had called in Otis's car.

He was an architect named Vreeling who lived in a precise, cantilevered mansion of his own design. Heading out early in the evening to attend a performance of *Rigoletto,* he'd been piqued by the sight of a decaying old clunker marring his pristine curb. To his greater irritation, the eyesore was still there when he returned just before midnight. He suspected it belonged to the live-in cook of his next-door neighbors, a couple with whom he'd long been feuding over their grove of bird-of-paradise that wept globs of sticky goo onto his polished cement deck. And so he had phoned the sheriff, demanding that the offensive car be towed away.

The deputies ran the plates. They discovered the car was registered to one Otis Wynne, a name that had popped up earlier in the day—a woman connected to the University Rape Crisis Center had phoned in a tip to check him out in connection with what the department had lately dubbed the Superhero Assaults. A car had been dispatched to the Wynne household, but Otis wasn't home, and a call to the Plum Mart that employed him reported he'd knocked off for the day. The deputies had smoothed the shaken nerves of old Mr. Wynne and told him they'd come back another time.

But now here was Otis Wynne's car popping up in one of the swankiest neighborhoods in town. One of the deputies had a brainstorm: She had the Plum Mart check what deliveries Otis had made earlier that day in that neighborhood. There was only one: Chandler, 1655 Polite Child Lane. The order had been called in at one-oh-six P.M.

And so a pair of deputies rolled up to that address and pressed the call button on the side of the gate. What they found was a hysterical college kid locked in a sauna, cooked to the color of a medium-rare filet, and more than willing to blubber to the cops about everything he'd been up to for the past few months.

Lally Chandler became a celebrity once again. The story—former Bond girl defeats sexual assailant with karate moves—was reported first in the local *Courier* and then spread rapidly to the national media. Both *TIME* and *Newsweek* ran photos of her brandishing her golden gun. She demonstrated her karate kick on Oprah, was reunited with her costar Roger Moore on Letterman, and guest-starred on *Law & Order: Criminal Intent* in the role of a vigilante madam.

Once again flashbulbs went off wherever she went. Once again her phones rang continuously all day and into the night.

When Perla buzzed her with a call from "a Barry Lewis from the Clemente Foundation?", Lally picked it up distractedly. A purry-voiced young man informed her that Mr. Clemente had viewed Lally's appearance on *Good Morning America,* on which she'd mentioned that she had become a board member of the University Rape Crisis Center. Would she be willing to do lunch to discuss Clemente Foundation's support for the center?

"Sure, you can arrange it with my assistant. She coordinates my schedule." Lally transferred the purry voice back to Perla and picked up another call.

The power of the press. Gotta love it! Jessica thought.

The Sunday magazine section of the *San Carlino Courier* ran its annual full-page photo spread of La Noche Para Los Niños Indigentes de Colina Linda Benefit Ball the week following the event. The largest and most prominent shot this year featured Sandra Bullock, Clint Eastwood, and Michael York caught serendipitously in a huddle. Second in size and position on the page was a photo of "local philanthropist" David Clemente, his arm proprietarily encircling the shoulders of "Colina Linda hostess" Jessica DiSantini. The blurry figure of the tall, shaggy-haired man almost out of the shot behind her was not identified.

Four days after the photo spread appeared, she was sitting in a ground-floor room of the historic San Carlino Courthouse (built in 1814; destroyed by the earthquake of 1843; rebuilt on the original foundation in 1868). Michael was seated across the rough-hewn conference table looking as eager to please as a puppy dog. He'd phoned her immediately after the *Courier* photo had appeared, gushed over how marvelous she looked and how glad he was that she'd hooked up with David. "He's a terrific guy. Fantastic. I've always admired him."

Gotcha! she'd thought. As long as he thought she wielded influence with a billionaire board member of Mission Mercy Hospital, Michael was going to change his child-support tune.

She was right. His attorney now presented his petition for revised support: The sixty-five-percent cut Michael had originally been seeking had been miraculously knocked down to fifteen.

Jessica's lawyer, Oliver Dietch, folded his hands on the conference table and cracked his knuckles. "My client is prepared to grant a twelve-and-a-half-percent decrease, provided Dr. DiSantini pays all forthcoming orthodontia and summer sleepaway camp fees.

Michael whitened, but continued smiling. He conferred in a low murmur with his lawyer, then nodded. "Okay, I can live with that."

Jessica was elated. Given the dizzying cost of braces and the skyrocketing rates for Rowan's tennis camp, she'd be at least breaking even. She might even come out ahead.

They spent another twenty minutes ironing out niggling details of the agreement. Then, with the proceedings concluded, everyone trooped out into a warm December drizzle. The moisture felt summery on Jessica's face. Only the plastic Santa Claus and reindeer strung between two Canary Island palms flanking the road gave any hint of the season.

"I'm glad we could settle this amicably," Michael said. "I'd like for us to remain friends—for the kids' sakes, if nothing else."

"I'm sure we can," Jessica said. It was strange, but Michael no longer seemed familiar. When had he developed that smirky little groove that came and went between his eyes? And had he always had the habit of hunching his left shoulder like that?

"So how's your mother doing?" he asked her.

"She's okay, thanks. She's got a suitor, a guy who lives in her complex and brings her strawberries he grows himself. It keeps her a little more in the here-and-now."

"A suitor. That's great." He chuckled in an avuncular manner.

I've got one too, Jessica wanted to shout. Her mind darted back to last Saturday night. She'd spent it in Tommy's bed, with a loganberry candle burning, the surf pounding below, and his hands with their long, tapered fingers coaxing sensations from her body she could never have imagined. She loved discovering things about him: that he kept his house surprisingly tidy; that his two Oscars (for best score) were stashed in the john, not as an ironic statement, but because they happened to fit in a niche built above the tub; that he habitually kept his phone off the hook.

She felt a wild surge of happiness.

It wouldn't last. She knew that intrinsically. Tommy was already being pulled back into a dazzling world of international high culture. He'd accepted a commission that would take him to Seoul in March, and this summer he'd be hopping from music festivals in Vermont, to Scotland, to the Czech Republic. While he was skipping across the globe like a flat stone over a lake, she'd be right here in San Carlino, glamorously chauffering her kids to birthday parties and bar mitzvahs, attending fund-raisers to lick cerebral palsy, battling the aphids on her roses.

But she didn't care. Right now the only thing that mattered was when she could get back in his bed.

She realized Michael had said something to her. "Sorry, what did you say?"

"I said I remember that dress you were wearing in the *Courier* photo. It was always one of my favorites. You looked smashing."

"Thanks," she said.

He gave a self-conscious little laugh. "Look, um . . . The Mission Mercy board is meeting next week for a departmental review. I'm hoping to bump up the funding of my department. Neurology has always been the stepchild of that hospital, and I'd sure love to see that changed. So maybe the next time you see David, you could put in a word."

"Sure, Michael," she said with a grin. "The next time I see David, I'll be happy to put in a word."

She had, of course, no plans to see David Clemente, now or perhaps ever. At some point Michael would find that out, and then maybe he'd set out to financially eviscerate her again. Today had given her some breathing space, but it was obvious she needed to get back to work. Maybe with a storefront law office—she could set her own hours and keep time free for Rowan and Alex.

The point was to ensure that she never again had to be dependent on the whims and favors of Michael DiSantini.

Michael clicked open the door of his Jaguar. "It's great to see you, Jess." He leaned over to peck her cheek.

"It's great to see you too, Mike," she said. But her thoughts were already drifting back to a room beside the sparkling sea.

"I've got a confession to make," David said. "For a long time I had you pegged as just another socialite. A Colina Linda lady who shops, like all those ghastly women Susanna used to run around with."

"So I had to karate-kick a would-be rapist in the head to make you think differently?"

"Actually that wasn't it."

Lally arched a brow. "It wasn't?"

"Nope. It was when you started that food fight at the Los Niños ball."

"Oh, good grief!" Lally slapped a hand to her forehead. "Don't even talk about that. It's too ridiculous. I was acting like a ten-year-old."

"Yeah, and it was fantastic. I can't tell you how many stuffy dinners I've suffered through that would've been greatly improved by somebody chucking a baked potato at somebody else. In fact, I think that at any event requiring black tie, throwing food should be mandatory."

Lally laughed. "Okay, I'll remember that."

It was their second date. The first was lunch at the Five Cranes, ostensibly to discuss Clemente Foundation involvement with the University Rape Crisis Center. Lally had shown up assuming it would be a meal with the pertinent Clemente board members and executive staff, with or without David.

But the maître d' had swept her past the larger tables in front to a sheltered table for two by the box bay window in the back. David was seated at it alone. He had greeted her almost shyly. And for a while he seemed a bit stiff, deliberating too long over the wine, awkwardly soliciting her choices from the dim sum cart. After some initial small talk, Lally found herself relating the story of her now-famous escapade, embroidering it just a bit to make it seem as funny as possible. She emphatically denied that it had displayed any extraordinary courage on her part. "Just instinct and a bit of luck," she said airily. "If you want to know the truth, I was actually scared to tears."

In turn, David had related to her a story about being mugged at gunpoint in New Haven when he was at Yale. He'd handed over his watch and wallet and then the mugger fled, dropping the gun. "Turned out to be a stapler," David said. "Your basic Swingline desk model. I felt like a complete and utter wimp."

They both broke up laughing at that. The ice was broken. They began to talk as easily as if they were picking up a conversation that had been running between them all their lives.

After they had consumed the first dishes and he still hadn't brought up the business at hand, it began to dawn on Lally: It was an undercover date! His interest in the Rape Crisis Center was, at least partially, a ruse. Like her own silly ruse to lure him to her disastrous Indian education–themed dinner party.

She laughed out loud.

"What?" He smiled.

"Nothing. I'm just having a very good time."

She could immediately have bitten her tongue. It was far too revealing a thing to say.

His face lit up. "I'm glad. Because I'm having fun too."

They continued talking, inclining closer toward each other until their foreheads were almost touching. Before they realized it, the lunch crowd had melted away, and the waiters were setting up for dinner. The first early-bird dinner patrons had begun to trickle in when they finally disengaged from their absorption in each other.

"I guess they're going to want this table," David said.

"I guess you're right," Lally said.

He paid the bill and they strolled out onto Kittredge Street. "Is it after five?" he said. "Come on!" He grabbed her hand and led her quickly around the corner to Mission Street.

The Luminaria Procession was in progress. The parade of white-robed children was ghostly in the dusk; their faces, lit by tiny flickers of candlelight, held expressions of solemn and self-conscious reverence. They were singing "O Come, All Ye Faithful" in alternating English and Spanish verses, and their voices were raggedy and sublime.

Every year Lally had resolved to come and watch the procession. Every year she'd been too busy getting ready for whatever social events she was attending that night.

"But it's wonderful!" she whispered.

"Isn't it? It's always been one of my favorite things about this city. No matter what, I always try to be here for it."

They continued to clasp hands and stood watching until the last robed ghost had drifted out of sight. And then David had asked her to have dinner with him the following night.

She was happy that he suggested his own house rather than going out. She was even happier that they were eating in an intimate little domed solarium instead of the coffered formal dining room. The food was delicious, but Lally had scarcely paid attention to it. She was too enthralled in the conversation that once again flowed effortlessly.

And now suddenly there was a pause. David fiddled with the stem of his wineglass. "My divorce was finalized yesterday," he said finally.

"Oh. Should I say I'm sorry or congratulations?"

"Neither, really. We were over long ago. This just makes it official. I don't know why I even brought it up." Another pause, and then he cleared his throat. "About Christmas. I'm going to spend the holidays at my place in Barbados. I'll have Noah for part of the time, and my sister and her family will be there, and, well . . . Would you like to come?"

"Oh . . ."

"You wouldn't have to bunk with me. You could have your own bungalow."

"That's not it," she said quickly. "The thing is, I've made plans."

"Right, yeah, of course. You've probably been booked up since July."

"Actually, no. It's something that just came up. I'd love to spend Christmas with you, really I would, but I'm going to New Jersey."

"Damn. No way I can compete with the glamour of Jersey."

She giggled.

"So are you going to tell me what's there, or are you going to make me guess?"

"It's a family matter. I've got, well . . ." Lally took a breath. "I'm going to see my granddaughter."

He stared at her with surprise. "You've got a granddaughter?"

She nodded. "Three years old. I didn't know about her until recently. I've been on bad terms with my own daughter. We stopped speaking to each other for some time. It was my fault, really—my own stupid stubbornness." Lally paused briefly; then the words came tumbling out. "Sienna, my daughter, had a baby three years ago with a guy who was knocking around Europe pretending to be an Italian count but turned out to be from South Paterson, New Jersey. His parents are taking care of the baby right now. They seem like very nice people; I've spoken with them several times. Sienna leaves the baby with them while she goes jetting around the world." Lally smiled tightly. "I can't really blame her for it. It was exactly the same thing I did to her."

David was silent, glancing down at the table. What was he thinking? she wondered. Was it dawning on him that she was not as young as she appeared? Calculating that he could have his pick of twenty- and thirty-somethings, so why waste his time with a woman who was not only well into her forties but a grandma to boot?

He looked up with a somewhat impish grin. "Why are you waiting till Christmas? It's almost three weeks away."

"Oh, well . . ." Lally said. "I had to make arrangements. This time of year reservations are tight."

"Well, you know, I have this plane. It's a pretty comfortable ride. It's got toothbrushes and stuff stocked on board. We could be there by morning."

"Oh!" Lally said softly.

"So what do you think? Are you game?"

"You bet I am," she said.

EPILOGUE

The Perfect Day for a Wedding

"I actually expected something a lot more lavish," Jessica remarked. "More on the lines of a coronation. With flocks of white doves released in the air and maybe a gilded coach."

"It's not exactly Spartan," Janey said. "There've got to be at least five hundred people here."

"I love the way they've floated all those millions of candles on all the pools," put in Caitlin, sitting between them. She edged away as Jessica swung her head, nearly thwacking Caitlin in the eye with the brim of her Edwardian picture hat. Beautiful straw, Caitlin noted automatically. She could move it in a flash on eBay.

Jessica glanced around the sea of wedding guests that filled the padded gilt chairs under the bowers of the palest pink roses. Everyone who counted in the city had been invited—*le tout* San Carlino, as Lally would say—as well as scores of notables from all points of the globe. Jessica picked out a London restaurateur with his own reality show, a slightly cross-eyed actress who'd had marquee value in the nineties, and a Wall Street high roller who'd recently been exonerated in the strangulation murder of his male lover.

It was a glittering day in late March. The only traces remaining of the rains that had drenched the state for the past three months were an abundance of new leaves on the jacarandas and a riotous pointillism of early wildflower bloom in the canyons.

"Well, it's the perfect day for a wedding," Jessica said, "no matter how simple or elaborate."

Caitlin nodded. "I hear David and Lally intend to give away all their money."

"Can you imagine Lally Chandler without any money?" Janey sniggered. "It would be like the pope without the Vatican."

"It seems to me it would be hard to give away a billion dollars," Jessica said. "It probably keeps making money faster than you can dole it out."

I don't know about that, Caitlin thought. All you had to do was write a check out to whatever person, place, or thing you wanted to enrich and just keep filling in zeroes until you reached a billion.

Though admittedly, she herself had never experienced the sticky problem of having money come in faster than she could spend it. The sale of the Fitzgerald had bailed her out of her credit card hole and even provided a little nest egg; and she'd had a reprieve on her job, thanks to the fact that Lally had adopted the center, this time for real. But money was still going to be tight. New expenses were constantly popping up. This wedding, for example. She'd miraculously scored the dress at the Pioneer Daughters resale shop—Prada, and hardly worn!—but it had needed expensive alterations. And then there was the issue of the gift: Lally and David had requested donations to World Aid "in lieu of presents," but how much would Caitlin be expected to give? Would fifty dollars be enough, considering her circumstances? A hundred? Whatever size check she wrote, it would still be a pittance compared to what most of this crowd would be coughing up.

She fidgeted, pondering the problem, and crossed her legs. The iris-colored chiffon of the Prada tightened across her thighs.

"You know, I think Lally had the exact same dress," Janey said with a knowing smirk. "Like from about two seasons ago."

Caitlin felt herself redden with horror. Could she possibly be wearing Lally's hand-me-down? Would anybody else notice?

She was saved from having to reply by a rustling that arose from the seats in back. "I think they're starting!" Jessica exclaimed.

The small orchestra (culled from the finest of the San Francisco Philharmonic) segued from Schubert into a stately baroque pavane—Rameau, Jessica happened to know, since it was Tommy who had directed Lally's choice of music. She rose along with the rest of the guests and peered expectantly down the narrow aisle dividing the banks of seats.

A tiny flower girl appeared. She had violets and daisies entwined in her curly hair and she tossed fistfuls of white rose petals in her path.

"That's Lally's granddaughter," Jessica whispered. "She's called Chiara. Isn't that a lovely name?"

"She's darling," Caitlin said.

"Lally a grandma. Who'da thunk it?" Janey chortled.

Of course, by now, everybody in San Carlino had heard the story: how Lally Chandler had discovered she was grandmother to a three-year-old who'd been abandoned, Victorian orphan–style, and how Lally had swept in to save the day. Some said the newlyweds planned to adopt Chiara; others said Lally's daughter, Sienna, wouldn't allow it and that it had fanned the bitter feud between them. Still others said that all three—mother, daughter, and granddaughter—were going to reside under the Clemente roof as one big, happy family.

The little girl was followed by Noah Clemente. He walked briskly, looking somewhat stuffed into his formal suit, bearing the ring cushion on the tips of his fingers as if it were slightly too hot.

The kid that cost me a billion dollars, Caitlin thought ruefully. Though to be honest, she knew it would never have worked out between her and David. All that do-gooding, the speeches and ceremonies and so on and so forth, it eventually would have driven her nuts. And frankly, how was she supposed to care about solving the problems of the world when she could hardly make a dent in solving her own son's?

Aiden . . . There had to be a scenario that would make him happy. If she could just find a new father for him, a guy who was loving and reasonably rich and *sane,* she was positive that Aiden would begin to bloom. Her eyes briefly swept the sea of guests, wondering if such a personage might exist in its midst.

Hard on Noah's heels marched a bevy of bridesmaids, seven of them, dressed in pale green, on the arms of an equal number of ushers. Jessica recognized none except for Juliet Shapiro, postchemo bald beneath her bridesmaid's hat.

Janey observed this procession sourly. After all her efforts to help Lally get to where she was now—sashaying her ass down the aisle to become Señora Billionairess—the *least* Lally could have done in return was ask Janey to be a member of the wedding. The fact that Janey had spiked Lally's chocolate mousse with a quadruple dose of extra-strength laxative—well, really, Lally had had it coming. And everything had worked out for the best, so why shouldn't they just be laughing about it now?

Actually Janey did feel a bit like laughing: She'd discovered a darling little internist down in Thousand Oaks who was delightfully liberal with prescriptions, and the two Xanax she had swallowed before taking her seat were kicking nicely into gear.

"Here's Sienna," Jessica whispered. Lally's daughter—the girl she'd once mistaken for Tommy's lover—was the maid of honor. Having been so seldom seen, she was a matter of considerable interest to the crowd. Everyone knew that Lally had had to bribe the girl to come—some said with an emerald necklace; others said with a seven-figure check.

She's exquisite, Jessica thought. A shimmer of gold and silver. Like a living moonbeam.

The moonbeam suddenly caught Jessica's eye and scrunched up her face in an expression of insolent disgust. Jessica gave a start. She wondered if she could have imagined it; she glanced at the girl again, but Sienna had already glided by.

The orchestra segued with a flourish from Rameau to "The Wedding March," and here came the bride.

"Wow, she looks fabulous!" Caitlin exclaimed.

Jessica agreed. And not in that eerie, unyoung way she used to—

there was a diffusion of happiness that had nothing to do with young or old that now transfigured Lally's face.

She was escorted by Tommy, so romantic-looking in his dark gray morning suit and with his tangle of silver-and-ash curls. He turned his head and saw Jessica and smiled, and for several moments Jessica was aware of nothing else in the world.

"Who made the gown?" Caitlin whispered to Janey. "Is it Vera Wang?"

"Badgley Mishka," Janey hissed back. "In champagne duchesse satin. Of course, Lally couldn't exactly wear white. I mean, what with her past, she should really be wearing scarlet."

Several rows farther back, Taller Kern, who was not an invited guest but was escorting Celia Roederer, watched Lally's stately ascent up the aisle with a certain satisfaction. The competition between the exes had been a blast. The winning of the dark horse, Lally—hey, he couldn't have planned it better himself. Of course, now he needed to promote himself back into her good graces, as quickly and efficiently as he could. Shouldn't be hard, he thought. With her life turned upside down, and that big-trouble daughter lurking about, Lally was going to need some familiar old pals to keep herself grounded.

He shifted his eyes to a few rows ahead, where the remaining exes—Caitlin, Jessica, and Janey—were seated, watching the bride with no doubt misty rapture. "And then there were three," he whispered to himself, and smiled.

The strings are playing Mendelssohn, but to Lally, gliding up the aisle on Tommy Bramberg's arm, the only thing she hears is Old Blue Eyes. The fairy tale has come true. It has happened to her. In a few moments time, Lorraine Siplowsky-Bramberg-Grass-Willman is going to become Mrs. David Alderson Clemente.

It's almost too amazing to grasp.

The truth is—and this is what's so wonderful—she really loves the guy. Truly and deeply. There's a connection between herself and David that (she's certain) she never felt with any of her exes, and it continues to grow stronger every week they are together. Moreover it has nothing to do with his wealth. If he were to go broke tomorrow, she'd still be gaga over him.

Though she has to admit the wealth doesn't hurt. The announcement is going out shortly that Lally is to become the executive director of the Clemente Foundation. She's thrilled about accepting this new role. It's the chance to make a difference in many, many lives as well as to accomplish something significant with her own. Lady Di was one of her heroines, and Lally envisions herself following in her footsteps (though presumably without the bulimia).

It can happen to you. . . .

Lally looks ahead to the top of the aisle, where she can see Chiara clutching her basket of rose petals and squirming, the way three-and-a-half-year-olds do. Lally's heart swells. From the moment she first glimpsed the little girl, she was head-over-heels in love. If everything else were to disappear—if David were to leave her and all her money evaporated—as long as she could sometimes hold Chiara in her arms, she believes everything would still be okay. A slant of sunlight suddenly burnishes the little girl's honey hair. This is the true pot of gold at the end of the rainbow. Lally smiles to herself.

But it's a hot sun. The day, which had started so cool, seems to be turning into a scorcher. Lally dabs away a little rivulet of perspiration that has dribbled from the tendrils of her elaborately dressed hair.

Tommy glances at her with a quizzical arch of his brow. It was so sweet of him to agree to give her away. Artie—sweet Artie—would also have been willing, but he's recuperating from a double hip replacement, and marching down the aisle beside a wheelchair . . . well, that just doesn't jibe much with the fairy tale come true. Tommy, with his Victorian-poet-about-to-perish-from-consumption look about him, is a far more suitable accoutrement.

God, it is hot! She suddenly feels like she's burning up.

On her left she spots Janey Martinez among the guests. Lally had hesitated before inviting her, but then decided to let bygones be bygones. Now she's glad she did—Janey looks elated to be here.

Beside Janey is Caitlin Latch. Lally's been seeing quite a bit of her since Lally has been in training to become a volunteer counselor at the University Rape Crisis Center. Caitlin's smarter than Lally had given her credit for. A bit rough around the edges, but with a certain amount of potential.

But the dress Caitlin is wearing looks familiar. Could it actually be that Prada chiffon Lally had sent to Pioneer Daughters a few months ago?

Jessica DiSantini is sitting next to Caitlin. No doubt she has eyes only for Tommy. For some reason, this gives Lally a little prick of jealousy. She proprietarily squeezes Tommy's arm.

Strangely, he doesn't seem bothered by the heat, even though he is wearing heavy formal attire. Nor does anyone else seem to be discomfited. In fact, several women seem to be pulling their wraps tighter around them.

And yet Lally is burning up. Beads of sweat are forming on her lashes. She's afraid to blink.

She's just several paces now from the wedding bower, where David stands waiting for her, looking eager and handsome. As Lally approaches, she suddenly knows what's happening.

She's having her first hot flash!

It can't be! She's far too young. And she'd almost OD'd on green tea and antioxidants.

But there seems to be no other explanation for why she suddenly feels like ripping the veil off her head and using it to wipe her red-hot face.

This cannot be happening! This is absolutely not in the fairy tale.

She consoles herself that David has already seen her at her very worst—looking foolish and childish and, as Taller Kern pointed out, deathly green around the gills—and he seemed to fall for her anyway. And maybe he'll just take her flaming cheeks for passion.

A train moans somewhere in the near distance. Funny how you can always hear a train in Colina Linda. Stepping under the bower, Lally lets go of her ex-husband's arm and reaches to take the hand of her husband-to-be. With streaming mascara, she gets ready to begin the happily-*ever-after.*

TURN THE PAGE FOR A SNEAK PREVIEW OF
LINDSAY GRAVES'S NEXT EX-WIVES NOVEL,

To KEEP a Husband

Coming soon!

PUBLISHED BY BALLANTINE BOOKS

Lally Chandler Clemente had come back to San Carlino in great style.

"Lally's back!" Word spread like cannon fire through salons and spas and the ecru-toned waiting rooms of the city's high-end dermatologists. It crackled over cell phones and ricocheted across plates of thirty-two-dollar luncheon entrées. San Carlino society, which had begun settling down for the more relaxed pace of summer, began primping itself for a second social whirl.

Fabulous Lally! She'd been a Bond girl in her twenties (opposite Roger Moore in one of the late-eighties flicks), then married a succession of famous men—a rock star! a cinematographer! a game show host!—before waltzing off with local billionaire David Clemente (CEO of the Clemente Group International, and currently tied for number 163 on the *Forbes* Four Hundred Richest in America list). The couple had married in mid-March, then embarked on a lavish honeymoon trip, the details of which had preceded the newlyweds back to town—a trek around the world via the Clemente private jet and an ocean-going ketch once owned by the late Prince Rainier of Monaco, as well as by more exotic forms of transportation—camels through the Draa Valley; some sort of customized junk for the tricky backwaters of the Yangtze. They had toured the Pyramids and the Parthenon and gazed with wonder at Angkor Wat, and they'd been wined and dined in the villas and palazzos of wealthy acquaintances on three continents.

And knowing Lally, her old friends sniggered, she had managed to shop up a storm—a speculation confirmed by the blizzard of boxes and baggage that had been Fed Exed back in advance.

The Clementes arrived home in the middle of June—the time of year on the California coast when thick fog billows in from the Pacific each day at dawn, stoppering the sky with a gray cottony quilt, retreating for only a few hours of sickly sunshine in the late afternoon. June gloom! But there was no gloom on the Clemente estate. Within a week after settling in, Lally and David threw open the doors of their baronial mansion and began to entertain. Select little dinners and butt-up-against-butt crushes. Coffees and cocktails and elegant little high teas. The invitations flurried onto the city like New Year's Eve confetti. "Are you going to that thingy of the Clementes'?" became the first question on every Zyderm-plumped pair of lips.

But, as everyone quickly came to realize, all these "thingies"—the dinners and crushes and high teas—were actually in the service of a higher purpose. David Clemente also presided over the Clemente Foundation, which was endowed with a billion dollars (give or take a couple hundred million), and he'd appointed his new bride as Executive Director. Word had it that the couple had combined their honeymoon with a humanitarian mission, and that the new, *serious,* Lally had inspected sub-Saharan irrigation projects with the same verve she used to apply to picking out the perfect Hermès handbag; that she now courted Carmelite nuns working for famine relief as assiduously as she'd once pursued A-list actors for her dinner table.

And so everyone who attended an affair at the Clementes knew to bring along a checkbook.

Caitlin Latch arrived at the Clemente estate with her checkbook tucked into the bottom of her bag, a knock-off Louis Vuitton monogram tote.

It was just after seven on a Thursday evening. The affair she was attending was a largish wine-and-finger-foods bash "in honor of Suraya Burab, founder of the Afghan Female Literacy Project." Caitlin considered this a marvelous cause. Educating oppressed women was something she supported wholeheartedly. She would love to contribute generously to it.

Problem was, her checking balance currently stood at minus seventy-six dollars and eleven cents, and her savings account was zilch. She'd already spent fifty bucks just to accept the invitation, which accounted for most of her negative checking balance. This meant that sometime during the speeches, after the elaborate thank-yous and just before the appeal to cough up an additional donation, she'd have to try to melt inconspicuously away.

The Clemente estate occupied nineteen breathtaking ocean-view acres in Colina Linda, the swanky village nestled like a crown jewel on San Carlino's northern crest. Caitlin snaked up the long, crushed pink stone drive, her rattletrap Volvo wagon sandwiched between a Mercedes sedan and a Range Rover. She surrendered her car to one of a pack of mauve-jacketed valets and entered the foyer of the enormous main house.

It had been nearly eight months since the last time she'd been there, and she was immediately struck by a sense of both familiarity and strangeness. Nothing much had changed—nothing, that is, except her relationship to it all, and *that* had changed decisively. And there was that awful Clemente butler, a terrifyingly haughty man named Eduardo. For one dreadful moment, she was certain he was going to stop her: *You've got no business being here! I'll have to ask you to leave!* But if he even recognized her, he gave no indication: His heavy-lidded gaze slid past her without even a flicker.

Another mauve-jacketed functionary checked her name from a digital list. "Follow the arrows," he barked.

Fluorescent orange arrows were taped to the walls, pointing the way down a spacious hall. *Kind of tacky,* Caitlin thought. Not quite what she'd expected from the haute-stylish Lally.

She dutifully followed them to a cavernous room she'd never been in before—the ballroom, she guessed you'd call it—all butterscotch and rose, with high, coffered ceilings and soaring rectangular multi-paned windows, the walls hung with the huge contemporary canvases that David famously collected. It was already packed, people spilling out of the tall French doors into the gardens. Women outnumbered men, Caitlin detected in a glance. This was almost always true in San Carlino: The city had unattached females in the way Venice had pigeons—arrayed in huge, pecking, and almost identical flocks that gathered in the most advantageous places. The only singular thing about this particular flock was that a sprinkling of them sported Islamic head scarves.

Caitlin immediately spotted Lally. Hell, you couldn't miss her: Lally towered over six feet tall in the stiletto Jimmy Choos she favored. Flanked by the guests of honor, a gaunt elderly lady in a sari and a blooming young woman in a scarf, Lally was constantly in motion: She kissed, waved, laughed, hugged, vigorously pumped hands. Her husky voice blared like a train station announcement above the social babble: *Nice to see you! So very nice to see you! It's so very good of you to come!*

Caitlin paused hesitantly. When you were attempting to move in social circles superior to your own, it was crucial to never give the impression that you were in over your head. This, she had discovered, was Rule Number One. Look and act like you belonged, and you could pretty much soar along with the current. But one slipup and chances were you'd be savagely pecked apart.

So okay, she was pretty confident in the way she looked. Her teal-green DKNY pantsuit (80 percent off retail at the outlet in Camarillo) was properly understated and de-emphasized her spectacular figure. The Vuitton bag might be a fake, but it was a really good one—only the sleazy vomit-green lining would give away its counterfeit status, and no one was going to get a look at that.

But here was her real dilemma: What was the proper etiquette for attending a function at the home of newlyweds, when, several months before the wedding, you'd been sleeping with the groom?

She pretended to examine a massive painting that looked like Chinese writing—slashes of black on a white background—while she puzzled the problem. She'd had a brief fling with David Clemente the previous autumn, shortly after he'd separated from his first wife and before he'd astonished the entire town by taking up with Lally, so it wasn't like she'd gone behind Lally's back or anything. Really, it was no big deal. And Lally obviously didn't hold it against her—she'd even invited Caitlin to the wedding. True, there'd been seven hundred other guests, but it still indicated she harbored no hard feelings.

And, Caitlin reflected, nobody else would even remember that she and David had ever met.

"I suppose you're thinking all of this might've been yours," cackled a voice at her ear.

Caitlin whirled. Shit! It was Janey Martinez.

In a city that teemed with moneyed and snobbish divorcées, Caitlin considered Janey about the worst. Hers was the type of snobbery that arose from old wealth—the sort that made her take it for granted that she was superior to you, despite her thunder thighs and a grate-on-your-sinuses personality and an ex-husband serving time in minimum security for some kind of Internet fraud.

"The big fish that got away," Janey added with an unpleasant smirk.

Caitlin forced a breezy laugh. "Oh, Janey, of course not. David and I were never anything more than friends."

Janey's smirk stretched wider. "Oh yeah, I'm sure. The very best of friends." She tugged at the hem of her Chanel jacket, which had the effect of widening the V-opening, exposing a bit of prodigious cleavage. Janey had been a Grade-A frump, all oatmeal-colored cardigans, and eyebrows that scraggled into a unibrow, until Lally had taken her under her wing and performed some radical makeover action. Janey was now waxed and streaked and Botoxed into what would be a semblance of chic, except for one peculiar thing—in the process, Janey seemed to have acquired a gargantuan new pair of tits. D-cup at least. Possibly double D.

Could Lally really have suggested those? Caitlin wondered. Hard to believe.

"So are you still working at that college rape place?" Janey asked.

"The Rape Crisis Center? No, the university consolidated it with another department, and my job was eliminated."

"What a shame. And yet here you are generously supporting one of Lally's pet causes. Good for you. It must be quite a sacrifice."

"Not really," Caitlin said crisply. "I give to a lot of charities."

"Well we all know you support thrift shops." Janey gave a nasty giggle.

Caitlin reddened. She knew exactly what Janey was referring to: Caitlin had worn to Lally's wedding a practically new Prada chiffon she'd scored at the Pioneer Daughters Resale Shoppe on Village Road, only to have Janey gleefully point out that it was one of Lally's own cast-offs.

Fortunately, Janey's attention suddenly flicked to the center of the room. "There he is!" she muttered and, wheeling abruptly, made a dash to a man emerging through the milling crowd precariously conveying two over-filled glasses of wine.

A remarkably good-looking man, Caitlin noticed, tall and lean, with bronzy hair flopping into thick-lashed eyes, and that kind of humorous, long-cornered mouth that made you think irresistibly about kissing. He glanced at Caitlin and gave a quizzical smile. She felt a flutter-kick of excitement in the pit of her stomach.

Then Janey grabbed one of the glasses he was holding and linked a proprietary arm through his and steered him efficiently out of sight.

Who was he? Caitlin wondered. And why in heaven's name was he with someone as singularly unappetizing as Jane Kern Martinez?

But of course she knew why. Because they belonged to the same tribe. The boarding school and sailing club and never-think-twice-about-price tribe. The bottom line was, it didn't matter if you liked one of your purebred shar-peis, or if you possessed the personality of one of your rottweilers, being a member of the tribe was the main thing that counted.

She was suddenly swept by a bitter feeling of rejection—the geeky girl left on the sidelines at the high school dance. But there was a trick she'd picked up some years ago from an article in *Cosmo:* When you were feeling insecure, you repeated to yourself the words "I'm glad I'm here, I'm *glad.*" Not only did this act like a bit of self-hypnotism, reinforcing your confidence, but when you ended with a stress on the word *glad,* it left your lips curved in exactly the right pleased-to-be-here smile.

She mouthed it now: "I'm glad I'm here, I'm *glad*"; and then she threw back her shoulders and arched her back and plunged into the fray.

The milling crowd carried her out into a garden that formed a crescent around a water lily–strewn reflecting pool. She fought her way through the crush to a bar positioned under a bower of old-growth olives.

"Chardonnay, please!" she shouted.

A glass of red wine was thrust in her hand. "Excuse me, I asked for white," she called to the retreating bartender. A pink-faced man muscled in front of her, roaring for a Glenfiddich on the rocks. With a sigh, Caitlin turned with the glass of red and began edging back through the packed bodies.

Thank God, a friend! Or at least someone she had a friendly acquaintance with—Jessica DiSantini, who used to be a lawyer and was divorced from a brain surgeon, and was now romantically involved with a world-famous composer. *No question of whether or not she fit in with the tribe,* Caitlin thought wryly.

She started to wave. Someone jostled her from behind, and wine from her glass splashed onto the silk shantung sleeve of a woman beside her.

"You clumsy idiot, look what you did!" the woman snarled. "This is a brand-new Saint Laurent!"

"I'm so sorry!" Caitlin exclaimed.

"You've ruined it!" The woman glared at her. Others were gawking with contempt or grins of snide amusement.

"I'm really very, very sorry," Caitlin muttered again. *I'm glad I'm here, I'm glad!* Her lips gelled into a pleasant curve, and she slunk back into the house.

Jessica DiSantini, who had just stepped away from the bar with the San Pellegrino water she'd virtuously asked for instead of the merlot she craved, observed this little mishap with a great deal of delight—not over poor Caitlin Latch's embarrassment, but because the despoiled shantung sleeve belonged to Kiki Morrison; and Kiki was a) the wife of Stu Morrison, a kill-the-earth shopping-mall developer who'd bulldozed most of the few remaining orange groves in the county; b) the bossy and officious chairwoman of half the charities-that-counted committees in town; and c) a bony-assed slut whom, several years earlier at a yacht-club Christmas party, Jessica had stumbled upon vigorously tongue-kissing Jessica's then-husband, Michael, in the staff ladies' room.

Of course, that had been just a sneak preview of what the louse Michael would later do. But it hadn't left Jessica with any residual tenderness for the bossy, bony-assed Kiki Morrison.

Jessica lingered for an enjoyable moment to observe Kiki futilely dab club soda on the purple blotch, which now roughly resembled the head of the Energizer Bunny, while a coterie of fellow socialites fluttered and simpered around her. Assured that the stain was indelible, Jessica headed back into the mobbed ballroom.

Many familiar faces. If she were still Mrs. Michael DiSantini, i.e. Mrs. Lord God Chief of Neurosurgery at Mission Mercy Hospital, a lot of these faces would be lighting up with hundred-kilowatt smiles, beckoning her to approach.

But as the discarded ex-wife of the Lord God, she knew that she was the one now expected to do the approaching.

She spied Taller Kern in a huddle with the mayor, the mayor's sister, and a couple of men wearing Wealthy Guy uniforms: blue cashmere blazers, gray slacks, dopey-patterned ties. She considered barging in on them: Taller was her mixed-doubles partner and (since her divorce, at least) her best friend. But he'd been weirdly distant lately: For instance, instead of lingering for their customary martini after a tennis match, he'd taken to hurrying off mumbling excuses about having to do vaguely this or not-quite-clear that; and he'd stopped calling two or three or six times a day to swap gossip or leisurely chew over the latest details of Jessica's sex life. Not that he'd dropped her completely—nothing as drastic as that. It was just that he wasn't acting quite the Vince Vaughn to her Owen Wilson these days.

She veered in the opposite direction and through a momentary gap in the throng caught sight of Caitlin Latch's varicolored blond head.

"Cait! Oh, Caitlin!" she called.

Caitlin hurried over to her. *Funny how she always wore that same expression,* Jessica thought—the kind of pleasant little smile a surgical nurse might wear while prepping you for a particularly nasty procedure.

"Jessica, how great to see you," Caitlin burbled. "I noticed you outside by the bar, but it was such a mad scene I couldn't get to you."

"Yeah, I know. And look, I saw what happened with Kiki."

Caitlin flushed. "Oh God, I feel terrible about it! That stunning jacket!" She hesitated slightly. "Do you think I should offer to pay for the dry cleaning?"

Jessica gave a snort. "I think it's beyond dry cleaning. And I'm pretty sure that Stu Morrison can afford to buy her another, so don't even worry about it."

"I still feel terribly bad," Caitlin muttered.

"Darlings!"

As if materializing out of the ether, Lally Chandler suddenly towered at their side. It was amazing, Jessica marveled, how Lally had managed to so instantly transform herself from a somewhat glitzy ex-celebrity into the hushed-luxe personification of a tycoon's spouse. Gone was the high-spouting ponytail that had been Lally's trademark since playing the Bond girl character, Priscilla Much: Now her burnt sugar–colored hair fell straight to her shoulders, lifted from her flawless forehead by a velvet headband rimmed with pearls. Her mole-colored trousers suit was both rich and subdued. In fact, the only things that flashed about her now were the mega-carat diamond on her ring finger and her white, white teeth.

She double air-kissed Jessica and Caitlin. "Thank you both so much for coming!" she exclaimed. "It means so incredibly much to me to know my friends support the causes I believe in."

Was she being sarcastic? Jessica wondered. For a brief time the year before, the three of them had been involved in a fairly intense competition for the attractive, newly separated, and dizzyingly rich David Clemente. But unless Lally had become a far superior actress than in her starlet days, she appeared to be sincere.

"It's an important issue. I'm happy to do whatever I can," Jessica said politely.

"Absolutely," Caitlin echoed. "Whatever we can do."

"Thank you, thank you! You know, I've had the chance to visit some emerging nations in the past few months, and I can't tell you how much needs to be done! Did you know that in Afghanistan the female literacy rate is less than twenty percent?"

"That's terrible," Caitlin clucked.

"A catastrophe! But we're going to change all that, no matter what it takes. In fact, David is in New York right this moment, coordinating funds with several U.N. agencies. And in just a little while I'm going to shamelessly beg you all to give as generously as you can." Lally flashed her perfect white teeth. "Where's Tom?" she asked, swiveling to Jessica. "Did you bring him along, or is he globe-hopping?"

"Globe-hopping. He's at a music festival in Vienna, premiering a new woodwind concerto. Then he hits a symposium in Montreal, and after that, I get him back home for a few weeks."

"Fabulous! You know, I often pat myself on the back for getting the two of you together. I suppose I'll always take an interest in Tommy's well-being, probably till the day I die."

Jessica smiled thinly. The fact that Tom Bramberg, the man she was furiously in love with, had been the first of Lally's four husbands, back—way back—when he was a minor rock star and Lally still a teenager, was not something she was eager to be reminded of.

As if prompted by her thoughts of rock and roll, a tinny rendition of the Ramones' "I Wanna Be Sedated" suddenly insinuated itself into the babble of the crowd.

"That's my cell," Caitlin said sheepishly. She opened her bag, just a crack, as if she had something embarrassing inside that she didn't want anybody to see, and dug out her phone.

Lally leaned intimately toward Jessica. "Listen," she said in a low voice. "I really, *desperately* need to talk to you. Not now, sometime in private. Could we do lunch tomorrow?"

Jessica glanced at her, startled. What in the world could Lally Clemente need to really and desperately discuss with her?

Before she could reply, she was distracted by Caitlin who had just flipped her phone closed. Her face had paled, and for once her surgical-nurse smile had disappeared.

"What's wrong?" Jessica gasped.

"I've got to go," Caitlin said. "My son has just fallen out of a window."

PHOTO: PETER D. GRAVES

LINDSAY GRAVES has worked as a journalist, a scriptwriter, and a television producer. She lives in the Hollywood Hills and is currently not an ex-wife.